Door to Heaven

Christine Young

Published by Rogue Phoenix Press
Copyright © 2016

ISBN: 978-1-62420-296-4

Credits
Cover Artist: Designs by Ms G
Editor: Christie Kraemer

Prologue

Hot and sultry, the intense heat of the day had continued into the night, and the blackness that descended offered no respite. It was curious. Normally breezes flowed off the Pacific Ocean and more often than not mist hung in gossamer veils over the landscape. A land where frequent rains fell in a solid deluge and roaring temperatures rarely insinuated themselves on this part of the coast. All afternoon clouds had gathered well out to sea, and as day turned into night, they grew larger and darker, menacing, turning the sky black.

Finally, when the two diametrically opposed air masses collided, the storm began.

The day had dawned so very still; the sky clear, marred with nothing, and the sun fed off its reflection in the sand, building gradually into the inferno yet to come.

A mysterious day, strangely foreboding, it turned into an ominous night.

Possibly the most terrifying part of standing on the auction block was hearing the lightning scald the night. It wasn't, though, because now the male population encircling the stage gaped at her, so very near that some pawed at her and dared pull on the thin white gown clinging to her trembling form. Her body encased in a transparent mist, teasing the men with her beauty and the promise of sensual delight.

She might have preferred death to the auction, but she had never truly considered that someday this could happen to her. Never believed the torrid night she had spent with Roc could have had a far different ending. Mortality had no place in her thoughts until now. And she had never thought it would come to this. She had never believed Roc.

"It's about to start."

The lecherous volley of anticipation exploded in the sultry air around her, taming the storm outside, yet the tempest warring within her dwarfed the other. The men surrounding her laughed and jeered, seeking to reduce her, somehow to discount her as a human being. All of them cried out impatiently to begin the examination then the bids. She had steeled herself against this final humiliation yet she knew more waited for her upon the sale.

"Stand back!" The voice assumed control of the room and she cringed, praying for deliverance. Raymond Pierce had sworn vengeance against her stepfather, James Lawrence, and now he would have it.

"One at a time. You'll all have a chance to see what you'll be getting yourself into. Patience, gentlemen!"

Another voice cried. "There's no hurry. Each man will be given the same opportunity, but only if he shows his cash. Five thousand dollars, sirs, five thousand, and no credit."

"Damn."

"I haven't got that much," someone groaned.

"Five thousand?" A man from the back cried out.

She thanked God they didn't. She remembered the evil in their eyes when they looked at her, sending revulsion sliding into the pit of her stomach.

"Ah, but do you think he has set the price too high on this...this hot little spitfire?" someone else dared to wonder.

"Gentleman," he stood arms outstretched, "do you think she is worth five thousand dollars?"

"I think he has not over estimated the lady's charms, but then we haven't seen them all, eh?" A man chuckled softly before digging in his pockets for his money clip.

"Do you think he'll let those of us who haven't the cash to bid stay and watch? I surely wouldn't mind a long look."

"Don't know, but there are some who believe it won't come to bidding." The man paused, clearly amused by his conjecture. Men stared at each other, almost frightened, for there wasn't a man in the room who didn't wonder if Roc Newman would appear.

"They say he'll be here," another spoke softly, camouflaged behind the leering affluent men. "Her breath, her life, her love... He'll come for her as surely as night and day. He'll come."

She could hear them, the men. Sorrow filled her, pervaded her heart and soul. He had warned her and she had listened. Then they came and she had faltered.

Excitement rang in the men's voices, and the noise horrified her for she could not give them what they wanted. Her body shook, trembling, terrified of the future. This would not take long, this peddling of flesh before someone would own her, could command her and she would have to obey. She whimpered and fought for the courage that had at one time been her trademark, her way of life.

She saw Raymond Pierce; Sterling Rutgers stood beside him. They spoke softly to each other and grinned. Sweat popped out on her brow, and she could not still the earth shaking beneath her. No, she had evaded them for so long, defied them, thought to defeat their evil, but still they managed to capture her, and everything she had worked for could not save her.

Now she had nothing, not even her wits for they had deserted her. Her heart, her soul, and the man she loved, gone. She had to admit that possibly, she had tempted the gods and destiny one too many times.

Even if he appeared, he could do nothing. She witnessed the security and it would take more than one man to break through the number of guards surrounding her. His life would certainly be sacrificed, and just as certainly Pierce would enjoy making him watch her humiliation. He had planned and plotted this since the day so long ago, a day she would never forget. Though Pierce had fled the country, he came back to savor this sweet moment of revenge, and now the only missing link was Roc Newman. Seizing a man such as Roc and humbling him would surely be a noteworthy accomplishment, but he had to show his face and it didn't appear he would.

What man would rush into such danger, risk his life, even for...

A woman who had in turns infuriated him, fought him, bested him, but a woman who loved him with all her heart. Ah, but she had never told him she loved him, and he previously claimed she was a regrettable accident, a selfish childish brat.

Once he spoke of compromise; once he had trusted her and had given her every opportunity to prove herself.

Yet with each new conflict she let him down.

A soft drum roll came from somewhere behind, building slowly, capturing the attention of the men. The jovial mood of the auction quieted.

"Tabasco Cat!" his cry snapped her mind to attention. Pierce stood before her, smiling, pointing to her. The audience applauded and whistled. The thunder grew. "A hot piece!" he went on when the noise fell to a low rumble. "Now, my friends, who among you can come up with five grand? A minimal price for such a delicate beauty."

A pause hung on the air, and she swallowed apprehensively because the game was about to begin. Her skin prickled. "Hot," she whimpered and it was the only sound inside the room. Men licked their lips and another soft sob ripped through her. Merciful heaven, they had drugged her. She wavered and closed her eyes against the humiliation, remembering another place and time.

The thought shattered her mind, for she knew first hand the potency of this aphrodisiac and realized she would have no relief. The heat and the anguish would build and her body would crave more than she was willing to give.

"Plank down the cash before you can look, and touch as much as you'd like," Pierce told his audience. His smug gaze rested on her and he strolled to her then, with a cold drink of water. She sipped and understood she'd made another mistake. They had used the water, the drug, and now heat flamed within her stronger than before. Her craving grew and the rosy flush it gave her enticed the men even more. They would not let up, not quit, until she moaned and pleaded for relief.

Six men stepped forward. Sterling Rutgers accepted and counted the cash from each man, carefully labeling and placing it in a safe.

"No..." her breath whispered piteously in the room, sultry and provocative, capturing each man and holding him captive, her moan of anguish, erotic and seductive.

"One at a time," Pierce continued, clearly enjoying her discomfort and the men's growing need to possess and consume her. He motioned to Rutgers then approached her with more of the liquid, forcing it upon her.

She trembled with the heat. Her skin so very sensitive she wanted to rip the transparent dress from her body. Wanted a cool breeze to ease her tender flesh, but the room was scorching and stuffy. Every place the fabric touched betrayed her and she prayed for respite. She ran her hands down her skirt, attempting to ease the pain. The movement seemed enchanting, magical, tantalizing. Pierce smiled and he looked to the men who stared in transparent wonder at the inviting touch. It seemed as if she beckoned to them, encouraging their attention, tempting and seducing them in her innocence.

Her faint moan, carnal and alluring, added to the fire that all ready inflamed the men's senses.

The first man stepped forward. Her breath caught in her throat, and she flinched back. His gaze traveled the length of her, seeming to undress her in his mind. She imagined his touch and loathed the thought. Trembling rocked her slender frame, flames ignited within and she hated. She hated everyone here. Despised the man who stood so arrogantly before her. A man who sought to take something that was only hers to give, so she fought the all-consuming power of the drugs.

"Nice," he said. And the heat of his breath singed her cheek. "An exquisite piece of flesh."

"Please," she sobbed.

She felt repulsed by the flames of betrayal, unable to control the heat of unwanted passion. A man approached, "Ah, but you'd please me," he sneered.

The man stepped back, studying her, appraising her one more time and moved to his chair. A second man stepped forward and the assault continued. With each man her fear and her hunger grew with the inferno of desire. She turned her mind inward and fought through the caresses and lewd remarks, the horrid intimate intrusion, but she could not fight the staggering effects of the aphrodisiac Pierce had given her.

The only chance she had now was herself. Roc had told her that once sold he might never find her. Had told her that her wild impulsive actions would propel her into trouble. Told her a female had limited abilities when pitted against a man.

And she had listened. It was only when she settled into a quiet peaceful life they had come seeking vengeance. Roc had convinced her.

Whatever his convictions he had understood and finally compromised. No matter what his mandates or commands, he had given her freedom, even when she had willingly given it up to him as her concession.

How curious this all seemed clear to her now. How terrible she would never hold him again, touch him, feel the warm security he had offered. Now that she realized how precious every moment was with him, she could not tell him.

Tell him she loved him as completely, as passionately as she had ever fought for her rights.

She would fight this. They could not keep her forever enslaved, prostituted in some far away place. She would not submit.

These men would pay. Pierce would sell her, but that was not a reason to die or give up. Even though she could see no way out of her immediate fate, it was not the end.

Never the end.

The last man finished. It was the last touch upon her sensitive skin. The room in its opulent splendor shuddered against the tempest. Lightning slit the sky apart and thunder boomed overhead. Men waited, eager to begin the bidding. Wild and untamed they stomped the floor, whistled, and clapped, building the tension and the anticipation. She whimpered and moaned and again she saw the light of passion or lust fill them, but she could not silence the raging fire within.

Upon the block, hands tied with a golden cord, she stood now high above the men. Her white dress floated uselessly, provocatively around her, shielding nothing from their view. A golden ribbon was tied to the neckline of her dress and one pull would unveil the prize.

She stood upon a stage, and she prayed for courage, prayed also her pride would not desert her.

Her transparent gown rippled slightly. A door somewhere had opened, letting in a breath of air, but no one noticed.

Pierce stepped forward. "Tabasco Cat!" he cried again. "Sweet savage innocence all in one hot package. A cherry ripe for the pickin'." He brushed her hair to the side. One flick of his wrist and the gown fell away, leaving her exposed to the gaping men.

She hissed at the men and glared, yet her discomfort only furnished more entertainment.

A muffled "Awe," rumbled around the room. The pause intensified the drama about to begin.

She felt the breeze against her flesh and stiffened. Her chin thrust upward with silent furious dignity.

An explosion shattered the stillness, muffled by the thunder above. Blackness swallowed the room.

She trembled, terrified, and her knees gave way. Jessica Lawrence crumpled to the floor of the stage.

Pierce pulled her back to her feet then caressed her intimately with his gaze, taunting her further. The lights flickered on once more.

Time stood still. A hushed silence settled around her then another explosion lit the room. The chandelier rocked, tinkling glass the only sound, and once again the light vanished. Shots rang out. Men ducked for cover and she was forgotten, left on the block in the middle of the chaos and the terror.

And the fear.

She nearly shrieked out loud with the sudden bombardment of men and bullets sweeping around her. Maybe this was her chance. No one came for her. No one seemed to care.

After all the battles she had fought. The many times she had rushed madly into danger. She could not give up now, but her limbs did not move, even though she forced her thoughts to that end. The drugs, the nights without sleep...she sobbed.

Roc... She pulled herself to the edge of the stage. Her arms and legs trembled then she fell and she was swept into unconscious oblivion. *Roc*... his touch. She needed him desperately now, his strength to counter her vulnerability and his stubborn determination to overshadow her impulsiveness. A chair crashed beside her jerking her awake.

Was this his doing?

Had he come for her?

Bullets whined overhead, and she continued her desperate bid for freedom, crawling along the floor, naked and terrified. She groped at the material lying next to her, fumbled with it a moment then draped it around her shoulder, tying it.

"Son of a bitch! Jessie!" The curse knifed through her thoughts and she listened more intently. She pushed herself off the floor, searching for the man who fit the voice and the curse. Still unsure she hadn't dreamt the words.

Suddenly her prayers had been answered and she leaned against the block, pushing her hair from her eyes. All she could see were masses of humanity surging around her.

Far away she heard Roc curse again. Doors flew open and more men filled the room, a host of shadowy figures in the night, illuminated occasionally when the raging storm took pity on the blackness.

Her gaze suddenly focused on a tall form, and her heart beat alarmingly.

A single man overshadowed all the rest. He stood unmoving, searching the room, lingering on each figure before passing it by.

Furious, he moved forward, stepped high upon a chair, continuing his search.

She tried to signal him. Her breath caught in her throat. Helpless and vulnerable a sob tore through her. Roc!

He had turned away from her now and she sobbed, trembling with defeat and fear. He had to see her. He had come so far to find her, to save her from Pierce's vengeance. If she could only meet the silver flame of his gaze. If she could see him.

He had come for her! Sweet Jesus, he cared.

He turned again. A flash of lightening. His gaze fell upon the small bundle of white near the stage.

"Roc..." she reached out to him.

She saw the fury plainly etched in the lines of his face. Felt the anguish when he turned from her then fear encased her.

"No..."

He had seen her and deserted her.

He would never forgive her for this, for placing him in danger, for making him come to her rescue. He had warned her and now he would believe she lied to him again.

He hadn't known. Hadn't been there when they came...

Chapter One

Salem, Oregon 1886

No one would have ever guessed the little spitfire could create so much havoc in Roc Newman's life. He would never forget that first bizarre meeting with the pernicious but lovely Jessica Lawrence. That night set the tone for their tumultuous and stormy ride through life.

She had shown her true colors; the wildfire that possessed her soul, the passionate spirit, and the will to triumph even when the battle seemed lost.

When the moon appeared as a silver slipper in the sky...

He waited for her, primed yet not prepared, forewarned through the political grapevine that Jessica Lawrence stalked him.

Jessica Lawrence was a five foot four inch pest. In the midst of it all, no matter how precarious the situation, she seemed to remain, completely, almost unerringly, on his trail--until now. At the window, Roc scrutinized the black form below, fighting the overwhelming urge to give her a shock she would remember forever.

She seemed hell bent on suicide. Consequently, he followed the young lady one day, dodging her path, keeping in the shadows. He had seen her enter an office mysteriously from a side door and discovered it housed a private investigator. The sign, etched in his mind, Jess Law, PI, alias Jessica Lawrence. It hadn't fooled him for a second, just gave him pause, and the fury seizing him rocked his usually placid facade.

He gambled on her naiveté. Perhaps because he had thought her harmless, a mere girl in a man's world, inadequate. Perhaps it had even been the notion she would eventually become distracted and quit. Whatever the reason, he had made a Herculean mistake, and now he pondered her next move. Dressed to blend with the night, she was out there, an apparition of darkness, wrapped in ghostly shadows.

He moved through the house, turning off lights, banking the fires, before settling in a shadowed corner of his study where he could watch Jess. Purposely, he waited until well after midnight to lower the lights. Roc was tense, ready for the intrusion of his privacy. He was peering through the lace curtains, wondering at the girl whose appearance would have shocked most men. A long rope looped over her shoulder, the lone woman strode surefooted across the gardens.

The sky was clear, except for a ribbon of low clouds and a sliver of moon. The house, a bastion against the silent assault about to come. A soft wind blew through the open window from the south; it cleared his head as he watched the approach.

Jess Law shrugged the rope from her shoulder. Silhouetted against the sky, he watched the cord snake upward, grappling hook deftly clenching the chimney. He stood in awe of the mastery. Jess Law pulled on the rope, tightened it, and with a proficiency contradicting her sex, ascended. The lady moved cautiously, and when she reached her goal, she smiled. Her even white teeth glowed against the blackness of her face.

With lithe movements, she swiftly opened the attic window. One jean-clad leg moved through the opening. She balanced precariously, for a moment, as if she were a bird ready to fly. Then her foot rested on the hard wood. The rest of her followed quickly, dropping to the floor; silent, ready to spring.

He felt the tension, knew she listened for the sound of footsteps. She was inside. He watched the window, imagining each moment, each breath, sensing the emotions that must surely riffle her body. Roc listened for the soft whisper of her steps as she descended and thought he could almost hear the wild racing of her heart. Only a moment passed before the sounds became audible. Once on the first floor, she made her way through the house. Her fingers rested on the tumbler of his safe and turned. He heard the click, saw the handle as she pushed down. The door swung open.

Then, without warning, he gripped her mouth. She wrenched away, turning quickly, groping for the documents, even while she tried to avoid him. Her actions, quick and agile, proved adept, throwing him off balance, but he would not relent and managed to grip her arm. No matter how swiftly she countered his moves, he still held mastery. He turned her, prepared to hog tie her if necessary. She allowed him, relaxed then surprised him, maneuvering expertly.

Jess swiftly shoved her elbow into his chest, and he gasped for air. With a skill he didn't suspect she possessed, Jess Law threw him to the floor, and Roc bellowed, landing at her feet. The force of her action amazed him. For a second time, the breath rushed from his lungs, and Roc found himself on the cold floor. Papers, pens, and books clogged the air and littered the Persian rug then a sudden crash reverberated in the once cozy room. His shirt dampened as cold seeped through to his skin. She hadn't just thrown him upon the floor in his private sanctuary. No. She had humiliated him, threatened life and limb, and sent a pitcher of ice water on top of him. If he still held a breath of air in his body, he would have retaliated, a throw for a throw.

He inhaled swiftly, contemplating revenge, thoroughly irritated. He'd held his own in every fight, every barroom brawl he'd ever participated, and now, in the middle of his study, he had been deflated by a plague upon the female persuasion.

Studying the ceiling from this new vantage point, heaving, feeling the stab of mortification against his gender, he looked into the leering countenance of what was rapidly becoming the bane of his existence. Then she spoke, surprising him, since he had expected her to run. Her voice, soft and feminine, one that pinned him to the floor with its arrogance. "To the victor belongs the spoils. Would you like a repeat performance?"

Fury overrode all common sense.

She had not won this contest yet. What did he look like, some old geezer? He rose on his elbows. He was seated in a puddle of water, his hair dripping, feet crunching on glass. He willed his self-control to return, shaking his head while glistening splinters of water flew in all directions and confronted his opponent.

It seemed she was not the least bit apprehensive. He registered that with his first glance. Feet, shoulder width; knees, bent slightly, she rocked on the balls of her feet, relaxed and confident, yet poised tensely, a contradiction at best. Recognizing the pose, he groaned. Hair swept tightly beneath a black cap, while a few tendrils escaped to lie damply against her neck. Streaks of ivory skin peeked out from behind the soot she'd layered on her face and neck. It was a perfect oval, delicate in shape, with a small, very straight nose, and lips slightly too full. If one could really tell beneath all that grime and eyes that seemed fathomless within the darkness of the night. Clad as she was and positioned to fight, she seemed like David come to slay Goliath, ethereal, frail, and totally unaware she was about to regret this assignment.

~ * ~

Jessica Lawrence was not quite so self-assured as she was attempting her damndest to appear. She did have her black belt, but...

She was lucky because she'd never before met with this much success. Oh, she'd tried, but the leverage, the technique, nothing had come together before. Now she intended to brazen it out, fearless, confident, yet beyond her ability.

She had not expected him to emerge from the shadows and frighten her into a corpse. But now that he'd appeared, she had no choice left except to fight him. She had thought he'd retired for the night. This was supposed to be an easy job. She wanted to bundle the papers together, stick them inside her shirt, find Rupert, her hound, and head for home. In the very worst way she wanted to escape this man and the retaliation she knew would soon come.

She eyed the open safe, the papers scattered on the floor, no longer neatly stacked, and the man was in the way. So close she could almost feel the texture of the documents beneath her fingertips. She wanted to succeed at this. If she didn't, her stepfather would inevitably put a stop to her fledgling career. Alex, Jessie's stepmom, kept the secret longer than she had thought possible, yet when the news broke and the summons came, it devastated her, for she knew exactly what her father wanted. "You're twenty-four years old, Jessica," he would begin, making her feel inordinately guilty. "And it's about time you began to act like a lady.

Naturally, I expected you to stop cuttin' didoes a very long time ago, but now you seem hell bent to continue making mischief into your adult life. I won't have it, Jess. I won't," then he would mumble softly. "This is your mother's fault," and Jessie would smile sardonically.

Jessie and Alex would look at each other, knowing who held the upper hand with her father. They never told him. It would have deflated his ego considerably to find out Alex and Jessie always got exactly what they were after. And though her mother gave her the reassurance and the knowledge she needed to excel in a man's world, it was still just that, a man's world and, according to Alex, it would be for a very long time. Alex, the only mother she had ever known, was exquisite, soft, gentle, and carried the will and strength of at least ten men within in her stubborn hide. She had taught her, coaxed her out of her shell of vulnerability, urged her on to greater heights. Jessie knew she could do anything she set her mind to.

Not to take credit from her father, he had a hand in all this too. Jessie knew he adored her mother and herself; for that reason alone he could never deny them. The two of them, Alex and James, were stubbornly happy, mismatched, but even after so many years crazy in love. When her father was in one of those moods, Jessie stopped listening.

She had mastered this technique before she reached the tender age of six, before Alex appeared.

Not that she didn't listen to his advice when it was sound, or when it was something she could agree with. Now he lived so far away, and she was forced to make major decisions every day of her life. She would do what she wanted then she would gloat. In her favor was the fact she knew her way around town and the people. They trusted her and her name. The Lawrence name rendered respect and, sometimes, awe; a powerful family from the west coast to the east coast. It helped her immensely. So, despite the hurdles thrown in her face from a few chauvinistic men, her life and career were moving along admirably. She advertised in the paper, clients didn't flock to her door, but she maintained her independence. Something she had long coveted. Verbal abuse from her schoolmates had hardened her fragile ego, and she steadfastly refused to fall into a subordinate role.

There seemed to be a tiny glitch in her plans however. At the moment she stood fully aware of the tenuous nature of her chosen career.

Unless she could step by this man, she was doomed, and failure was not something she would accept.

It was a spine tingling thought. Right now she had no time for such a foolish endeavor as thinking. The fight or flight syndrome, firmly entrenched itself within her, and she prepared for flight, the first being no choice at all.

Perhaps she entered this mission a bit recklessly, but she had felt so sure of herself and cautious, until this terrible, audacious man had the nerve to surprise her.

Positioning herself above him, she waited, praying for a chance, a small opening, a mistake.

"If you value your life, you will stay there, on the--"

"The question is, do you value yours?" Roc Newman whispered. He'd been waiting for her to make her move, studying her. His temper flared. "I should tan your backside and hand deliver you to your father."

She seethed, "As I've said, sir, stay where you are."

"And I suppose you have a mind to stop me?"

With deft cautious movements, she eased around Roc's legs, eyeing the scattered papers as she edged closer. Her heart thundered in her chest, glancing between the man and documents. It would take only a flick of her wrist and luck, but she could do it. "I can--"

"You expect me to believe that nonsense?"

She felt his gaze skate insolently from her toes up to her eyes. His tone laced with amusement.

"Do tell, if you care to remember, I put you where you are now."

"Lady, you give yourself more credit than you deserve, and if I were you, I wouldn't assume too much," he told her.

"Sir, it is you who should not assume. I can lay you flat on your back as easily as I breathe," she informed him.

"Shall we try it again, eh? Go the whole hog?"

"Sir, not with the likes of you. I choose my own partners. And to your great misfortune, I have picked--"

"My dear little pest, I was doing my best to avoid humiliating you."

She trembled, stifling it with a great deal of effort. "I am *not* a pest." She leaned closer, closer, so close she could almost sense victory, the parchment white and blindingly near. "And need I remind you that you are the one on the floor."

Roc watched. "It won't happen again."

"Now who's arrogant? I think, perhaps, you do need another lesson," she said, deceptively still, with her gaze on the documents.

"You have no idea what you are getting yourself into!" he suddenly exclaimed, seeming to tire of the game and his tone spoke of more than just a skirmish on the floor. She eased toward the papers once again, still trying to convince him she merely fidgeted, that her well-calculated moves meant nothing.

"You're wrong," she said. "I know what I'm about and it seems you're meddling in my affairs, conceited man that you are."

"Oh, lady, you go too far," he whispered.

"And, this is none of your..." she began.

He grinned, his teeth gleaming in the dark. "What a fix." His muscles tensed.

She saw the slight movement even before he could spring.

She let out a soft sound of terror but had the presence of mind to dive for the parchment. A flick of the wrist, quick thinking, and lady luck landed the papers in her hands. She stuffed the contents down the front of her shirt in less than a second then sped past him.

~ * ~

Perhaps he should have let her go. The impact to the political scene would shatter so many lives, and he planned to unveil those reports within the week. Her stepfather as well as her cousin were friends of his as was her younger half brother. They would have expected him to handle Jessica with tenderness.

But tonight...

Something about this brazen little chit irritated him. No, it was more than that; she had bested him and done it at his own game. He prided himself on his ability to defend his home and himself from any attack. And she could certainly use a lesson.

He watched her snatch the papers, and his grin broadened as her black form dashed toward the door. He rose from the floor in time to catch her boot before curling his hand around her ankle. He tugged mercilessly, flipping her in one swift move.

A terrified squeak was rapture to his ears. His smile widened as he pulled her beneath him.

"Now who needs a lesson?" he murmured, chuckling as she struggled for position. She relaxed against him, and it seemed she waited for another opportunity. To his chagrin he found himself aware of the little scamp in a physical manner, more intensely than he wanted to admit. He covered the length of her body, and her attire left nothing to his imagination. He could feel the hard tips of her breasts pushed flat against his chest, his legs rested between hers; he slipped so easily between them as if he belonged there. He held her waist between his hands, could feel his fingers touching, before the soft swell of hips. He was conscious of her soft fragrance, as a fresh breeze touched with spring, yet so compelling his breath caught in his chest. She caused his sanity to catapult and his common sense to ebb and flow. For several seconds, he reveled in a swirling lethargy, images stamped in his brain, bewitched by something unique and tantalizing in this woman. Perhaps he could have avoided this moment, perhaps not. Annoyed by his response to her, surprised, even bewildered such as this could happen so swiftly.

Idiot. She's a thief, the daughter of a friend, a woman who professes to take on a man's role in life, who came to his home, who thought to steal.

Yet he could sense this curious, frenzied craving for a girl he had felt only mockery for; a yearning different from anything that had ever touched him. A desire conceived by the feel of her beneath him, her breasts tracing an unforgettable imprint against his chest, by the flash of blue-violet eyes deeper than the darkest amethyst, her hair now flowing loose, black as night.

He tore his vivid imagining and the unforgettable feel of her from his thoughts, determined to keep the issue clear.

"Get off." She pushed at him to gain the leverage she needed to accomplish the feat, and snatching his recalcitrant notions back to reality.

His hands flexed around her waist. His lip curled dangerously. "Ah, lady, and I use the term vaguely. Indeed, it seems you were a bit too arrogant. But considering your reasons for being here in the first place, I don't believe I'll leap to your defense." He let his confidence override his practical nature, releasing her a moment too long in an attempt to reach for her arms. She took immediate advantage, one second throwing herself away from him before scrambling to a safe distance.

"You're not capable of such a chivalrous act," she sneered, smiling wickedly, poised for battle once more, but he was agile and well versed. Catching her by surprise and offering a devilish warning, he caught her wrist and wrenched her against him.

"Chivalry has nothing to do with this. But then dressed as you are and acting in this manner, you never know what might happen. Take heed now..."

Her strength could never match his, yet her wit and audacity met him evenly. She was intrepid, bold, the type who would never cry off. "You take heed or I will see you pay. You can not treat a lady in this manner."

"If you recall, your status as a lady is debatable. We knights have a decidedly different manner with a common tart or thief if you would give yourself--"

"Never." Her eyes could surely pierce a man's soul and rip it apart. It seemed she planned her next move, relaxing against the hard planes of his body. "You give it up. What I seek belonged to another, and you had no right to it. If you would allow me to leave, we can call this night a draw."

He held her shackled against him. Her fingers wound around his wrists, tighter, tighter still, intriguing him. He relaxed, guessing he had her in a position she could not defend.

"It's hardly a draw when I hold you," he told her. He moved through the hallway, dragging her with him. For the moment, at most, he held the advantage but was startled by her sudden submission. Then he realized his mistake, determined to act before she knew he understood her ploy.

But the moment of knowledge came too late. Jess turned the situation to her favor. She moved swiftly, perfectly and with remarkable strength. He was so surprised and so unbalanced the sudden leverage she used against him threw him hard against the wall and she ran, which was, in truth, precisely what she must have designed.

"Why you little dickens," he cried, and before she could humiliate him further, he caught her around the waist. She screamed, hurtling herself toward the front of the house, but his hand held and she plunged to the floor once more. Roc regained control, finding her lithe body pressed against him, and for a moment feeling a shudder deep within, for she had not responded to him, and it occurred to him perhaps he'd treated her too harshly. He lunged upward, struggling for balance then grabbing hold of her, hauling her to her feet. For all his worries, he felt the vicious strike of her bare hand across his face. They staggered through the front door, tumbling down the steps.

"Sakes alive, what are you trying to do, kill me? And all because I bested you twice?"

"Kill you? I was trying to save you from yourself. But I forgot cats have nine lives. I wonder, does that pertain to cat burglars too?"

"With that kind of help a lady could find herself in deep trouble, sir. I'd prefer it if you left me."

"I'm afraid I can't do that, because you possess something which is mine," he replied.

She was flat on her back again; papers crinkling between his weight and her breasts, her eyes shimmering pools, fathomless, cloaked in secrets. Secrets he meant to unmask. "Damn," she cried then shoved against him, desperate now he had her pinned once more. She clawed at the walkway; before he knew, she had showered him with a fine coating of dust.

"Why you little..." he cried, astonished and resolved this battle would end; he would retain the documents once again, even if he had to strip her to achieve the goal. "You deplorable little hoister." He wasn't sure how he was going to retrieve the papers, but he gripped both her wrists, holding them above her head then straddled her. She screeched and tried to buck him off. His hand rose above her shirt, hesitating. He grinned wickedly, settling the bulk of his weight across her hips.

"How dare you. You have no right," she warned, seeming to guess his intentions.

He quirked an eyebrow, "Ah, kitten, it seems you've misread the situation once again." His fingers toyed with the top button, insulting, insinuating, threatening. "Oh my, stealing is a crime, a punishable offense, and you, little one, are going to pay the full--"

"I'll cry rape."

"You would ruin your reputation the very moment the words came from your delectable mouth. No, I daresay you won't try that because it's not true."

Yet he had gone too far, come too close, and he would never dissolve the memory of her pressed against him, the feel of her breasts, the sizzle of her flashing eyes.

"I'll make your life miserable," she cried. "I'll see that no one will do business with you. You'll starve..."

"Silence, someone should have paddled your backside," he insisted, reaching swiftly, most decorously inside the loose fitting shirt and claiming the documents. He waved them beneath her nose taunting her futile attempt at robbery. "A quick message to your cousin should put you in your--"

He stopped, startled by the deep rich baritone speaking behind him. Roc turned, the daring cat burglar still held beneath the grip of his thighs.

"What have we here?" Jessie's cousin laughed. Then turning to his companion, Senator Drake, he winked. "It seems, friend, you saved yourself a message, and I'd be delighted to see Jessica home...to Jacksonville."

"What, and spoil all this fun?" the senator asked. "I for one would like to hear all about this."

Chapter Two

The beribboned dawn cast a hazy glow across the figures silhouetted against the night. Amusement turned to apprehension when the impact of the evening's events became clear. The men no longer laughed, Jess Law bristled and Roc Newman cast a wary glare at the men who had found him in such a dehumanizing position. He had never meant the fracas to go this far, but this woman had sorely pricked his ego.

Senator Drake, on his way home from a frolic at the governor's mansion, never looked better; his mustache twitched with unshed humor then horror at the complication in front of him.

Roc knew he had gone too far; this was the daughter of a highly influential man, a powerful leader in the state. Despite the provocation of the girl who still lay sprawled on the ground beneath him, he could hardly press charges or allow Drake to.

However, her cousin Trevor was at Drake's side, and he looked eager to see his recalcitrant relative sent home, thus out of the way. Naturally, Roc thought, the young man would do everything in his power to see to it, yet he didn't believe Trevor would succeed. No, if he handed Jessica Lawrence over to her cousin, she'd be plaguing them once more within hours.

"This is fascinating in truth," Drake said to Trevor, and it sounded almost as if he meant it. "I do wonder who the real victor here was. It seems Roc has ended up with the documents. My sweet child, Miss Jessica, you must grow up sometime and cease playing these silly games. It quite scares me what you could stir up. Your father can remain tolerant only so long."

"Leave my father out of this," she tried to squirm out from under

Roc.

"Ah, my dear, I find I can't do that. I'm quite sorry. I'm afraid someone has misled you, blundering into something that is far above your meager understanding. Politics, my dear. Well, this issue is beyond a woman's intelligence, and, Roc, my good fellow, you must learn to treat the fairer sex with a bit more tenderness. It was not good of you to rip the documents from beneath her shirt. It puts her in what one might call a delicate situation--compromised. Since her cousin here is the only male relative in town, it does make him responsible, does it not?" he chuckled. "Don't you think it's about time you helped her up?"

Compromised. Delicate situation. He should have foreseen this, should have taken everything into account.

Roc frowned. His guts churned, then he turned to gaze at the rope still dangling across the attic window and back to the trio. "Senator, she gave me no other choice." He stood up and offered Jess a hand.

She snorted, politely ignored the gesture, pushed herself off the ground, and dusted her pants then turned on him, "Of all the nerve." It sounded as if she were choking on the words as she said them.

Senator Drake cleared his throat. "Roc, you might consider an apology."

She glared at Roc. He fumed silently then grinned, unmindful of her cousin and the senator.

"For what?" he inquired innocently. His gaze fixed on the girl, her shirt still slightly open, revealing the ivory swell of her breasts. Indelibly, the sight was imprinted in his mind.

"Roc," Trevor warned.

Roc's attention wavered from the view beckoning innocently to him. He could hear Jessie hiss, scrambling to arrange her clothing and for a moment, regretted his boldness.

"Roc, perhaps you don't understand, perhaps I should--"

"Oh, I understand all the wild implications and the demands you could make," Roc assured Trevor before starting for the house, documents clutched firmly in his hand.

He could imagine the claws the girl was about to display and smiled. It was one hell of a fight.

"A gentleman! Hah! Implications! Nothing happened!" Jessica cried.

Roc turned, studied the girl a second. "She lies; quite a lot happened, and I do assure you, Jess Law, if I choose to, I can ruin you."

"Jessica Lawrence," Trevor commanded. "Perhaps we should go inside and talk about this. It seems you need a bit of guidance."

Roc was certain Jessie needed more than a harsh reprimand or guidance for that matter. Jessie needed a man, a husband, someone to put her in her place. The Senator had looked at him as if he'd fit snugly in the role before his sparkling gaze had gone back to Jessie.

The unscrupulous little private investigator seemed more interested in getting the documents into her hot little hands than finding a husband, and that suited him fine. In truth, he marveled at the malevolent stare of her darkening eyes seeming to knife through him then cringed when he read the delight in Drake's expression.

"We have nothing to talk about, Trevor," Jessica replied, "And you are hardly dry behind the ears. So a lesson from you would be foolish indeed."

"She doesn't need a mentor. She needs a firm hand, I am afraid," Roc said.

Drake's grin widened. "And you're just the man to do it too. James has often suggested you would suit Jessica well. A man's man he proclaimed once."

"Roc," Trevor nodded his approval, his mustache twitching almost as if he strained to hold back his laughter, "your words have a certain amount of truth to them. Indeed, I regret I must leave for Astoria soon. I simply can't stay around to administer that firm hand. And Roc, if nothing is done to subdue her nightly excursions, everyone will talk."

Roc flinched, finally catching the drift of Trevor's thoughts. He was right. But it wasn't up to him to keep her safe and her body sound. Why, she'd claw him to shreds.

Trevor's speech annoyed him. Everything he'd thought and Trevor voiced held true, but she wasn't his responsibility. Roc didn't want to look at her again, yet he couldn't help himself. His gaze turned to the girl. Her hair swirled around her shoulders. Black skeins fell almost to her waist; soft, heavy, inviting a man's touch. Trevor was wrong. No man alive could change the little dickens into an angel. She was a talented and exceptionally intelligent woman, willful, independent and tough; she might well cause a man more headaches and heartaches than imaginable. To add to it, even smeared with fireplace soot and completely unkempt, she remained breathtakingly exquisite.

She'd certainly amused Senator Drake.

Roc frowned suddenly, catching Trevor with a conspiratorial wink directed at the senator. Oh, no, they weren't going to gang up on him. They wouldn't sink that far. Absurd, this idea; he wouldn't allow them to railroad him. "Well, young man," Roc said directly to Trevor, "I do believe you have your hands full. Senator," he turned to Drake, "if you'll excuse me, I have some sleep to catch up on, and few documents to secure."

"This hasn't been resolved," the senator said, "since the only alternative left for the girl is the cooler, and that is no alternative at all."

"How sad," Roc said flatly, still glowering at Trevor, the man responsible for setting the flavor of what he knew would come. "I, for one, have no qualms about seeing a hoister pay for her crimes."

Drake had found the perfect solution to everyone's problems, but he refused to accept it, even though there was no other choice. It seemed inevitable he would serve as jailer and protector. Despite his grave misgivings, he would have to allow Jessica Lawrence to stay in his home.

Jessica smiled at the senator then whistled shrilly, calling Rupert II. With three long strides the hound was at her side. "I could command him to kill, you know. Senator...Trevor," she glared at them.

"Ah, she not only has claws but fangs too. We must not let you go away disappointed," Roc insisted. He dared and challenged her with his unshakable confidence, still resisting the inevitable. He turned again to stride toward the house, leaving the senator bewildered and Trevor laughing at his cousin's antics and wondering what devil possessed him to gamble with his life.

Rupert II whined as if he'd let his mistress down before nuzzling her hand, licking and nudging her fingers with his nose. "Oh," she fumed, and it seemed she was furious with the man, the dog, and her cousin, "I'm leaving. Any more of this outrageous talk and the gossips will beat you to the punch. Since I no longer have the documents, I see no need to even think of punishment."

Roc had put one foot on the steps leading into his house when he heard her last statement. He whirled. "Perhaps they are not thinking so much of punishment and protection for you, Jessica, as they are about the poor people of Salem. Who will protect them?"

Roc moved further up the steps and clenched the papers tightly. Rupert barked. Trevor laced his fingers around Jessica's arm and followed by Senator Drake, pulled Jessica along.

Rupert sat staring at the retreating backs and whined.

They strode into the house. Jessica looked over her shoulder, whistling for the hound.

In seconds Roc was upon the porch and through the front door. Roc climbed the steps to the second floor two at a time. Everything, every blessed little thing seemed to have spun out of control. Even the hound made himself at home, finding a cozy place on the braided rug in front of the fireplace. If Rupert wouldn't kill in the literal sense, he would undoubtedly drown everyone in drool.

Jessie sat in the rocker near Rupert, absently stroking his head. She expected to get away with this.

In the room below, he heard Senator Drake pacing absently across the floor, pausing every so often he was sure, to gaze up the staircase or out a window. He spotted Trevor beneath the banister, watched him arch a brow then shrug at Drake.

"Is he going to come down?" Drake demanded.

Trevor shook his head. "Roc is volatile, unpredictable at times; I don't have a clue what he's up to." He pounded his fist on the banister, staring upward. "We should have followed him, convinced him of the plan. It is the only way."

But they hadn't, of course. If they left Jessie alone, Roc thought, she would vanish. He had to agree to keep her in his house, and she most certainly would have to acquiesce to his wishes. She was in grave danger. He could only pray she hadn't read the documents she had stolen. Trevor and Drake had allowed her to play at this game, hoping she would come to her senses and quit. Maybe they had given her too much room, encouragement when they should have stopped her. A shiver suddenly seized him. He wasn't eager to confront Jessie, but he was impatient to hand over the responsibility, and he knew it was impossible to shirk his duty.

"You need to write Jessie's father," the senator commented to Trevor. "This is too important to leave to chance. I mean to be the most thorough senator ever, even if, in my worst nightmare, I have to tread on a few people's toes. But so far my nightmares haven't bothered me overmuch, and I know what we proposed here was right. No matter the outcome, I will always proceed with thoughts of my constituents as a group and how they will benefit. In my mind they will always come first."

Roc snorted at that little speech. It was helpful, however, to have wealthy and powerful friends. Drake had secured many and it made him a force to reckon with in the legislature. Now he risked everything, but, as Roc knew, Drake pondered the question many times, and the senator had found no other alternative.

"I did that yesterday when it became apparent Jessie intends to see the elephant, wants to experience it all before she's twenty-five. I never dreamt she'd take on a commission quite so foolhardy," Trevor wrinkled his brow. "I don't cotton to Jessie's actions, and I also don't understand why Roc is acting so churlishly toward Jessie, so why am I willing to leave her in his not so tender care?"

"Oh, my boy, you do know. The two of them charge the air with their searing exchanges, sparks fairly fly from Miss Jessica's eyes when she looks at Roc; until now I've never seen her react to any man. And, as we concluded earlier, Miss Jessica needs a man, not a sorry excuse for the masculine persuasion. She needs a real man. Roc fits the bill. They might be the most brutal of opponents--

"And..." he conceded, "I've never before seen the mercurial shimmer of her eyes..."

Mercurial shimmer of her eyes? Roc snorted. No, he attributed the shimmer to fire works, and a seething desire to best him. Yet he had come to terms with the situation. He would allow Jessica Lawrence to stay in the attic room. He turned from the conversation below and moved upstairs to check on the accommodations.

~ * ~

"He is the only one who can handle her," Drake went on. "I would hate to lose him as a friend, yet somehow I doubt it will come to that." He frowned. "Bizarre, isn't it? Upstairs is a man who has negotiated treaties, traveled the world over, and conversed with diplomats on the most genteel of levels. One of the most accomplished martial arts experts in the world, he's determined to outfight a mere slip of a girl."

"Ah, but he underestimated Jessie's talents," Trevor assured him.

Drake's eyes shimmered. "I love a good mystery. This, it seems, rises above others at the moment. But what talents?"

"I taught her all she knows. Roc schooled me."

"She has half his strength."

"Strength is important but quick thinking and the skill, Senator, the skill of it all."

"He will not allow her the upper hand again. A lesson learned..."

"She has a woman's wiles. I doubt the little scuffle we witnessed was enough to harden the man so thoroughly," Trevor told him, chuckling. He looked up the staircase and started toward it. Drake, frowning curiously, followed on his heels.

When Trevor reached the third step, he stopped. "Jessie..." It seemed he had already forgotten Jessica, sitting so deceptively silent by the fireplace.

The senator remembered at the same moment, whirled and returned to the room, murmuring quietly to himself. "By thunder, Trevor, she almost got away. We do agree on that."

Trevor nodded, still moving up the steps. "Where it concerns Jessie, one can never turn his back." He paused, absorbed in his thoughts then, "This is important. Despite your confidence, I'm worried about Jessie and the gossip, Senator, the gossip that will surely follow. Roc is a virile and healthy man. Charming when he wants to be and devilish, and capable of seducing anyone's maiden aunt if he chose. His exploits are well known, envied at times. Perhaps we have unwittingly cast Jessie to the lion.

"Perhaps it is for her own good," Drake countered.

"I don't know. It makes me nervous to think of Jessie powerless against a man twice as experienced. Despite her age and her penchant for trouble, Jessie is as innocent as a new born babe."

Roc could just make out the words as Drake spoke to Jessie from below. "He is not a fiend, Jessica, if that is what worries you about staying with him. It will only be until your father can come and take you home. He's an honorable man, really. A gentleman from head to toe. And though I regret it has come to this, I would not put you in the hands of a seducer of innocents."

"Do tell, you're too noble," Jessie clipped sarcastically.

Drake grunted and turned from the girl, looking to find Trevor more amenable. He paused, the noise from above catching his attention.

"I had hoped to find all of you gone," Roc said dryly, looking down from the top of the steps. Trevor stood mid-way, and Senator Drake had one foot on the stairs. "I've prepared the attic room for her stay. All in all she should find it comfortable."

Roc shuddered then swore, astonished at Jessie's daring when he looked into the sitting room. She had vanished. It had not taken but a moment and now she no longer sat by the fire. Indeed, Roc hit the banister with his fist, swallowed his fear for her and turned to Trevor, furious, ready to throttle her again.

"Where is she?" Roc asked, searching the room. "I suppose she has eluded the two of you," he said. It seemed he was about to say something more but hesitated, glowering. "I have to retrieve the little dickens, don't I?"

"It might not be as difficult as you think. Fetch Jessie," Trevor commanded and the big dog took off after his mistress.

Drake waved a hand in confusion. "That will work? I thought the hound was hers."

"He is, but I trained him. He obeys me first."

The Senator smiled at Trevor then Roc, his sky blue eyes sparkled with humor. "It so happens I should enjoy seeing the indomitable Miss Lawrence brought to heel by her hound."

"So will I." Roc began, but he could see the fight wasn't over. He paused, tensing his muscles, and it seemed he knew the next few days would try his patience. "You will take the hound with you, I presume," he said to Trevor.

"Of course," he replied.

"Here they come now."

Rupert had Jessie well in tow. Obviously, she had not made it very far.

"By thunder, I would give just about anything to have a picture of this. I'd hang it on my wall," Drake said. "We'll leave now. I believe you are better prepared to handle the young lady on your own than with a crowd of well-wishers hanging around to give advice. Join me, Trevor? If you'll come with me, we'll finish the transactions and you can be on your way."

Roc scowled at the two of them, looking apprehensive then he glared at Jessica.

~ * ~

Ah, well, Roc would have to learn how to deal with her soon. Let him struggle now. Trevor chuckled softly before leaving with Drake, and he didn't take a second glance back. Somehow he thought he wouldn't survive if he did. "There will be heck to pay for this. I don't want to find myself caught in the cross fire," he told Drake.

"Hmm," Drake murmured, clearing his throat. "Heck to pay, yes, I do believe you're right." He had ventured a look back, yet the shrieks that came from inside offered enough information to send the two men scurrying away.

Trevor shuddered. Rupert growled. Drake gave him a reassuring wink, quite unlike the man. He and Drake were both enjoying and fearing this at the expense of Roc. But then again, Roc was the only man they could trust with the precocious piece of baggage.

"Hang up the fiddle, Jess. It's over."

They could hear Roc swearing although the sounds were growing dimmer. He and Drake were moving down the street. Out of earshot, Trevor began to chuckle, and the senator joined him, and several moments later they laughed, caught up in the humor and of the challenge, the intrigue. Then Trevor who had much on his mind directed the conversation to business and the two of them forgot Jessie, forgot Roc and hurried away to Drake's office.

~ * ~

Raymond Pierce was an entrepreneur; rich, decidedly without morals, the power behind the conspirators. He was above reproach, both socially and politically, covering his crimes with such finesse it terrified Trevor. Trevor's latest assignment, or mission, had come to him from Senator Drake himself; he had called Roc in to assist. Raymond Pierce was heir to a vast fortune and land that covered thousands of acres. Since it provided a healthy shield for the laundering of money and the sheltering of his victims, he maintained each piece of property with diligence. He also involved himself with underworld leaders from back east, their hold over him confusing, yet something Roc had looked into. All his crimes had gone unprosecuted, this, their last chance because rumor had it he intended to leave the country. Of course if they managed to accumulate enough evidence, both the senator's and his career would soar. Scandal and crime always topped the news, and the people of Oregon would show their favor. They would both profit. Senator Drake had pointed that out himself, so he knew his plans were not completely selfless.

Pierce had basked in illicit profits long enough, yet without the damning evidence, he would continue to reap the rewards. He had his own plans, and they did not involve meeting his punishment. Raymond Pierce was meticulous, intelligent, and careful.

Naturally, that was one of the reasons no one had discovered his perfidy, until now, until he made one mistake. The documents that rested in Roc's safe had fallen into the wrong hands, or in the state's interest, the right hands. Quite by accident, Drake had come across evidence that shook his own self-confidence. He had always admired Raymond Pierce and his solid position in the community. When presented to Trevor for further scrutiny, he'd felt sick. So much so he could not condone actions that transpired through this man's hands. He had determined to work with Drake to end this.

Maybe he and Drake had waited too long, going about this deliberately and painstakingly. Roc admonished them for taking so much time, collecting, sorting, and categorizing the evidence. In truth they had enough to put Pierce away for years, yet they wanted more, so much more, they wanted Pierce's life blood. They wanted to stop him and people like him. They owed no one an explanation, except Jessica perhaps, and she would have to wait. Still, for her sake, he hoped she would not remain locked in the attic room for long.

Trevor grinned, thinking of what could happen between Roc and Jessica. Indeed what he hoped would happen. Sometime soon, if everything went according to plan, they would reveal the damaging testimony.

When they reached Drake's office, they slipped in the back way. Trevor Lawrence moved inside the dark cool room. Drake had poured himself a drink and collapsed into a comfortable chair. It had been an extremely long night, one without sleep but not without a victory of sorts.

"Help yourself, Trevor. It will calm your nerves. Did I tell you I can hardly wait to see who wins? She's a feisty one and full of the very devil, a huckleberry above most people's persimmon, eh? Of course you'd know first hand. Ah, but I could use one just like her."

Trevor stared, astonished at what Drake had said. *One just like her, hmm? Wouldn't that be a treat? The devil, but one's enough in the family.*

"Well, what do you make of it? I've seen worse combinations than those two. And I take that back, I'd never make it past the first round with anyone as determined as Jessica Lawrence."

Drake pulled out the drawer of his desk, rifling through the contents until he found a notebook. "In here is a map and directions to the warehouse. I want a detailed accounting of everything that happens."

Trevor reached for the book, clenching it tightly against his chest. "You'll not be disappointed."

The senator leaned back and closed his eyes. When he had thought a second, he opened them, "I'm counting on you." He stood, and for a moment it seemed as if he'd say something more. But he didn't. Then...after clearing his throat, "If you're not back in a week, I'll send Roc after you."

Trevor wanted this as much, maybe more. "I'll be back. The rendezvous is only three days away. If I'm to..."

He broke off, noticing Drake's answering nod. It was bad luck to talk of this any more. The senator reached out a hand. Trevor grasped it in his and they shook.

"Take care, I'd never forgive myself if anything happened to you," he whispered.

"You would, but nothing will happen. You've given me a chance to prove my mettle."

"Trevor, you have nothing to prove."

"I'd like to live up to my family's reputation without using their name. No sir, I do have a lot to prove, a hell of a lot to live up to."

"Just be yourself and don't forget to use your head," he told him, frowning. "Intelligence is often of more use than brawn or your martial arts you're so proud of learning."

"You're so astute," Trevor said laughingly. "I'll not forget that either."

"Good, I'm glad to hear."

"Walk with me to the Wells Fargo Station."

They headed down Liberty Street. A wolfish grin touched Drake's face. "She is an exciting woman," he said simply.

"I'm afraid Jessica took Roc by surprise," Trevor laughed.

"He won't like that."

"No, but he'll get used to it. You don't suppose anything will happen while I'm gone?" Trevor asked.

Before Trevor could stop himself, he was thinking of so many things. Jessie could provoke. Roc would grit his teeth and hold his ground. But if they touched, yes, if they met each other flesh against flesh, Jessie would melt. Roc would counter the invitation, and there would be the very devil to pay and a wedding to negotiate. Yet, he knew Jessie didn't want marriage. It wasn't part of her plans and Roc, what did he want? What every man wanted, his freedom. Yes, by the time he returned, all the furies from hell couldn't stop the chain of events put in motion this day. It could have been worse. No, in Jessie's eyes nothing was worse than marriage, a forced marriage at that. He could pray.

As Trevor Lawrence waited for the stage, rocking on his heels, long minutes later, he thought how he'd hate to lose her. She'd blame him, hate him for a long time, no, a very long time. Maybe Roc would fall madly in love with his hot little cousin and sweep her off her feet. The devil, she swept him off his feet and no love was involved.

The worst was yet to come and it seemed unavoidable.

He laughed again at something Drake said.

"By thunder, that wasn't funny, Trevor. Where's your head?"

"Drake, you are a senator, a member in good standing. You must look out for my cousin. I'm feeling decidedly guilty all of a sudden as if I've somehow shirked my duties, left her with that known womanizer. No matter how dear a friend he is, my conscience is bothering me."

Trevor heard the senator chuckle softly. He could tell Drake thought his sudden wave of guilt humorous. Senator Drake would do almost anything for him. He knew that, but they had agreed to let nature takes its course. The Senator wouldn't change his mind now.

"Drake..."

"Trevor, Jessica's stubborn, impetuous most of the time, and needs a strong hand from what I've seen. Last night's escapade is proof."

"Needs to understand the dangers," Trevor added with a heavy sigh "Jessie's high-strung."

"She might well have gotten herself shanghaied and transported to some rich whore house, Trevor, she doesn't think of the--"

"True, but, she forgets her abilities amount to nothing against a man like Roc. She doesn't realize he let her have the victory because he was trying not to hurt her."

"He let her have the win?"

"Jessie doesn't even realize he held back."

Drake laughed. He pointed to the stage. "Once you're on board, forget those two."

Trevor grimaced, once again guilt taking over, "I don't think I can do that, but I'll put her in the back of my mind."

"Good..."

"Drake," he hesitated, "I can't forget her completely, but I won't let her distract me." He winked, staring at Drake before looking down the street in the direction of Roc's house.

"But Trevor..." Drake began, harshly.

"No, Senator." Trevor held up his hand in warning.

"This is the last piece of evidence we need."

"You've impressed me with that fact."

"Well, you can't fault me with concern. We've waited over a year for this moment, and I don't want it lost because you can't keep your mind on the job. Besides, if we fail here, we'll give our hand away and Raymond Pierce will skedaddle."

Trevor scowled.

"Another shipment of Chinese ladies are due in port. They'll auction them off the same night. Rumor has it Pierce picked up a couple of natives off the island and one white woman, a minister's daughter."

"A minister's daughter," Trevor repeated.

He nodded seriously. "They stopped in San Francisco first, spent almost a week there. They've never sold a white girl before. Honestly, Jessie could find herself in the same position if she isn't stopped."

Trevor paled. "Jessie, Jessie, Jessie..." he groaned.

"My sentiments exactly. But still..."

"She's locked in his attic," Trevor said, quickly. "The devil, but I pray he keeps her there and damn that pretty little hide of hers. I'd give anything at this moment if she was buck toothed and fat." He groaned again, mentally calculating all the tight spots he'd saved Jessie from, all the scraped bruises and cuts he'd cared for. And nothing had stopped her, nothing. Now only one man stood between trouble and his conniving little cousin.

Drake smiled. "She's not dear, boy. She's not."

"So we pray?" He arched a brow.

"Well, you're quite right. It's one of the reasons I acted so fast. She needs to be held down for the week. At least until the immediate danger passes."

"Well, Roc has his work cut out for him. He has a wildcat in his house, a wily one at that. Promise me you'll check in on Jessie everyday. I mean it."

"Perhaps you have a valid point. Roc may find himself in need of another pair of hands before the week is out."

"Just remember to handle her with tender loving care."

"Even when I find myself backside on the ground? I don't have the skills Roc does."

"I know."

"You don't have to act so smug," Drake said. "Raymond is our concern at the moment. He hired her to retrieve the documents. When he discovers she failed, he'll come after her. And though he is respected here in town, he is capable of..." He hesitated. "He loves the game as much as the money, Trevor. All and all, Raymond Pierce doesn't care for anyone, except himself. He'd stop anyone who got in his way."

"Murder?" Trevor scowled.

"It's only a game..."

"Everyone plays games, not everyone plays them with human lives. Raymond Pierce does. As to Jess Law, or Jessie, she doesn't have an ounce of common sense. She couldn't have known what was in those papers, or she would have never agreed to work for that scum Pierce. If she did know, she deserves what she gets."

"Trevor, you don't mean that."

"What if I did?"

Drake paused. "Just a few days ago, Trevor, I helped pick up the pieces of one of his girls who managed to escape him. It wasn't pretty," he said dryly. It had been worse than that, but knowing Trevor's temper, he refrained from supplying the details. Instead, he told him what was necessary. "I'd been out riding on my property, and I found the girl nearly curled into a ball, cowering with fear, naked except for a scrap of cloth that left nothing to one's imagination. She was incoherent and mumbling. But Jessie had come upon us and relieved me of the responsibility. Her uncanny ability to soothe the distressed woman had been so magnificent I allowed her take over and help Raymond Pierce's victim to my house. The poor girl will never be the same again."

Drake inhaled sharply. It seemed the scene he played over in his mind once more affected him. "It matters not you're frustrated with Miss Jessica and would like nothing more than to ring her neck, but no one deserves that fate. Jessie behaved admirably with the girl and the look in her eyes touched my soul. It strengthened my vows to see Pierce come to justice."

"What was wrong with the girl?"

He waved a hand in the air. "It was unspeakable, really. Sold on an auction block then raped by several men. When we found her, she hung on tenaciously to life even after having suffered so. But I'll never, as long as I live, forget the haunted look in her eyes."

"Senator, I'm sorry, I would do anything to bring this to an end. You're right, of course. I wouldn't wish that on any woman, even my willful cousin."

"Now I want no more thoughts of Jessie, only the business at hand."

Trevor entered the coach and settled himself on the seat.

"I'll see you in a week," he assured Drake. He remained silent, a grim line creasing the corners of his mouth. Within moments, Senator Drake stood alone on Liberty Street.

To Trevor's great annoyance he could not relax. He remained tense and wary, envisioning the woman Drake described, the horror of it all. The terror Roc would keep Jessie from, he hoped. In truth his cousin had fallen in so deep, knew too much or nothing, but it was the promise of what she could possibly reveal that threatened.

He shuddered, startled by the stark fear then the wave of guilt he held in check these hours turned to unease. Roc would keep her safe. A beautiful woman such as Jessie would bring a great deal of money at auction.

There was no need for Jessie to ever know what she had come so close to revealing. If she had succeeded in gaining the documents, Pierce would have had no choice but to rid himself of her.

And he could not still this feeling of terror.

His cousin was trouble, he knew first hand. Bad trouble. She just wanted her independence, her freedom.

The devil, he prayed she never found it.

Chapter Three

Raymond Pierce strode the length of his office, pausing only to stare out at the first blush of dawn. Pierce was approaching middle age; a slight twinge of gray dusted his dark hair, his eyes, the color of flint, seemed to smoke with the hint of anger. He kept his body trim, his stomach only beginning to lose its youthful hardness. Yes, he should have been a very happy man, and would be when he got his fingers around Jess Law's scrawny neck. His smoky gaze roamed the well-furnished office. Papers cluttered his huge oak desk, stationary that had a corresponding set, documents that should have been in his hands an hour ago.

And Jessica Lawrence should have been on a fast packet to Seattle.

Somehow, he thought his plan had failed. He'd never been able to tolerate failure, and now he'd have to cut his losses and run before things here got too hot. As soon as this boatload sailed into the Astoria harbor, things would most definitely smolder. He wasn't quite sure how he was going to manage his escape, but he'd think of something. For now, liquidating his assets plagued him, took all his concentration and time.

But, he thought with a smile, he could take a few of his more delicate possessions with him. Ones he could not bring himself to discard. Naturally, he had his favorites and they were ever so much more interesting than the others.

"It's time to move on," Sterling Rutgers told him.

Pierce nodded, frowning out the window as he watched Trevor board the stage to Astoria then turned his gaze back to his partner. Rutgers was a lanky man, un-intimidating, meek, yet intelligent and crafty; he liked that. Everything about Sterling spoke of wealth and breeding, from his silver gray hair to his spit polished shoes and his immaculate clothing.

But he was no gentleman, not Sterling. He had a subtle way of turning one man's failure into his gain, and he thoroughly enjoyed the baser things in life. Pierce needed him because he didn't have the imagination or the intuition Sterling had, and Sterling enjoyed all Pierce's little streaks of cruelty, seemed to enjoy watching. He knew Sterling would never betray him. As with his other associates, he picked them carefully, never let them close to the inner workings of his empire until he had a trump card to play. Blackmail, he did it so very well.

Jess Law had been his one mistake. He could find nothing to hold over her head to keep her in line, and so he knew in the end he would have to deal with her in a unique fashion. He could never risk the little brat and her honest streak, as strong as the wild one that got her into so much trouble.

"It's a damn sight too soon," Pierce told him wearily, letting the curtain fall back into place.

"Because they've protected Jessie Lawrence?" Sterling inquired.

Raymond Pierce scowled, turning back to his desk, noting with some dissatisfaction his hasty search had resulted in nothing. He slammed his hand down hard and Sterling jumped. Then he sat down only to lean his head on the chair, gazing at the ceiling.

"I have always wanted revenge against the Lawrence's," he said, and it was true. James Lawrence had outbid him on the land James now owned in Jacksonville. The pear orchard that flourished there should have been his. Instead, he settled for less than the best. That wasn't a habit of his, and it still didn't sit well with him. James Lawrence was a thorn in his side, even if the entire state worshiped the ground he walked upon. Damn Lawrence, his adventurous daughter, and her failure to bring back the damning papers he employed her to retrieve.

But Jessie...

She'd pay for it all. He'd see to that before he left the states. More than anything in his life he wanted revenge. If there had ever been anything that could taste so sweet, promised so much, anything that could ease the frustration simmering within him, it was what he planned to do with Jessie Lawrence, when he got his hands her.

Jessie was someone he could never quite understand. Everything about her was contradictory; something he couldn't put a finger on, and it disturbed him.

Then there was Trevor.

Yes, indeed, the epitome of a Lawrence; proud, strong, arrogant when it suited but always honest to a fault. Trevor Lawrence was always off on some mission of goodwill to save the country from evil and men such as himself. Pierce chuckled. Well, the lad would meet more than he bargained for when he reached Astoria. Oh yes, more than he'd ever thought possible.

When this ended, Trevor Lawrence would never set foot again in Oregon, not in this lifetime anyway. It bothered him he couldn't be there to see it. A little humility was always good for the soul; he thrived on watching a man humbled, and he would have witnessed it first hand.

Jessie Lawrence had thrown another blockade to his plans.

"They've put her under the protection of Roc Newman," Rutgers said with little emotion then leaned against the desk. Papers shifted under the weight of his arms. "It must have been one hell of a fight. The Senator, Roc, Trevor, and Jess Law. Just thinking about it makes for a good laugh."

"And you were there to see it. So you know just what they plan."

He paused. "Yes, I was there, waiting for her."

A knock sounded on the door, and Pierce could hear the hasty shuffling of feet. *Lilly, she's come for the girl.*

"Damnation, Lilly, couldn't you wait?" Pierce thundered.

Lilly purred from behind the door, and he could almost hear the claws scratching. Then the door swung open. She stood, provocatively framed in the doorway. A sweet smile curved her lips, disarming and completely suggestive.

She moved into the room.

"So, what did you do with her, Pierce. I thought I got first look-see. If you've gone and sold the little cherry off without a by-your-leave, you'll pay. You promised, Pierce, and I mean to hold you to your word."

Sterling moved to close the door. "It wouldn't do to let the world hear of this," he said smoothly. "It certainly isn't as if our underworld activities were common knowledge." He reached to the shade to draw it down and moved back.

Lilly grinned broadly at him and pursed her overripe lips. "No, and it wouldn't do for your business associates to see me in here. I know what side of the street I walk on. You don't have to hit me over the head with it."

She was once an exquisite woman, but the years had taken their toll. In a way, she resembled every woman who had wished for something better in life and never found it, but that's as far as the comparison went. Lilly had found exactly what she wanted. Her eyes were green, almost the color of emeralds, her hair a deep golden red, and she was well rounded, abundantly so, in all the right places.

She didn't ply her trade any longer, didn't have to. She had a stable full of girls who did it for her, paid a pretty penny for a clean room, food and a place over their heads. Yet he'd never heard one of them complain. Lilly treated her girls right.

"Sterling," Lilly dipped her head, lowered her lashes demurely then turned to Pierce.

"Good day, Lilly. Your visit is a bit premature."

Amusement curled her lips. She walked to the cabinet where Pierce kept his liquor, shuffled the bottles around before finding something she liked, and poured herself a stiff drink. She moved to the desk and sat down, crossing one leg. She posed, smiled, and sipped the alcohol.

"So, the girl bested someone."

Pierced frowned. "Roc Newman."

Lilly laughed softly. "Well and blazes, if that isn't a sound I thought I'd never hear. That little scrap of a girl got the drop on Roc Newman. Delays your plans a might though, I suspect. If it weren't so damn serious, I could enjoy the thought. Now what? Surely with your devious and crafty mind there is some way you can rectify the matter."

Sterling growled. "Don't jump in without thinking."

"Shut up." Pierce snapped, "Unless you've got a brilliant idea."

Sterling leered at Lilly. "Lilly, we are going to need your help, and I know Pierce will see you well rewarded. He always does."

Lilly grinned. Pierce knew she hadn't made it this far without taking a few risks. He had treated her right; she owed him this, even with the added danger. Just the mention of Roc Newman obviously sent delightful little shivers down her spine.

"Tell me the plan," Pierce insisted.

Sterling grinned, moving closer to Lilly. He traced the length of her leg with his fingertip, stopping at the edge of her gown. Paused a moment. Emerald lights spit fire at him; he moved his hand to her bodice and touched the swell of her breast. Silence lingered too long. Sterling cleared his throat, tapped her on the chin then turned. He walked to the window and stared out at the street. "It's easy. The players, the scenario, they're all ripe for the picking. They've even very cordially arranged themselves. Ah, Jessica, a little spit fire, but innocent, so angry with Roc she'll believe anything. She trusts you Pierce. Then we have the good senator, the snoop; he's been at your back a long time now. He's waited too long. Then, of course, the gallant Trevor Lawrence and finally Roc Newman. We just have to see that they sail on the tide."

"That easy, huh?" Pierce said.

"If we all do our part," Sterling assured them.

Pierce thought he was running out of time, but reciprocity had become an obsession.

"All right," Pierce finally agreed. If anything went wrong, just one mistake...

Sterling inhaled a long steadying breath. Mistake...

~ * ~

Roc was beside himself. It had taken him fifteen minutes, fifteen earsplitting, muscle straining minutes to get Jessica to the attic room without hurting her. His temper had risen so high he barely restrained himself, threatening her life if she dared create more chaos. By the time he'd barred the solitary window and locked the door, he'd cursed Jessica, the senator, and Trevor to hell and back. Now she summoned him and he couldn't get in because Rupert had returned. He stood sentinel over the door. So, until she called the hound off, he wasn't going nearer than the bottom steps.

"I want out of this place now!" Jessica hollered.

He heard the cursing that followed, blanched guiltily but didn't move. It was as if he could see the wild little creature pacing the tiny room.

Captivity didn't suit her. With his eyes closed, he could see her raven black hair spilling across her shoulders, flying with each turn she made. His fingers itched to feel the silk, caress the length, and he damned himself to a thousand hells.

"Call off the dog, little wildcat. I won't come until he goes, you can rest assured of that."

"Afraid of poor Rupert?"

Her taunt grated on his nerves.

"He's my only protection. You're a horrid creature to think of it." She pounded on the door until the sound reverberated down the long stairway. "You're detestable."

His eyes smoldered. His guilt turned to anger as he thought of all the things she had demanded, all the things she had done to him in the last twelve hours and the worst yet to come. He had a sinking feeling his life would never be the same.

"Never the less, call the hound off. Your claws are enough of a threat to my well being."

"I'll sheath them."

"Ah, sweet Jessica, you expect me to believe that?"

"Believe anything you want. If you don't come up here this minute, I'm going out the window."

"Do that. I'll be waiting to pick up the pieces." He chuckled softly. Didn't believe for a moment she'd actually dare that feat. Yet, the sudden stab in his gut brought his head up fast. His gaze met the closed attic door at the same instant the explosion of shattered glass filled his ears and Rupert's loud barking drowned out all conscious thought.

Roc waved a hand impatiently in the air. "Son of a bitch! I don't believe it. She doesn't have a brain in her head, the little idiot. She certainly doesn't think of anyone but herself. The blasted hound will undoubtedly follow her out the window, and I'll have to rescue him too. If Trevor thinks for one moment this will end up in matrimony, he's crazy as a loon." Roc was out the door and around the side of house, mumbling profanities. His thoughts were on the girl above. Yet, even as he threatened to murder the little dickens, he saw her clinging tenaciously to a weathered gable.

The sun sparkled down, enfolding her in its embrace.

He smiled. She wasn't going anywhere. The no-account Rupert howled from the window, mourning his mistress's predicament yet smart enough to know better.

Roc stepped back, shielding his eyes from the sun, soaking in the vision. Ah, how long should he let her hang on the ledge? Long enough, he mused, for her to come to terms with the danger. Long enough, but how much time would it take? For an ordinary person perhaps a minute would do. Jessica...well, he'd wait it out and see.

She'd have to beg.

"Jessica." Roc called out with undisguised humor.

No answer. He laughed again, settling himself against a huge old oak tree. It was a sight he'd never forget.

Perkins, his valet, servant, and sometimes confidant had followed him outside only to stare at the young girl in horror. "Mr. Newman, do something." he sputtered.

Roc grinned, "I am."

"But..."

"She's fine." He looked back just in time to see her foot slip. Perkins moaned. Jessica scrambled, only to slip again. Roc's heart flew to his throat and he lunged forward. His better instincts took over; his fears calmed. Jessica froze almost in midair between the clouds and the ground, had found a foothold and now rested, apparently unfazed by the near mishap. Roc cursed violently. "I need a drink."

Perkins turned, moving toward the house; he looked as if he wanted nothing more than to fetch the desired liquid and return where he wouldn't have to witness this travesty. Yet, when he saw Jessica, he slowed.

From where he sat, Roc was sure he could see violet fire, liquid with fury, and the sun sparkling on a tear. His imagination. Damn, he wanted her to cry, wanted her to understand fear. It seemed the girl had none and that terrified him. He'd promised to protect her at all costs, but dear God, he had to have her cooperation and all she wanted was her freedom.

"She has to learn," he said suddenly, staring at Perkins who was walking backwards, gazing at the tiny figure above. "This entire affair is too hot for her to involve herself in, too dangerous. Lord, she doesn't realize it but she could have ended up in a brothel or as some man's prized whore.

Her father spent all those years teaching her everything she didn't need to learn and her cousin didn't help." He thought of his bruised backside and ego, all at the hands of the little wildcat perched above. Even in that precarious position, she appeared ready to spring.

Perkins moaned once again. "Sir, I know you've a bone to pick with that girl...up there." He pointed a shaky finger in her direction. "But you have to do something. If anything happens to her, you'll regret it. Trevor and the senator..."

"Are both crazy," Roc finished for him.

"True, all of it, but..." Perkins said, looking distressed, and clearly urging Roc to remedy the situation. Roc could be very stubborn and resolute once he chose a course of action, and in his anger he might well linger over much.

Roc tensed his muscles so hard he shook. "She's fine," he said again, as if to reassure himself, yet he knew better, could sense the fear. She clung to the roof. "Cats have nine lives; she's hasn't used half of them yet."

Perkins looked as if he wanted to scream. "Roc, you've never acted this way before. I'm afraid Trevor Lawrence placed you in a dastardly position. One very thin line separates you from a fate you've so far managed to escape quite handily. But truly, Mr. Newman, couldn't you save the girl yet manage somehow to fall in with Trevor's plans?"

"Whose side are you on?"

"Yours, sir, but if you don't do something soon, you'll find out first hand how many lives she's used so far. My guess from the way Miss Jessica handles life, she's got to be on the ninth one," Perkins warned.

Roc knew instantly what Perkins meant. Jessica Lawrence had always been a little wild, a spoiled child. He remembered another meeting five years ago, when he'd run across the little lady sitting on top of a thoroughbred hunter, surrounded by a pack of forty hounds. She had intrigued him even then.

On top of everything else, Trevor had wired James, Jessie's father, and he was bound to cause trouble. Roc didn't want to deal with the man on these terms. Particularly when he felt it was not in Jessica's best interest to place her in the hands of her father, a father who denied her nothing. If he did, they would be back to the beginning. Although James was a powerful and determined man when it came to his cunning little daughter, he was spineless.

"James Lawrence," he said dryly to Perkins. He hesitated. "I hope he never discovers what I've done...or not done...or. Damnation," he whispered fiercely, and so very frustrated. He felt as though he'd tied his hands and been swept into a tornado. "I can't let him near Jessica, or this house. He's her father, but I vowed to protect her. Heaven help me. I'm supposed to see that her virtue is kept safe," Roc groaned this time. His gaze flew heavenward, stopping to rest on the sleek form nestled snugly in the eaves, her long slender legs encased irresistibly in pants. He didn't have to imagine a damn thing. And her virtue...

Perkins gaped at what he saw, Roc's reaction to the girl evident. He stepped back apparently to chastise his employer but stopped short. "If you don't mind my saying so, she's perfect for you, sir. Jessica Lawrence is just what you need to give meaning to your life. A woman made for you as if you'd ordered her."

Roc's eyes looked smokey, sending hazy signals of desire toward the girl, in sharp contrast to the casual lock of hair that fell across his brow. Flaming lust, smoldering burning desire, radiated blatantly from him. Roc's casual elegance belied the tightly sprung coils of fear that pierced his gut, suddenly realizing the precarious position she had placed them both in, damning him if he gave in to his protective nature and rescued her. Rumors had it he was the most eligible bachelor on the west coast. There were also strange rumors he kept a harem of waiting and very willing women where ever he travelled, and the lucky lady to find his favor might find herself most amazed at his skills, and never question the short term relationship.

Roc didn't pander to gossip. All of what was said had some basis in truth. But then one could find a grain of truth in most anything if they looked deep enough.

"I think you've waited too long, Mr. Newman," Perkins told him.

Roc stared, glued to the sight above. Her audacity amazed him. Then he cursed, "How the hell am I supposed to get her off that perch? She certainly has the unmitigated ability to make me miserable."

"You could try the fire department, or perhaps send her a rope. I suppose she could find her way down."

Roc grinned, raising an eyebrow. "Either might work, but I'd still prefer to see how she plans to handle this."

"Well, I don't believe what I'm hearing," Perkins said. "Does she look like she can get down on her own?"

"She, yes," He shrugged. "She found her way there." He groaned, surprised to feel the subtle rise of guilt. No, he refused to let her twist him around that lily-white finger of hers, the one she'd used to deck him so handily. He'd wait. She didn't look as if she were in immediate danger. With her jet hair and glorious eyes shooting a mercurial warning his way, he'd be willing to believe she was just biding her time, hoping he'd leave. Well, he had news for her. When he first thought of this, he'd known Perkins would bring him whatever he needed. He had been sure of himself from the moment he managed to throw her into the attic room. When he touched her, he felt the wealth of soft feminine curves. He had to admit her physical appearance might have momentarily robbed him of his senses.

"No, Perkins, I'll not help her, not unless I have to, but I doubt that possibility. You see, she looks quite at home up there."

"Well, I had thought..."

Roc narrowed his eyes and Perkins had the good sense to close his mouth. "Go fix something to eat. My stomach seems to need a little fortification."

"I'll not mince words. I don't like this, but I'll do as you say if only because the young lady up there is bound to need something also."

He left Roc leaning against the oak tree and started toward the kitchen. Roc watched Perkins retreating back, deep in his thoughts, when he heard a sharp cry of distress. His gaze flew swiftly to the roof to see Jessica had inched closer to the open window but somehow slipped and once more scrambled to regain her footing, clinging desperately to the ledge from which she had just perched and glared at him.

She pulled herself to safety, flattening her stomach across the window ledge. Rupert barked then licked her cheek. Roc held his breath, finally exhaling slowly when he realized she managed to seize the moment. Unless Rupert hindered her climb over the windowsill, she was out of danger. "Very nice," he drawled. "Is the entertainment over now?"

Perkins raced outside at the first sound of peril. Rupert's barking frenzy had seemingly terrified him. "Mr. Newman...Roc." Perkin's breathless demands startled him.

Jessica climbed into the house. Roc continued to stare at the window long moments after the girl disappeared from view. His frown hardened, molded itself into ice.

"She did that splendidly," he told Perkins.

Perkins's shocked expression drooped. He turned on his heel and strode back to the kitchen, leaving Roc to grin at the empty window. Rupert vanished, no doubt to give solace to his mistress. His brow rose questioningly, and his lip curled into a contemptuous smile. "Why, Jess Law," he murmured. "Whatever will you try next?"

Just as if she'd heard him, her head popped up, "I'll make you regret this."

"You already have, my dear, you already have."

It was anything but that. He enjoyed watching her antics as long as he didn't have to come in contact with her. Yet he had a certain duty where it concerned her, and he did mean to keep her safe. Unfortunately, the attic room would no longer suit this purpose. His smile widened.

"Are you going to stay there all night?"

"No, I intend to have something to eat. Would you join me?" He called up to her.

Roc imagined Jessie's wrath, expected a sharp report, but when he was met with silence, he knew she couldn't find the words to counter his politeness.

Perkins called from the front door. "Everything's ready." His voice sounded clearly disgruntled and angry with his employer.

Jessie must have seen Perkins at the door. She leaned way out from the window and waved, but Perkins seemed entirely too absorbed with his hostility to fall for her obvious ploy. Roc didn't miss it though. He didn't reply, just signaled for Perkins to stay put and watch the lady in question. He strode to the house.

By the time he reached the attic, he found his good humor had returned, but with the first warning growl from the drooling hound, he forgot all good intentions.

"Call off the dog, Jess."

He pounded on the door, heard the scuffling and knew she meant to leave by the window again. Fury seized him. He forgot the dog, forgot the fangs and the threat.

He karate kicked the door. Splinters flew in the deepening twilight. Shattered, the door hung from its hinges and Roc lunged for Jessica.

"Dash it all," she swore just as his fingers closed around her waist, finding purchase within the belt loops. He yanked her from the open window. Harmless and enjoying the fun, Rupert barked and scampered around the room, delighting in this new game. Jessie legs whirled, arms flailed. She wrapped her leg around the back of his knee and applied pressure; he dropped to the floor but not before he turned, pinning her beneath him.

Their gazes met.

Silence fell ominously, surrendering the moment, knifing between them while they parried each other's thoughts.

Her breaths came in gasping heaves. She lay beneath him, and he refused to move, rejected her opportunity to turn the advantage, enjoyed the sight of her subdued for the moment.

"Ah, Miss Lawrence, do you have to make life so difficult?"

"In truth, I was thinking this was your doing," she said coldly.

"It was you who thought to fly. Didn't your father teach you humans have certain restrictions?" he inquired, his dark head coming unerringly closer to her, his whisper fluttering against her cheek, and exploding a wealth of sensations within. Her common sense seemed to evaporate whenever he appeared.

And with the heat came the oddest of chills, tumbling throughout.

"My father taught me I could do anything I set my mind to, sir. In the matter of flying, suffice it to say it was not my intent."

"Oh, but that seemed the only way to find the ground, flying." Roc knew despite her arguments Jessica understood the truth of his words. She hadn't thought before leaping through the window.

"I am afraid, Mr. Newman, that due to your untimely arrival, you were unable to witness my agility. I planned to climb down. Most gentleman would have avoided causing a lady to act so haphazardly to life and limb."

"Most ladies would not act like a spoiled child. You refer to something you obviously know next to nothing about."

His words seemed to cut deep, and he watched her struggled to contain her rising temper. He'd already lashed out, condemning her behavior even when he'd provoked it.

"Do tell but it's just as obvious that you are incapable of behaving as a gentleman," she countered.

"I see, so you imply this is my doing, this precipitous flight through the window?" he asked.

She pushed against his chest, budging nothing, moaning at the horrendous position he'd managed. "So you finally figured that out," she said.

He grinned, pleased. "Well, people say I'm intelligent."

"You haven't the wit God gave you," she replied.

He yanked her from the floor with a sudden jerk. Rupert rose, barked once before settling back to the rug. It was time for Jessica to understand what he intended. Amazed to realize he wanted her to stay with him willingly; tired of fighting and baiting her. Once the week ended, she would go her own way.

"If you'd promise to behave yourself," he began, but before he could go any further, he realized the way things stood between them, it was futile to expect her word to mean anything. To complicate his evening, he could distinctly hear the rumblings of guests below.

"Where's Newman? Upstairs with the sweet little private investigator I imagine," a male voice stated with mirth.

Jessica gasped and Roc felt a sudden surge of protectiveness while he watched the slow flush of embarrassment on her features. The men would not let this go unheralded. Sterling Rutgers had always reminded him of a weasel, with his cunning eyes. The other man, the one who had spoken so rudely, was Raymond Pierce, Jessica's client and friend of her father. A powerful man who wouldn't allow her failure to stand in his way. Roc discerned Raymond Pierce had come hunting, come in quest of the documents.

Roc pulled her to her feet and escorted her down the stairs in pursuit of quelling waging tongues. Avoidance the better part of valor then hesitated, winded from the exertion. Jessica had not followed complaisantly.

"So, there they are," Sterling announced, his gaze roaming Jessie's slender curves, provocative in the tight fitting pants. He smiled slowly then turned his attention to Roc. "I see you two met, dear Jessica. I'll be pleased to pass the news on to your father."

"Mr. Rutgers, this is none of your concern," Jessie began.

"Call me Sterling, Jessica. Your father and I are fast becoming friends."

"Mr. Rutgers," she said, her voice shaking. "I have no reason to believe my father would ever do business with you and least of all call you friend. I do not intend--"

"My dear, Miss Lawrence," Sterling interrupted her, "I am partner to all of Pierce's businesses. That in itself gives me a certain closeness to your father. I believe Mr. Pierce and I have your best interest at heart." He glanced toward Roc. His gaze crept slowly back to Jessica, lingering too long on the tight fit of her Levi's then rising slowly to meet her watchful gaze.

Roc didn't doubt Jessica had longed for someone to come along, a person to spirit her away from him before he could protest, but he knew she wouldn't go with either of these men. They even made him shudder. Sterling goaded her and threw out insinuations she couldn't defend. Now Roc understood she would see him as the lesser of two evils, a savior perhaps, and he intended to take advantage. Yet the look of revulsion on Jessica's features almost made him laugh, and he wondered if Sterling reminded her of a weasel too.

"Let me begin then, Mr. Sterling," she said quickly, "I intend to stay here with Mr. Newman. He has opened his home quite magnanimously to me, for the week, until my cousin returns."

"But, my dear, your reputation…" Sterling hesitated.

"Sterling," Roc said sharply, disliking the tone of the conversation. "I don't like the insinuations. It seems you could find a more suitable topic of conversation, such as why you have stopped to pay a visit. I, for one, am interested. And I hardly think, sir, you are in a position to condemn her reputation."

Jessica snorted, crossed her arms over her chest before she turned her back on the men.

"Oh, but what will people think when I explain where Miss Lawrence is spending her evenings and the scandalous way she is dressed?"

"This is far from improper, and I see no need to discuss it with you," Jessica said, turning suddenly. "If you'll excuse me..." she began again.

Roc understood the full implication of her dismissal. Furious, proud, and not intending to underestimate her again, he tightened his grip around her arm.

"Jessica," he murmured, next to her ear, "don't get any ideas. You're not leaving." His focus fell upon Sterling then Raymond. "What is it you came for?"

"Roc, I'm really tired. I'd like to excuse myself."

"Don't be foolish," Raymond said suddenly. "You must stay."

"I'd really like to go."

"You needn't consider Sterling's threats. He was only teasing. I'm sure Roc is the epitome of a gentleman. Personally, I'd consider it a great honor to see you home."

"No," she said, suddenly afraid. "I can't... Well I mean..."

"The lady is staying here," Roc cut in.

"I see," Pierce said coldly. His brow arched smoothly, studying the situation then handed the paper to Roc. He had brought it with deadly intent.

The last thing Roc wanted to do was demolish Jessica's reputation further. With each notch, it seemed he dug his grave, yet he could not let her leave with Raymond Pierce. When Pierce handed him a copy of the newspaper, he swallowed his contempt. He never believed anyone would go to such length. He found the article confusing and uncomfortable, all of this was taking on a strange aura, dragging him deeper into some fathomless pit. He felt more protective of Jessie each time the men raked her with their eyes, and his hands clenched with unbidden fury.

Roc wouldn't let either man near her. Determined beyond reasoning to keep her, despite the article, despite the threat of her father, and despite herself. He stood with his arm firmly around her waist, holding her closer than proper.

"If that's all you wanted, I'll have Perkins see you to the door." Roc turned swiftly. And to his relief, Perkins had anticipated his call. As they left, Pierce hesitated at the door, daring to look back.

"Jessica..." He paused, and Roc scowled at him, wondering what he was thinking.

Then he spoke swiftly. "Roc, you and Jessica should be very careful."

"Is that a threat?" Roc's hard voice cut the air.

Jessie merely glowered at them all, at the attempted manipulation.

"Think of it as you like," Pierce said then left.

Jessica wilted against Roc. Despite his irritation, he was glad she leaned on him, trusting him. She looked at him, and he wondered at the strange flood of emotions surging within.

No, she couldn't stay here with him. Didn't want her so close, temptation overriding common sense. Didn't want to feel the need to shelter and shield her.

But Jessica had no opportunity to make a choice. He still held her and with little ceremony, he ushered her upstairs to the master chamber, calling once more to Perkins.

Chapter Four

He was impossible, she thought with dismay.

Hysteria threatened to explode within her. This was truly bizarre.

She didn't know how to fight Roc. Only that she could not remain in this room with him. One look at the man and she melted inside.

Why had she ever thought to best him?

She relaxed, wooing him into compliance; he seemed to fall for the charade easing his hold upon her arm. Rupert slept at the top of the step, mindless and content.

His hand brushed hers and sweet wildfire raged within. She gasped, pulling away, hating the confusion. So far she had managed to resist, managed to hold to her purpose.

"I won't go with you," she whispered.

One dark brow arched. "You will."

His conceit infuriated her. "That's what you think." She tensed, her gaze suddenly scathing.

"That's what I know," he countered. Swooping her resisting form into his arms, he marched up the stairs.

"Oh."

He grinned audaciously. "Please forgive my manners, my dear oh-too-confident private eye. You deserve this and more. I want you to know I find you the most annoying woman I've ever had the misfortune to come across, and therefore, my sweet, as perturbing as it might seem, you will do what I say, when I say it. My aversion to your actions has no importance. Of course, since you feel the same, we will deal well together. I would not marry you, sweetheart, were the hounds of hell after me, abstinence would

52

be more desirable. There now, do you think you could cooperate?"

"Never."

For a moment his lip curled into a smile, but when her struggles almost sent them catapulting down the steps, "Son of a bitch," he cried, clinging to the railing while he pulled her closer. "I didn't think so," he murmured, "cooperate, that is."

"You can't make me stay. I'll find a way..."

"I'm sure you'll try."

If he held her any tighter, her delicate bones would break. "Could we call a truce, Jessica? At least until your father or your cousin arrive."

She screeched. What an idiot. He should have never treated her so roughly. Humiliated, she meant to make him pay. She sobbed again. "You're hurting me."

He groaned and his expression turned serious. "I don't mean to," he said in all innocence. "I am curious to know how. Perhaps I could oblige as you seem so eager to blast recriminations. But a gentleman, sweetheart, would never allow a lady to bully them into reprehensible acts, by any threat, and by any means. He would strive to treat a lady in the most tender of ways. Let me emphasize the term *lady*."

Her struggles slowed somewhat. "Oh, so you agree now that I'm a lady. Why then you should trust me?"

Amused, he nearly shook with laughter. "I'm not agreeing with anything."

She was silent, rattled. Persisting, "I *am* a lady."

Laughter swept through him once again. "And just what have you done recently to indicate that, Miss Lawrence?" he demanded. "Was it your hasty climb up the side of my house? Or perhaps the scuffle we had in the dust? Maybe it was when you got caught with your hand inside my safe. But your clothes, Jessie, your clothes resemble that of an urchin rather than a lady. Admit it, Jessica, you don't know the first thing about being a lady."

"Dash it all."

"Of course there is the uncanny use of words setting you so high on a pedestal."

"Mr. Newman, there is no reason for you to feel responsible for the likes of me. Let me go and I will never bother you again."

"I'm afraid I can't do that and I may just enjoy teaching you. Jessica, it is a man's world and you are at our mercy, mine to be more exact. You are a valuable pawn in dangerous intrigue, nothing more, and it is my responsibility to keep you safe, even against your will if necessary. Perhaps your father has neglected the finer points of your education. It would please me to fill in the gaps."

Jessica struggled, futile against his hold. All she had accomplished was to wear herself out. He did not intend to let her go.

"I don't need your words of wisdom, nor do I--"

"Too bad sweetheart. I am extremely eager, I do hold a wealth of knowledge, and I am the only one offering."

He was so damned conceited. She longed to put him in his place as she had done earlier. Yet all the while she felt the most unusual heat cruising through her. Humiliation, possibly, but where his hand stroked, brushed, and even caressed. Oh...

She needed to distance herself more than she had ever needed anything in the world, but she was astonished at the determination in his touch, the taunting casualness of his words, and how thoroughly they frightened and made her tremble. No matter how he irritated her, he caused her to feel completely vulnerable, yet ready to denounce the feelings he evoked, hot, flushed, annoyed past endurance.

"Would you please set me down," she demanded.

"I like you right here," he told her.

She wriggled in his arms and groaned. Fine. He moved up the steps infuriatingly slow.

"Perhaps if you'd act the gentleman, I'd find it easier to act the lady."

"You think so?"

"Of course, it follows doesn't it? I am a lady, my mother made sure I learned how one acted. Where lies the difference between us. You don't have a notion how to behave the gentleman."

He arched a brow high, and it seemed he took a curious interest in her statement. Then he chuckled softly. "Oh, darling, I'd love to teach you the differences between us, but I'm afraid of your claws."

"Good. I can wield them with deadly force."

"I'm not surprised."

"Umm. Then you will stay far away from me?"

He laughed. "I would like nothing better but, no, I can't trust you farther than I can throw you and right now that's as far as the bed." He swiftly released her, shocking her as she flew through the air, landing solidly on the huge master bed. He came swiftly down beside her, his voice most tender. "Sweet kitten, so wild and reckless. Some lucky man will find a way to harness that energy. I pity the fellow. Yet perhaps there is still hope. If your reputation isn't completely tarnished this week, why then..."

She stared at him wide eyed, shocked, furious, and speechless. "And you will do your level best to see it tarnished, I suppose."

He paused, gazing down on her their bodies so close. A transient, unexpected moment struck her when she thought she saw a glimmer of compassion in his steel gray eyes. "Jessica, I doubt your father would have allowed you to put your life in jeopardy. And Raymond Pierce is not as he appears on the surface. He is dangerous and a threat to your existence. I'm not at liberty to elaborate at the moment. Maybe when the week is up things will be different; I've hoped we can effectively put a stop to the conspiracy of Pierce and Rutgers. But at this moment, Jessie, no woman is safe on the streets, not even you."

Ironically, she felt the sting of truth in his words. He seemed to be speaking with sincerity and wisdom, and she didn't want to believe him. No woman safe on the streets?

"Preposterous. You're mistaken. It's perfectly..." She froze, remembering the young lady she'd found, disheveled, forlorn, a shell of a woman. She vividly recalled the haunting look in her eyes, the fear.

He inclined his head, watching. "What is it Jessie?"

"Oh, I..."

"The girl, is that what you're thinking? You and the senator?"

He watched her slender frame shudder and it seemed he yearned to reach out and console, but hesitated only to berate himself.

Jessica saw the change in his expression, but she didn't want his tender touch, not now, not after he treated her so poorly.

Shadows seemed to cover his expression, hiding the light, the warmth, then vanished swiftly. The man cared.

"How did you know?"

"Drake told me when he enlisted my help."

"Then you can understand why I won't let you stop me."

"No, I don't see how that has any merit. This is deadly sport and a woman--a woman could find herself in a position..."

"A man is not immortal."

He smiled, with a tender glint in his eyes, as if she meant something more to him than a responsibility.

"True, but, Jessie, he is not nearly so vulnerable."

"What difference does that make?" she murmured. "Don't you see I must follow my heart? I have a mind and strengths you could never dream of."

He laughed at her words, and for a brief moment, she was once more aware there were, possibly, justifications for the man's tremendous concerns. When he spoke to her he was sincere. A touch of candor crept into his voice, his expression, seen through his eyes sparked with silver flame, and his mouth curved with unspoken invitation.

"You have listened, Jessie," he told her, and she found his breath caressed her skin. He had come so close, very close, though still watching her intensely searching for capitulation.

"I have, to every word. It's just I don't agree," she murmured even while she found truth in what he spoke.

"And you would never acquiesce."

"I would never surrender my principles," she said.

"Son of a bitch, Jessie. What am I going to do? I suppose you would never give your word. Your word you would not try to leave?"

He pushed away from her, moving through the room, to the window, back again then running his fingers through his hair. He gazed at her, long and hard.

"You have no right to keep me here," she said. Innocently forgetting she had, only a few hours ago, tried to rob him.

"Oh, my, sweet, Miss Lawrence, how soon you forget. If not here, brat, then the county jail."

"I'd prefer confinement to these accommodations." Yet she knew she wouldn't. Her words were pure bluster.

"Umm, you would? Well, my quarrelsome private investigator, your cousin Trevor, as well as the senator, are quite concerned about you. And until your father arrives to take you home, out of harms way, I will protect you."

"You have to sleep sometime," she said taunting him with the truth, "and when you do..." But she wouldn't leave and neither would she give him her word.

"You push me too far, Jessie," He spoke slowly. His distaste for his thoughts evident in his tone, "but, Jessica, I can think of nothing to do save sleeping with you or tying you to the bed, and I'm not sure I can go that far."

Jessie smiled. "I won't stay..."

"I haven't figured out how, but you will remain in my home. I've a promise to keep. Trevor expects to come back and find his cousin here, not in some expensive brothel. I don't think Pierce would go that far, but if he's threatened, he could strike out at you and he wants revenge. What better way than with the man's daughter?"

His words stung with fact. "I don't believe you. Pierce is a friend of my father's. He'd never harm me and you know that. I don't understand any of this. I want to go home."

"That's not possible, Jessie. I'm truly sorry. There is so much you don't know, and I wish I could tell you."

"I will not allow you to keep me here," she said.

"No? You're incredibly stubborn. Haven't you comprehended a thing I've said? Jessica, neither you nor I have a choice in this matter. One way or the other you will stay."

"And you haven't heard a thing I've said."

He laughed. "Oh, I have and I haven't forgotten anything. You will have your say, but I will see that you remain, and at this point I don't care how. I'm tired and you've managed to bruise my body quite handily, and, Jessie, I'm ready for bed."

"Don't let me stop you. You should certainly get your rest. You will need it."

"So will you." he laughed. His smile lengthened; regardless of her efforts, she felt a languid heat stir within once more. The man was incredibly handsome.

"Damnation, let me go. You don't want me here any more than I want to stay. Don't worry about me, I can take care--"

"I wouldn't be able to stop worrying. I wouldn't be able to sleep or eat for thinking of your welfare and my lack of chivalry. If anything happened to you because of my neglect, I would never be able to live with myself. So you see..."

Worry? Would he worry about her? She couldn't let her burgeoning feelings sway her. She longed for the advantage, the strength of attack, the chance to unseat him. She would find it, surprise him at his own game, and she would go home. She smiled as innocently as she could manage. "Chivalry, Mr. Newman? You have no idea what it means."

His brow arched. His eyes narrowed. "And you, Miss Lawrence, have run free and wild far too long."

"Cad, reprobate, take your pick, you are an insufferable bore and I will count the seconds until I am free of your horrid manhandling. There isn't a man alive who can keep me locked away for very long. I will not be here in the morning. You can make book on it."

The moment of tender concern had vanished. She surprisingly found herself wrenched against him, and tightly so. His eyes smoldered, steel hard, unmovable as they met her fiery glare. "You had best understand I am up to a challenge. I don't take threats lightly and you, sweet lady, have issued a mouthful. You sorely tempt me to tie you hand and foot to this bed. A more prudent man than I would have already done so. Tempted also to wash that filthy mouth of yours with soap and teach you how to, at least, speak as a lady would. Perhaps your father never saw fit to teach you manners, but if you remain in my company much longer, I will not have the patience to restrain myself."

She struggled against his hold yet could not free herself. He pinned her arms uselessly to her sides. She stared hard at him, amethyst fire blazing within; her fury barely restrained. "My father is a gentleman and you're right, he never laid a hand on me, never had reason. Now, sir, unhand me or I swear I'll..." If only she could give her word. Curse her stubborn self.

He smiled and she saw the gleam in his eyes and it sparked an answering flame within her. It wasn't that she had intended to fight him. It was the principle of it all, and he was so unbending, unyielding in his strength. He meant to prove something to her. Prove he was a man, she just a woman, a thorn in his plans. She hated the philosophy, reviled that is was indeed a man's world and there was so very little she could do about it.

"Get your hands off me," she whispered.

He held her too long. Heat and the hard planes of his body pressed against her; begging her to touch, and Jessie, even in her innocence, was aware of the powerful force of his hold, the solid strength of his arms, the fire radiating from him; the curious trembling suffusing her body. She understood sexual need and told herself it was just his proximity to her.

"Now." Panic seemed to rise within, and she forgot every lesson, every move, the technique she had laboriously mastered. She struggled harmlessly, writhing against his length, igniting the simmering fire within her, passing all restraints. She resisted once more until her strength vanished, falling weakly against him. She had proved his point.

She heard the heavy sigh, not an elated voice of the winner. The struggle had been a serious mistake. One she refused to admit. She nearly sobbed from frustration for she knew eventually he would goad her with it. He pressed a hand against her back, and she found he could still close the distance between them.

"Miss Lawrence..." he began, his voice husky and slightly amused. Then he hesitated. In the ensuing time Jessie became thoroughly aware of him in every microscopic detail. She noticed the smoky sheen to his eyes, saw the tender curl of his lip, felt the powerful force of his muscles. She inhaled the scent of him: clean, irresistibly masculine. Against her cheek she felt the subtle whisper of his breath, the slight brush of his lips, soft lips, very tender, seductive, pulling her into his web. The cloth of his shirt touched her hands and she gasped, astonished at the heat lying beneath her fingertips, a fire that seemed to creep within her against her will, overwhelming, questioning her existence and all her noble intentions.

"No," her voice barely perceptible.

The sun dipped beneath the western hills, throwing the room into dusky shadows. He slowly pushed away, holding her at arm's distance, muscles tense, prepared for anything. It seemed he had felt the magic too. Like a mysterious enigma, plaguing, tormenting them both, foretelling of an enchantment that might weave beautifully and strong.

"Behave yourself then," he warned. "Don't throw caution to the wind."

"I am only defending my rights," she told him. "And if I have to take every opportunity offered, Mr. Newman, don't be surprised. I will find a way."

He let his hands fall away from her, confusing her more. "Miss Lawrence, falling into the enemies' plans. It can not happen."

"But you are so sure of the enemy; in this game their numbers increase with every throw of the die."

"I am the only one you can trust," he said. "With each moment more players reveal themselves, and the plot deepens; an intriguing, mysteriously dangerous scenario, one I am well prepared to deal with, Miss Lawrence. You are naive, an impetuous headstrong woman, and you've yet to find the danger you're seeking. But beware, it could well end up more than you can handle. So take my warning."

"I will choose my own destiny," she promised him. "You will not gainsay me." She was adamant because he had frightened her. He had told her a truth she had long suspected. Now, he had given her a clue, pointed her in the right direction and it terrified her. Even though she couldn't verbalize the promise to him, she vowed to herself she would be prudent and would stay in his house under his protection.

Night shadows lengthened in the room. Cool air floated through the windows, sending chills racing within, apprehensions of warning. He seemed to notice it too. His hands fell from her and he stood, striding to the window, staring long moments into the distance.

"I will do my best to protect you, Jessie," he finally said, and he seemed sincere, not mocking this time, but truly afraid for her.

"Mr. Newman, I don't want your help."

She had dropped her guard but a moment. With a swift step he was upon her. A startled cry escaped her, alarmed to find he had pulled her against him, held close to the warmth and security she was beginning to long for, drawn against him. His fingers wove themselves into her hair, pulling her head back so the silver flame of his gaze met hers. "Don't you ever listen to reason? You are the most tenacious woman I've ever run across."

She couldn't move, once more aware of the raw desire he fanned into raging flames when he touched her. It was so curious, for he even seemed caught within the web he had woven mysteriously about her, and it seemed, against his will.

Perkins cleared his throat. He had knocked softly at first but when there was no response he pounded on the door.

"Mr. Newman, a...your dinner..."

Perkins was standing at the open door, watching them both. She cringed, embarrassed to the tips of her toes.

Roc inhaled sharply, his hands falling free from her hair, his gaze riveting hers.

He moved back immediately.

"Oh, Perkins. Set it on the table by the window. Pour the wine first and I'll take care of the rest. I can't speak for Miss Lawrence, but I'm ravenous. She seems to have calmed down some since this afternoon, and I believe you can retire for the evening."

Perkins moved with great deliberation around the room. He inadvertently watched the couple. An amused grin curled his lip now that the seeming shock of interrupting their ardent embrace had dissipated. He chuckled softly.

Jessie didn't realize how hungry she was until the heady aroma of the chicken and the freshly baked bread filtered to her senses. The day had exhausted her, and it wasn't over yet. Now though, she had one thing on her mind.

Their discussion had revealed so much. Raymond Pierce was not the man her father had come to trust, but what was he about? She suddenly realized the answer might lie in Roc's safe, in the documents she almost had in her possession.

She was ready to change her mind. Perhaps escape was not what she should concern herself with. Perhaps she should bend her efforts to getting back inside the safe and reading those papers. The plots, the plans, the conspiracy, she would know more. The Senator, bent on protecting her, would not exclude her from the scheme. Trevor, just as bad, had no confidence in her expertise; an expertise he had honed to a razor sharp edge. Well, she wanted to know everything, every sordid detail; she wanted to know why. Tonight was not soon enough.

She suddenly knew what she had to do. "Mr. Newman, my regrets. I'm thoroughly exhausted. Please, I'd like to rest. Roc, would you leave?"

She wanted to laugh at the curious expression on Roc's face, instead, stifled a yawn and turned her back to him. Jessie looked again but it seemed he'd backed off, considering her request.

"My dinner?" he began then sighed deeply, turning to leave. "Very well, Jessie, but don't get any ideas." He moved to the door. "It's a straight drop to the ground from here right into several large holly bushes. I wouldn't advise it," he told her then left.

She found he'd taken care of security. Rupert had turned traitor and now guarded her door. But she'd find a way around the wily hound. Jessie began to plan. Schemes of her own making fit her constitution much better. She yawned again and realized she truly could not keep her eyes open.

She sipped at the glass of wine Roc had poured earlier and crawled to the bed. It was soft, tempting. She closed her eyes, willing her mind to rest.

Seconds slipped into minutes. Hours later, her eyes jerked open. The moon had risen and cast soft beams of light through the lace curtain. She stared out the window, certain she would succeed this time then listened long moments to the natural sounds of the house, creaking and groaning. Nothing out of the ordinary presented itself. She heard Rupert rub against the door then pad quietly down the hall. Even her dog cooperated.

She rose from the bed, trying to concentrate yet kept seeing the silver flames sparkling within in his eyes, hearing his voice so caressing her flesh with warmth; the safety she felt within his arms.

The documents, she reminded herself.

But she must proceed cautiously. She almost had them in her hands, a wealth of information. He would not outwit her again. Still he tormented her thoughts. She could feel the steel gaze of his eyes, haunting her, watching. She trembled, suddenly believing that even now she schemed against him. He had seemed so frustrated with her, so angry.

Yet she would never understand the silence.

It seemed ridiculous to keep the truth from her.

And still...

He did it to protect her. She could almost accept that, almost, but she had climbed too many mountains. She would not go back. She opened the door, walking stealthily down the long hall then the stairs. Fear suffused her. Minutes ticked by. The old grandfather clock chimed once.

She imagined him around every corner, lurking, waiting to pounce if she made one mistake. Fear, terror, second thoughts...

She breathed deeply, calming herself, willing her mind to remain focused, remembering the safe, the combination, the documents lying within. Information, so coveted, she risked herself. For if he discovered her...lord...if he caught her again. She could see the den in her mind's eye, dark with no light illuminating the room, only shadows cast from the moonlight. She stepped inside. The threat eluded her. Time froze, mystery encompassed her and she trembled then apprehension forced her to reconsider.

Thoughts of discovery by him made her pulse throb, her stomach somersault. She stiffened, forewarned, possibly, but only silence penetrated the room. She closed her eyes and felt him behind her then in front of her. He stood so close she could feel his presence; wonder at the haunting emptiness. Cautiously opening her eyes, she turned on her heel. No one, not even Rupert had entered. Deadly silence permeated the air.

"Dash it all," she murmured. "He's making me crazy."

Then she gulped a mouthful of air and lit the candle. She set to the safe. His every warning had filled her mind to terrify her, to hold her back; it had, indeed almost worked.

She smiled. Finished. Slowly Jessie pushed down on the handle. A tiny sound emanated from the safe, beautiful, then the door opened. She stifled a hysterical giggle before burying her face in her hands. There they were. All she had to do was reach out, touch them, put her fingers around them and run. She'd have to run forever for suddenly she knew he would find her. No, she'd read them and put them back. No one would be the wiser.

Trevor, she had to find Trevor. His life was in jeopardy. Truly, how could he do it? So damning, the woman, the one she'd found that day, dear lord she had escaped and the senator hadn't told her even then. He'd known. The secrets they had all kept. She could hardly believe it. It was there, plain as the nose on her face.

She hastily folded the evidence, clutching the papers tightly, swiftly looking around the room. The house seemed deserted. She moved to the door. Behind her, under the desk, she was certain she heard something. Fear seized her. Rational thought left her. He wouldn't hide under a desk; she knew that. He'd throttle her, but he wouldn't hide.

Her heart pounded furiously, a startled cry escaped without warning, and a frog croaked. Rupert charged. All hell broke loose before she could curb the terrified screams. Her knees buckled as her hound shot by in deadly pursuit of the horrid amphibian.

Tears welled in her eyes at the pain when she landed hard on her back, cherished papers flying through the air. She realized she had sealed her fate. Within seconds, Roc would descend from wherever he'd kept himself and she'd pay for this night's work.

She scrambled, searching the floor for the coveted evidence but couldn't find all the documents. She swore under her breath, cursing the fates and her stupidity.

Rupert lost interest in the frog and now barked furiously at her, dancing around her kneeled form, wagging his tail; creating havoc throughout Roc's den. Books fell from the cases, pens littered the floor; Rupert played.

"Hush, Rupert," she commanded.

Rupert responded with a mournful wail. He sat now, baying at the moon. Jessie groaned, lunging for the hound. Her fingers closed around his muzzle, shutting off the awful noise. He looked at her with huge sorrowful brown eyes.

"Stay, Rupert." She pointed a finger at the dog. Slowly releasing her hand, she began to back away. What could Roc do to her? He had, after all sworn to protect her. Still, she didn't want to find out.

"If you know what's good for you, you stupid hound, you'll stay," she threatened.

Rupert grunted and settled himself on the rug. He rested his head on his paws and watched his mistress.

"Good boy." Time was running out, sounds from above created an uneasy stir within. She backed away, knowing she should turn and run. Her feet didn't seem to get the message.

The time had come. She might never get a second chance.

But she wanted to stay and help. Trevor, the senator, even Roc they needed her. She didn't want them to hide her away. Damn them all.

There might be women out there, forced into lives of virtual slavery, sold at auction to the highest bidder; she could find herself in such a place if she persisted with this, but it was the principle.

Such things happened and she would take heed. She promised herself she would do nothing without thinking it through. She would act with prudence and concern, not risking herself.

Rupert's ears rose sharply.

"Stay, Rupert."

He rose suddenly and barked a greeting.

She swirled around, intent to run.

Newman. He caught her in his powerful embrace. "A little late for a stroll through the house, isn't it, Jessie?"

Panic sparked through Jessie, but she didn't struggle. She relaxed. "You know damn well what I was doing," she whispered, furious he'd caught her.

He swept her off the floor and carried her to a chair, placing her there, oh so carefully. She felt Roc's eyes rip her apart with their volatile fury. Felt the fear of the silence as it built around her; she prayed, knew the moment his gaze left her only to move across the damage and the papers strewn haphazardly around.

He raked his long fingers through his hair, cursing under his breath. She knew how angry and frustrated he felt, knew also he didn't know how to deal with her. The curl of his lip was familiar, the arch of his brow. Everything.

She lowered her lashes swiftly, praying he wouldn't deal too harshly with her, wondering what he'd try next to keep her in one place. Every thought she had terrified her.

Still, it seemed he went out of his way to treat her with care and tenderness. To protect her as he vowed but she appeared bent on a collision course with this man. How long would he remain gentle?

"Perhaps, Miss Lawrence," he suggested, "you could return to your room before I lose my temper completely. It seems Rupert isn't as good a watch dog as I assumed, yet he did serve a purpose."

"Alright," she murmured softly. She wanted to snatch the papers from him and run, to scream he couldn't keep her here and he had no right.

But she knew his strength was mightier than her inalienable rights. Unless she could overpower him, she had lost what little freedom he had given her. But her nightly stroll, as he had put it, gained her the knowledge she sought. She knew now why her cousin and the senator and even Roc Newman wanted her out of the way.

"Come along, Rupert," she called. Newman held out his hand to help her from the chair. They moved up the steps and to the room again. As he closed the door on her, she heard a bolt slide across then a key turned in the lock.

She stared, frozen at the sound.

~ * ~

Across town, in a well-lit room, Sterling Rutgers gazed blankly at the brilliant stars etched in the sky. "We have to move fast. The girl doesn't know a thing, forget about her. We have other more urgent problems."

"No, I won't forget her. She's part of this," Pierce told him. "I will have my revenge. It is all I care about. Jessica Lawrence will learn the hard way what interfering in the affairs of men can cost."

Rutgers turned on his friend. "Don't lose your focus."

"Indeed, the plans go well. Thank God. The minister's daughter was easily subdued," Pierce said tonelessly.

"Ah, so, they laced her water with opium. No relatives to come after her?"

"None that could change her destiny." He paused, looking over the stock of liquor in the cabinets. "And if Trevor interferes, we will certainly put an end to his career. It would please me to add one more insult to the Lawrence family."

"That's a little more than a mere insult."

Pierce smiled pleased with the progress of events. "As I said, revenge is sweet and when that revenge is doubled, ah...so sweet. But time and timing are so important now."

"We have no room for mistakes." Rutgers said.

"No mistakes," Pierce agreed.

Far away a dog howled mournfully into the silent night sending an icy warning.

Chapter Five

Roc groaned and stretched, squinting against the sun that signaled a new day. The ground felt hard as rock. Perkins looked forlornly down at the irascible man lying on the grass beneath the old oak tree. He held hot coffee, a tray of bread and jam, and a note from the lovely Miss Lawrence.

Hope you slept as well as I did.

Roc drank his coffee and scowled at the freshly penned words. Perkins stood placidly at Roc's side waiting for a reaction, and looking curious. They both waited to see what would happen next.

"You could have trusted her. She didn't budge from the room," Perkins said.

Roc looked to the window. He'd had a horrendous night. The last thing he wanted to do was spend the next minutes bantering with Perkins, since Jessica would surely be the topic of conversation.

Perkins frowned and after a very long pause. "Sir," he began, "I don't understand. I'd have thought...well..."

"Little you know."

Perkins followed Roc's gaze. "You did lock the door?"

Roc nodded his head slowly. "After she got away."

"The devil," he said, purely amazed.

"The little dickens, you mean."

Perkins chuckled softly and it seemed to Roc, Perkins was enjoying this all immensely.

"You mean...that...that," he laughed again. He began to pick up the remains of Roc's breakfast, still laughing and grinning wryly at Roc. "She bested you again then."

"I wouldn't go that far. She's in the room."

Perkins shrugged. "I'm sure she'll agree with you. How did you manage to get her back to the room this time?"

"None of your business," Roc said incredulously. He growled at Perkins then thought better of it. "She knows everything. I'm afraid she's determined to help," he said, wishing the words weren't true. He looked back to the window. Perhaps he was wrong and she would behave. Perhaps he should marry her just to keep her safe, but somehow he didn't think even marriage would stop her.

He knew better than to get his hopes up. Truly, he did. He stood up, shaking leaves and dust from his clothes. He felt a curious premonition of doom sweeping over him, just thinking of the woman. He had his work cut out for him. She was obstinate, selfish, and horribly convinced of her own prowess, and that was the crux of the problem.

All in all, despite all the things about her that troubled him, he had to admit she was a good private investigator.

His gaze wandered to the note again.

Impertinent little devil, she knew how well he'd slept; he'd bet tonight's sleep she'd find a way out of that room. He gathered his composure, thought a moment, breathing deeply, hoping he'd have the strength to keep his sanity. He didn't know what he'd do if she kept pushing, kept putting herself in harms way. No, Jessica Lawrence wouldn't get her way this time.

"So, what do you have planned?" Perkins asked.

"Nothing," Roc told him.

"Nothing? Why..." Perkins sputtered.

"I'm going to wait and see what she does."

"Isn't that a little dangerous? What if she gets away before you realize? She'd find herself in his, Pierce's, hands and--"

"She won't."

"The possibility always exists. You have to find a way to make her understand, before she does something irrefutably dangerous," Perkins warned.

Roc flashed him a quick warning. "That's what Trevor told me. Oh, all right. Wonderful. Now tell me how to go about it, because I haven't a

69

clue," Roc demanded.

Perkins walked to him and extended his hand. Roc took it, springing easily to his feet. "I think drastic measures are called for here. Perkins, you may have to look the other way. Chivalry be damned. I may have to wed the girl after all. At least then she'd have to obey. Why did the senator and Trevor put me in such a tenuous situation?"

"Roc, you're the only man in these parts who could handle her gently. Look on the bright side. She's still safe. One night down and there can't be too many left. Naturally, I wouldn't relax yet." He hurried into the house, but before he strode inside, he looked to the chamber window and grimaced. "Never relax..." Perkins whispered.

Roc followed more slowly. He, too, hesitated before entering, his gaze cutting to the window. A figure silhouetted behind the curtain vanished as suddenly as it appeared. He scowled. "Perkins," he murmured, "you have it right. And if it takes drastic measures to hold her safe, why then..."

The door slammed behind him. Roc made his way to the kitchen.

"So, you don't plan to starve the poor child. Do you intend to take her the tray or do want me to?" Perkins asked, his old eyes twinkling with merriment. "Of course we could both take it. I'd like to see how you convince Miss Lawrence, or she convinces you," he added suddenly.

At least Perkins found something amusing in this. He picked up the tray and started up the steps, thinking of all the things he could say to her, nothing new, nothing original, nothing he hadn't already told her. He wondered why he suddenly shivered, felt the cold penetrate to the bone and an icy dread envelop him. He shook off the feeling. Perkins was right. It wouldn't do to let down his guard. He moved farther up the steps, balancing the tray easily on one hand and stopped in front of the door. He closed his eyes and inhaled quickly, almost afraid to meet her head on. Prudently, he set the tray down, preparing for another battle.

~ * ~

Perkins whistled as he walked down the long walkway, relieved Roc would treat Miss Lawrence delicately. He had held his breath the long night through, hearing all that had gone on below. He knew what the papers contained, knew also Roc ventured into deep water with the Lawrence girl. He saw the sparks they exchanged, the way his gaze followed her every move. He heard footsteps behind and slowed then turned to see Pierce and Rutgers and behind them two others.

"If you want something you'll have to wait. Mr. Newman is busy," he said quickly wondering why the two men behind Pierce seemed so huge.

"Don't want to see Newman. I just want you to give him a message for me," Pierce told him. "Tell him I want the documents he keeps in his safe."

"Don't know anything about that," Perkins murmured offhandedly. Tensing, waiting for the blow he knew would soon follow.

"You shouldn't lie, Perkins. It won't do either of you any good," Rutgers added.

Perkins stiffened. "What's in Mr. Newman's safe is none of your concern." It seemed only a matter of time, and Perkins sifted through all the moves Roc had taught him.

To pile on the agony, Perkins inadvertently allowed them to corner him against a perfectly nice picket fence. He groaned, realizing too late this would not end well.

"I'd think twice…" he began nervously.

"You see he stole something from me. I'd have it back," Pierce said slowly, threatening.

"I'm afraid we just can't allow Mr. Newman to hold what rightfully belongs to Mr. Pierce. As for the girl, it would be in his best interest to release her," Rutgers added.

"If he keeps her, he'll regret it," Pierce agreed.

Perkins studied the men waiting behind Pierce and Rutgers. He would have to deal with them and knew the intended message. It wasn't so much the words but what would follow. "No," he began brazenly, "you will--"

He wasn't allowed to finish.

Pierce and Rutgers separated. A fist plowed into Perkin's head and he sank slowly to the ground, fleeting images of his lessons before he felt nothing more. Blackness descended.

~ * ~

Roc was pacing and in the midst of indecision. He hadn't a clue what to do about Jessica Lawrence. Everything he mulled over in his mind he discarded. All the underhanded tricks he thought of to keep her bound to his chambers and protected held shades of the dark ages, and he detested each thought even though a few of them brought a curl of amusement to his lips. He realized suddenly that Perkins should have returned.

He stepped outside and was greeted with the sight of Perkins, staggering along the street, his hand held to his head. Roc raced down the sidewalk. What had he done? If he hadn't spent innumerable hours tutoring him, he would have expected as much. But then, he had, and it seemed Perkins once again lost.

Roc met a grateful Perkins and assisted him into the house. He settled him on the sofa, a million questions coming to mind. The attackers had thoroughly beaten him, his face and eyes puffy from the blows to his head. Roc could tell by the way Perkins held his ribs at least one was broken or badly bruised. Doctoring first, questions later, he mused, the cold cloth he held to Perkins bruises relieving the pain.

"Warning, sir..." Perkins murmured, closing his eyes, an effort it took to say those few words.

"A warning or a threat, Perkins?"

"Both, I believe. It seems they don't like your possession of the girl or the documents," he winced.

"Ah, I see, then they think I should turn them both over."

Perkins nodded carefully, before licking his dry throbbing lips, "Think they belong to them, Pierce..."

"Perkins, did you forget everything I taught you?"

"I wasn't quite ready..."

"You forgot."

"No, there were two of them. Big brutes, came up from behind. Planted a hard one to my chin before I could blink. Took me by surprise they did then they pulled foot," he grunted.

"A likely story, Perkins," Roc commented dryly. "I suppose you need a few more lessons. I could approach Miss Lawrence on the subject. I'm sure she'd lend her expertise."

"If you don't mind me saying so...sir, with all due respect I don't think I'd like that. Speaking of the girl, have you checked on her lately? You know with her penchant for running off."

"Son of a bitch." Roc whirled and started up the stairs. No, she was there; he'd know if she'd left. He would know, he reassured himself, taking the stairs two at time. His breath caught in his throat. *Damn, but she had to be there.*

~ * ~

For her part in this, Lilly had managed to procure clothing fit for the fanciest brothel. She spent the better part of the day sorting through black lace underthings and revealing red satin dresses. Of course for the auction she'd clad Miss Jessica Lawrence in virgin white. She hoped Jessie would still have that thin gossamer veil proclaiming her maidenhood.

She had to admit being excited. She had thought of this for so very long. The riches this one girl alone could bring her had her reclining in wealth for the rest of her life. And she'd see to it personally the wealthiest gentleman attended. She had potions, more than enough ways to fool nature, concoctions to stupefy even the most knowledgeable, and she wouldn't hesitate to use them. She was a powerful woman and probably the least obvious. At times she imagined herself as powerful as a man, and with that thought she fell back on the bed, laughing softly. They, men in general, were so damned easy to disable. All it took, all it *ever* took was an exquisite woman willing to charm their way into the man's confidence. She had, over the years, used her power wisely and her money as well. This last escapade would set her up for life.

Sheer black stockings, satin and lace, her trademark for now. Other obvious signs of her profession littered the floor and scattered around the rooms, things no lady would understand or even recognize. She had lived with them for so long she took them for granted.

But Lilly had bided her time through the years and through the hardships. The new era, the 1890's, was approaching, a time when opportunities for women blossomed; all the signs pointed to that. A woman private investigator; who would have thought that possible? Perhaps not many as yet, but they would soon come around. Not in time to save Jessica Lawrence from her fate but soon enough.

Lilly fingered the delicate fabrics that lay before her. She could imagine Jessie in them, a beautiful woman that one. She'd make some man a fine mistress if he could tame her wild spirit. That bothered her for some reason, so she put her mind to work on something new. The drugs she would use would have to be mixed in the right portions. Yes, measured careful doses of each item and Jessie Lawrence would end up putty in some lucky man's hands. The magic would cost. It wouldn't come cheaply. She'd make sure whomever purchased Jessie knew. Now she had to get to work. She couldn't afford to waste time.

Before she could rise, a knock sounded softly on the door, and it slowly creaked inward. A very old lady moved cautiously through. "You're on time, come in. We have much to do this evening."

Sabrina entered the room. Her toothless grin brought a smile to Lilly's face. The old lady was just as she had expected. She stood, stoop shouldered, no more than four feet high. Long sliver-matted hair hung to her waist, torn ragged clothing fell loosely from her body. But her eyes sparkled clear, gray, cold as ice. She carried a huge shopping bag filled with all manner of things Lilly shuddered to think would undeniably end up in the brew they would create.

"Tell me the exact nature of the potion," Sabrina commanded.

"I need something very special."

"Ah...but you must be more specific."

"I have thought long on this," Lilly fingered the red velvet curtains hanging from the window. "There are a few...problems."

The old lady cackled. "Come along then speak of them. We'll give each one full consideration."

"Something to transform and humble. Something to give an illusion of falsehood, yet nibble at the truth. Seduced, but still a virgin, she must remain pure," Lilly told her.

"Impossible, an aphrodisiac holds no guarantees."

"Then we must find a way to interrupt them before it goes too far."

Lilly's bosom heaved. She strode quickly to the cupboard, motioning the old lady to follow. Events now set in motion, irrefutable, viable, suddenly chills swept through her an overpowering sense of failure. Lilly shook the feeling away. Her scheme would work.

"It seems your plan has holes in it. Just how do you plan to administer this potion?"

Lilly waited to enjoy the drama. "That's not my problem. It is up to someone else. I will see he has the magic. That is enough."

The old lady smiled. "Remember, nothing is as it seems. I will give you what you need but do not come to me begging if it fails." Sabrina warned.

"I know, but it will work. Too much lies at stake now to turn back. No, there is no returning, no chance. If the drug does not work..."

Sabrina dug through her bags. She found what she wanted and held it high above her head, studying the contents through the hazy light of the room. The bottle shimmered. Light splayed around it and mysteries resided within.

So much enchantment, so much intrigue, Lilly thought. Pierce and Rutgers wanted to play with human lives, enhance their desire but leave them unfulfilled. She wanted to write her own play but had only a meager outline. Well, she, Lilly, would give Raymond Pierce what he needed, but she could not write the final scene. No, the players were too illusive and the script poorly written. Anything could happen if the actors decided to improvise. She was silent for several moments, rehearsing perhaps, or maybe even wondering at the conclusion of this.

Then she watched Sabrina set the bottle down and search once more through her numerous bags.

Another knock on the door. It swung open and a giant of a man stood before them. He dwarfed Sabrina.

"Noah will see to the delivery of the girl and the potion. He will make sure to keep her under the influence until her transfer." Lilly held the white virgins gown in the air, smiled, then laid it back down. Tomorrow all their plans and schemes would be well rewarded.

Sabrina gave the mixture to Lilly. "Thank you, I'll see that you're paid well," Lilly told her. "Remember, not a word of this to anyone."

Sabrina gathered her bags and slipped silently through the door. Ah, the enchantment and mystery of it all.

~ * ~

Jessica obviously threw his emotions counter clockwise. She waltzed out the bedroom door. Straight laced and proper, head held high without a second glance at him, as if she'd done nothing untoward. She had scarcely left the room when he snapped his mouth shut and followed her down the hall.

She heard his soft tread, paused and looked back. He reached her side, easily capturing her arm in his hand and ushering her the rest of the way, food forgotten momentarily.

"Fine day, isn't it, Mr. Newman, sir." She wondered what he intended to do next.

"You never cease to amaze me, Miss Lawrence. Let's see, a count, once two nights ago, once again last night. Why imagine, the thought that you might try once more, one more time to wrest the papers from my safe keeping."

"Would you please stop harping on that? I've no intention to take those documents, not after I read them...anyway."

He chuckled softly, holding even tighter to her arm. "You expect me to believe that? You do not seem that naïve."

"I am anything but, Mr. Newman, sir. Naiveté is for the foolish and weak. I am neither."

"If you wish to believe that, don't let me dissuade you." He was suddenly staring at her. "Do you have any idea what I could have done to you if I hadn't tried so hard to be gentle? Ah, perhaps you think you possess greater skills and even believe in your own mortality."

"I know what I am," she responded, "I have no delusions of grandeur, nor do I think of myself as immortal. Trevor spent many hours teaching, perfecting my skills."

"And Trevor learned everything he knows from me," he advised her. "You are as ignorant as a babe just beginning to crawl, pulling itself along with the greatest of effort. Each time you fall on that pert little nose, a lesson, yet unlearned."

He watched, seemingly amused, as her fury rose beyond control.

She drew away from him, spacing the distance between them. "Just what is it, Mr. Newman, you are so afraid of? I have proved myself beyond redemption. Is there something that irritates you? Something that would embarrass you if the truth were known?"

"Embarrass me?" He asked smoothly, his brow arching high. He grinned. "Dear Miss Lawrence. You forget the rules of the game. If someone is shamed, or humiliated here, it will not be me."

"Do tell, the infallible, Mr. Newman," she said. "Truly? I think you are insufferable and a bore, sir. As I've told you, I bested you. You're old now. Your time is over. Be that as it may, it seems you should take heed. I warn you, don't get in my way lest you find yourself on your derriere in the mud."

A slow twinkle brightened his eyes, and his brow arched high again. "Miss Lawrence, you are a stubborn woman. A slip of a girl, too smart and full of daring for her own good and unwilling to accept what fate has dished out. If you wished to best me in a battle of strength, then you would do so?"

"It takes as much wit and skill."

"Are you implying I lack these traits?"

Her body trembled violently. She was acting beneath her intelligence, but he must know he brought out the anger and the frustration she'd harbored since learning, indeed, it was a man's world. She lifted her chin and gave him a bone-chilling glance. "I imply nothing, sir, only that brute strength is not always important. But rest assured, in all my life, I have never met a more supercilious, overbearing man, with or without the proper credentials. I would meet you again one on one, if I could be sure of a fair fight," she finished.

He drew her closer, his body tight against hers, his hands suddenly around her arms. "Now you have the gall to call me a cheat?" He seemed frustrated, more so than he'd ever been. Surges of intense heat seemed to consume him, spilling forth. When he pulled her to him, encasing her within his strong hands, she shuddered against him. Sparks flashed, burning the space between them, the room surrounding them. His gaze traveled her length.

"I meant nothing by that," she said. "Take your hands off me. I would not fight you in any case."

"Why, Miss Lawrence, do I detect a note of anticipation in your voice? A man could take your word as a challenge, needs only to see the defiance in your eyes to know he should pursue until the prey is captured."

"You presume too much." A shriek escaped as he drew her closer, tight against him. "I am not prey to be captured by any man, especially you, Mr. Newman. Especially you."

"Ah, but in this you are wrong," he said, his eyes never wavering. "Jessica, Jessie, Jess, so wrong. When I hold you, there is no other thought that speeds through my mind. Yes, your eyes blind me with their fury; cut through my heart without a tender thought, the heat of your flesh upon mine reminds me how much I want you. I must admit you are tender prey, indeed yes, and worthy of capture. Any man would react the same, therein lies the danger. Listen to me, Jessie. Trouble brews and you are the bait. Without me your life is threatened, Jessica. In my hands you stand to lose only your woman's modesty, but with Pierce..."

"How dare you. Your audacity knows no bounds." She struggled within his grasp, his hold loosening. It seemed that with each encounter her temper flared higher. He set her into a chair, towering over her. "I am bait for nothing, Mr. Newman. Don't concern yourself with my virtue. No doubt you think yourself as a dandy, but you don't hold any interest to me. I wouldn't surrender to you." She smiled at him innocently, abruptly changing tactics. "But then again you mention Pierce in the same breath and I have no intention of winding up with him either. Perhaps you would consider a small iota of trust and let me help."

"You help?" Physically separated from her now. "You've made quite a spectacle of yourself, Jessica. First you dangle from my attic window then you wrestle with me on the front lawn. With each moment the list grows, and with all that in mind you ask to help?"

"I don't want anyone to get hurt," she said. "In truth you all could learn something from me."

She pushed from the chair, attempting to stand, feeling the palm of his hand against her shoulder, restraining her.

"And what pray tell could that be?" he asked, curious now at the absurdly feminine notion she had.

"Patience," she whispered and stood this time successfully, only because he allowed it, but she didn't know what to do with herself so she sat down again. The moment lasted too long as did his gaze. For the smallest moment, she thought she imagined something within his look, something she'd never seen before, a hunger. But it vanished quickly and she knew she was wrong. He winked at her and turned away, walking to the mantle and leaning against it.

To her bewilderment and dismay she felt a moment's loss at his withdrawal, then a fleeting notion he might allow her to help. Perhaps, if she acted prudently...

And with extreme caution.

He stared at her hard and she quickly lowered her lashes. When Rupert nuzzled her hand, she absently rubbed his ears, sparing a covert glance at him.They had come to an impasse, Roc and Jessie, a stalemate seeming to stretch on forever. Their impressions of each other seemed built as solidly as a fortress, unmoving and incapable of bending. Long hours of thought molded and shaped the flavor in which character flaws had, indeed, highlighted the assessment. On one hand bringing them together, binding irreversibly their destinies, yet, in another way setting them incoherently apart. Noise from the kitchen shattered the silence. Deliveries of food and drinks, joined with Rupert's wild dashes back and forth sent a harmony of discontent within him.

~ * ~

Jessica's nerves jangled. She wondered who would break the staggering silence and if she could bear to argue with him one more time. It set her teeth on edge and made her mind rattle, this arguing. She hated it. Before her thoughts could wander farther afield, she discovered Perkins hovering anxiously at the door. The dining room, readied, appeared magnificent, much too sumptuous for two people. She suspected they might have company and yet...

No, her mind played tricks on her with wishful thinking, nothing more. Perkins stood, looking much like an expectant father, hovering, wringing his hands. Jessie thought he must be in the midst of a prayer; praying he'd survive their presence and possibly, with luck, the feast set before them would somehow reach its proper conclusion. She giggled, seeing the peas flying through the air.

"Do sit down, Miss Lawrence," Perkins said, suddenly surprising her. "I hope everything is as you like it."

She licked her lips, whether from hunger or nerves she didn't know. "I'm sure it is," Jessie agreed, meeting Roc's eyes. He moved to her, touching her elbow lightly, bringing her to her feet then escorting her to the table. She moved hesitantly through the house to the table, swallowing hard, petrified. Why, she couldn't fathom, but sheer terror engulfed her. Once again, he was so close and the same feeling magically heated her body, confusing her. She looked again at Roc, and he was grinning. Damn the man, he was grinning at her.

Dash it all, but he had a way of making her lose her appetite. And just a moment before her stomach had rumbled its displeasure. It seemed since he'd snatched away the documents and she'd set him on his rear, he had deprived her of food non-stop.

"There you are," Senator Drake called, making his way unceremoniously into the dining room. "I've a splendid bottle of wine, here, delivered just today by one of my constituents, a gift, a peace offering perhaps to the two of you. I'll pour."

Roc met him with a wide grin and a handshake. Jessie welcomed another person, a friend, someone to breach the silent tension surrounding them. Perkins breathed deeply, clearly relieved by the senator's presence. "Be my guest," Roc nodded.

Jessie glanced between the three men then let her chin raise a notch. No, she wouldn't allow him to capture her heart or bend her to his will, even though she surmised she might like to be loved by him. She'd fight them until she convinced these two she could stand with them, assuring she wasn't in need of protection. Despite herself, she wondered what it would be like if he ever included her in his confidence.

Drake procured the glasses and poured the wine, filling them. He turned the conversation from business, the treachery at hand. He didn't know she'd broken into the safe and now knew everything, so he rambled on. Jessica studied Roc throughout the innocuous conversation.

Roc managed to down part of the glass of wine, even while he and Drake plotted the next move against Pierce. Jessie, on the other hand, had barely touched her food but found solace in the wine. Roc poured her a second glass and laughed outright when she gulped it down.

Jessie heard the unspoken words, the silent command that after dinner the senator and Roc would find privacy and discus the issues. She looked up from the table and found Roc watching her. He winked. She wanted to hit him over the head with something.

He poured her more wine. The laughing smile never left his face. She wanted to dump the contents of her glass in his lap, but she needed the false courage the liquid seemed to give her. No, she told herself, she didn't need it, and this time sipped the wine slowly, hoping Roc hadn't noticed. They droned on and on and still said nothing of importance. Oh, she knew they waited for her to leave, but she wouldn't. No, not until she'd heard every piece of superfluous gossip they could think of. Dear God, they were men. They couldn't possibly talk about such trivial things for so long.

The senator excused himself and pushed away from the table, his glass still full. He moved to the door and waited for Roc. Jessie grabbed it and swigged it down. Her head buzzed and the room seemed to whirl, but she ignored the sensation. Instead, she wondered fleetingly if Roc cared for her at all. Perhaps he had felt the same heat at their touch. Perhaps he had the same curious melting feeling when their gazes met. But no, he disliked her intensely. Didn't he? Ahh that was the crux of the matter. She was everything he didn't like, impetuous, wild, stubborn and the list was never ending.

The floor seemed to undulate. She felt the warmth of the air upon her flesh, swirling within the confines of the room. The deep resonant laugh of Roc and the senator filled her senses. Her gaze moved to them and they wavered fuzzily, heat waves rising around them. Warmth radiated from her. Inadvertently, she dipped her fingers into the water glass. Droplets seemed to sizzle when they hit her face. A low moan rose from her throat and she wanted to hide. Jessie was trying very hard to listen to the men, but they moved away. She wanted to follow but her feet didn't like what she told them. Everything had turned topsy-turvy. She didn't understand. Those few glasses of wine shouldn't affect her this way. All her senses heightened to a curious awareness. Yet, she could barely hold her head up or keep her eyes open.

What was wrong with her? What had Roc done to her? He had threatened so very much; had admitted he would try anything to keep her safe. No, he told her to take heed, to listen to his warnings, and she had willingly drunk the wine he'd poured. Oh, she remembered the smile, the curl of his lips, the volatile blaze of his eyes. He'd done this to her. He'd put something in the wine. Then her mind wandered, no longer wanting to examine his motives. She didn't care, for now she seemed to float on a golden moonbeam, wonderfully light. She licked her lips again, watching Roc. He smiled then nodded. Her head bowed, and she jerked up to meet his gaze again. Now he no longer grinned. Surely, he would help her to her room. But no, he turned, about to leave with the senator, and she wanted to scream but she could no longer command her voice. Perkins would help. He would take her to the room. Oh, dash it all, she just wanted to lie down.

She motioned futilely, her voice strangely hollow. "Roc...please," her whisper, light and airy, floating away from her on a wisp of a cloud. She looked to the senator then Roc for help, but the senator hadn't heard. The outside door closed, and she knew they had left her alone.

Her head pounded. Suddenly a very large man stood in the room glowering at her. He laughed and muttered they weren't paying him enough for this when Perkins backed in with a pie in one hand and coffee in the other. The man had his hand on her arm, wrenching her up from the chair, and she didn't have the strength to resist. He heaved her over his shoulder.

"What are you doing to Miss Jessica?" Perkins demanded. He looked askance and Jessie would have giggled again if she could, but her head dangled uselessly and she had the strangest thought she'd surely lose her meager dinner. The man growled and dropped his hold, intent on doing away with Perkins. Jessie slid helplessly to the floor. For once Perkins remembered the lessons Roc had so painstakingly given him and retaliated, or at least, part of the lessons. The pie flew through the room, directed most calmly by Perkins hand. It landed on the man's face, hard. He staggered a moment, wiped the peaches and cream from his face and lunged. Perkins adeptly sidestepped the furious attack and yelled. The man turned swiftly and was met by a strong kick. It landed squarely on his chest. He gasped for air, panicked and bolted from the room without further retaliation.

Perkins white brow knit, concentrating on the man's fleeting back. Then, as if nothing happened, he began to pick up the mess, whistling. She listened to the tune, suddenly feeling incredibly peaceful, and swept a juicy piece of fruit from her nose.

Roc barged through the doors, horrified by the noise of the brawl and Perkins's yell. He stopped almost as swiftly, studying the scene. "By all the saints," he began then broke off, "the room is tilting." Even as he approached Jessie to help her from the chair, he swayed. She could only smile and look to Perkins then back to Roc. The wine, she thought suddenly. He drank it too.

But her heart seemed to beat so rapidly and the room grew hotter and hotter. She couldn't think. Everything she touched, the brush of the linen tablecloth across her arm, the cold smoothness of her wine glass when she pressed it against her cheeks then her forehead. The satin and lace swirling around her legs, touching, tempting, heating...

"Are you all right?" a masculine voice whispered, hot against her neck.

Roc. No, it was the senator and he stood behind her, helping her, watching Roc with the most curious expression. An alarm sounded in her brain, but she didn't comprehend the message. She couldn't help herself. The senator swept her into his arms, carrying her up the steps. He called to Roc to follow. It seemed so very curious, the strangest... Rupert licked her hand then padded along behind, whining. The world ceased to move. Her eyes fluttered shut.

"I don't feel well," she stammered.

"I can tell," the senator told her. "Roc, help me undress her and put her to bed."

"No..." she began but the whisper didn't seem to penetrate. At least no one stopped to do her bidding. She heard the click of the door and rose to protest. The bolt slid home and she thought she was alone. She closed her eyes, sighing, hoping the spinning would stop. For a long time nothing happened. She could hear her deep raspy breathing. Her skin began to prickle, tingling heatedly, sensuously. She moaned.

"It's all right, sweetheart," Roc said. His voice caressed her flesh heating it even more. "It's only the wine. You drank too much."

"I'm so..."

Clothing fell away from her. Cool breezes wafted in from the window teasing and touching the skin now revealed. Heightened awareness and a horrible need pervaded, moving from deep within slowly outward, inflaming every part of her.

"Hot?" she heard. "You look ill, Jess. Here, you have to help. Can you sit up? There, that's a good girl."

She felt her chemise slip over her head. Her moan sounded distant, so far away. "Roc, please..." she murmured.

"Oh, sweet darlin', you don't know what you ask." She thought she heard a note of distress in his voice.

~ * ~

"Do something," she pleaded. Her eyes huge luminescent spheres stared at him. And he'd never seen her look so vulnerable and trusting.

He ran his fingers through his hair. His gaze fixed on her. Lord, he only began to guess what was happening. Skin so flushed, breath heaving, and her hair spilled across her white shoulders. Son of a bitch, he felt it too and he'd only had a few sips of the wine.

"Jessie, there's only one thing I can do that will help and I don't think you'll appreciate my efforts in the morning."

"Please, Roc I'm on fire."

"I know, honey. It was the wine."

He sat next to her, bringing her into his arms. She ran her hands across his chest. The flames, the inferno raged, and nothing she could do stopped it. The nightmare continued. With his tender caress, her blood began to boil and she plummeted out of control. He tensed, "Please give me control," he prayed. His body shuddered and strained with the effort.

It seemed he lost the battle somewhere between the golden mist of the rising moon and his tormented soul.

"Sweetheart..."

She cried out once more, trembling with the intensity of the raging wildfire burning within her. She hungered, needed, longed for something she could not define but knew somehow Roc could ease the pain and cool her feverish soul. Her body writhed uncontrollably, seeming to push Roc to his limitations. Jessie tugged at his clothes, wishing for the feel of his skin meeting hers, naked flesh joining. He was helping her rip his clothing away. Hard bronze muscle rippled beneath the tips of her fingers, and she explored the width of his chest, down its length, stopping only when her fingers met his belt. His hand clamped solidly around her, holding her against him, pushing and she didn't understand. The warmth, the heat, surrounded them and he seemed golden and perfect, a God.

"So beautiful, Jessie. I tried, truly I did, but the wine, the drug, I can't stop. I'm not sorry Jess. I've wanted this since..."

His mouth descended, softly, brushing against hers then harder. Control came then, momentarily, his tongue teasing her lips, tasting, pushing against them urgently now as if he wanted to tell her something. Her tongue swept across her lips and they met. She shuddered from the searing heat and the passion. Now he surged on, pushing within, sweeping the sensitive recess of her, dueling, parrying each thrust. She trembled and cried out.

The light of the moon shimmered through the open curtains and a moonbeam, glanced across the lovers. It was hot, so very hot. She rose high above, looking down, detached; her soul seemed to float above, free on the golden light misting in veils of enchantment.

Roc, he had come to her to help and he eased the discomfort but then it grew, the power soaring out of bounds, beyond the horizon, limitless. It seemed nothing could stop the agony or define the mystery. She clung tightly to him, a lifeline she didn't dare lose. Even in her wildest imaginings she had never thought such sensations existed, the swift spiraling of heat, low and so deep inside her. Not until he had fallen upon her, teasing her with his caress. Then she had known a wild sweet yearning but for something indefinable. The fire, the agony, the need for something that existed, called, and dear lord excited.

Ah, yes. Ah, the man had said he would stop at nothing. Yes, Roc. It was him and she wanted him. Hard as steel, potent, inflaming and she trembled from the secrets. Roc caressed her, stroking her so very intimately. She lay with him, locked naked, inside his room, and she offered no protest.

She writhed beneath him again, she burned, and wanted, and still the heat raged. He should end this now before it went too far. He should stop the burning and ease the pain.

Or did he want her to stay this way because, in truth, she didn't want him to stop. She didn't want to open her eyes, afraid this was a magical enchantment and he had truly bewitched her. And if she dreamt then it would mean he didn't hold her and touch her.

Ah, yes, Roc.

His mouth, tongue, tasted her. Fingers touching, needing, the soft brush of his thumb across the crest of her breast. Feathery kisses exploring the smoothness of her flesh and the whisper of his breath sighing so close. This was Eden, enchantment and paradise, a fire burning, a longing she could not deny. She moved against him, writhing beneath his solid length. He pulled her close, finding heavenly delight. Hot and fresh, naive for only a short while more. His teeth rubbed against her nipple, lips closing over, swiftly tugging, setting the tempest raging wildly once more. And still he teased her with the unknown, with the mystery, with secrets she had yet to learn. It seemed, though, her body knew. Oh, yes, her body knew everything, and it swiftly urged her mind to claim the knowledge.

Now his lips demanded hers again then moved to her eyes, gently closing each one, exciting, intriguing, seducing. A caress, which left no room for denial, claiming her as his own.

His fingers threaded through her hair, reveling in the fullness, the silken length of it. His grip closed around her neck, pulling her closer still. It seemed they had become one and she moaned, soft sounds, unrestrained.

"Oh..."

Fire spiraled from the depth of her, commanding once more. Demanding something, everything.

He moved. The weight of him bore down upon her, rubbing against her flesh. His hands, stroked everywhere, his mouth following, giving no respite. Sweet Jesus...

Rational thought surfaced for a brief moment, and she knew this couldn't happen. Yes... She had to stop him. His tongue brushed her lips then delved within hindering the thoughts, tamping them down.

She had to stop the burning heat. His touch made the fire sear and her flesh so sensitive she couldn't think. No, he wouldn't do this to her. He didn't want this anymore than she did.

Yet, it seemed she had found her Garden of Eden, a paradise of sensual promise. Roc! Blunt, gentle, caring, generous...

She wanted him. Wanted to know what this was all about. And it seemed he meant to teach her. His hands slid over her waist, her hip, lower. The provocative allure of his mouth followed, feathering heated kisses, whispering fire. She moaned, writhing, mindlessly.

Her eyelids fluttered against her cheek, trying to recover from his bold touch. Impossible, she relaxed. It seemed useless to fight this enchantment. He had bewitched her, setting her within his spell.

She gasped as his fingers stroked the inside of her thighs. Moving intimately against her, pushing them wider. He shifted, falling between her legs. She was powerless, melting, his kiss paralleled his fingers, touching, heating, setting the fire burning hotter, hotter still. The stroke of his tongue. A gentle touch, lingering then exploring higher, hotter. Her heart pounded and she closed her fist over it, willing it to calm. His mouth charted unknown territories, so intimate, so commanding, so fervent. Liquid fire exploded within, hotter than she could withstand. She fought the sensations, his touch, his burning flames, but to no avail. The wild hot tempest blasted her, swept hotter, higher and coming harder, swifter, unyielding. She cried out and tried to touch his naked flesh, but he still wore his clothes. Feelings, violent, shuddering, claiming, consuming, shattered down upon her until she thought nothing would be left of her. The tempest calmed but it was only the eye of the storm. The peacefulness was nothing but an illusion conjured by her imagination, for suddenly the coolness vanished once more and she felt the slow burn begin once more.

Then a moan ripped through him. Her hands tugged at the fastening of his pants, but he pushed them away.

"No, sweetheart. No." He swept his hands across her body and once more she burned with pleasure she'd never thought possible. Heat wrapped around and within, shocking, dousing her from the sweet reverie she had just enjoyed. She cried out, but his mouth descended swiftly and covered the sound. It didn't end, the heat, the electricity ripped through her. Tears slid down her cheeks and she responded to his touch, moving in rhythm until the pleasure consumed her and the burning heat dissipated.

"I'm sorry," he whispered. "I don't want to hurt you."

His words did nothing to ease the reality of this situation even as the heat began to build.

"What is happening? Why won't it stop?"

"Be still," he whispered softly, his breath feathering her ear then following along the column of her neck. "I hope you find some pleasure in this," he murmured, and she felt him shift above her, gently now. So very tender and slow before she was on fire once again.

She moved beneath him. His solid length pinned her to the bed. Now he touched her, magically, the warmth, the mystery of it returned. Purposeful, sure, so defiantly. More and more he gave to her. She bit her lip then licked them. Her muscles tensed. Suddenly, she wanted to look at him. Intense, hot, the movement of his hands upon her, the tender care he took with her, refusing to see to his needs. Her eyes opened, memorizing the man, the sheer masculine power that dominated, commanded then coaxed her senses to unparalleled heights. On the brink once more, the culmination of magical secrets, the force of it all, the sweet, restful, bliss following.

He surrounded her, encompassing, unrelenting. His body rigid, he held back, denying himself.

She cried out, shuddering, gasping for a breath then relaxed against him, still enjoying the feeling of his body so close to hers.

It seemed an eternity he lay heavily on top of her. Her thoughts traveled back to the meal and the wine and the heat. It began to build again and she moaned, moving beneath him. Her body, exhausted, sore, yet still she craved him, more and more...

Even then her eyes closed, the wine, the drugs, the heat, but she no longer cared. She didn't care. Once again he brought her to a magical climax. Blackness descended, wrapping her in the arms of Orpheus. She slept and dreams filled her. Her world had suddenly changed.

Paradise, a fantasy fulfilled yet her loss still lingered. She moaned and rolled over only to encounter naked flesh. Her fingers touched, explored, felt the crisp hair, the hard muscled tension. A gasp stopped her short, and she was suddenly wide-awake. Silver fire burned above her as she met his gaze.

She tried to move away.

She felt as if she'd done something horribly wrong. She wanted to die of embarrassment. Guilt washed over, and she looked to find a way to hide from the memory.

Someone had drugged her, and Roc. She could see it clearly but like a fool, she had consumed it all. Almost all of it...Roc had some too. But who was responsible?

She froze, fingers gently touching his chest, barely feeling, aware of her ragged breaths and the horrible ache seeming to fill her. The devil, but she didn't know what to say to him. Not one word came to mind. Thank God he still wore his pants. He looked damn uncomfortable.

Ice suddenly rushed through her veins; fear, terror; she knew he'd think the worst. Perhaps even blame this on her. But she had known nothing.

Valiantly, she tried to push him away. His arms tightened around her; still he stared at her, seeking, and she knew he looked for answers. She had none to give him, not one. All she could offer were questions of her own.

She couldn't deny what had happened. She felt the rapid beat of his heart, and the warmth of his body next to hers.

No. It was a dream. She had only to wake up and her imagination would find its way back to reality. This wasn't real. Somehow all the magic had disappeared.

She flattened the palm of her hands against him. Licked her dry lips and felt the heat penetrate her flesh and she could forget nothing. The breeze through the window blew cool and fresh. A strong arm curved over her, holding her flush against the bed.

A sob tore at her throat, terrified she had set events in motion. Roc didn't want her and now... He would not have a choice. Panic tore through her at the thought. She wouldn't allow this to happen.

Sunlight bathed the room and nothing was as it seemed.

Roc.

She heard his deep chuckle and didn't understand, then his voice calling to her. "Are you all right?" It was tender, full of concern. Pain settled deep in the pit of her stomach and she couldn't face him. Not yet.

Tenderly, he held her chin gently forcing it up, compelling her to look at him and meet this head on, but she couldn't bear it. Her eyes opened again. In dazed terror, Jessie watched as Roc brushed his lips lightly across hers then paused, touched his tongue to her mouth and raised his head. A smile curled his lips. "You never answered my question."

She gulped in air and courage and nothing mattered. She couldn't speak or think. Still he grinned.

"Yes, yes I'm fine."

Roc frowned and his silver gaze met Jessie's. She nearly bolted in a rising sense of fear. He moved away from her, breathtakingly splendid, shoulders broad, hard as steel. As if he knew her thoughts and her fear, the guilt embedded deep and fast, he traced her cheekbone. "Has the drug worn off?" he asked thickly.

"It has. I..." Jessie tried to reassure him. Her amethyst eyes radiated all the heat and passion she had felt in his arms. She closed them. Nothing she could say now would change what happened.

Roc smiled gently. "Of course," he said. "I'm sorry."

For a moment, he stared at the bed. Regret seemed to lace his feelings and shone in his eyes, yet it seemed to vanish quickly. He gazed out the window. It was a beautiful day, Jessie realized. She had allowed him intimacies she had never even imagined. Her clothing lay scattered on the floor. He walked to the window, purposefully. The curtains billowed gently with the breeze. Fresh air filled the room. His fingers stroked the material then he turned suddenly, calmly as if he had resigned himself to the inevitable.

And he smiled at her again. Volatile flames danced in his eyes. So hot she thought surely the inferno would reach her. She pulled the sheets up to her chin and stared back at him.

She taunted him, fought him and he ended on his rear, humiliated. She'd mocked him foolishly without understanding. He had the graceful bearing, the wit, and the technique to best her. Not to mention the brute strength appearing so evident now. Mindless of the situation they inadvertently created, he continued lazily to gaze at her. He stared at her as if she wasn't there, as if he could make her vanish into the early morning dawn.

"You know what we've done," he said, his voice deep and husky. "Even though we did not have sex, I will have to make an honest woman of you," he went on smoothly, ignoring the furious expression that suddenly played across her face.

"Honest." Even though she had been a virgin and was still a virgin, her stepmother taught her she didn't have to wed a man because she'd had sex with him. And marriage or no marriage didn't have anything to do with honesty. She tossed off the sheets, furiously rummaging for her clothes, unmindful of her nakedness. "Honest. Dash it all, I had nothing to do with any of this. It was the wine you poured, and you taunt me with honesty," she cried, tripping in her haste to dress.

Too amused to help, he doubled over with laughter. She whirled around, intending to lash out at him. All momentary concerns for him vanished. She managed nothing against him simply because he finally learned his lessons well. And she thought as he lifted her from the floor she would never best him again. Their eyes met. Humiliation suffused her body with heat. She realized her scant covering had slipped. He held her naked, against him.

"Wildcat, I didn't want this, but now that I've held you in my arms and tasted your sweetness, I find I cannot live without you."

"No," she cried out swiftly. "Just because we slept in the same bed doesn't mean I want a permanent arrangement."

"But I will wed you and it will be forever," he told her softly, all traces of humor gone.

"I won't," she panicked, wishing he would set her down before she begged him to make love to her. Their bodies touched. The inferno igniting, curious sensations that no longer seemed so strange to her welled within. He smiled tenderly, softly, placing her on the bed with reverence and perhaps admiration shining in his gaze. She grasped her chemise, holding it tightly against her breasts.

He leaned over and brushed a wayward strand of hair from her face. "You will learn. The threat... I should have paid more attention to it, and the intruder last night. I wonder..."

Confusion whirled though her. She listened, no longer fighting the deplorable situation and the unavoidable. She wouldn't concede to a wedding. She didn't have to. Alex, her stepmother, would stand beside her. He didn't love her, and a marriage between them would never work. Stunned now, she stared at him, slowly shaking her head, denying.

"Go away. I'd like to dress."

"I can't do that, Jessie. You see, I have an obligation to fulfill, one I will not shirk from. I owe you your innocence, and I will marry you."

"Why? You don't want me." Her voice shook, and he had to bend forward to hear. So softly she spoke, tensing, fearing she would never convince him. Tears stung the back of her throat, her eyes, and slipped down her cheeks.

"I will never marry you, Roc. My father, Trevor, they will never allow it. If they find out what happened..."

"They will insist," he finished for her.

"You can't believe that." She let her face fall into her hands, trembling she couldn't meet his gaze. She shuddered and her thin shoulders wracked with sobs.

"You're innocence has been compromised," he said. "I will arrange everything. He turned from her, quickly dressed then moved toward her. He crouched beside her and held her face in his hands. "I will make this right for you and for me."

He left her and in two swift strides, he reached the door.

A cold breeze blew through the window. Jessie shivered and stared into the dawn of a day no longer holding promises, only regrets.

Chapter Six

Roc walked out the bedroom door and down the steps, calling for Perkins. He could have sworn the senator locked the door. Damnation, but why hadn't he tried it one more time? Locked or unlocked, nothing would have changed.

Senator Drake rose from the sofa, hands uplifted in supplication. "By thunder, you'll never believe what's happened...last night...this morning. All hell's breaking loose...impossible to stop," he said wearily. "It seems Pierce and Rutgers fled last night after their aborted attempt to kidnap Jessie. Trevor has disappeared without a word."

"And you locked the door last night."

"Yes."

"You had no right," Roc replied. Suddenly furious that with one small act his ability to choose was wrenched from him. Yet he felt an undulating current of gratitude.

"It was the only way. Jessie's life..."

"You knew what would happen."

"Did I?" he asked but didn't wait for the answer. "Damn it, stop a minute to think. The auction... Jessie was billed as the main attraction, you know. I suspected as much, but after the wine..."

"You drugged it?"

"Of course not, I simply saw the results and understood what happened. I sent my man to investigate, and it didn't take long before I had all the answers. Now what happened between the two of you can't be changed, and you will have to take responsibility, but it kept her safe, for the time being anyway."

"Safe?" Roc queried. "Forgive me, but I fail to accept that. She was not kept safe..." his voice trailed off, and he paced the room with long strides, seeking solace with his thoughts. He accepted nothing more from Drake but stepped outside, and walked.

For several long moments, he was undecided, but his steps never wavered, he continued on his way, purposefully. He meant to discover for himself the truth of Drake's words.

Once he had confronted several sources, it became evident. They'd been set up. Only the plot failed. He had Perkins to thank for that. Pierce intended to spirit Jessie away, sell her at the brothel run by Madame Lilly. Instead, Roc spent the night with Jessica Lawrence. At least with him she'd only lost her reputation not her virtue. Trevor had vanished, and he feared for him, but now he had major obligations to fulfill.

He wanted to remember everything about last night. Needed to memorize how she filled his arms and his soul. The peace he felt with her beside him as if he had come home. He didn't regret a moment with her, and she had been everything he hoped for. She had enchanted him.

He intended to see this through to its proper conclusion. Miss Lawrence was his now, and he'd never let her deny it.

Never accept the word no from her.

Jessie had told him she would never marry him, but he had to find the words to change her mind. By this evening they would be man and wife. If he couldn't convince her, her father would.

She would not get away from him. He wouldn't allow it, so help him God; she would come around to his way of thinking. He'd fallen hard for this beautiful spirited lady.

He walked through town. He threatened, bullied, and bribed, until satisfied, but he still had to confront James, who had conveniently arrived in town this morning; most likely Drake's work. He headed for the hotel unaware James was with his daughter. Nor did he realize Jess poured her heart out only to find James unsympathetic. It would have made him laugh.

The hell of it was he felt insecure. In all his wanderings, he had never wanted a permanent mate, and now when he found a woman, she refused him. She had fallen into his arms wantonly but only because of an aphrodisiac, a drug he had succumbed to, also, and now he had no idea if she felt anything for him.

He might never know. He was going to marry her before she could put together a good rebuttal and seek sympathy from James.

Actually, he left so determined, it was only now, when his good sense had overcome his stubbornness, he realized Drake had uncovered everything. He had found out nothing new. The only notable accomplishment was the acquisition of his marriage license.

Roc fell into a comfortable chair; distraught, jaded, grim. He closed his eyes, feeling guilt steal over him. He prayed Trevor had not found himself caught in a trap, and he wondered once more how he would ever persuade Jessie to marry him, or if it was, indeed, a lost cause. Breathing deeply he tried to remember every word that had passed between them. She was strong and resilient and he didn't believe any of the arguments he offered so far would change her mind, unless...

He wanted to have a child with her.

He sank farther into the cushions, feeling the frustration and guilt, tearing through him. He should have been with Trevor in Astoria and none of this would have happened, yet he didn't regret a moment.

Trevor was capable. He would never let Pierce or his men get the upper hand. Rutgers was the clever one. Rutgers had surely been behind this.

That made little difference. He had a score to settle even though they had done him a favor of sorts. The manipulation, the drugs, none of that he'd wanted.

But Raymond Pierce and Sterling Rutgers weren't fools. They left town before the bottle of wine was planted in his dining room and heated the night, even before the unnamed constituent handed it over to Senator Drake.

And he couldn't forget Jess Law.

A strange foreboding shot along his spine. His body shuddered and he longed for a brandy to dull his nerves. He could vaguely hear Perkins and Drake arguing in the distance, and he didn't care.

He rose from his comfortable chair, wondering if some part of his confusion and eagerness had its source from the drug. He speculated too, if perhaps it still flowed through his veins. Yet he never wanted to forget. He savored the memory even though it seemed encased in magic and enchantment.

She had bewitched him; Jessie had responded sweetly, innocently yet so very passionately. And he didn't want to believe the reaction was due solely to the drug.

But it could have been. Jessie had never known a man's touch before, and she acted as if she'd had a wealth of experience. He thought a magical veil had descended and wrapped itself around them creating the mystery, the heat, and the delight. Holding back, not making love to her, had taken every ounce of strength he possessed.

How he had needed her. It was hot in the city last night. He would never forget the taste and feel and scent of her or the velvet smoothness of her flesh beneath the tips of his fingers, the pulsing of her heart, and luscious feel of the perfect softness that was hers alone. He never once denied he wanted her, never denied the current surging between them with each encounter, and because of this, he decided he could risk everything for one night in her arms.

He hadn't wanted that one night shrouded in gruesome intrigue. Hadn't planned it that way at all; he couldn't deny he'd schemed and plotted searching for some manner to bring her willingly to his bed. He couldn't refute he'd enjoyed the night, but, in truth, he hadn't wanted it that way. Even though some of the aphrodisiac flowed through his veins, he'd done his best to act the gentleman.

But the senator locked the door.

Looking into her eyes when she woke had been the culmination of his wildest fantasies. It was all he could do not to taste her again. He held himself rigidly in check, knowing it would not further his cause. Oh, but how he'd wanted to come inside her.

He groaned aloud. All that had happened saved her from the auction block. So he should pat himself on the shoulder, complimenting himself for a job well done. Perhaps he could proclaim her innocence in the affair, but it would not solve the problem they created.

He stiffened, ready to confront everyone, including Jessica Lawrence's father. The marriage license, he'd called in favors to get, burned his fingers.

"Drake."

He called, moving into the parlor. Suddenly, he stared into the stern, cold face of James Lawrence, Jessica's father and now soon to be father-in-law, though Roc would have chosen a different time and place to confront the matriarch of the Lawrence family. Roc stared at him, surprised to see him so soon. He had only penned the message a few minutes earlier. Perkins couldn't have made it to the hotel and back. He should have felt relieved to see James. The man, after all, had the authority to command his daughter; Roc knew James Lawrence had never disciplined Jessie but allowed her to run wild over half the continent, so what made him believe he'd make her do anything she didn't agree with.

"James, just the man I wanted to see. I'm glad you could come quickly."

James raised a brow sardonically. His expression never softened. "I'm supposed to believe that?"

Roc's eyes narrowed swiftly. "I don't lie. I sent for you. Perkins delivered the note. I presume that's why you came so quickly."

"No, it seems the gossip preceded the note. I've heard an ear full and came promptly only to see that you lived. When my wife gets here, you'll find yourself in mortal danger."

"You don't say?" Roc sat back in the chair, watchful, anticipating more of the same treatment. After all, he deserved this and more, but he lay odds James had no idea, as of yet, what transpired in the heat of the night. "I believe a short explanation and subsequent commitment can rectify the matter."

James nodded and strode the length of the room, turning to stare back at Roc. "Explain yourself then. Drake has told me some of the story, and I believe Trevor has some accounting to do likewise but for now I'm waiting." He made a growling sound deep in his throat, nodding his head again. Roc thought he'd never seen a man so furious, and it would get worse. "I can't think of anything you could say that would improve the situation, but I'll listen. I'm a patient man."

So, what had she told her father? Roc sipped the brandy Perkins had poured earlier. It went down smoothly, and the heat of it warmed him. He offered James a glass, biding his time. James lied. He was anything but patient, and his speech amused Roc. The wedding would take place, he knew, just by the look in James's eye. *Where to start?* He ran his hand over his jaw then explained as quickly as possible that Trevor had disappeared along with some missionary's daughter. His daughter had been drugged and marked as the main attraction at an auction the previous night. To keep her virtue in tact, he kept her in his bed. He waited as the silent moment ticked on, watched as fury seized James. Then went on to explain the scenario, concocted by Raymond Pierce, and Sterling Rutgers had only begun. Jessie would not be safe until she found protection as his wife.

"She neglected to tell me about the auction or what happened between the two of you," James whispered fiercely. "I had almost agreed to her request, and yet I knew, oh, I knew I had to hear the other side of the story."

"Somehow, I'm not surprised. I suppose the rest of it was a little warped also. Did she tell you how she came into the house? Or how she attacked me?" he asked James. He sipped the brandy, loath to continue in this way, as he wanted a swift resolution. His cynicism would get him nowhere. He set his glass on the end table and waited for James to digest all the information he'd received. The silence fell heavy around them, and Roc found breathing difficult.

All of Salem knew now that James Lawrence had come, seeking retribution, and Pierce, Rutgers and Madame Lilly had plotted against the family, and Roc Newman had hastily obtained a marriage license and a minister.

Senator Drake and the minister waited in another room. Roc hurried in without waiting for James to give his consent. He knew it would come, albeit begrudgingly. Perkins stepped forward, looking worried for his friend and employer. To Roc's surprise, he found James had followed him. The men stared at each other, waiting to break the silence; neither one did. Roc hesitated and let his gaze move upward to the root of everyone's thoughts. James's eyes followed and he frowned, clearly angered by his imaginings.

"Is everything in order, Senator?"

Drake nodded. "Indeed, everything except a certain young lady's consent. It seems," he chuckled, "Miss Jessica has given Roc the mitten. She refused his proposal quite adamantly. I had thought you more persuasive, Roc."

Roc stiffened and pulled up a chair, straddling it before resting his arms on the back. Perkins offered coffee. Roc shook him off, preferring his brandy and the quiet calm it gave him.

"I don't know what to do about that. I hoped her father would help. As for Trevor, we need to find him," Roc said. "As well as the infamous trio. You know the city is a buzz. My hat's off to you, Senator. Your predictions have held true."

The Senator arched a brow.

Roc turned to James. "I need your help to convince Jessie. It's the only way."

James leaned casually back in the chair he'd taken, rubbing his fingers on his temple. He stared hard at Roc. Then he breathed deeply. "Do you love her, Mr. Newman? I can't let my daughter bind herself to a loveless marriage."

"Even for her own sake?" Roc shot back without stopping to think. "I care about her, but for love..."

"Roc, Please, listen to me. This has to be Jessie's decision. I can tell her what I think, but she's a stubborn woman with a mind of her own. She has never been one to allow any person, especially a man, to force an opinion on her. And, Roc, we're talking about a life long commitment. This, she won't take lightly. It's a serious issue and she's said no. I don't have a clue what I can do to change her mind."

Shocked, Roc felt the anger and the frustration simmer.

"You have more influence than you think. Talk to her. Remind her there could be damage to her reputation. Threaten, warn, I don't care, but tell her now that she will wed with me tonight."

"I don't like this."

"Son of a bitch, no one's asking..."

"Roc, I cannot say the words for her, any more than you can. She has to stand in front of the preacher and willingly say I do. Heed my words, I may be her father but I cannot make her marry you. When I think of what she can do to herself if left unprotected, it makes me shudder. But neither will I coerce her into a marriage she doesn't want. I will talk to her, but I think you will have to convince her."

"Whether she says yes or not, I will have her." Frustration meddled with his sanity. "I will find a way, and she will learn to obey."

James leaned forward suddenly amused. "I wish you luck. She will never obey, but she might come to love you."

"Luck? Hell, it's going to take more than that."

"Perhaps you should have thought of that before you compromised her. If either of you can find a way to give an inch, then a happy union might result. But I know Jessie, and she's almost as stubborn as her mother."

"Impossible." Roc stood up suddenly, the chair slamming to the floor.

James didn't move; Drake gasped at the sudden violence.

Finger combing his hair, he paced the length of the room. "What would you have me do? Forget all I've promised, a vow to her cousin and to myself to protect her?"

"Hers, too. But you've put events out of sequence."

He glowered at James.

"I know." His voice emphatic, as if he harbored no doubts. Roc let the words fall into deathly silence. They sounded curiously strange to his ears. Jessie would understand, at least it seemed as if she did when he'd made his pronouncement only a few short hours ago. He strode to the steps and rested his hand on the solid mahogany banister, anticipating. Jessie's words were clear and concise in his head. There wasn't the smallest waver in her words. She had told him no.

"Have you heard from Trevor?" he demanded of Drake, changing the subject. He would have time with Jessie; he'd see to it, soon.

"Knowing Trevor, I think I can say he's waiting for the right time. He has the girl with him, and I'm sure he feels a certain responsibility, but he wants Pierce. So far the two have outwitted us at every turn. It's almost as though they have an informant."

"What if he needs help? I can't let those two get away."

"Smuggling, prostitution," Drake said flatly, "they won't get away. It's only a matter of time and patience. Trevor seems to possess much more of that quality than you."

"What do you mean by that?" Roc remarked, lifting an eyebrow.

Drake sighed. "Only that under the circumstances, I chose the right men for the jobs."

"That doesn't give you the right to sit in judgment."

"No. But until we hear from Trevor, I have no other recourse than to wait. I won't blow his cover and neither will you. I forbid you to run off to Astoria. You can do nothing except damage whatever progress Trevor has made and, in the process, leave Miss Jessica unprotected."

Roc inhaled sharply. "And how am I supposed to protect her when she fights me at every turn? Pray, how does any man stand a chance against that woman?"

"Being the wise parent that I am," James interrupted shrewdly, "I will ignore that. Yet I would encourage you to seek her out and perhaps tell her some of the things you have told us. I believe if she is approached in a gentle manner, she will listen. You have hurt her terribly."

"I know."

"Now, have you forgotten who waits in this room for you and the girl to settle your differences?" Drake asked wryly, with a quick glance to James.

Roc stiffened. "Of course not, but I've reached an impasse with her."

"Indeed?"

"I can think of nothing more to say. Her father doesn't have a word of encouragement for me or Jessie." He grilled James with an icy glare.

James smiled irreverently. Drake arched a brow. "We've been over this ground many times already. I am beginning to think the young lady upstairs has you cowed. Indeed, she has bested you so many times you probably fear for your life if you come remotely close to her."

"I need not remind you how close I was and survived."

"No, you don't. My daughter was a virgin. Knew nothing of the ways of men and you saw fit to teach her," James swore. He stared hard at Roc. "As your future father-in-law, I'm telling you to see this to its proper conclusion. If you harm her again, I will have your hide and nail it to the wall."

Roc fought the rising tide of fury. "Your daughter is still a virgin, and I believe I've made my intentions clear from the start. I--"

"She is? I wouldn't have believed it. But you haven't talked to Jessie.

You left this morning, executed the proper arrangements, and came back expecting me to deliver her in a neatly wrapped package," James said, his voice deceptively softly.

Roc stared, amazed at the man, remembering her words. *I will never marry you. I am an honest woman without your help.* Had she or hadn't she been adamant?

"I've asked her and she refused."

~ * ~

James glared at Newman, his mind raging against the indiscretions this man took with Jessie. He wanted to strike out. At least he hadn't stolen her virtue. Jessie was not a woman to bestow her love or loyalty easily, but when she did, she did so completely. James knew he would have to defend her honor and see to her marriage. He closed his eyes, very sorry Jessie's life had come to this. Perhaps he had given her too much freedom, a man's freedom, and now it would be so much harder.

He was her father. A father who had to do what he felt was right. After years of treating his daughter as if she could think for herself and had the right to do that, he would have to make her obey. He'd watched her grow, held her close when nightmares overwhelmed her dreams and she cried in the night, sweated by her bed when she almost died of diphtheria. He could remember the moment she conquered the disease. In her guileless way she'd brought Alexandra and himself together when it all seemed so hopeless. Now it was his turn to do something for his daughter. Roc would make her a fine husband.

And Roc knew none of this, knew so very little about her. But he knew Newman, better, he thought, than Roc knew himself; knew he would have taken advantage of Jessie and the situation if he didn't feel a great deal of concern for her, even perhaps love. There was so much about Jessie's childhood Roc needed to know, things that molded her into the woman she was now and her passionate fight for women's rights. He should know Jessie as a little girl had seen her mother raped and murdered during the war. But it was up to Jessie to tell that tale.

He hadn't offered to help because he thought it best solved between

Roc and Jessie. And above all else, he wanted to keep his distance for the simple reason he could barely control his fury.

And yes, Jessie needed Roc, and the senator needed Trevor, his calm perceptive personality, capable of dealing with the craftiest mind.

James found it hard to believe the animosity and the hate exuding from Pierce and Rutgers, but as he thought back on his dealings with Pierce, he understood. He was tired of battling, fighting for those who sought to lay claim to his empire. An empire won with hard work and perseverance. Tired of men who sought riches at another man's loss.

Watching Roc now, his concentration on Jessie, he knew, for his peace of mind he would have to land at least one blow. A father's duty, he supposed, even though he backed the marriage, even though some of what happened was not Roc's fault. "I have known you, followed your career. I have seen you at your best and now your worst. I have given my consent to the marriage even though I abhor the way you went about this. Yet now it seems you lack the courage to confront her. How can you forget how deeply you wronged Jessie?"

Roc grimaced "I've forgotten nothing."

"Then prove it."

"I already have."

James strode toward Roc, bent on violence. "I don't think so. You haven't felt the pain, or the fear she feels now. Have you ever been afraid, vulnerable, forced into a situation with no choices?" James asked. "I'm warning you now, whatever happens I hold you responsible, and you will not get away without some form of suffering."

Roc stood firm, his hands held loosely at his side. It was obvious he wasn't trying to defend himself against James. It seemed he would allow his soon to be father-in-law his restitution. As he waited for the inevitable, Roc's muscles tensed.

Bloody hell, how his daughter confused and infuriated him. She had manipulated all this so easily.

The blow came swift and sure. Blood gushed from his nose and he reeled backward, no longer willing to capitulate. He yelled and kicked high, hitting James squarely in the chest. James gasped for air and staggered back. Roc balanced, waiting.

James watched, intent. No words passed between them. Suddenly, the setting sun flung beams of light through the window. Drake and Perkins looked from one man to the other. The contest had only begun or had it ended?

James threw his head back, laughing, breaking the deadly tension. "That wasn't enough, but I suppose it will have to do for now. She'd never forgive you if you beat me half to death now would she. And as you well know, you have a great deal of convincing to do. I don't suppose you're ready to get started now."

"Not really."

"Then I suppose I will have to continue this." James charged suddenly, taking Roc by surprise.

"James..." the rest of his sentence ended in a gush of air.

"Roc." James persisted. They rolled on the floor, punches coming fast and hard. Impossible to tell whose arm belonged where.

Drake and Perkins surprised them, stepping into the middle of the contest, pulling them apart. Drake ducked too late, and the punch hit him solidly. He reeled backward obviously wondering what his supporters would think when they read the front page, for surely this would headline the paper because nothing seemed to get by the reporters who dodged his steps. He almost laughed when he saw Perkins topple James with a well-executed move.

All four men, in some state of dishabille, watched each other, motionless.

"Have you all had enough?" Perkins asked.

They glared at each other. Tension and anger, perhaps some frustration still enshrouded the little gathering. "Yes," Roc admitted.

James nodded. But he would have liked to say not nearly enough.

"Fine." Drake dusted off his pants. He motioned to Roc. "Talk to her, convince her, do whatever is necessary, but bring her to her wedding."

"This instant?"

"Never a better time than the present," James growled.

Drake nodded his agreement. "We've wasted too much time as it is."

"She's never going to agree," Roc blurted, even while the minister stood patiently in the next room. Everyone waited for Roc to bring Jessica down, yet he looked ready to balk. Then he stiffened, and it seemed he remembered something.

Of course she will," Drake laughed.

Roc moved to the stairs. "I'll do my best."

He left then, taking the steps two at a time, lunging furiously toward the tempest inside, wondering what he'd find.

~ * ~

Jessie sat uncomfortably stiff, frozen, trance-like upon the bed. Doom paled the still air, while all about walls seemed to close in upon her. It was beginning to seem like eternity since the horrible morning and her rude awakening in the arms of Roc. Except for a few seconds with her stepfather, she had remained ensconced in the room, his room, staring at the undeniable proof the dream had reality. Tantrums had done nothing. They hadn't erased the memory, or the night she would rather forget, deny. Hate, the only emotion she wanted to feel; yet somehow she could not reach past the coldness within her to find the fury and the rage.

Fear for Trevor, at times, seemed to wipe her desperate situation from her mind. For truly, her life meant nothing if her cousin perished. Sick with worry, she swore to help him, go to him, if she could find a way. From what she understood, he had disappeared, his fate unknown.

She had listened and heard the words from Senator Drake even as she pressed her ear so close to the locked door. Knew Pierce and Rutgers had underestimated them, caught in their own game. Had heard they skedaddled out of town and Madame Lilly had planned a night's entertainment with her as the leading lady. She supposed she should thank Roc, but the hollow feeling in the pit of her stomach would not leave.

She heard a shallow, raspy, laugh echo through the empty room and knew what she had to do, determined Roc would become only a bitter sweet memory.

Jessie would find a way to leave. Intuition told her Pierce and Rutgers would not head for Astoria. They had lived in Oregon too long. The law waited for them in that bustling port town. No, they would find seclusion. A place where no one would suspect them and where news traveled slowly. She knew where they would head.

She paced the room, thinking, determined to find some way to leave, but even as she contemplated her escape, the lock on the door clicked, exploding through the quiet, shattering her plans. *Roc?*

Silently, he stared at her. Silver eyes, striding over her, cool, determined, relentless, dashing her hopes, bringing to mind his heated touch, the whisper of his lips, the force of him, and the sheer masculine power.

"We have to talk, Jessie," he said, his gaze lingering on the sheets that now lay piled on the floor.

"I don't think so," she denied him coolly. He didn't move. Except for the arch of a black brow, he seemed frozen in the doorway, an apparition in time, a force to reckon with, demanding and unbending.

"You have no choice, even your father agrees," he told her, and he looked as if he tried to keep his temper in control. If only he didn't know her so well, comprehend she harbored such animosity for him and even now she plotted to leave. She admitted to herself at times she did have no sense and sometimes an inflated image of her prowess. She blamed him though, blamed him for everything that had happened, but she hesitated. If she had not acted so rashly, if she had only listened to him even then. If...

"My father would never..." she began to repeat, but she fell silent. "Very well."

"Miss Lawrence, we must find a way to deal with this."

"Why?"

"Why? You are not stupid. We spoke of the consequences. And I intend to marry you. Today."

Jessie stared at him, unblinking, still so very quiet, and she didn't understand what could possibly be rumbling around in his mind. He didn't want to marry her anymore than she did him. "I know," she admitted.

He stopped in mid-stride, his breath quite taken from him by the unexpected capitulation. She knew the shock of her words would turn him to some emotion she'd rather not see; saw the fever simmering within his eyes, knew his frustration at the time lost in contemplation and fear she would tell him no. Now his every move charged the atmosphere, and she noticed the change of expression, his sudden loss of control, and knew he despised what she did to him. His gaze heated with the fire that burned within him, pierced her, terrified her and she cringed back against the bed, no longer calm and coolly collected.

"I understand," she gasped out again. "I realize we must for appearances, for the time being."

"Appearances? For the time being?"

"Of course."

"Never."

"An annulment, when all this is over."

"I don't think so. I have no intention of ending a marriage, sweet. Once I have spoken the vows, they will last my lifetime. Never forget it." His voice, softened for a moment, but it deepened suddenly and his gaze froze her.

"But you don't even care for me."

"Ah, but in that you are wrong. I care that nothing happens to you. I care to see you live a long and fulfilling life."

"I won't sleep with you."

"You will."

She felt cold descend even deeper, and she wondered if that were possible. Her body trembled wildly, afraid what he said was truth. He would sleep with her, and she would make love with him and somehow she knew he would give her undreamed of pleasure. "You can't force me."

"Never, Jessica Lawrence. Never would I force you."

"Promise?"

"With every breath I take."

"Very well, I will agree to marry you, but beyond that, the wedding is a mockery."

"I mock nothing, but once you wed me, we will see what happens."

She couldn't begin to tell him how wrong he was. All she knew was she had to agree to wed if she were to get out of this room. He was correct. She wasn't stupid. It seemed she said too much, spoken hastily and out of turn. He appeared, at the moment, ready to leave the room and never return. He would never do anything less than honorable. They had to reach a compromise, put aside their differences if only to make the best of this horrible situation.

"I will try," she said, cautiously lowering her lashes and biting her tongue. She knew he would never believe this sudden compliance. Somewhere she would have to find a middle ground. Somewhere it existed.

He grinned suddenly, but his eyes still glittered and shimmered silver fire. "Good. I'm pleased."

Jessie's gaze moved upward, no longer demure and pretentious. He knew. Damn his soul, he knew. "But..."

It seemed she'd lost her wits and now could only stutter in front of him. He only looked more pleased.

"Your father," he said, "has agreed to give the bride away."

She stared at him, shocked at the easy grace of his movement, at the penetrating heat of his gaze. She gasped, knowing the betrayal of her father, conscious he had done this to her, gone against his word and everything he'd ever promised her.

What would her mother say? Alexandra would never forgive James. They had both promised she would have the freedom of choice, and now James ripped it from her, smoothly, callously, and without thought.

Roc would never allow an annulment.

She fought the fury and the desolation threatening to swamp her. Struggled with all her will, knowing her choices were limited and her life in danger. He might not give her an annulment, but she would find away to escape the hatred he harbored for her. Because she knew he would never understand her need for freedom and independence.

"We must reach some compromise," she declared.

"We will take this one minute to the next."

"I don't think I can do that."

"You have no choice."

She inhaled sharply, fiercely trying to deny him and his closeness, for he was suddenly so near she could feel the warmth of his breath the subtle caress of his hand as he moved it against her cheek softly to brush her hair back. "You've said that before, and I find it hard to cotton to."

He dropped his hand away then pulled her close. They had come to an impasse. She gasped, realizing he meant to prove something. Roc brushed her lips with subtle and tender care. Heat surged through her; she meant to deny him, meant to remain cold and aloof. But when he nibbled at her bottom lip then sucked gently, she opened to him. She leaned into him, begging for more, for the continuation of the night before. A cry escaped her lips when he gently placed his hands on her shoulders and moved her back. Cold replaced the heat. Tremors ripped through her; hungry for denial, for recriminations she could not explain.

"Come now. The minister awaits."

Jessie calmed herself. She could see everyone, waiting. Her father appeared at her side, ready to escort her. James took her arm and waited for Roc to move down the steps. Her life floated before her, ethereal, mystical; she searched for a way to move back in time.

Hesitation overwhelmed her. She looked to her father and read cold determination. After all, she had brought herself to this. The blame rested on her shoulders.

"Jessie, dear child. If I knew of another way, I would see to it." They moved slowly down the steps. She didn't want this marriage, or any marriage. It wasn't because of Roc. Loss of her freedom had always held the greatest threat. She guarded it religiously. Now it was about to end.

"I've accepted it."

"Jessie, you will have to do more than accept. You must learn to live with it. He will protect you with his life."

She didn't want to argue with her father. In this she knew she'd never convince him to renege. The emptiness in the pit of her stomach rumbled and grew. Hopelessness descended to remind her of her strengths and the power she held within. She would hold fast to her demands. He would not make love to her with out her consent. At least he had admitted that to her, and when this had all ended, she would once more demand an annulment. For now she would not speak of it again.

"I will not promise to obey," she whispered. Her father heard and smiled.

"Indeed," he countered.

They reached the bottom of the steps, moved through the outer rooms to come to the huge hearth. Flowers, hundreds of flowers adorned the inside. And she wondered then, how? Haste and no time to plan, still, the house decorated to perfection. She caught Perkins smiling face; knew instantly he had designed all.

Everything so perfectly arranged. No one had consulted or asked her. Had never thought to consider her wishes.

James brought her to Roc, handing her over easily, swiftly. Roc kissed her fingers.

The minister began. His words droned on.

This was really happening to her. She tensed, shivering even while she smiled and tried hard to calm herself. She turned, meaning to comply, to read Roc's mind, perhaps gaze into his soul.

To her astonishment, Roc smiled back and it seemed tender, sincere. She could have thought he might want this marriage, but the smile vanished quickly. What she'd thought was only a figment of her imagination and hopes.

The minister continued. Calm settled around her shoulders. She began to hear the words of the ceremony. Roc held her hand gently within his own. Time seemed eternal. She held her breath, heard the soft timber of his words.

"I do."

"And do you, Jessica Lawrence?"

She couldn't talk. A lump had settled deep in her throat. Jessie gulped for air, yet the sound wafted softly through the room on a gentle breath.

"Jessie..." Roc whispered, his volatile gaze taunting her, mocking her every wish and the demands she had made. She remembered the kiss only a short moment ago and wondered if she could resist this man. His promise echoed in her head. He would never use force against her.

"I do," she said so softly the minister leaned forward, hesitating if she had indeed spoken. She could hear Roc's sigh, satisfaction and the gently teasing smile she suddenly wanted to touch.

A moment later, they were pronounced man and wife. Roc swept her into his arms. The kiss held promises, so very many promises. She was flush with him; he tasted her, it deepened, and she searched for the beauty and the hunger that would fulfill a dream. He set her down as if nothing had happened. It was binding and permanent, unless...

Unless she could convince Roc she didn't want him or care for him, that there was nothing between them. But that was not longer the truth.

She had just married a man for his protection, a man who hated her.

"A wedding toast." Senator Drake cried. Perkins grinned. Everyone else glowered at him, even Roc. Now that he had placed the ring on her finger, she thought dejectedly, he had no need of pretense. "To a union bound to sizzle, set the night on fire," Drake chuckled.

Even Drake mocked them. She closed her eyes against the laughter beating hollowly against her head. She felt ill, wanted to run from the jeopardy her foolishness had brought down upon her. But she couldn't.

"Truly, I am sorry it has come to this, Jess," her father whispered, bringing her a glass of wine. Of all the men, he had not laughed, only studied her with an implacable expression. She felt his pain and the remorse, perhaps the guilt because he'd allowed her so much room to grow and explore the world unencumbered by the strict values society placed on its ladies.

She was sorry too.

He kissed her cheek with fatherly concern. Drake followed. Perkins hesitated. She could hear him mumble something then he too kissed her cheek. She wanted to laugh, the adorable man. It eased her pain and she silently thanked him.

Then Roc held her hand. He pulled her close. His gaze threatened and intimidated, brooking no argument. Perkins began to clear away the glasses. The minister had left moments ago, a fat purse in his pocket.

"Please forgive me, but my new bride and I have much to discuss."

James looked reluctant. "Roc, I beseech you," but he faltered.

This was none of his concern. He had willingly given his daughter away.

Jessie gazed between the men, one so dear to her, the other unknown. She knew instantly her father relinquished any hold he had upon her. James was afraid Roc would hurt her, but he could no longer say anything. She wanted to reassure her father, but Roc wouldn't allow it.

"I won't hurt her, if that's what you're afraid of."

"Father, please. He won't, you see, well," she looked up. A becoming flush painted her cheeks and James nodded. He understood.

She didn't want them to go, but Roc was right about one thing. They did have a great deal to discuss. The consummation of the marriage listed high among her priorities.

His gaze found her. Silver fire smoldered within their depths. He whispered softly, close to her ear, "I will see you in my bed tonight."

She paled and turned away from him. Yes. She had agreed to many things. And she doubted his words, even while she steeled herself against them.

The next few moments appeared hectic. James kissed her good bye then turned from her. Drake and her father left together, laughing. Laughing as if nothing terrible had just happened to her. Perkins muffled a good-natured toast before he turned, also to leave them, moving through the house to his quarters. "Can we stay here?" she asked finally. The quiet of the house disturbing, intimating events she wished to forget.

"If you wish, but Jess, you can't escape the inevitable."

They were in the parlor, dusk slowly descending, and he was staring at her. Before she could ask, he handed her a glass of wine, and he was sipping his. She began to tremble.

He was gazing at her, knifing through her every defense, cutting each resolve so carefully planned, leaving her vulnerable. She felt as if he read through her carefully guarded thoughts and knew how much she wanted him.

"Please," she whispered suddenly. He arched a brow and motioned to the sofa. It sat in front of the fireplace which was filled with blossoms of every kind. The fragrance soft and delicate swirled around her enchantingly. The evening was a perfect midsummer night's evening, perfect for seduction, for his love, if it could only be.

"Truly, it would please me." He grinned.

She wet her lips and moved to sit, sliding to the far end, distancing herself from the power, the force of the man, afraid she could never resist him. "You wanted to talk?" she asked, humiliated at the fear her voice showed.

For a moment he was silent. He laid his head back, studying the ceiling or perhaps the waning light playing across it. Perkins had lit a few candles before he left and the shadows danced on the walls and flickered bewitchingly around the room.

Sometime in the silent relentless night, he moved to her, forcing her hand and her courage if nothing else. He could read her thoughts and her fear, it seemed. He caressed her cheek, and she heard the rustle of fabric at the window as the cool evening air brushed whisper soft against it. His fingertips touched her lips lightly, hovering and enticing, drawing her into his web of seduction. She didn't know how to fight him and, she thought, perhaps she didn't want to battle. When he came to her ear, tracing it, she shivered then stood suddenly and he reached out, pulling her back, allowing no quarter. He had said he would not force her. He had said it. She reminded herself. All she had to do, all she had to say was no.

But his hands roamed along her collarbone across her shoulders, pushing away the material.

"Do you think to slander this?"

"I don't want this," she said. "Please, don't touch me. Just leave me alone."

"Don't say it, Jess." His finger touched her lips. "Hush."

"I..."

"I'll never let you go. Don't you know that by now? I've told you a thousand times."

"But..."

"Jessica," he said softly. "You are my wife now. It is over. You are mine. My wife. If you do as I say, I will keep you safe." She watched his eyes, watched him studying her. But she knew just how far she had pushed the issue, because she had indeed pushed it past his endurance.

"I will try," she said. "But I do have a mind of my own, intelligence to match yours."

The mood changed, and she was glad because she didn't want to feel anything for this man, a man who created fire within her but confusion too. It was gone in a sudden flash of anger and sweet tempest. He held out his hand. "A truce," he said. "I never meant to imply..."

"Of course you did," she interrupted. "I wanted to talk and you wanted to seduce. It didn't work." She turned, giving him her back. It seemed her only recourse for he would see the desire shining in her eyes and the lingering flush where he had touched.

He walked around her, taking her hands in his, drawing her away from her thoughts and into his body. "Enchantress," he told her softly.

She felt the power, the breadth and the irrefutable desire pulsing, drawing her ever closer.

Then the yearning to run came over her.

She was in his control, prisoner to his calculating enticements, helpless within the sticky web of his trap. But was it really so bad? She loved the feel of his touch, loved the man.

His wife.

She had to remember to say no. Or there would be no excuse. He would never use force. He had promised.

"I don't want you to touch me again," she said suddenly. "You told me..."

"I know what I said," he countered. "But what harm in a kiss?"

She wanted to scream at him, tell him all the harm in the world. Because that's all it would take. One kiss. He must know it.

"Are you afraid?" He arched a dark brow.

"Surely you jest," she flung back at him. "Never afraid, but I would hate you forever."

Roc paused at the determination in her voice. His hand shook with constraint, trembled, even as their gazes met. Jessica knew he remembered the magic and the mystery and the fire and flame that had burned within both of them and she understood he wanted to taste it again. She wanted the same thing.

"Well," he whispered softly, studying her, "it is up to you then, a kiss perhaps if you can renounce the feelings," he shrugged.

"A trick, I want no part of it."

"No trick," he said easing his long length to the floor. A huge white fur rug lay beneath him. He patted a spot, encouraging her to come. "If you're not afraid..." he let the sentence linger on the breeze. Saw the hesitation in her step, he had found her weakness. His gaze flashed and shimmered, twinkling with merriment. She wanted to hit him, deny him, refuse his request, but it was such a simple one.

"Do I have your promise?" she insisted.

He frowned, stiffening suddenly at that. "I'm a man of my word."

She inhaled deeply, worrying, wondering. He arched a brow and patted the fur once more. She stepped closer. When he didn't move, she let out her breath and sat beside him. She faced him, casually and perhaps fearlessly, but her heart pounded beneath her breasts, and she was afraid of herself. He watched her and must have seen the desire in her eyes even as she tried to deny it and waited for the kiss that would come soon. "A kiss, just one."

"Only if you can still say no, but it must be a real kiss. Not a peck on the cheek, not a moment here then gone, vanishing, a veil of mystery."

"I don't..."

He smiled. "Of course you do. Think back to last night..."

She wet her lips, her breaths ragged and unsteady, her body shuddering. She wanted to get this over with. She gazed down at him for she sat above him. He had stretched out, leaning on his elbow, relaxed, confident and so very arrogant. "You won't touch me?"

"Not unless you ask."

"Fine." Tears, hot and fresh, suddenly welled in her throat. "I hate you," she told him. But she wanted to say I love you. Did she?

"I'm your husband and I haven't touched you. Force? Hardly, but if you are afraid..."

"I'm not!" she cried out incredulously. She struggled for the words, but they eluded her. He was wicked to do this, but she couldn't deny the strange power that one word held over her.

She would never admit to the fear. Never.

"But I don't want to kiss you or touch you, and somehow this seems like deadly force."

"Deadly? Oh, Jessie, never that. Kiss me and we will see."

"This is incredible. You seduce me, subtly but truly that is what you do and you know it." Panicked, she sought an answer to her question. His hands relaxed, non-threatening but she felt the overwhelming pressure and knew in a matter of minutes she would succumb to his caress. He had promised, but what had he said? If she asked for his touch. She wouldn't say the words. She was safe. If she succumbed and consummated this marriage, she would truly bind herself to him.

He chuckled softly, "This is seduction? My, you are inexperienced."

"Please..." she began. But if she backed down now, she would never forgive herself and she wouldn't allow him the victory.

"What ever you wish, coward," he taunted her softly.

"One, only one."

"No, I don't think so. I hate to see you trembling with terror. It shows in your eyes. Fear of deadly force, fear I would take unholy advantage of you, my wife. No, coward that you--"

"Oh, stop," she pleaded. She couldn't bear his mockery. He spoke the truth for she was a coward, at least about this. But she'd prove herself. She was trembling but not in fear but in anticipation. She was feeling the flames ignite and he hadn't touched her.

"I don't want you to do anything you will regret, Jesse," he told her softly. "And I will not force this issue. But I swear, sooner or later you will want me too."

"No...yes...I promised too. I'm not afraid of you," she told him.

He hadn't taken his eyes off her for all the time she had sat so primly in front of him.

And the reflection in his gaze soothed her.

"Then prove it."

"We despise each other."

"I care for you deeply," he told her, and leaned back from her, distancing himself. She moved closer as if she sought the warmth he promised. She watched him; he continued backing away. She suddenly discovered she had rested a hand upon his chest to support herself.

She flinched and jerked her hand away. He frowned but made no attempt to capture her hand. "You can touch me anywhere, anytime..."

"I didn't mean..."

"More's the pity," he said and sighed, his eyes dark and unrelenting. "It seems you still have much to demonstrate. Or have you forgotten so soon the lesson I taught you. Have you forgotten how sweetly your lips parted to my kiss? I would do the same for you."

She trembled. "I would forget the drug..."

"I would forget the drug and what we have said to each other in the past. We need to begin anew. A fresh start, Jessie, that's what we need."

"I don't know."

"Perhaps," he said softly, studying her eyes. He shrugged. "We do have to get past that first kiss." He rolled on to his back. His hands linked behind his head; his pose relaxed and casual. She wanted to lay her head on his chest and feel secure within his embrace. And she was scared, but she closed her eyes, prayed to the gods above and let her braver self take over.

She lowered her head; brushed his lips lightly with hers, running her tongue over the seam of his lips, enticing them to open. She tried to coerce and seduce, but he held them rigid and he wouldn't yield. He had told her to remember and she had.

She moved her tongue across his lips again then nibbled her way across. He groaned. His lips softened, and she urged them apart, felt the hardness of his teeth, the soft inner lining of his mouth and pressed forward. She employed every tactic she could think of until she trembled and pulsed with a fever she couldn't negate, but still he didn't yield and he hadn't touched her. She groaned.

"What do I have to do to end this?" she whispered and could feel the smile curve across his lips and the subtle softening of his mouth once more.

"You must ask."

"Please..." she could say nothing more.

"Please what?" He laughed softly. Still he didn't touch her, didn't move.

"Open your mouth," she gasped.

He complied, readily, easily, gave her the lead, allowing her to do as she pleased.

Then he groaned and held her tight against his heart.

He reached for her, pulling her hard into his embrace. She moaned softly, the magic, the music of the sound, swept his desire into a raging tempest. "Jessica Newman," he spoke her name softly and with the most tender care, close to her ear. "You are my wife. Forever. After this night you will harbor no thoughts of annulment or a marriage of convenience. And I pray you will have no regrets in the morning."

Chapter Seven

It was just as he remembered; the warmth, the enchantment, the mystery of it all as he held her. Fragrant roses, the scent of her silken flesh, and the feel of her hair entwined around his hands seduced him. Candlelight warmed her skin and bathed the room in a golden halo. Why had he taken the chance of her refusal? He couldn't remember and now he no longer cared. She had surrendered in his arms. She had not given him her heart but for now this was enough. Beneath him she was soft and willing and he realized the magic he had known the night before was real. He hadn't imagined it.

Each time her fingers moved across him, she fanned the flame and the tempest within.

"Jessie."

He touched her cheek, traced his fingers along the smooth column of her throat then cupped her face in his hands. She closed her eyes and a delicate sigh escaped her lips, forfeiture of the battle imminent. There was something intriguing him, inherent and different in every aspect of Jessica Lawrence's nature. Something she tried to hide and seldom succeeded. He saw it, all the untamed passion, the wildness and the urge to live life to the fullest possessing her soul.

He laughed softly, buried his hands in her hair, and leaned down to sample her lips again. His mouth demanded a response, and she didn't disappoint him. The wait had seemed like torture, but now, he knew the tender consideration he had given her would reap many rewards. His kiss was soft, slow; it allowed her to explore and perhaps understand. He raised his head, and he saw the warmth, the curious confusion shielded within the amethyst of her eyes.

She must know to return was no longer possible. They had progressed far beyond a simple no.

"Don't fear this," he told her huskily.

"I'm not scared."

"It will change everything, tonight, tomorrow night, every one after that," he reminded her. He touched her lips with the tip of his finger, frowning skeptically. "What did you believe? That I have no honor? And perhaps I do not take my vows seriously? Jessica, I promised to stay with you and protect you until death, and I intend to keep that vow. You would be a fool to think otherwise and you are no fool."

She shivered at his words. "I don't understand. I would think you would jump at the chance to annul this farcical marriage. A marriage where there is no love."

A sound of unease rustled the air. Love. For what seemed a lifetime, he had searched for that elusive butterfly, love. It didn't exist. Life had convinced him. Jessie could love him like a wildcat, and still the mystery would fly through the haze and the clouds and the sorrow in his heart. Ah, but love, he closed his eyes. This was as close as he would ever get to his door to heaven and to love. She had married him, come willingly to his bed, and he would see her safe and happy.

Now he could find some forgiveness for the senator and Trevor. A plot neatly hatched had come to fruition. He accepted it; that in itself was curiously strange. For the sake of her reputation and his honor he had agreed, but he didn't believe for a moment he would have if anyone besides Jessie had lain in his bed. He was not a man easily coerced.

No one had extorted his compliance or forced him to walk to the altar.

He grinned down at his beautiful wife.

His fingers sifted through the silken length of her hair. He gazed at her. "Touch me," he commanded her.

She drew a deep breath, nodding her understanding. "Where?" she whispered.

"Anywhere it pleases you. Do whatever comes to mind, sweet Jessie. This is your night, and I will see your dreams satisfied."

"You won't expect my submission? You'll allow me my freedom to come and go as I please, to continue my work? I intend to find Trevor."

"Then I'll have to lock the room again. I didn't think it would come to this." He wanted to give her everything she asked for, yearned to make her happy.

"This room won't hold me if I want to leave."

"So, I'll have to resort to the medieval methods I had contemplated earlier."

"If you expect to hold me," she said.

Crazy woman. She was unfathomable and too independent. The truth, she taunted him with the truth as if he'd allow her escape now that she'd exposed her plans.

He rose above her to study her features; clear, exquisite, honest. Trust, yes. He could trust her to do exactly what she said. She would be a perpetual challenge for him.

When he first saw her move silently across his lawn dressed for the blackness of the night, she had intrigued him. Then she had surprised him, taken him unaware with a swift elbow to his chest. Now this wild, hot, little cat of the night was his wife. Maybe she would learn he had only her best interest at heart.

But he wouldn't hold his breath.

And she would try to outwit him. He would enjoy picking the thorns from her nicely rounded derriere.

"Son of a bitch," he said softly, his voice low and husky, refusing to laugh again. A state that would surely betray his thoughts and render the mood he'd labored so hard to create, ineffective. "If I am going to protect your soft hide, I will need some manner of compromise here, and if I find you running off half-cocked into trouble...I'll...I'll...well, be assured I will do all in my power to see no harm comes to you." He roared out finally, shaking. His control lost, long forgotten in his fear for that very lovely hide he'd just referred to.

She was staring at him, amused and clearly set in awe by his lack of punishments and dire warnings.

He cursed again, realizing his rambling had far from put the fear of God, or even himself into her. He sat up, wrenching his shirt over his head.

He had never dreamed a woman could torment him like this, set his harmonious life into a tailspin. Even when she created chaos amidst confusion, he had his conscience and sense of right and wrong to hold on to. Now he groped for some lifeline, and she kept pulling it away. He had her practically begging for his caress, his kisses then he initiated a conversation. The atmosphere fairly exploded. Still, it sizzled, charged, but not with passion. He reminded himself again he'd not force her, this exquisite woman. Did he mean that for her actions outside the bedroom as well?

Time had tested his patience. Tested and tested, now it seemed he would have to begin again.

He met her gaze. Desire still evident within the jeweled depths. She touched his shoulders, traced the muscle lightly with her fingertips. No, it wasn't too late.

"I..." she began. Her fingers fumbled then hesitated and finally moved again. "I don't know if I want this still," she told him. So beautiful, she should have never looked at him. She could sound incredibly shy when she spoke like this. That amused him, made him realize the magnificent range of personalities she had. It was hard for him to believe this sudden shyness in front of him when she had fought him, battled him physically and with her wits. She bested him many times; didn't know the count, even now, he imagined.

"Of course you do, Jessie. And I'll prove it to you," he said smoothly. "You have, after all, pushed me past the point of return."

She inhaled sharply, flushing crimson. He regretted his words as soon as he spoke, but they were in the past now, and he couldn't call them back. It was a lie. He knew he could stop any time she asked.

"Go to the devil," she whispered furiously, pushing against his chest. He moved away, releasing her from contact.

"Please stay, Jessie. Would an apology smooth your ruffled temper?"

His words surprised her. He could see the shock in her expression and lay still, grinning at her, hoping he'd not ruined the carefully planned ambiance. She licked her lips, rising on her elbow as he methodically gave her distance then folded his hands over his chest. She rose higher so she could look at his face. Her gaze met his, roamed the length of his body, then back again. She closed her eyes, trembling. She wanted to run, he knew, except the threat of cowardice still hung in the air. He wanted to laugh. She had long ago fulfilled the threat, given him all he'd challenged her with. But now he wanted more, and he wouldn't let her go. She touched him, gingerly, hesitant, unsure of herself and the rising flood of heat coming so quickly to her cheeks. She bit her lip; her gaze locked with his, gemstones glittering, pulling at his senses and resolve. Her hands clasped around his.

"Roc," she began, her voice quavering between indecision and despair.

He turned her hands and pressed them against his chest. "Jessie, do you have any idea what you do to me?" his voice husky and so deep she barely recognized it.

She gulped back the fear surfacing once more, her gaze riveted on the candle flickering above his head. He released her hands and allowed her the freedom to explore. Her fingers touched, leaving a tingle of desire, whisper soft, and he tensed against his swift reaction, concentrating on his vow to her. She kissed his chest, his neck, trailing upward to brush his lips, innocently, tenderly. Her kiss moved to his eyes, to the tip of his cheekbones, to his ear, to the rapidly beating pulse at his throat.

A deep groan escaped him. He pressed his hands against her shoulders, separating them for a moment.

"Do you want me?" he asked quietly, praying the answer was the one he wanted to hear.

Their gazes met; she inhaled slowly, her eyes dark and sultry with passion. She shuddered, and nodded her head.

"You have to convince me. I won't touch you until I know for sure," he told her softly. She licked her swollen lips, gulped. "A nod won't stir me. You must ask. Ah, yes, perhaps plead your case. Perhaps not, for you've created a tempest inside me and truly, Jess, I don't know how much longer I can hold back."

"A tempest?" she returned with a strangled sound. "Perhaps only heat and fire and magic."

"A mysterious enchanting web, my sweet."

"I don't understand this...this..."

"Neither do I."

"I feel as if I will melt from the heat, that if you don't do something I will surely die. Yet I'm afraid too."

"I'll try not..." he began, afraid to tell her the first joining might hurt. At that moment, he knew he'd never look back on the events leading to this with anything but happiness. Her eyes were shining upon him guileless. Color brushed her cheeks with an artist's touch. He wondered what he said that would cause the sudden flush.

He only wanted her to think of the pleasure.

Her lashes fell across her cheeks, black against white, yet he knew so well nothing was that simple. He paused with his hands still resting on her shoulders, waited for her words. She smoothed his frown with her fingers and opened her eyes, gazing thoughtfully at him. "I want you tonight," he warned her gently.

"But I have to ask and I don't know what to say," she told him.

He battled the laughter, yearning for escape, her hands still on his chest, supporting her weight. He touched her lips gently with the tip of his finger until her tongue inadvertently met it but found himself at his own loss for words.

"You are going to have to think of something, soon," he muttered.

"Perhaps you will give me some hint."

"No," he countered, "I will have no recriminations in the morning. This must be of your doing or nothing will happen." He allowed his finger to slip downward, belying his words, noticed her breath came in ragged gasps, felt the gentle heave of her breasts.

By all that's holy, if he kept this up, she wouldn't be able to speak.

His hand fell away and he stared into her eyes, imploring the confirmation.

But Jessica Newman had set her mind to work, trying to force the words she so longed to say. He could almost see the wheels spinning. The evidence of her innocence was still so very apparent. Just thinking of the act, her face took on a rosy hue, caught in her own game.

Roc smiled, calmly waiting, knowing she'd ask him, watching her frustration mount. He'd ask a lot of her. Born a lady, even though her actions refuted the fact, she'd possibly never spoken openly of sex or ever thought she'd have to beg for it. She still sought a way to out-maneuver him, but he wouldn't allow it, drawing her farther into the enchantment of the evening he caressed the silken flesh he'd exposed, tantalizing her senses, leaving her no room to back down.

He toyed with the buttons on her shirt, slipping each one free before moving on to the next. She sat still watching him. And suddenly her bodice fell free. His breath caught in his throat. His heart seemed to cease. He had not realized the exquisite rare beauty she possessed. Her breasts perfect, flawless; her flesh ivory silk, her waist so narrow he could span it with his hands. He held them there, at her waist, tense, impatient with himself for moving too fast, pushing her too far. Already he had imposed his will upon her, and he'd never meant to do that.

The pulse at her throat beat alarmingly. She looked ready to panic and bolt rather than ask him to make love to her. He couldn't let her go now, so he hung on to her as if his life depended on it.

"Jessie, please... I don't know if I can honor my promise much longer," he told her softly.

She tried to speak. Her lips moved but it seemed her voice froze.

"Ask me to make love to you," he said softly.

A sliver of light entered the room. The tiny crescent of moon seemed to entrance her and she managed a gentle whisper. "Make love to me, please." The whisper so soft he thought at first he hadn't heard. Then a cloud slipped over the silver beacon, and he knew she'd finally asked. He groaned, pulling her close, delighting in his fantasy no longer but hungrily sampling the feel of her solid against his chest.

"I will be gentle," he promised her, "and come morning you will have no regrets."

He laid her back against the furs. Her eyes wide open. He hastily rid her of the rest of her clothes, pausing only to kiss each part of her he'd newly revealed, cherishing her. Perfection, he thought, touching the black hair cascading over ivory flesh.

He brushed his lips across hers, his hand cupping and cradling her breast. He played with the nipple, teasing it, drawing it outward. She moved beneath his touch, her fingers running through his hair, urging him closer.

His hand moved low against the length of her leg then began a steady movement upward, seducing, sending heat spiraling inside her, creating the magic she had known so well only the night before. He kissed her, long and deep, tasting the sweet wine; the delicate flavor of her. She writhed beneath him, responding with passion, fire and lightning.

Her gentle exploration increased. She returned his kisses, setting his heart to yearn for more. He lowered his lips to her breast, hesitated then slowly traced it with his tongue, savoring the taste, the texture, the incredible feelings racing through him. He stretched out beside her, drawing her closer, stroking her again and again, his hands leaving nothing untouched. He stroked and caressed her belly, the inside of her thighs, her buttocks then around her hips to her belly once more. He hesitated, brushing the black triangle at the apex of her thighs, his touch tender, then reaching closer, more intimate, his hands moving as he searched for the center of her desire and delved within. He had never known such wild heat and sudden longing to know more, to discover the depth and intensity of the mystery she held within.

He kissed her while he continued to stroke her. Her lips parted, opening to him as did her legs. Her eyes closed, and a strangled whimper escaped her. Her hands encircled him and he could feel the innocent caress on his back, the gentle exploration she launched lower until she reached the small of his back. He smiled and moved between her legs, urging them wider, and he remembered the feel of it, the naturalness, the longing he felt.

"Do you still want me?" he asked again.

A trembling whimper escaped her and she nodded, "Yes."

He continued his exploration. She appeared as a pagan idol, so beautiful, untouched except by him. He leaned toward her, his tongue drawing wet circles around her nipple. He met her gaze, assuring her, reminding her she had nothing to fear from him.

"Touch me, my sweet." He whispered near her ear and she clung desperately to him, writhing beneath his powerful form in an ageless and eternal rhythm. He brushed her lips, tasting once again the wondrous treasure he'd found. Then he followed the valley between her breasts, a fiery path lower still to her navel; lower still, an intimate touch with the tip of his tongue, before he raised his head. A tiny cry escaped her and she arched against him, driving him crazy.

"You like that?" he asked softly, grinning, for he knew the answer better than she.

He covered her, his weight pinning her beneath. Felt her hips move, begging for his entry. So hot, so very wet, and yes, she was ready for him. Still, he hung on to his control by the slenderest of threads. As if his body took over all rational thought, he slid into her inviting depths, stopped for a moment when he breeched her maiden's barrier. She seemed to encircle him fully, excepting the power of his sex, inviting him deeper, begging for completion. It seemed she felt no pain.

He shuddered, realizing he had indeed accomplished a miracle. Desire raged unleashed and out of control seeming to explode whisper soft but all consuming in its need. He urged her legs around his flanks and began to move, slowly and deep. Deeper still. Her gaze met his, lustrous with desire. She embedded her nails in his shoulder, holding on to him. She was heaven sent with her enigmatic eyes and her wild mane of blue-black hair framing the delicacy of her face. He held her firmly beneath him, whispering into her ear, encouraging her, claimed her lips, and continued his slow movement within her. He deepened his kiss, moved lower, kissed her breasts. She cried out, arching against him, her hips undulating beneath him. The sultry cry, her seductive movements, all created a magic encompassing them within its power. His body tensed against her, and he slowed wanting nothing more than to feel her pulse against his flesh.

But he couldn't hold back, she tensed and held her breath, suddenly crying out his name. She writhed uncontrollably and he let his body react to her wild impetuous craving. Heat engulfed him, sent him hurtling through a windmill of enchantment to a magnificent climax. It blew hot, hotter still and slammed through him. Deeper, deeper. One more time, until he thrust to her womb and became part of her. Shudders seized him, trembling, his muscles quivering. He fell upon her, weak and exhausted; she held his weight against her length, uncomplaining and ran her fingers along the sleek wet muscles of his back. She bewitched him, this innocent lady, this cat with nine lives.

He felt her withdrawal. She moved away, a curious, wondering expression in her eyes. Smiling, he caught her and pulled her back into the protective embrace of his arms, trying to read the thoughts behind the eyes. A useless battle; she had shuttered herself against him. Perhaps she had not felt the wonder of it.

"What's wrong?" he asked, brushing her hair from her face, saw the tears glittering in her eyes. "I felt your pleasure."

She gazed at him, fear shone clearly.

"Tell me, please. What did I do?"

"Nothing," she whispered. And her body trembled against him. It wasn't the truth, and he suspected he knew, understood she had given him far more than she had wanted. She had responded to his every caress, refusing him nothing and now when she thought about it...

He had vowed she would have no regrets, but now, gazing on her he suspected she hated herself. He had quite expertly seduced her, and now in the aftermath, she comprehended what he had done. She had to admit she had no excuses either for she had asked for him to love her. "Nothing, indeed. Don't forget you begged," he reminded her softly.

He could feel the horrible shudder of her body pressed flush against his. But she met his gaze, focusing and clear and he found a hardened resolve in her expression. Next time it might take longer to breech her defenses, yet he hoped not. Roc sighed, weary of the battle and the strain.

"It won't happen again," she said.

He had tried so hard to hold his temper in check. But now emotions he didn't understand suddenly seized him, frustration that she wouldn't accept him as her husband and lover. Only a few moments ago she had humbled him, brought him to the most shattering sexual experience of his life, and her audacity and the open refusal to enjoy his favors again left him confused and wondering what he could do to change her mind.

"Jessie, there is so much we can share," he told her. He moved with lightning speed, sweeping her into his arms. He rose, holding her tight against him then padded naked from the room, up the stairs and to the bedchamber. She was too stunned to move until he kicked the door shut and set her onto the bed, but it was too late for he came down on top of her, covering her once more and pinning her beneath him. She gasped for air. Her nose buried against a huge feather pillow. The length of his body fit solidly above her, his chest against her back and she could feel the rise of his erection against her derriere. His chin nestled sharply against the back of her head and she stiffened.

"Roc, please... give me time."

The words knifed through his frustration. He pulled Jessie to his side but didn't release her. His hand drifted lazily to caress her stomach. Teasing once more and he reminded her that now, after this, she might carry his child.

"I'm sorry," he said simply.

She choked, "You're sorry." Her echo spun around the room. "This wasn't meant to be, not a consummation of the marriage, not a commitment, never a child. I wanted nothing to do with any of this," she began, then broke off, apparently terrified at what she'd said for it seemed she must have remembered what she'd asked for. Recalled he'd waited for her to ask, no, plead for him to love her. She buried her face in her hands.

"Perhaps that's an understatement," he told her. "I wanted you to understand certain principles of this relationship. I believe now that you do."

She moistened her lips. "I no longer know what I want. Maybe your respect would help me understand this new role that has been thrust upon me despite my protests."

His fingers tightened against her. "Maybe we can find a middle ground," he whispered softly, determination in his words.

"But I don't believe you can give as much as I want," she said huskily.

She tried to move away from his embrace, and perhaps from the reminder of what she had given, had shared with him. Determined to see this through to the only conclusion he could imagine, he pulled her against him. Tenderness had not made a lasting impression. Now he couldn't fathom what to do. More of the same? Perhaps so much more he could leave her sleeping, exhausted and unable to find herself in the arms of Pierce.

"I want to give you the world, but I don't know if that will ever be enough," he told her. His hand moved along her abdomen, upward to hover beneath her breast, taunting the underside. He turned it palm upward, cupping its fullness possessively.

He watched her set her mind against the sensations he evoked with his gentle touch, watched her try to dislodge the hand that had taken possession of even more intimate places. "You can not deny this, my sweet," he told her even as he deepened the caress.

Her face flushed a deeper shade of rose. "I can try," she said determinedly, closing her eyes. She whimpered, small mewling sounds.

"No," he said. "I think not, wife," he stated, gazing at her. "It is amazing how swiftly you respond to the gentlest touch, light, soft; your reaction wanton and unrestrained, hot and so very fresh and innocent. See, your hips are moving beneath my fingers, begging, igniting the magical fires once more."

He withdrew and she froze, confusion shining in her eyes and her fingertips straining to touch him, but he had promised, and she hadn't asked.

Suddenly, she changed the subject. "I know where Trevor went, at least I can guess. I want to go to him," she told Roc honestly. "I won't entangle you in this mess, and I hold you to no responsibility over me."

Roc pulled back. "So, you still refuse to believe you're in more danger than your cousin. I can't let you go even though under other circumstances I would say yes. I would never forgive myself if anything happened to you, but you can tell me where he went."

"No." she turned into him.

Her breasts touched the light covering of hair across his chest. A spasm seemed to tremble the length of him touching his soul. The feather light touch seemed to capture his heart.

"I can't let you go on a foolish mission."

At that moment she jerked away, finally noticing their closeness and the ease with which she lay naked next to him. She flushed again, lowering her lashes and swiftly turning her back to him. "I have to find him," she murmured.

He let his hand rest on her hip.

"You could trust me."

"You've given me no..." she began and stopped, knowing the lie. He had given her every reason, had held her fears in highest regard, had held his needs at bay until she wanted him enough to ask. He had earned her trust.

"Damnation," he swore, pulling her against him; his eyes ignited. "What the hell was this evening all about if it wasn't trust?"

Silence followed, seemingly forever. She bit her tongue, and he thought she avoided his gaze. He knew she was afraid of the truth, afraid of what she might say.

"Possession."

He turned her again, seeming ready to do battle.

She didn't move.

"Hush, we've a lifetime to discuss this possession thing. For now, sleep, I know you're tired. I need the peace if only for the night. The last few days have tried my patience and my soul. I want clarification, an understanding of expectations, and I didn't want to fight. If Trevor would appear, half the battle would vanish and perhaps we could find a measure of solitude."

But Jessie didn't want to hush. She suddenly broke the silence and whispered, "If you'd promise to let me help, I'll tell..."

"I just don't know..."

"I'll tell you where Trevor disappeared. It's quite obvious."

"If it were so obvious, then we would have dispatched men to find him," he reminded her tiredly.

"Perhaps he doesn't want a bevy of foot soldiers mucking up the works," she whispered.

Of course, why hadn't he thought of that? Frustrated at this strange conversation and Jessie's refusal to see things realistically, he gave her proposition thought. Since Trevor had left for Astoria, his life had turned upside down. Not that he minded the side benefits of this relationship, but he hadn't planned on marriage either. Not when he had to convince her every time he touched her she wanted him.

He had thought once the ring was on her finger she would obey him unconditionally. But in all his imagining, he had never foreseen her reaction to him and her refusal to look at this logically or his wild desire for this violet-eyed seductress who had bewitched him with a snap of her fingers.

He had promised the senator. Yet he felt a kinship with Trevor, her cousin, and now related to him through these curious circumstances. He would have to secure Jessie and try to find Trevor. Short of tying her to the bedposts, he had no idea how to keep her safe. He was an idiot to leave without her or with her. He'd never find a moment's peace, for the hunger she created in him would not rest, and he would forever find his position infinitely vulnerable.

He would have to guard her back as well as his own.

But then he'd know where she was.

"Go to sleep," he sighed softly, frustrated with his every thought.

"Trevor?"

He rose above her. "Not now. You have put me in an awkward situation, fought me at every turn, and I cannot trust you to stay in one place. You've thoroughly tied my hands, and I won't tolerate your interference," he told her, his impatience and frustration rising again. "Through an accident, a regrettable accident I have become your husband. You rant on about your freedom. Your rights. Yet you think nothing of harming other people. In truth, Madame, you are the most insufferable, selfish, brat I have ever had the horror of--"

"You arrogant beast. A regrettable accident is it? I didn't want this anymore than you, so don't lay the blame on my shoulders."

"I'll lay it anywhere I please." he said, his voice husky. "You are not going after Trevor. You will stay here in this house until I give you permission to leave. Now, I don't want to hear another word."

"Selfish? What about you?"

"If you insist on battling, I swear you might have to seduce me again."

She used the point of her elbow to enforce her anger at his words. His breath rushed from his lungs; he doubled over, smothering her in his embrace. Her lungs labored to gasp air.

The magic had vanished.

The mystery surrounding their mating gone in a burst of disillusionment.

The enchantment only a vague and distant memory.

He stretched out, fitting her into his body once more. His hand resting close to her heart, pounding against her ribs and the palm of his hand.

If he could only forget the sorcery.

But it seemed an impossible task as he lay awake, dreaming of the incredible passion she had gifted him with, an innocent treasure.

In the end, he realized she had fallen asleep. He settled her head against his shoulder. Her hair tickled his senses, the fragrance, the silk of it and if he could, he'd love her again.

In her sleep, she looked fragile, vulnerable, in need of masculine protection, but he knew better and therein lay the beauty and the intrigue of her. She tested him, questioned every creative power within him, and he never gave up on a challenge, never backed down.

Maybe she would succumb to his wishes. At one time, he had prayed for just that but no longer. Now he relished the fight and the peace that would eventually come; the raging wildfire flaming out of control only to climax smoldering beneath his caress. And he liked the sound of her breathless, wispy, voice when she asked him to love her.

He swallowed hard. Damn, but he desired her again, and she was too asleep to give her permission. He drew tiny circles on her breasts, enticing her to wake. Stroked her legs, the back of her knee, the inside of her thigh. Higher until he claimed intimacies she hadn't allowed. But her quiet whimper delighted him and the acknowledgment that this perhaps was her way of asking him for more. He continued the gentle seduction then gently possessed her, moving slowly until she cried out with desire.

And he tried to deny the magic pulling him ever deeper into her warm loving impetuous nature. Tried to deny the possibility this woman might hold a very special place in his heart and in his life.

Chapter Eight

Thunderclouds grew over the Cascade Range and threatened the valley. Newman's elegant Queen Anne house stood, a silent guardian over the huge estate. Built and designed to his specific recommendations by W.C. Knighton when Roc had first come to Oregon, it was an elaborate home for a confirmed bachelor. Over the summer he'd added every conceivable convenience. As he became more comfortable with the idea of settling permanently, his additions took on more elaborate and expensive characteristics. Intricate stained windows graced almost every room including the fireplace window he'd dedicated to his brother who had died in a whaling accident in Alaska five years previous. And he'd used Eastern oak for the elaborate woodwork carved into Greek symbols.

It personified a new dynasty to him, a way of life long forgotten. It wasn't as splendid as the Southern plantation lost by his father during the War Between the States, but it didn't matter. This was his way of preserving a small part of his heritage, the grandeur and the beauty, only on a much smaller scale. Even when he watched his family home go up in flames and billowing smoke, he had known someday he would create a splendid home for himself. And when his mother finally broke down and cried, the boy managed to hold on to his pride. The slaves scattered, the crops ruined, trampled by the hundreds of union officers and he didn't cry. Instead, he held his mother in his arms and shuddered with each sob tearing through her frail body. She gained strength from the gesture. Then silently led her family away from the carnage and the danger. They hid with friends and neighbors until the officers took control of the area and the threat of rape was no longer a concern.

He had wanted to defend his home and his family. Frustrated because of his age and size, he could only lend a meager support. It was as if he watched everything through a tunnel. When it was all over, they left for the east; New York. His mother's family lived there. A travesty, it seemed to him, to run to the enemy when confronted and with nothing left except pride. Truly, they were left with nothing. Even their self-respect and dignity were lost, vanished in the smoldering ruins of their home.

Yet, because of the move, he attended the finest schools, had the best education money could buy. Even though he had to work for each advancement, his skill and daring gave him strength where others failed.

Perhaps that was why he eagerly accepted each new assignment and when asked to go west, he had embraced the idea enthusiastically. All his loved ones had died, passed away before their time. Senator Drake was aware of his history and welcomed him to Salem with eagerness, having lost everything but his pride in the same war that took so much from Roc Newman. Perhaps that was why Drake had set up the charade leading to his eventual marriage.

Drake had overstepped his bounds. The Senator had forced his hand. And he wasn't used to that.

He had now spent several days wondering what Jessica Lawrence would surprise him with next. If anything, his senses were more confused than they had been. She was an enigma.

He gazed out the upstairs window toward the capital building. Thunder rolled off the hills, and streaks of lightning seared the sky. Rain began slowly, the drops heavy, and the scent of water hitting the dry earth filled the air. He had wondered for several days now when she'd try to leave. His patience taxed thoroughly. All in all, he hoped for some type of conclusion to this horrible waiting. Trevor, still unaccounted for, and his cousin, the private investigator, seething in her boots to go after him, swearing she could find him, left his fortitude ironically lacking. His fingers drummed an errant staccato on the windowsill. The heavens boomed in unison.

He turned his attention to the muddy road below then back to Perkins who stood, speaking incoherently, in front of him. He realized before the words were out of Perkins's mouth, knew, simply because he had extracted a promise from Jess, a promise to stay here, on his land, in exchange for her freedom. It was an unholy idea, but Roc had simply twiddled his fingers long enough. And he hated keeping her locked away. So, to find out the extent of her honesty, he forced her hand.

Well, it didn't surprise him, not in the least. In truth, he had expected this sooner. After all he had unlocked the door thirty minutes ago. Now he had only to pick up her trail. Ah, but which way had she flown? He studied Perkins who seemed to have aged ten years in the last week. It was good to know he wasn't the only one Jessie had that affect on.

Roc had never expected Perkins to take such a shine to Jess. Roc had brought him from the Midwest. He was intelligent and trustworthy, a good man to have tending his affairs, and one in need of honest employ. When Roc had found him, Perkins's one venture at farming had failed miserably, and during a trip into a small prairie town, his family had been massacred by a band of Comanche; his home burned to a shell.

"She's riding hard, heading east, toward Sublimity. The groomsman reported she took her hunter, the hound, and bulging saddlebags. She's riding astride, sir. Has the same outfit on she wore that night."

"So, she's gone," Roc said.

"It appears so. I sent Dillon after her. He's an excellent horseman and can follow a trail."

"Jessica Lawrence isn't going east," he said softly, only a trace of bitterness to his voice. He could speak freely and he'd anticipated this. Perkins knew his fears and had berated him endlessly. "But then which road to the west? I hope you're right about Dillon, for Jessie's sake I just pray..."

He stopped.

"I've sent men to watch the roads leading to the coast and Portland," Perkins assured him. "Surely, they will see her and send word."

Roc knew they would. They were all hand picked, trustworthy, and thorough. Once Jessie committed herself, his men would inform him. Now all he had to do was wait, prepared to fly out of here on a moment's notice. Jessie had always thought she had control.

Now she had no idea what she would find.

It was all a throbbing fear within him, growing with the passing of each second Jess was out of his sight.

"You've had no further information on Pierce's destination?" Roc asked.

Sweat beaded on Perkin's head. "I believe, sir, they've covered their trail well. Jessie's idea is the best lead we have. I don't like using her like this, but I'm not sure what other options there are. It seems she will head somewhere other than Astoria."

"But the coast line is long," Roc mused softly.

He grasped his hands behind his back as he moved to the upstairs balcony to stare through the dripping rain to the west and the mountains stretching between them and the beach. Ah, but where? Pierce and Rutgers were smugglers, pirates of a sort. Rugged lonely terrain, a place where boats could land and go unseen. Where are they? Many an innocent had found himself shanghaied, and the white slave traffic still existed.

To his absolute consternation, he suddenly realized the garden below him was not empty. Rupert, running and setting up an awful racket, was baying, approaching the balcony below.

He couldn't believe his luck. Even her dog had the good sense to come in out of the rain. Perhaps the hound knew Jessie would find trouble and wanted to include him. Perhaps the dog was smarter than he had previously given him credit for.

It was doubtful though, he thought, amazed, and curious about the direction she had gone. He turned to Perkins. "Excuse me. It seems we should check on Rupert."

He hurried down the steps and out the front door, stopping just in front of the carriage house. Rupert whined and turned his great head to the west then dashed toward the road barking madly. "Come here, you old hound," he yelled, quickly gazing down the road at another rider galloping toward the house. He nodded grimly as the man pulled up next to him. "Tell me, did you see Jessie?"

"Yes, indeed. She's headed due west on the road to Willamina."

Cape Foul Weather, of course. She had thought this out, but he still did not understand why she believed they would go there.

"Sir, if you want to catch her, you'd best not waste any time," the man said anxiously. "She's riding hard."

"Thank you," he said suddenly. "I had no idea". By the time he reached the stable, his horse waited, saddled. The horse seemed to sense his mood, thundering from the stable.

She was at least an hour ahead of him, and, he had to assume, knew the road as well. Jessica Lawrence had to know he would come after her.

Within minutes, he had crossed through town, reached the Willamette River, and the Center Street Bridge. He slowed his wild mount, prancing recklessly before crossing.

The woods on the other side were canopied with green, dark and cool, providing shelter from the storm. He moved quickly, urging the horse forward until they reached the other side. Roc paused, resting the horse and searching the road.

He rode swiftly, following Jessie, never quite catching a glimpse of her, but knowing she was just ahead, riding at breakneck speed into trouble. He stopped several times for a fresh horse, learning Jessie had done the same. It seemed as though an eternity had passed. He'd been riding for hours. He could smell the crisp breeze off the ocean, heard the thunder of the crashing surf, and turned south, toward Newport. Suddenly, he caught a flash of light reflected off the bridle of her horse. She had paused at the top of a hill, for breath, or to gauge her direction, he wasn't sure.

Then she heard the whinny of his horse and seemed to panic, nudging her horse hard. He cursed. She didn't even look back but sent the horse forward, pounding toward the beach and the harder sand. She began a reckless race through the surf.

"Headstrong little fool," he muttered aloud, chasing after her. Salt spray and sand flew into his face as he put all his efforts into catching her. It wasn't easy. The race took them along the beach. Rocks loomed in front of them. The beach ended. She turned her horse away from the ocean, urging the mare up a steep slope.

"You're going to kill yourself," he roared above the sound of the sea. The tide was coming in or she might have tried to go around the cliff. She looked back. Her eyes widened but she didn't hesitate. Calm and terrifyingly audacious, she kept going. She reached the top and followed the edge of the cliff, heading for the lighthouse at the next point. She might be the best private investigator in all the world, but he didn't think she could possibly want to approach her destination in this manner.

"Hang it up, Jess," he swore, reaching out. He had come abreast of her within minutes of topping the cliff. She yelled when his arms found her, sweeping her from her horse to his own. The mare she rode slowed and stood now, waiting for her. Nothing would have happened.

Except Jessie was fighting him again, something he expected, and he thought prepared himself for. His horse reared, surprised by the unexpected thrashing going on above him. They slid off the back. Incensed, cursing, and falling, he still managed to protect her from the fall, coming to rest with her supple form lying bewitchingly on top of him.

"You're an idiot," she gasped.

He gazed at her stunned. "Me?"

"You have no business--"

"And you lied to me. Promised me--"

"I only wanted to go for a ride," she cried.

He laughed and arched a brow, watching the slow flush slide up her neck finally reaching her face. The audacity of it left him amused but still furious.

His eyes blazed and his voice was harsh, demanding. "A ride? How droll. All the way to the beach? How interesting. Of course I've known for a long time nothing you do is simple."

She shoved at his chest. His weight had borne her down, and he didn't intend to release her until she told him the truth.

"I planned to stay with a friend then ride back in a few days."

He wasn't at all sure how to get to the bottom of this. The whole idea she'd betrayed him hurt. She hadn't trusted him, although he had no intention of allowing Jessica to see that. She'd have him wrapped more thoroughly around her finger.

As he moved, he felt something hard against his thigh. It seemed to have an unmistakable feel. He started to move her, intrigued now. He lifted her above him. She took advantage of his precarious position and leapt away from him, eyeing her horse as if she thought to run once more. He moved quickly, following her. He didn't miss her look of hope as she glanced at the horse. "My little love, what do you have in your pocket?" He stalked her now.

"None of your business."

Christine Young

But he moved too fast for her, pulling her into his arms and reaching for the gun he knew she had hidden. She was dressed as a man, but the weight he'd felt came from her coat. He reached within and discovered the small derringer. She fought him, and when he removed the gun, she did not give up the fight.

He held it in front of her, his anger evident in the curl of his lip. "Why, how interesting. I gave you more credit than this. This is a worthless weapon, at least you could have had the intelligence to carry a real gun."

She turned crimson but kept herself away from him. Her gaze steady, blazing wildly.

"My choice of weapons is none of your concern."

"Even if you do something irrational, I still want you to stay alive."

"I couldn't hide a real gun in my pocket."

"Again, our minds are different. But that is not the point here, little one. Just what did you plan to do? Attack Pierce and Rutgers or merely get in Trevor's way, perhaps threatening his entire operation?" he asked boldly.

The sudden paleness sweeping her features betrayed the truth. It was clear she hadn't thought beyond herself. He swallowed back his words for a moment, battling the wave of anger and of terror winding around his heart. Perhaps she had no fear for herself, but he meant to protect her. In a few days she had managed to worm her way into his life and his thoughts. He would not allow this, this, idiotic rush into danger. For whatever reasons, he cared what happened to her. And when he thought of what danger she could confront at the hands of Pierce, unprotected, with her face and figure and the revenge Pierce meant to exact, he felt sick. He had no trouble picturing her naked, standing on the auction block.

"My love, I should have stripped you of all your clothes and tied you to the bedposts."

She should have shown some fear, but she didn't. It seemed all she could do to keep from laughing at his fury. "But you wouldn't dare," she told him. The smile she fought back nearly broke through. "I know you even better than yourself. And you might think of it but you're too much the gentleman to see it done. Perhaps in another life..."

"Don't hold your breath."

She grinned and moved toward the horse. "Perhaps you would like to help. If you are so concerned about my welfare then," she pointed toward the cliffs and the sheltered inlet they had raced across only moments before. "I believe the smuggling operation comes in at night between these two points. If we mean to catch them.--"

"You are not to involve yourself," he snapped.

"You simply can not accept the idea I can handle this."

"And I'll also not accept that you put yourself in danger."

"You waltz into my life and start laying down rules and regulations..."

"Because I want you to live a long healthy life." A touch of frustration tinged his voice. Frowning, he moved toward her, catching her hand. "Very well."

"What do you mean?"

"If you insist on helping, then we'll do this together. But you'll have to do it my way, follow my directions, and Jessie, if you fight me on this, I'll drag you home, bound and gagged."

"I don't believe you," she told him, her beautiful face, proud and very cautious this time.

He helped her mount her horse, holding the reins for assurance before leaping on his horse. They started toward Newport.

"I can take the reins. This is absurd."

"You've forgotten one very important fact. I can't trust you."

"Why..." she stopped, regretting that one word.

"Why, my sweetheart? You've proven yourself adept at breaking promises. I'm going to see you stay close to my side from now on."

"But..." she started, then fell silent, gazing straight ahead, and it seemed she meant to ignore him.

He chuckled softly, beginning to enjoy this immensely. He suspected she had thought of his swift compliance as an alternative. Oh, she was smart and devious. But once he caught her, he wouldn't allow her to escape him again; wouldn't allow her out of his sight.

They made their way quickly to the small town. It wasn't much more than a handful of cabins, roughly built, and flanked by an Indian camp across the sand bar. A small hotel stood at one end of the town. Children played in the streets as they passed.

"So, you have a friend who lives here?" he queried.

"I..."

"Don't bother yourself with another lie," he told her. "We'll see if there's room in the hotel."

~ * ~

As they moved swiftly along the street, Jessie watched with curiosity. She'd lost this battle. But wondered what he had in mind. She didn't believe for a minute he would let her near the lighthouse again.

Roc would have his way.

And he had done this for her safety.

"Doesn't this make you happy, luv?" Roc asked.

She tried to ignore him so he wouldn't see and read her emotions. Happy? She might have been happy. It might have pleased her if she thought he spoke the truth. Perhaps she could have told him everything he did made her happy, and he'd filled her nights with a raging tempest that left her breathless and yes, happy. But she wouldn't admit to anything.

She could never make him understand she needed more from life than nights of seduction and love. The days left her empty and yearning for something more fulfilling.

He had slept with her every night.

It had been days since he'd left her locked in the chamber: days since he'd given her freedom back, days since he'd wrenched that horrid promise from her. She knew he had spent so much time searching for information, hunting for some clue that would lead him to Pierce and Rutgers, and perhaps Trevor. Though she realized he'd only made her promise because he'd given up on his other sources, she had fallen neatly into his trap, no longer content to wait for the night when he would return to her.

A regrettable accident. He had said it himself. His heart wasn't hers.

"You can't mean to keep me locked in this," she told him, staring open mouthed at the hotel.

"But, sweetheart, it's the best accommodations in town, unless you can come up with that friend of yours you mentioned."

"She's moved. I just remembered. And I can not fathom why you insist on locking me--"

"You can not fathom?" he queried. He sounded most amused.

"I only want to find Trevor." She waited for the rebuttal she was sure would follow. But it didn't.

He took her hand and strode forward before talking to the landlady who had a room to spare. "And you think he's here, in Newport."

"Yes," she said stubbornly.

"Very well, then I will look for him," Roc assured her. "And, since you seem to know the area, you will come with me," he said lightly enough, but he continued with, "and you will not leave my sight again or run off recklessly with no thought of the danger."

Jessie stared at him, frowning before she turned, ignoring the smile curving his lip and the raised eyebrow.

"Jessie, I mean it."

She sniffed but didn't answer, moving up the steps to their room.

~ * ~

"Jessie!"

She stopped in front of the doors. He unlocked it and let it swing open. He caught her hand, pulling her inside.

"Damnation..."

"I don't believe you," she said softly. He leaned against the bedpost. "I don't. Oh, you're truly awful." She didn't allow him time to defend himself. She ran to the window, throwing it open in a last feeble attempt to escape. Even as she threw one leg over the windowsill, the uselessness of her efforts evaded her. He moved with swift precision, catching her around the waist and dragging her back inside. Jessie lashed out, but her sharp elbow caught him in the arm, instead of the chest. He wanted to shake her, but controlled his anger, both because her little endeavor had created an audience below, and because he was a gentleman, and he didn't want to hurt her.

"Damn you, Jessie," he whispered fiercely, holding her tightly against him. "I don't want you to put yourself in the way of these men. They will think nothing of stepping on you. The women these men find are sold into slavery and degradation with virtually no way of escaping. You wouldn't find yourself locked in a crib like the Chinese women. Instead they would sell you to the highest bidder. White slavery exists, and you are too exquisite a treasure to overlook. Jessie, I might not ever be able to find you. Do you want that? Listen to me."

She gasped softly as he turned her. He wanted to see her eyes, read the expression. He had to know if she understood. Her cheeks turned white as new fallen snow when she realized the captivated audience below had heard every word.

"It is true, Jessica, all of it."

Jessie and Roc whirled to confront a tall slender girl. She stood in the doorway watching them. Her hands clasped tightly in front of her were almost white.

Roc let Jessie go and she moved swiftly, "Who are you?"

She cleared her throat. "Charity."

"The minister's daughter?" Roc asked, his eyes on Jessie. His body tightened into knots. He had done everything in his power to tell Jessie the truth.

But he had not managed to change her mind. Each time he thought he'd made headway, she would come back more determined than ever. If Pierce got hold of her, he could only guess the outcome. He had seen prostitution of all sorts, and the Chinese slaves sold into the cribs were the worst. It made his stomach churn. He could smell the stench from the cribs, hear the few words the sing song girls knew. And it went on through the night seemingly without end crying: "Two bittee lookee, flo bittee feelee, six bittee doee." When he closed his eyes, he could see the wild-eyed creatures staring at him full of fear and hatred.

But he knew Jessie's fate wouldn't lie there, not until she got old and worn out. No, Pierce would drag her to the auction. He'd seen a few of those, also. Naked and forced to stand in front of prospective buyers, the girls were punched and prodded and even examined by any one wishing to inspect the merchandise.

Yet no matter what he told her, she always seemed to ignore him, denying the inevitability of her capture by this man who wanted revenge against the Lawrence's and seemed determined to use Jessie.

With each night he wanted her more. No anger over her

stubbornness could stop the longing that seized him when he looked upon her. He had planned to make love to her so many times exhaustion would overcome her or until his obsession with her diminished. But it didn't and to his knowledge she wasn't with child. Each time, it only seemed his fear for her increased, as did his hunger.

Now as she studied him and listened to Charity tell her story, her lashes lowered over her eyes. She looked up to meet his gaze. "You've told me the truth in all this?" she asked softly. "Those things really happened to those poor girls?"

"In truth, Jessie," he said. His voice lowered. "Whatever you had hoped to achieve, Jessica, and whatever purpose you set out with here today, you will have changed your mind. Although you are the most stubborn woman I have ever run across, you are not stupid; I promise I will see these men brought to justice. I will do my best, even if you do spend your days seeking new ways to bedevil me."

She flushed. "I haven't changed my mind, Roc. If anything this has only served to make me more determined," she said proudly. "It's just I think we could have worked well together, but you have forever denied that." She pulled Charity farther into the room, beckoning her to sit.

He watched the two women, suddenly more afraid than ever before. They sat, their heads bowed together in deep concentration then he understood he couldn't allow this, realized also, he couldn't think of anything to stop it. Charity was talking quietly, but her words held Jessica in rapt attention.

"It would be best you hear this, Mr. Newman. It concerns all of us."

"Really?"

"Please, if I may speak," Charity said, clearing her throat. "Trevor was shanghaied two days ago, at the lighthouse. We were watching the smuggling operation from a cave running below. A rock slipped and we were discovered."

Roc gazed thoughtfully at the girl. Damn them. Damn all of them. Everything, every piece of evidence sucked Jessica farther into the intrigue. She couldn't deny a mystery anymore than she could accept that she was immortal. And his little speech had not quelled her ardor at all. If anything, it had increased with each breath she took while listening. It had sent her on a crusade to right the world's wrongs, and this little piece of baggage sitting next to her seemed to be cut from the same cloth.

"But you managed to get away," Roc prompted.

"Yes," Charity said with impatience.

He shut the door. Now the two women were staring at him. Roc ran his fingers through his hair. "Am I supposed to read minds?"

Charity scowled at him. "I can see you have no reason to guess that Trevor made sure they would not find me. He allowed me to get away, sacrificing himself in the process. Believe me, I had no idea he was not directly behind me as I ran."

He arched a brow and walked into the room settling himself on the opposite side of the bed. He smiled and waited for more.

But Charity had said as much as she intended. She smiled back at him and quietly moved to leave the room.

Roc cursed softly and reached out an arm to hold Charity back then thought better of it, letting his hand fall away.

Through slitted eyes, he watched her walk out of the room, and he did manage to keep his temper in control. He didn't speak. It seemed the time stretched on forever. The landlady brought them food and drink. Still he couldn't bring himself to confront Jessie. After a while he rose and walked outside, down the trail to a sight overlooking the ocean. He watched the waves crash against the rocks, spray flying high into the air. The sun slowly dipped beneath the horizon, leaving the sky just above the sea, golden and streaked with ever darkening clouds.

He started up the hill to the hotel, wondering what he would say to her now. Ah, yes, he would tell her she could have her way. That he no longer cared what became of her and knew she could handle herself as well as any man. She would smile as if it were the only conclusion he could have come to, then she would turn from him and he knew he could no longer protect her. If he insisted on his way, she would fight him with every breath she took, and they would get nowhere.

But in truth, he couldn't do that to her, for he would ever harbor a guilty conscience. So, as he did every night, he would come to her, pour out all his feelings for her in the only way she would let him, and even then she would sometimes fight and deny the signs of her love. Jessica Lawrence might try to battle him, but she was innately sensual, and could not deny the beauty and pleasure they derived from each other.

Still, he was tired of the stubborn streak coloring her good sense. He entered their room, closing the door behind him. He strode quietly to the bed, stripping off his shirt as he did so, folding it over the railing at the foot of the bed. He sat on the mattress and pulled off his boots, then turned, furious.

She wasn't there.

He threw his hands in the air, cursing himself and his foolishness for leaving her unattended.

But just as he was reaching for his shirt, his heart raced unchecked and his temper escalated to near explosion. She came through the door, an apparition in white. She was standing, framed by the door, ghostly, enchanting, and completely bewitching. Only her gown flowed gently around her as the summer breeze caught the gossamer threads and lifted them gently. Her long black hair cascaded to her waist. A letter she had held when she entered slipped from her fingers and floated gently to the floor.

Amazingly, he had frightened her. And for once, he thought, she must realize how vulnerable she was.

He rose and walked to her, holding out his hand. "Jessie." His fingers closed around hers. They felt cold, lifeless. "Jessie, please you can not go through with this madness. You'll come to find out in spite of all your knowledge and your strengths, of which I know there are many, you won't win." She stirred slightly. He pulled her toward him, and she moved with a willingness that surprised him. The warmth of her body settled around him, and scooping her into his arms, he lifted her.

Whisper soft material imposed a slight barrier between them, for she wore nothing else. While he gazed at the pounding surf and the exquisite sunset, she had bathed and somehow she reminded him of a sacrificial virgin.

His fear rushed in on him, and he tightened his hold, wishing he would always find a way to protect her. It seemed she had planned this seduction.

Her eyes shimmered as their gazes met. They widened, almost welcoming his embrace and knowing his intent, then, surprising him, she lowered them shyly, a gesture he seldom associated with her. Her head rested against his chest. Innocently. Provocative.

"What?" he asked her.

"I'm afraid."

"You came back," he told her, carrying her to the bed. Her eyes fixed on his, and she looked frightened, as he laid her down.

Yet as he watched her, she rose on her elbows then sat against the headboard. He undressed, wondering at her behavior, curious and slightly cautious still. If anything, he had expected more anger and steadfast refusals to back down. Not this. Not her fear, but it pleased him she had begun to see things realistically. After Charity's appearance and her news of Trevor, he had truly thought she would have left on her crusade.

But she hadn't and perhaps that boded well for their future. She waited for him. The long white gown entwined around her limbs, promising so much. She reached for him, beckoning him to sit beside her, the rise of her breasts enticing then he pulled her into his embrace. She felt warm and soft, the magic and the enchantment would begin again but would she ever listen to his fears or heed his cautions. He covered her with the length of his body; she kissed his chest, then his throat, and her nipples hardened against him.

She seduced him, but for what purpose?

He froze. He didn't dare respond. She ran her fingers through his hair, along his back, her gaze touched his, her lips brushing his, lightly at first. It seemed as she hesitated, wondering what she should do next. He felt the tip of her tongue tracing his lips.

He changed the cadence of the dance, sweeping away his thoughts, taking over the rhythm. He kissed her deeply, letting her feel the hardening rise of his desire. The need to possess her overwhelmed common sense and he battled it. Fought the urge to succumb to her enchantment and the silken web she wove so easily around him. He had to know why she had come to him.

Across his chest, kissing him, nibbling ever so softly; that erotic flutter of her tongue. She experimented with him, he thought. Indecisive, hesitant, reveling in new found knowledge. Her fingers wandered across his chest, fell lower, still so innocent but no longer the sacrifice. She shadowed her fingers with the enticing play of her lips. She stroked, fanning his desire, liquid hot magic. Still he hesitated, holding his breath. One last lingering thought to her plan as his body hummed with passion.

He moved his hands to her breasts, unlacing the gown, sliding it off her shoulders. He lightly traced the contour of her breasts, again, then once more, watching her delightful response. He could hear the raged whisper of her breath; feel the warmth, soft against his flesh. Her head thrown back now, the softness of her hair entwined around him, across his chest then teasing him. He fought against her charm, tensing. Ready to encourage the teasing seduction she had begun. But he didn't have to. She moved, continuing without pause, without hesitation, continued the mystery. Lower, the liquid heat of her enchantment, teasing, mocking, and yet he wouldn't change a thing. Touching him, her fingers innocently exploring, learning his hard contours, brushing lightly against him. She touched his stomach, her lips taunting and sexual, then he gasped, surprised by her boldness, for her tongue had fluttered shyly against him. Control vanished. She had vanquished him easily. Before he could stop it, a blinding climax swept through him. He cursed, pulling her back to reality. She trembled, subdued by the power she wielded so expertly yet unplanned.

"I only wanted to give you pleasure," she said softly. Her amethyst eyes were wide with longing; her body was silken velvet beneath him.

She had given him more than he ever thought possible. He would treasure this forever. Yet he wanted her to experience the same pleasure. The very thought of what she had done for him brought him near climax again and a sweet aching tenderness grew within him. Even as he held her in his arms, he wanted to possess her, to love her, to be part of her, his body one with hers. He groaned, closed his eyes and felt desire surge into him; he forced control, to feel the rhythm of her body, to watch her eyes. On his elbows he held himself above her, watching a soft flush cover her, the flutter of her lashes, and the gentle rise and fall of her breasts. He watched his possession of her and the arch of her hips as she welcomed him. Observed the subtle movement of her tongue, licking her lips. She gave everything of herself this time, holding nothing back. Her body shuddered, arching suddenly against his, almost pleading. She cried out his name, in the dark, the soft glow of the moon sending beams of light downward, haloing their bodies.

He held her tenderly, finding a second release within her, claiming her irreversibly for all time. Praying she would conceive so her mind would find another avenue to pursue and she would no longer welcome the excitement she seemed to crave.

He let his head fall softly against her, knowing he would never find anything, or anyone, as exquisite as this lady. He smiled, perceiving also that he would never seek to change her only protect her.

He distanced himself from her, pushing away, before sitting against the headboard as she had done earlier. Uneasily, he wondered what had happened as she pulled the covers against her, holding them just below her chin. His gaze met hers. She closed her eyes tightly then trembled.

She whimpered, surprised when he pulled her between his legs, her back against his chest, his arms pinning her to his body. He rested his chin upon her head, smiling, wondering what truth or half-truths he would uncover.

"So, sweetheart, to what do I owe this incredible seduction I just enjoyed? You have fought against this for so long I can't help but wonder. Why? What reason prompted this?"

She didn't meet his gaze. He brushed his hands along her arms, feeling the slight tremble and the cold seeming to penetrate his flesh. She gazed at the moon, following the slender fingers of light out to sea.

"I have to find Trevor. After this afternoon and knowing what happened to him, I couldn't sit by and do nothing and so I thought... perhaps, I could make you understand I can't wait here, alone," she told him.

"Well, I guessed as much."

"I didn't mean for this to happen, well, not quite like it did," she amended swiftly, and their gazes met again. She blushed and lowered her lashes.

He inhaled deeply, wondering if she knew she had prostituted herself for a favor, but pushed the idea away not willing to think of it. The thought left him cold, and after all the heat and the tempest he had encountered with her, he shoved the image from his mind. If it weren't for the accident that brought them together, and the horrible situation threatening to consume her...

Yet perhaps when this was finished they could find something between them. Perhaps the desire was not just born from the fear and the danger shadowing her existence.

"Then what did you mean? Surely you must have guessed that one thing would lead to another."

She blinked back a sudden tear and lowered her head. He turned her in his arms. Touched the moisture lingering on her cheek.

"You don't understand."

He smiled, brushed her lips lightly with his own. "That's the problem, sweetheart, I do."

"Trevor has stood by me for so long. He encouraged me when I floundered and defended me when others made fun." She looked at him but couldn't smile. Her eyes narrowed and she lowered her head. "I have to do this, not just for him, but for me. I have to prove something to myself and you have to know I won't let you stand in my way."

He felt the anguish deep in his soul and the fear. Dear God, but she scared him to death, and he couldn't protect her from herself. Oh, he could try to keep her with him always, but that was futile and he knew it.

"Well, Jessica, I will concede to you on this issue, but rest assured I don't intend to let you out of my sight. This evening was a mistake, the walk to the beach. It won't happen again. Somehow, we will deal with this together."

She turned back around, resting against him, tears beginning to flow in earnest now. He held her close, whispering huskily. "You must promise me that you won't do this alone."

"No, please," she murmured. "I can't do that."

"You can." He softly stroked her neck, then her cheek, feeling the moisture there. Her features were so very fragile, her skin flawless. "Tell me," he demanded. "I won't let you go until you do."

"Please..."

"I won't, Jessie."

She shivered in his arms. She murmured something he could not understand. "All right then, I promise," she said suddenly, surprising him.

"And I can expect you to keep your word?" he queried. "You broke it only today. It doesn't seem to mean much to you," he teased.

He could imagine the rosy hue that must certainly tinged her face, but now her head rested against his chest, and he could not read her thoughts. In one swift move he turned her and pulled her beneath him.

Again, he made love to his wife. Gently. Thoroughly. With no thought of time, he stroked her, bringing her to a heated plateau. Wanting her to hunger for him as he did her and to understand he would care for her, protect her, but he needed her help, for he could not do it alone. He wanted to love her completely. Unselfishly...

But even when he thought to make a point, he realized he could not escape the mystery that seemed to enshroud them each time they came together. She aroused in him emotions he never thought to feel. And there was so much he needed from her, things he would see that she gave to him. She would never have the annulment.

"Ah, sweetheart, you are beautiful. I will never let you go. Never."

"Roc..."

She whimpered and cried out his name again, pleading for release.

"You will keep your word, Jessica."

"Yes, please, Roc..."

His fingers held her still and he thrust within, held her for a moment before he moved again, deeper and stronger. In the soft light of the moon, she clung to him as if her life depended on his strength and wildfire surged within sending her soaring into the night. She cried his name again, and for a moment he knew victory, knew also it would never last, and he would have to battle again.

He held her close, entangled in the fear of her fierce pride and the fire of her stubborn personality, danger a constant threat.

He slept, dreaming of a way to keep the wonder of her amethyst eyes from drowning.

Chapter Nine

"So, what do you propose next?" Roc asked her. He was leaning against a giant boulder gazing out at the wildly churning sea that raged into a narrow cavern between two cliffs, throwing waves onto the jutting rocks. The spray hit and danced off the cliffs, sea green to dark blue, foaming on the top of each crest. The trees were wind-blown, the foliage facing east as if to shield it from the storms frequenting the coast line; Newport was due south, Astoria far to the north. Although the culmination of this, their haste to find Trevor and confront Pierce, was long overdue, it seemed as if they had found God's country. Long hot sunbeams fell through the slight cloud cover. Light glittered like diamonds farther out on the ocean where it seemed motionless and somehow calm. It was a peaceful scene.

Jessie stood on the edge of the cliffs, hair blowing wildly around her face. The light framed her in a golden halo. She wrapped her arms around her, just beneath her breasts, and looked to the horizon, concentrating. She didn't think she'd ever felt so frustrated amidst such tranquil beauty. It seemed strangely odd to have such powerful emotions pulling her in two different directions.

She tilted her head back to catch the wind and studied Roc, knew for a moment the thawing of her heart.

Don't let your emotions fool you. You mean to betray him, and he will never forgive you when it happens. The warning came too late, just as it had the very first time she saw him.

He had a vulnerable side even though he hid it well. Patronizing, brazen, demanding, she simply found herself swept too quickly within his control.

Into the domination of a man who looked on her as a regrettable accident.

She didn't want to be reminded of her husband and his ways, but she was. She didn't want to care for him and least of all love him. Anguish and a broken heart would come from falling under his spell; that was all too apparent. And she had no plans in her future for a husband. An annulment was the only way. She only had to convince him.

It seemed something unceasingly gentle, unfathomable, had entered into their relationship. She hoped someday he could look on that first horrible night together as something other than a rueful mistake, at the very least. Perhaps he would let her go with no recriminations.

She prayed each night she could sweep the fear and past from her life and become the person he envisioned. But she couldn't. She could never change for him or anyone else, despite his assumptions. She knew he spoke the truth; she could not stop this plan of hers, because her heart called to her and she had to pursue the path she had chosen.

How strange that now she knew her mind, she had found someone she might share her life with, and that person demanded she give up the one thing making her feel whole. He was right. It was dangerous, but no more for her than him. She could accept that and expected him to do the same.

But he never listened. Yes, she hadn't explained it all. Not the way she intended. For all his promises and innuendos, they would continue together. He just didn't realize she saw through the ruse, and he would only allow her so much freedom. She had to have it all.

The time would come when he would leave her alone, waiting, wondering where he was and what had happened to him. What then? What of her needs and fulfillment? She'd never let him change her, dominate her, dictate to her. A career and love too? Was it possible? She admitted she wanted it all, and he had been in the front of her thoughts since that first day when they'd tumbled down his front steps together locked in mortal combat. Captivated by the silver flame of his eyes. Enchanted by the sweet wildfire of his kiss. Delighted by the way he cherished her with each caress, so tender and gentle, yet left no doubt of his possession.

She had never expected this side of him.

Since the night Charity came, he had changed. Several days passed, and they followed much the same course. He asked her advice, allowed her to accompany him on his excursions. He was always with her, never letting her out of his sight and loving her constantly. Wherever the mood struck. Sometimes zealously. Always enchanting her.

He brought her along to the wharf, rode with her when he seemed to want solitude, and allowed her most of the information he was privy to.

Last night he shared a note he received from a man in Astoria, a pilot on the Columbia. But when he'd folded the note and placed it in his pocket, it seemed as he'd sealed it away from her. A token gesture. Nothing more.

Now he had ridden with her to this place of enchantment, a place where he meant for her to forget her intentions. He meant to leave her here, waiting, one more time. Yet when his eyes touched her soul and their lips met, and when he held her against him, she did almost forget.

"Someday I will build you a house overlooking the sea," he said softly. "When I roamed the plains, wondering if I'd ever see a mountain or a crystal clear lake, or the vast endless ocean, I vowed I would find a place I could build a home and raise a family then I found Oregon."

Jessie understood him completely. She grinned, wanting to add her sentiments to his. "When it rains for ninety days and nights non-stop, you'll change your mind," she laughed softly. "You'll pray to see the sun just once before you die and you'll think you've truly found heaven when it peaks out from behind the clouds."

"Oh?" His eyes studied her. Humor danced across the sensuous curve of his lips. "And for you this is heaven, today, before the rains come again?"

"Yes," she whispered.

"And what about when the sky opens and drenches us?" he inquired.

She smiled. "It's still paradise on earth. I'd like nothing better than to find a cozy shelter and watch the storm until it plays itself out. A warm fire and perhaps a hot drink to sip."

"And my arms around you?"

"Yes." She lowered her lashes a moment then looked back at him, wishing she could tell him of the feelings simmering within her and how much she wanted him to believe in her.

He sat down beside her, scooping a shell from the rocks, idly turning it in his hands. His volatile gaze bore into her. "What makes you so different from other women?"

She arched a brow. "Different?"

He nodded.

She stared out at the breakers crashing below. Never liking to talk about herself, she paused, hesitant to give too much away. "Well, my mother, stepmother that is, brought me up to believe I could do anything I set my mind to. She convinced me women are every bit as smart, independent, and capable as any man. My father humored her or finally, I think, began to believe the truth of her words." She hesitated. "When I got older, she saw I had the finest education possible," she murmured. "In a way, though, she taught me more than any school she sent me to." She smiled at him. "My father used to call her a witch when he was angry, and sometimes I thought it was true because she knew things, knows..." Jessie hesitated to say any more.

"What did she know? Tell me what brought you to this point in your life where you are willing to risk your life for a cause."

"Roc, I...a confidence. I don't know if I can."

"I'm your husband. Tell me," he laughed.

"Alexandra has a way about her," she began but smiled. "The future never surprises her and sometimes at night I could hear the two of them laughing about things. Absurd things. I never understood, but father would laugh and I knew there would be no more conversation," she said, suddenly falling pensive and knowing what it was they did. It all seemed so clear to her now, and she wondered how she ever had the audacity to listen at their door.

She paused, feeling as if she had said too much about herself, about her family and eccentric mother. Perhaps she had given away too much. But he had leaned back on an elbow, playing with the white shell and gazing at her implacably with a glimmer of amusement in his eyes.

"I'd like to understand the way you think, what pushes you to act so out of character. She taught you well, but perhaps it has done more harm than good. This knowledge, this fiery determination to live in a man's world could well become the death of you. So I find it hard not to assert my husbandly rights and deny you this folly."

"Roc, it is just that I have earned my freedom, my right to do as I choose. And I have worked hard to set up a business, earn respect, become a person of trust and reliability. Now you seek to rip it all from me in the pretense of my mortality."

He clapped his hands together, applauding her speech. "Spoken like a true suffragist," he teased her. "But tell me, do you really believe all that nonsense?"

"It's hardly trivia when all over the country women are finding a way to survive financially without a man's support," she answered him, holding her temper in check.

He gazed out at the boiling sea. "It's a hard concept to understand or even accept," he told her.

"You could try. You've seen first hand what I'm capable of. I don't need you or your money."

He ran his fingers through his hair, grinning then chuckled softly. "Yes, I've seen the havoc you can create without blinking an eye."

"What?"

"You heard me. I disagree with your major premise that you don't need me. If it wasn't for my protection, Jessica, you might now find yourself in a very tenuous position."

"You will never see my side," she said, moving swiftly, angry with herself and her ramblings. Surprised, he watched her stride away from him and his lip curled in amusement. She whirled back around, glaring, wishing she had kept her thoughts to herself. "Of all the nerve. You made me think you might care."

"Hold it right there, Jessica. I do care. It's just that I don't understand. I suppose if it means so much to you, I could try harder to see things your way," he told her softly, rising to follow her. "I don't mean to belittle the crusade you are hell-bent to follow. I was curious about the way your ingenious little mind works, that is all. All I knew was my sweet wife was the most novel woman I had ever run across. I have never thought a woman could want more out of life than a husband, children, and a home to care for, or that you might want some of the things a man assails to. I remember planning my future with great diligence. It seems strange, but you have done the same."

"I have," she murmured uneasily, caught suddenly within his arms.

His breath, hot and whisper soft, stirred her senses. "Perhaps I could change your mind. Perhaps you might learn to care for me and hopefully our children with as much enthusiasm as you charge after criminals. In all of my travels and the time I've spent on this earth, you are the most intriguing woman I have ever known." He feathered his mouth across her lips, easing them apart with the tip of his tongue, gently gliding across their fullness then delving into her only to retreat again, teasing with each pass. He sank to the ground, bringing her with him to sit upon his lap. He kissed her cheeks then her eyes and came back to her mouth, hungry to taste once more and to capture her heart and soul.

The wind off the ocean swept around them. The spray misted and floated. He kissed her again, easing her back to lie upon his cloak on the soft sand. His fingers ran through her hair, fanning it around her face, caressing the silken length of it. Watching, studying, concentrating on the subtle play of emotions dancing within her eyes. "You once threatened me with an annulment to our marriage. Do you still feel so determined?" he asked her.

She closed her eyes for a moment, the anguish almost unbearable. For that was the last thing she wanted. "You called that first night we had together a regrettable accident," she reminded him.

"And if I lied?" he asked her.

"Did you?" she asked. "Why did you ever insist we marry?"

"We both agreed," he told her huskily, "because I thought you might have found yourself pregnant and I didn't want a child of mine to go without a name."

"The child would have my name and it is a good one," she replied indignantly. He laughed, seeming to ignore her statement.

His fingers toyed with the buttons on her dress, slowly revealing, inch-by-inch the swell of white flesh. The wind and his fingers teased, until finally the warmth of his hand closed over her breast. She gasped for air, tensing against the wayward sensation she battled. "We are out in the open," she reminded him.

"Ah, but no one would dare intrude," he assured her. "No one would venture to interrupt what I am about to begin. Well, I suppose I could think of a few, but since we can not find them..." His voice faded into nothingness. His mouth found her again, lightly at first then possessively as if he meant to convince her she needed only him.

Then he was studying her again. "Why do you insist on pursuing Rutgers and Pierce other than the fact they might have had Trevor shanghaied?"

She was having trouble thinking let alone speaking. He teased and tasted her body while he asked questions she would have trouble answering at the best of times. She tried to ignore the liquid heat flowing within and the soft caress of his fingers as they stroked and explored every inch of her. Her concentration vanished with the salt air as it moved inland and the thunder of the waves seemed to match the cadence of her heart.

She opened her eyes; saw the flash of his as their gazes met. He didn't really want to know, she thought suddenly. "I can't abide the way they use vulnerable women to their own selfish ends. I intend to see they pay; everyone of their kind who think women are useless chattel put on this earth only for their horrid needs."

He laughed. "You mean the horrid needs that occupy our time right now?"

Her eyes flared and darkened, gazing upon his. "It is not the same and you know that, Roc. This is different, beautiful..."

~ * ~

She had learned a great deal in such a short time. Innocence still a part of her though, and because of that she couldn't accept the reality of her sex. The belief she could do whatever she set her mind to still played a major part in her actions, and he was at a loss to convince her otherwise. If given a chance, a man could easily pay a small fortune to posses her even once. With her hair spread out around her, her rich dark lashes fallen over her eyes, her lips provocative and full, she appeared an angel sent from heaven or a temptress from hell. The long column of her neck made to feather kisses down, and her breasts, spilling from her bodice, were a fantasy of delight. Sometimes he thought one more time would appease his craving for her, but the mystery and the intrigue surrounding her cast him beneath her spell. It was so easy to forget the fear and the danger, the intentions she had made clear to him, the promises she had broken.

And the way she refused to give him that last piece of herself. She held on to it, and it seemed the price soared with each passing moment. He couldn't help wondering at the way her mind worked. How she had grown into such a confusing, beautiful, stubborn woman, hell bent on her destruction. For, if he could not convince her or change her mind, she would eventually push too hard and too far, and he could only pray he would be there to pick up the pieces.

He brushed the hair from her face, touching her cheeks gently with his knuckles. "I think you once told me I could trust your word. That you would stay in the house."

"Yes," she murmured. "But I lied. It was for a good cause. I had reason and I believed that soon it wouldn't matter. You would seek your annulment and leave."

His lip curled mischievously. She smelled like the fresh air, the salt spray and innocence. The scent mingled with his desires, the sand and the pine trees surrounding them on one side. He shifted his position, slipping his hand into more intimate quarters.

Her body jumped, tensed, startled by the invasion. Her eyes flew wide, embarrassed and shocked, wonder clouding the brilliant amethyst sparkling like a million stars.

"Roc, no. Not here..." she paused for breath, her cheeks flushed to a rosy glow. For all her claims and ambitions to succeed in a man's world and all of the time they had spent together, her shy innocent nature never failed to surprise him. "Anyone could see us."

"They wouldn't dare," he laughed softly.

Her fingers tightened around his shirt, clutching the fabric as if she had found a lifeline. Realizing he would not change his mind, she pushed on his chest. He held on to her shoulders, moving her back to the sand. A whimper, a soft sigh, then his mouth claimed hers tenderly, intimately exploring. He searched and teased, tasted her lips until they responded to his plans. His hand followed a different course, pursuing recklessly the soft skin beneath her skirt, higher, stroking and teasing. She trembled under his caress and gentle touch. He hesitated, coming in contact with the soft curls of her mound, embracing the crevice between it. Melodically, tantalizing, he penetrated her with his fingers. Teased the soft velvet he craved. Found the sensitive little pearl of her deepest passion; caressed and touched winding her in a mystical wed of sorcery.

"Roc," she cried out against his mouth. Her fragility and honest pleasure were his delight. He wanted to be a part of her. Quickly, he shifted and undid his Levi's then pushed her skirt aside. He impaled her, slowly, intending to give her all the pleasure he could and perhaps to convince her she had created a place of her own and she had nothing to prove. She gave herself over to him, winding her arms around his neck.

The waves thundered, crashing against the rocks in front of them. A soft drizzle had begun to fall from a patch of gray clouds overhead, yet in the distance the sun shone on a large expanse of the beach. He could smell the salt and surf upon the wind. Hear it as it ruffled the needles in the trees overhead. It seemed to set up a cadence all its own, one of perfection, and he followed along, making love to Jessie with his heart and soul. Desire surged through him, possessed his mind, lured his body into temptation.

Still the mystery and the power of their union enchanted him.

Now he could hear her soft sigh rushing gently past him. He flinched at the way he had taken her, without a care or concern. She looked so vulnerable, yet her mouth formed a tender smile and he could only hope it was for him. He moved off her and adjusted his clothes then hers and gently caressed her cheek.

She was his. In all his life he had never known such a fascination with a woman. Or such an insane madness for a woman he could not stop thinking of.

And he would give anything...anything at all if he could exact a promise from her that she would keep, a promise she would stay where he left her. Or did he dream of something so futile he wasted his time. He wished he could convince her she teetered on the edge of insanity when she thought to go after Pierce. Even when she smiled and pretended to agree with him, he could read her mind and cringed at what he saw there.

As he lay next to her, he knew he had to return. Their paradise here in God's country could not last forever.

Jessie accepted his hand. Her eyes still darkened with the passion they had just shared. He pulled her to her feet and escorted her to the horses. The ride back seemed idyllic, peaceful.

"What now?" she asked suddenly when the little town came into view.

"The same, at least until we find some clue," he assured her quickly, which seemed to put her at ease for the moment. He nudged the horses to a faster pace.

He left her behind, urging his horse forward. Charity ran from the boarding house. Her arms waved frantically in the air with a piece of paper clutched in her hand.

~ * ~

Jessie relaxed in the saddle, smiling. Everything was going as planned. The wind had picked up and the few shafts of sunlight that had once pierced through the cloud cover had vanished. She watched the exchange that passed between Charity and Roc with grave indecision. She saw Roc's expression lighten. A tiny smile curved his lips then watched as he held the missive and read.

Roc seemed to relax also as if he had held his breath for an eternity. He turned to her, motioning her to hurry then headed toward the house. He reached the door, and Jessie was sure their mission would be successful after all.

"Charity, tell my wife what has happened," he called.

Then he hurried into the hotel and raced up the steps to their room.

Jessie grinned devilishly, excited he had fallen so neatly for the letter, in such haste to leave her with nothing to do but wait, and elated he had not taken time to question the unexpected news.

"Jessica..." Charity began quietly.

"Not yet," Jessie told her firmly. She slipped off the horse, tethering the mare next to Roc's, and followed him. But when she reached the stairs, she hesitated, turning back to wink at Charity.

Charity clutched her hands in front of her. "I understand."

"We can discuss this as soon as he's gone."

Charity looked up to the rooms, shifting nervously.

"Are you sure you want to go through with it?"

"Of course."

"Good. If you have even one misgiving, I want you to stay here and wait for Roc."

"It would take more than one doubt to keep from going with you," she said and looked back to her room.

"I want you to consider this carefully," Charity whispered.

"I already have, a very long time ago. Nothing can stop me."

Jessica fought the battle raging within. Had she only known how hard this would become, she might have never begun what was rapidly turning into the fiercest battle of her life. He had known she was determined. Jessie desperately wanted to bring Pierce to justice. Alive and well, able to stand trial, but first in her mind now that she knew Trevor was safe she wanted to help the poor Chinese girls Pierce had enslaved.

With the storm threatening out to sea, she had her chance. The patience she prided herself with would pay off. Roc would leave for San Francisco to rescue Trevor, and upon his return, would learn of her flight to Astoria with Charity. He would never forgive her.

Before he left, he might force another promise from her. A promise she would have to break.

"Dash it all," she breathed. "Why do I feel compelled to go to him and tell him goodbye?"

It seemed Charity saw the battle she fought and her heart went out to her.

"You love him," Charity said simply. "Tell him. No one should have to make such a choice."

She fought the hot sting of tears welling in her throat and rising to the back of her eyes. "He'll go now and I won't see him," she told her. "And when he gets back, he will seek vindication."

"He will get over the deception, Jessica. If he feels anything at all for you, he will realize he gave you no choice."

Jessie turned away, determined, stubbornly hoping he would, perhaps, never find out. Indeed, if everything went as planned, she and Charity would arrive in Salem before Roc.

"Jessica," Charity said softly. "As soon as he rides over the first hill, we'll leave." Her voice was steady and firm. It gave her confidence and strengthened her will.

Oh, yes. They would ride swiftly and deal with the injustice. Charity had sent the messenger ahead this morning with money Trevor had given her and directions to buy a wagon and horses. She pushed the warnings her mind kept insinuating away and the feeling of doom that surfaced periodically.

But she was terribly afraid.

How curious. It was not so long ago she had held herself in high esteem and believed no one could vanquish her. Now she knew different, understood her talents were feeble at best.

She stared at Charity again, a weak smile before she pulled her hair away from her face, tying it in a knot to keep it from her eyes.

"We're horribly unprepared," she whispered.

Jessica tensed, then raced up the stairs. When she reached the top, she walked cautiously to the room they had rented, shared, made love in.

She left the door open and stepped inside. Silence hung on the air like a death knell, but she ignored it, standing motionless before him.

He had finished packing, and she watched as he buckled his gun belt around his waist.

She swayed slightly, wanting to run to him, tell him the truth. Tell him the letter was a hoax she and Charity made up. His eyes caught hers, pulling, coaxing the truth from her. It seemed he read her thoughts and she flinched.

"Be careful," she whispered.

"You're concerned for my welfare, Jessie?" he said. "I find that touching and strangely intriguing. You surprise me, sweetheart."

"Of course." She hesitated then looked away, considering her next words. "I've come to regard you with great affection. I'll miss you. As you have told me so many times, this is dangerous. You are mortal just as I am, and I wouldn't wish to see any harm come to you."

He arched a brow to her. A curious smile rose slowly to his lips. "What are you up to?"

"Nothing, Roc," she said too suddenly and with too much force.

He was ready to ride now, prepared for anything. At least he gave that appearance. He strode to the door but paused there for a brief moment. "I'm not going to seek a promise, Jessie, if that's what you're afraid of. I know what your word is worth. But, if you are not here when I return, I will see you never set foot out of our bed chamber until you are old and gray and can not do further harm to yourself."

She understood he would never do as he suggested even though he would have every reason to do just that if he knew what she planned. Guilt welled inside her.

"I won't disappoint you," she said quickly. But she knew her words were lies. "You..." she broke off. She couldn't say the words she wanted to. His words kept tumbling around in her brain. Regrettable accident. And she could not, would not risk the anguish she felt knife through her heart.

"Trevor is important to both us. I must go. Is there something else?"

She couldn't tell him she might be falling in love with him and she didn't want the annulment, didn't want to disappoint him either, but she had no choice.

"You might not get him off the ship."

"I'm his only hope."

"You might find yourself shanghaied also."

"I won't. No one would dare, besides I can take care of myself, Jessie."

That's what Trevor thought, that's what she thought about herself, but anything could happen or go wrong, accidents, a lapse in concentration.

She hesitated, refusing to divulge her secret. "I am still worried for you. Take care, Roc."

He smiled, looked at her, and it seemed he understood she had lied to him. But she knew he didn't have time to discover the ruse. He cupped her chin, raising it so he could see into her eyes, frightened suddenly for her. She couldn't move from him.

"Jessie..." he murmured, his voice trailing off. "Jessie, please don't do anything foolish."

It was too late for that. She had already made plans that sounded crazy to her. He was leaving and she had only her expertise to rely on. She thought suddenly of how much experience she lacked. She didn't want to feel guilt, or fear, or insecurity. At the moment she was determined to concentrate on the work that lay ahead of her. "Go, Roc. Go find Trevor for me. I would go with you if you let me."

"No, Jessie. You know I can't risk that." He pulled her to him, drawing her against his solid muscled length. Feather light kisses seared her neck, her cheeks then found her lips, drugging kisses, filled with longing and passion. Guilt overwhelmed her, and the wrenching pain inside made her cringe away from the heat of his mouth.

"I would have you return safe and unharmed," she whispered, trying so very hard to fight the repentance surging through her. He could have tried to understand. Now all was lost.

He stepped back and laughed softly. "You never cease to surprise me. I will do my best." He hesitated then kissed her deeply one last time.

"Be here, Jessica, when I return. I don't want to have to search for you," he whispered.

"I will be here," she said. But it didn't matter. He had left her side.

He stared at her. Their gazes met. His looked hollow and pained, but he turned swiftly, gathered his saddlebag, and left the room.

Jessie walked to the window and pulled the curtain away. She had a clear view to the grounds below. His horse pounded south across the rolling dunes.

Most assuredly, Trevor would hear of this, but not in San Francisco. And she wondered how long it would take Roc to discover the trickery.

But Jessie had no time to waste, for Roc was no fool, and she thought he might even put it altogether before the day ended.

If that was the case, she and Charity might have only a few hours head start.

She leapt up, suddenly ready to prove herself. She was going to Astoria.

~ * ~

Trevor wavered as he studied the bay and the docks. Boats of every kind moored here; fisherman, whalers, merchants and a few navy vessels were placed in strategic spots. He tried not to think of the deception he had played with Charity, but he could not allow her underfoot. So he had faked the attack at the lighthouse, met Senator Drake in Eugene, and traveled via the railroad to San Francisco in search of Pierce and Rutgers.

He had found his way to the Queen's Room.

Once he had discovered the room and its purpose, he had pulled in a dozen favors so he could see first hand what went on there. In these rooms Chinese women were taught the trade of prostitution. Taught how to please men and how to entice them into their cubicles. Taught, also, the English words: "China girl very nice. You come inside please, and I make you happy." When the girls appeared well schooled, they found themselves at the auction.

He was determined to prosecute the men who perpetuated the slavery. Pierce headed the list. All in all, he found little difficulty understanding Jessie's stubbornness when it came to these helpless women who suffered so at the hands of greedy men. And he could comprehend Roc's fear for her. Jessie was beautiful. Impetuous. Trevor had seen the sparks of desire electrocute the air when they had not realized it themselves.

Yes, Jessie was trouble. And, he thought suddenly, so was Charity. He had just penned a note to Roc but he wasn't sure if it would reach him in time. He wanted to return to Salem, but the next shipment of Chinese women was headed for Astoria. As much as he needed Roc's help, Trevor thought dryly, he couldn't risk informing the girls of his plans. Once he let it slip, he might have his hands full, and he didn't want his cousin and the determined Miss Charity to get in his way.

With Jessie wed, he had foolishly thought Roc would control her. But Newman was too soft where it concerned his little cousin. It seemed she wound him around her finger as easily as she did the rest of the men in her life. If Drake had not told him first hand of their exploits, he would have never believed it possible.

Drake was in their host's great parlor, looking out the windows toward the San Francisco bay. A sudden foreboding stole over Trevor, a fear he had somehow neglected a detail, an important detail, one that needed his attention immediately. But since Drake's arrival, the pace they had set was fast, and he'd had no time to concentrate on anything else.

Drake heard his entrance and looked up from his musings. It was evening and they had planned to set out with the rising of the moon. The train was scheduled to leave in an hour. When it reached Eugene, they would finish their trip in stealth then pray they'd reach Astoria ahead of the ship which was scheduled to leave San Francisco in a few days, its hold full of women.

"Ah, Trevor, are you ready?"

He walked into the room, frowning, still trying to remember the detail he had missed. Coffee sat on the table, hot and black. He poured himself a cup and sipped it slowly, cautiously gazing out at the harbor. "Rumors have it the ship will land in a week," Trevor told Drake. "If the train arrives on time and we're lucky..."

"Yes, provided we don't run into any unforeseen problems," Drake interjected thoughtfully.

"All right then. You have the same fears I do. I know Jessie will find some way to involve herself."

Drake grimaced. "Charity, too, from what you've told me about her."

A shiver spiraled down his spine. "I don't doubt it for a minute."

"And what part will Roc play in all this? As soon as he gets your message, he'll go to Astoria, but it might be too late. You know the girls will follow him, but if that's the case, we know they won't get into mischief because everything will have reached its proper conclusion before they arrive."

His fingers clutched the cup, hoping beyond prayers that what Drake said was true. But the feeling of desperation wouldn't leave, his cold chills continued. They had to hurry. "Let's go now. No one will follow and it's dark. Truly, we have no time to waste."

"If you insist," Drake said, rising to follow Trevor.

"I have this horrible feeling we will all reach Astoria too late to do any good. Pierce and Rutgers seem to know what we are about even before we do. The girls, stubborn, unpredictable, bait for that man and I'm afraid for them, afraid that even Roc has fallen into a trap."

"Roc is hardly an amateur," Drake said coolly. "You don't give him enough credit."

"Perhaps you give him too much," he insisted, suddenly wary. He still felt the urgent need to leave. And gathering his things, he strode from the room, Drake behind him.

"Perhaps..." Drake said, his hand resting on Trevor's shoulder, stopping him suddenly.

"But then..." Trevor's voice trailed away.

"You have to have more faith in Roc. Remember, we hand picked him for the job, and give him credit where it is due. That way, perhaps we can all trust each other."

"Trust. You speak of it so easily," Trevor told him.

Drake shrugged. And Trevor thought, perhaps it was too easy for Senator Drake to speak of trust. A man in Drake's position relied heavily on it and learned to gauge his friends and enemies; trust was a precious commodity.

And, Trevor told himself, Drake believed the two men he hand picked deserved his trust.

"Yes," he said flatly. Then grinned boyishly. *As long as I have you and Roc behind me, I have no fear.* "Let's go so you can put your mind to rest."

The night breeze was cool and the sky was black. In a matter of minutes, they had reached the outskirts of the city and were traveling north. Wheels pounded the rails and the terrible fear within Trevor grew.

Doubts assailed his mind. Chills traveled his spine, making his flesh crawl. After leaving the train station behind, he set spur to his horse. Traveling swiftly, he could smell the salt spray. Feel the soft caress of the moonbeams. But nothing could shake the terror that tore at his heart and wound its way inside him.

Guilt swept through him.

He should have never left Charity alone or disappeared without a word to Jessica. He had, after all, known she would chase after him. All the way to Astoria if she thought he was there.

Dear God, what had he set in motion?

I am not too late. I've sent the messages. One should arrive in time for Roc to take protective measures. He had to hurry.

It didn't help they could only travel so fast. Then he froze, sifting through his thoughts.

A traitor existed within his circle. A traitor who seemed to know everything they did. He glanced to his side. Senator Drake had pulled even with him. Someone had betrayed them.

Chapter Ten

Pierce stared at the mouth of the Columbia, frustrated beyond measure.

He turned his attention to Rutgers, the man who had orchestrated all of their schemes until now. The ship sailing into the river would eventually leave for Alaska to get rid of the girls they didn't sell here then back to Hawaii. He would sail on that ship only after the culmination of his plans.

Rutgers had been incredibly anxious to reach Astoria and settle the accounts; to see this last shipment of women sold before moving on to other enterprises.

Sterling Rutgers strode down the pier, coming to its end, staring from the ship to Pierce where he waited for its arrival. The warehouse was ready and the auction set to begin. The women already schooled in their new art, students of the 'Queen's Room' in San Francisco.

"Damn, but this is making me nervous," he said, shielding his eyes from the glare off the river. "What's taking so long?"

"She should dock in less than thirty minutes," Rutgers said cautiously. "And then we can see to the girls. The auction will take place at midnight. Nothing will go wrong."

Pierce stared from the ship to Rutgers, still nervous. They hadn't heard a word about Trevor Lawrence. He'd just disappeared. Roc kept Jessica guarded night and day. He would slip up sometime. No one could keep her subdued forever.

He should have left the states. They had planned to, but the money from this auction would give them a sizable bank account until they could set up a new base of operations.

The ship had arrived on time. He heard that the warehouse in Swilltown had been cleared in preparation. The building belonged to an old friend who had given his permission for Pierce to use it, assuming he meant to store merchandise. Well, he did in a manner of speaking. Invitations sent days ago to the wealthiest madams, pimps, and gentlemen in the Northwest. The girls not sold to brothels would be used in the cribs. And Roc Newman was out of the way for the time being. Pierce couldn't figure what information Newman had come by, but he thanked his lucky stars for it.

They should have no trouble tonight. Roc would discover this too late of course. They would have already sailed.

Roc had played unexpectedly into their hands by heading away from Astoria. Now even if he rode hard, he could not reach them until they had gone.

Sterling was grinning, as if he'd finally realized there was nothing to fear.

"I am looking forward to this evening then sailing with the tide," Sterling said. "I believe I'll quite enjoy this show."

Indeed, Pierce thought. He would too. It was always a pleasure to watch one of these in the process, and he would have first pick. When the ship docked, he'd make his selection.

Sterling smirked and rocked back on his heels, anticipating the evening.

Pierce paced the width of the dock, still watching the ship, his mind working quickly. The sails trimmed. The anchor dropped. Nothing would stop him. Nothing at all.

If Roc hadn't interfered, he would have had his revenge. Now, of course, he would have to wait patiently until he could come back to the states, until he could take them by surprise.

Failure didn't suit him.

Sterling didn't care for his plan to return but...

Could he find Jessica Lawrence and take her with him?

Hmm. Perhaps he could persuade the captain to put in at Cape Foul Weather. If Jessica Lawrence were still there as his sources informed him, he would take her with him. Without Roc she would have little defense against a ship's crew. Everyone knew how impetuous and wild she was.

Perhaps he should have more patience. Sterling was nervous and the authorities were closing in as the evidence piled up against them. If there was ever a trial, at this point, prosecution was a foregone conclusion. He didn't want to spend the rest of his life in a federal prison. He had other more elaborate and pleasurable ideas as to how to spend his time.

Then there was the matter of Roc Newman. The man had tracked him and his crimes across the United States, relentlessly. Determination stole its way into Pierce. He would have his revenge against Lawrence and Newman. The solution lay in pulling back and waiting patiently until his name was no longer synonymous with crime in Oregon. He would come back. In a year or two, when no one expected him.

He would no longer have to worry about Jessica Lawrence because... Jessica would become a high priced whore in one of Lilly's houses.

Pierce smiled. He wore the look of a smug arrogant bastard. The look was always razor sharp. He moved in a dangerous world of intrigue and subterfuge, and it was best to be primed.

He stepped back into the shadows, watched the ship dock and begin to unload its valuable cargo. "This is all going to work out," he told Sterling. "Perseverance is all we need now."

"Just the same, I'll breathe easier when we're on the boat," Sterling murmured. "If Roc hears of this, he'll notify the authorities."

"Roc's on the road south," Pierce promised. "He won't have time. Confidence, Sterling, confidence."

Sterling held his breath and ran his hand nervously across his stomach. While the moon passed behind a cloud, the first of the girls walked silently from the ship. Pierce and Rutgers slipped into the night and directed them to a large warehouse.

Only the soft sound of water lapping along the beach was heard.

The door swung open and the girls filed inside.

Pierce closed the door, locking it behind him. "The last stage almost completed," Pierce whispered. He waited for his eyes to adjust to the blackness. No light penetrated, and he had to blink once. The captain had lined the girls up against the wall of the warehouse to wait. Some rested, others slipped down to sit on the cold floor, but still silence haunted the room. All he had to do was wait another hour and see to it that each girl brought a high price. He'd be a very wealthy man.

There had to be a way to get Jessica Lawrence here. She was too far away. Then Pierce decided he'd send someone to get her. Now, as to getting Jessica here, unhurt...

Ah, a righteous plan. The gullible little thing who had risen to his cause once before, easily swayed. Her sympathies would reside with the poor women so abused here and she would come. The girl would react again without a thought of the consequences, and he wouldn't have to wait for his revenge.

This would work to perfection, completely flawless. Everything he had dreamt of for the last half of his life.

Leaving the Chinese women alone, he and Rutgers strode swiftly from the warehouse. Pierce bent on putting his hastily prepared plan into action.

~ * ~

Once Jessica and Charity had learned of the delivery and subsequent auction in Astoria, they wasted no time in implementing the arrangements. From her saddlebag Jessica dug out the gun her father had given her when she had first opened her office and the knife she had expertly learned to throw. She dressed in her men's clothes, pulling her hair back tight and winding it beneath a hat then donning her favorite buckskin jacket, even though the jacket wasn't hers. Thus prepared, she set out down the hall to find Charity, nearly crashing into her when she flew through her door.

"Jessica, slow down. We have plenty of time."

"Somehow I doubt that. Every time I look over my shoulder, I swear Roc's standing there," she told her. "Charity, we've got to hurry. Roc's sure to figure this out before he reaches San Francisco. It was all too contrived, sudden."

Charity watched her stubbornly without moving.

"Charity, whatever are you thinking about? It's not like you to take this for granted."

She didn't move.

"Hurry, please."

Charity studied her a moment longer then nodded, agreeing with her. "I wonder, do you underestimate yourself or give Roc more credit than is his due? Needless to say, you're right. We must not postpone this a moment longer."

Jessica sighed, feeling almost giddy before tapping her foot impatiently while Charity stuffed a few more items into her saddlebags.

Charity inhaled deeply then signaled she was ready, calling over her shoulder as she made her way down the stairs of the little hotel. "I hope you're wrong, Jessica. But I won't take any chances. What will he do if he catches you at this? Hmm?"

Chills spiraled out of control down Jessica's spine. No, she wouldn't think about that now. And he wouldn't catch her.

~ * ~

Roc made good time, yet when nightfall came, he kept on, traveling swiftly, the urgent need to help Trevor always in the back of his mind. Peaceful night sounds filtered through the air, giving the urgency of his quest a sense of frustration. A lonely owl hooted above then swept suddenly, capturing a field mouse in its deadly claws. A light mist of clouds overhead encircled the moon casting a halo of color around it.

Sometimes eerie shadows seemed to crystallize from behind the trees. All types of animals came to life by night, and it reminded Roc of Pierce and Rutgers.

All types of animals.

Honest men rarely traveled in the bleak forbidding hours of blackness. But this night he was about.

Still Roc had more urgent business to concern himself with. He had Jess Law on his mind and the sudden missive calling him away from her side and Charity's. He had the sinking feeling in his haste he had overlooked something important. He rode, striving to recall every detail of the day and their parting. Too exhausted to think, he dismounted, finding a suitable place to camp for a few hours.

A soft fog drifted through the clearing, rising from the tributary of the Alsea River. A salmon jumped, and a bullfrog croaked, and still he could not pinpoint what bothered him about the afternoon and his swift ride through the Oregon countryside. The smile. He could clearly remember the smile on Jess Law's face and that puzzled him now, although he hadn't considered it at the time. He ran it through his head again. Jess Law, P.I.

Damnation.

Yet, with all that had passed between them, he didn't think of her as Jessica or even Jessie, only Jess Law the implacable private investigator. He'd think on it later when he had his senses intact, for now he needed to rest.

Still, sleep was elusive. He leaned against a log and watched the firelight dance with the shadows. He was barely relaxed before an ember sparked and popped, landing next to him. Reflexively, he moved for his gun then sighed once more, shaking the exhaustion from his clouded mind, honing in on Jess. On the smile. Remembering. "Go, Roc. Find Trevor. I would go if you'd let..."

And of course the smile curving her lips haunting his thoughts. The swiftly lowered lashes meant to hide something.

No fight. No argument.

She was a master at deception, but she could never lie to him without him knowing. Not when he could see her eyes. She was bent on investigating this, the smuggling, the white slavery, the whorehouses. She intended to catch Pierce and Rutgers. When he warned her, she responded with complacency, clearly meant to deceive.

She would do as she pleased. He knew that but what he didn't know was what it entailed.

Roc laced his fingers above his head, reworking each word, each expression. Something had turned her into Jess Law. It was up to him to figure it out before she got herself into trouble. "I would have you return unharmed."

Roc stiffened impatient with himself. "I will be here." She had promised. That was it. Everything she had said then the missive, so surprising after the days with no clues, no evidence to point them in any direction. San Francisco, miles out of the way, miles from Astoria. "Best you again." Ah, yes, perhaps she had bested him quite handily. The note a forgery, he was sure.

Her eyes had flashed, filled with intrigue and secrecy. He felt the heat of them upon his back as he rode away, felt the guilt of leaving her, felt the stab of betrayal. It pierced his heart. The girl had honed the knife to a razor fine edge.

His fingers vised around a rock. She had lied easily and expertly to him, aided and abetted by Charity. What had they intended? He would find them on the road to Astoria. Discover them up to their lovely necks in trouble, no doubt.

Stars shone from above and he prayed a silent prayer he was wrong. His stomach clenched in anguish and he choked, barely able to gulp a lungful of air so terrified for her. God almighty, he couldn't close his eyes without seeing her dressed in virginal white, standing on the block, countless buyers hungrily circling her. He could see the dress ripped from her, tears spilling down her face as men examined her.

He bolted upright, unaware of the sound of hooves filling the air, intent on only one thing. "Jessica Lawrence, when I have you safe, I'll never let you from my sight."

Roc stared grimly into the dying fire, kicked dirt into it, watching it smolder a second then go out. "I'll find you, Jess Law." He saddled his horse, quickly leaping on its back.

Roc urged the horse north. "Son of a bitch," he swore.

He rode swiftly. When he reached the trail, he hesitated, listening. His horse nickered and he placed an affectionate pat on the horse's neck. Roc dismounted and led the horse off the trail then waited.

He stood silently, his gaze wary and cautious. Two men rode hard from the south, oblivious of the watcher. Did he dare present himself? He carried nothing of value, but something about the way they rode gave him pause.

He only looked for news and a swift journey to Astoria. He was a powerful man, but he didn't wish to fight. Still, they looked familiar, and in the blackness of the night unless he hailed them, he wouldn't know for sure.

They rode closer, hooves pounding a rapid staccato on the hard packed earth. He waited. Concentrating. He inhaled sharply, suddenly aware the lead man was the one he dashed off to rescue, surprisingly whole and in no need of deliverance.

Roc shouted, stepping from his place of concealment, raising his arm high in an attempt to stop the men. Trevor's horse reared, startled by the suddenness.

"Stop, Trevor! Or I will surely lose all patience and shoot you. Between you and your cousin I..."

"Roc?"

Trevor brought his horse under control. He patted it soothingly then stared at Roc, obviously furious. A wealth of unanswered questions seemed to race through his thoughts but Roc Newman was in no mood to answer them. He couldn't wait for one. "Where's Jessica?"

Ironic, Roc knew, Jess Law had bested him once more.

"Jess Law is undoubtedly, at this very moment riding into a rat's nest, and with no protection except your friend Charity. Too put it simply, I was duped."

~ * ~

Jessica and Charity knew exactly where to go, just not what to do once they arrived in Astoria. She was glad, though, she had someone to back her up. They had ridden together, silent with their thoughts for quite some time, but she had eventually breached the silence and the subject at hand. Not once had she questioned the source of Charity's information. Now she did. She had acted surprised, quite put out, being Charity, and prayed they would find a way to extricate the Chinese women from their servitude without joining them. Jess told Charity to let her do it alone since she was the P.I. and trained. Charity refused, reminding her adamantly she wouldn't even be near Astoria without her amateurish help, and therefore had earned her a spot in this escapade. With Charity at her side, there were at least two of them, double the chance of succeeding.

Jessie refrained from reminding Charity neither of them knew where the auction would take place or what they would do to rescue them once they had the knowledge.

Jess Law told Charity she would have to learn to take orders and move swiftly. Everything would hang in the balance.

When nightfall came, she was heartily glad Charity had not backed down and thoroughly aware of just how impetuous they had been to start out on this dangerous mission alone. She had never been to Astoria; Charity had, but that had not been under best of circumstances. Neither of them knew of a respectable place to stay, nor for that matter knew if they had time to find one before the sale.

They were on the south side of Astoria, separated from it by a river smaller than the Columbia. Charity had built a small fire for warmth and cooking before they started out again.

Jessie was too nervous to eat. Her stomach churned and the guilt of betrayal hung heavily over her head, weighing on her thoughts. Only fear of enslavement and the dangerous situation that loomed hauntingly in front of them kept her alert and ready.

She didn't know how to find the warehouse, and if she did find it, she didn't know what to do next. But she was here and she had to find a way to get into the auction and a way to get the women out and on the road to Salem undetected.

Jessie gazed across the river at the lights of the town. She insisted they discuss their strategy before crossing the tributary and setting their course.

"Where is Roc, do you think?" she asked Charity.

Charity grinned devilishly. "Jessica, you worry too much, he's somewhere between Newport...hmm," she glanced Jessie's way, "and no danger to us, I believe, following an outlandish trail, expertly devised."

"Then you don't think he's figured..."

"Never, Jessica. Not in this lifetime he hasn't."

"I wish I felt as sure as you do."

"Me, too. But, Jessica, I think he will come here after we're gone. In a couple of days, there will be nothing he can do then. It will all be finished, for good or bad. It's too late to think about it now."

Jessie grimaced. Charity set down the cup of coffee she'd been sipping and walked to stand before the fire, warming her hands.

It was then Jessie noticed a movement in the shadows, near the riverbank.

A man strode toward them, confident, purposeful. He had left his horse tethered to a tree near the riverbank. He reached the campfire, ignored the gun Jess pulled on him then helped himself to the lukewarm coffee and grinned.

A moment later Charity and the man talked as if they had known each other forever. Jessie stared, incredulous. Charity, the ever quiet but efficient young lady, had arranged for a law enforcement officer to meet them. She had planned this without her help, planned it even before she had met Jessica Lawrence Newman.

Jessie looked at one then the other. "Well, are you going to include me or leave me sitting here by the river while you and your deputies charge into the warehouse?"

Jessie blinked once before she glared at them, looking last at Charity as if to say *You could have told me*. Charity rubbed her hands together in self-defense then set her hand on Jessie's arm. "I didn't mean to leave you out. It's just this was so important and I was afraid."

"Afraid I'd tell Roc?" Jessie's eyebrow rose at the thought. Never would she have told him. But how could she have expected Charity to understand when she wasn't sure herself. "I wouldn't have." But now when she listened to the conversation, she had a different impression of the girl who had come from Hawaii on a slave ship with the threat of prostitution prevalent in her every thought, the naive minister's daughter who had needed rescuing a few weeks ago.

"I should have trusted you." Charity began.

"You had no reason to," Jessie told her without hesitation. "I would have felt the same."

She reached out her hand to shake. "Jessica, I don't know what to say."

Jessie smiled. "Don't say anything, just include me. I'll warrant that you'll need an extra hand before the night is over. And I'm an expert with a knife and a gun, not afraid to use them either. Include me in this, Charity, not on the outside looking in but in the middle. I promise you, you won't regret it."

She winked then and turned to the officer. "Good, Jessie. I really had no intention of leaving you out. I just wasn't sure what you'd do under pressure. Now, sit down, we still have a few details to discuss. This is John

Clayton."

Jessie studied the sheriff.

"The doors will open in two hours, midnight," Mr. Clayton said.

"I should have guessed," Charity murmured.

Jessie flashed her a warm smile. "Superstitious? Now, how could that happen, you're a minister's daughter. Midnight...hmm. The witching hour, at least that's what my father always called it. Said strange things could happen."

"Stop. You're making me nervous."

"Sorry. I suppose that's the least of our worries." She turned to study the landscape, the river, the town, and beyond, the Columbia.

A tinge of guilt seared through Jessie. But she threw off any approximation of convention or conservative behavior when she first chose to defy Roc and pursue Pierce. She had to follow her conscience wherever it lead, or she wouldn't be able to live with herself or her nightmares.

She turned and swiftly gathered the few items they'd unpacked, easily finishing before Charity. As she had suspected, this would take a considerable amount of determination and luck.

She mounted her horse and waited for the officer and Charity to do the same. It was not so hard to forget Roc's warning. In the midst of all the excitement, Jessica could only concentrate on the night ahead.

Perhaps they would be in Salem by tomorrow. It was possible, if they took a boat up the Columbia to Portland then a train south to Salem.

Nervously, she bit her finger, wondering what Roc would say to that. Not in Newport but in their home in Salem, safe. "There's the wagon," she said softly.

"Jessica. Stay behind me and don't do anything sudden. Quiet now."

They had crossed the river ten minutes ago and now they huddled together outside the warehouse on 7th street. Jessica shivered and drew her buckskin jacket closer. She could hear muffled noises coming from the building. Every so often a man would enter through the back way. No one came out. No lights. Nothing. Blackness. It seemed her imagination had taken over.

"Ah, but they won't take any chances, you see. No one has come without an escort and by appointment. They use this warehouse whenever someone extra special is auctioned. Then, when they've made their purchase, they leave through an underground passage," the sheriff told her.

She gasped. She had her knife and her gun, but she suddenly felt lacking. Already, even as they watched, sales were taking place and they had done nothing. Nothing. "What are we waiting for?"

"Reinforcements, though you might not believe it. We will have the warehouse surrounded in a matter of minutes. Then, my friend, and only then, will we move against them," Clayton said.

She tensed and watched as another man entered the building. Then a shadow emerged from the far corner, an almost imperceptible nod and it seemed a year passed.

The sheriff turned his attention to the river, waiting once more. He started to rise then hunched back down.

"Now?" she asked him quickly.

She could hear Charity calming the horses and the creak of another wagon moving slowly along the dirt path. Her soft crooning voice a whisper on the wind.

"Stay behind me, Jessica," he warned her. "If anything goes wrong, I'm the man responsible for your welfare, and I want to know where you are. When we get the wagons loaded...go. Don't look back."

"Yes..." she murmured, then she held her breath, waiting.

A lantern swung from the roof of the warehouse.

She gripped her gun, ready to use it. "What now?" she whispered. "What's happening?"

"Wait," he said, his hand holding her back when she would have plunged ahead. "They've entered. We'll move on in a moment."

She longed with all her heart to rush in and confront the two men who had created such havoc in her life.

But she had to wait. The confrontation would come later.

"I don't know if I can," she said.

"Now, Jessica Lawrence, come on. It's time." They crouched low, running. The sheriff's men rammed the door, shattering it. The smugglers retaliated. Bullets ricocheted off the walls in the warehouse. Men yelled, women screamed, but it died almost as quickly as it started.

Sounds of weeping filled the empty space inside the building.

Jessie's eyes began to adjust. A lantern swung lazily on a far wall. All around her she could see women moaning; despair, fear, terror etched forever on their faces and in their hearts. She fought the urge to cry. Instead, she began to lead them to a new and more pleasant future.

Charity met each group at the wagons.

The tension eased slowly in Jessie muscles. Her face was strained and ashen from what she'd seen. Charity looked very close to tears herself, her dark brown eyes shimmering with a liquid film.

God. Tremors seized her. She steadied herself on the edge of the wagon, these poor helpless women.

Nausea churned in her stomach. Her knees threatened to collapse.

She turned to see the officer who had led the raid.

"Did you find them? Pierce and Rutgers?" she whispered.

"No, they got away, the underground tunnel. There was more than one. We didn't know."

"Then they're gone?"

"No, nothing will sail until we find them. The roads out of town are blocked."

"When you find them, what then?"

"They will stand trial. Trevor has accumulated a wealth of evidence, enough to convict them. If they find a way out of the net we've dropped, they'll search you out. Stay alert. They'll want to blame this on someone, and believe me, I heard your name mentioned several times. You must get the wagons moving. Take the road to Portland then go south from there. It's safer."

"And Roc will assume that we'll take that route. So, we'll have to find an alternate."

"No. There's no other way."

"Of course there is."

"Not one that's safe. How can you risk your lives and these women's so callously?"

"You have to trust me."

Jessie tried to toughen her stance. Her head throbbed. Everything he said made sense then nothing did. She closed her eyes, praying for guidance, thinking, concentrating on every word they'd said. She turned to

Charity who seemed oblivious, content to soothe the shattered Chinese women in the wagon, some no more than children.

"You have to do as I say," he told her. "You have to stay along the Columbia River then turn south when you reach Portland."

"Why?"

"I've told you," he said. "Lady, I know the territory. I know that to take another route would be foolish. I know what I'm talking about."

His eyes were focused and steady but, she felt uneasy. Suddenly, Jessie didn't trust him, and she couldn't quite put the facts in order, but she didn't like what he said or the way he said it. He had another reason, and she had no wish to fall into a trap.

She inhaled sharply. She didn't want to deal with this. But she had to find another way or all would be lost.

"All right," she murmured.

He smiled, solicitously helping her into the lead wagon then Charity. "Good, now I can rest easy, Jessica. I'll trust that everything will turn out for the best."

She looked at him, her expression frozen. "I'll send a message when we're safe and the girls are placed in homes."

He nodded, smiling.

They were on their way, but not down the Columbia River as the sheriff had demanded.

~ * ~

Roc sat on his horse, listening to Trevor and Senator Drake inform him of all that had happened. "Found out Pierce had a shipment of Chinese women coming into Astoria. Said he intended to auction off each one and if he could, he'd cap the evening off with two white girls. No, you don't have to guess, you know. I imagine by now you've met Charity, and the white girls, Jessie and Charity. Pierce didn't like losing Charity in the first place then you married Jessie. There's a warehouse off 7th street, right on the river, perfect for unloading merchandise. The owner looks the other way. Of course, Pierce sees to it he doesn't go without a reward."

"When's the auction?" Roc demanded.

"If my informant was right, last night. I thought Drake and I could make it in time."

Trevor kept talking, but Roc's attention had drifted elsewhere.

A creak of a wagon and the low whinny of a horse, then a soft crooning whisper drifted from the bushes. Someone was hiding just off the road. Roc slowed and moved his horse toward the sounds. A small campfire glimmered in the clearing. He hesitated.

Long black hair caught his eye. He saw a woman dressed for the night and a long hard ride. Noticed a buckskin jacket, one he would recognize anywhere, because it was his.

"Son of a bitch..." he began.

Then he smiled. Jessie. He had found her quite easily. Remarkable. Skeptical, he started to dismount then swiftly changed his mind. He had worried about her for days now, ever since he ran into Trevor and Drake and found out the message he received hadn't come from them.

She had defied him, ignored his warning. If Pierce had found her...

He was going to put the fear of God into her. Damnation, the woman, what had she thought to do? Why in hell had she risked herself?

He gazed at Trevor who had just ridden up beside him, catching his first glance at the cozy little scene. "What do you make of this?" he asked Trevor. "I think I'd like to hog tie her." He dismounted then, moved silently toward the women.

"My sentiments exactly," Trevor said dryly.

Jessie cocked her head, listening, then shrugged and turned back to the fire, staring at the embers then the sky, pensively.

He came up behind her, one hand over her mouth, the other hard around her waist. She gasped, trying to scream, then she seemed to know who it was and she squirmed.

"Not this time, sweetheart. Don't fight me for it will go infinitely worse for you if you do. Remember the warning." He removed his hand from her mouth.

She froze, shivering. Chills swept through her. "I've done nothing wrong, she assured him.

He tightened his hold on her. "Ah, Jess Law, that's not the way I see it."

"I don't' care a fig what you think," she insisted.

"Jess, you will."

A twig snapped behind them. Roc loosened his hold, turning to see into the dark. Jessie whirled, determined to distance herself from him. The fire played across her face, illuminating its perfect features and alabaster skin.

"Charity," Trevor cried out.

"Hell," Roc cursed, sweeping her off her feet and hurdling across the Chinese women to set Jess down at the edge of the clearing. "Trevor! Drake!" he called out. They had ridden into the midst, heading toward the ambush that had awaited them. Roc drew his gun, a warning to those who circled the camp.

"The hell with the China dolls," someone cried out. Those two white girls are worth their weight in gold,"

"To hell with Pierce, we'll keep them for ourselves."

Two shots flashed and Roc hit the ground, rolling for cover. He looked for Trevor and Drake only to find himself pinned down by the crossfire. Roc shot wildly, hoping to cover Jessie, hoping she'd have the nerve to grab his horse and run. Charity cried out then he heard Jessie calling to her. Not again. Damn. She had caused this mess by striving to be something she wasn't, a man.

"Give it up," Roc cried in a harsh voice. "Your men will die, I assure you, if you don't."

"Ah, it's a joke," a man called. "There's only the three of them. Get 'em."

But fortunately for Roc the rest of the ruffians were not so bold. Suddenly, more men joined them.

"It's the sheriff and a posse." More shots echoed in the night. Drake was at his side, Jess Law behind him. He and Drake set up a rhythm, covering each other, bullets flying, and slowly, with the girls, backing their way to the horses.

"Go on, Newman. Get out of here," Clayton said.

From the shadows, he noticed a movement coming up behind. He whirled ready to fire.

But too late. Jess Law had sent her knife hurtling through the air straight to the man's heart.

Perhaps she was more adept than he had given her, his wife, credit for. She was a private investigator, Jess Law, P.I., and skilled. Roc didn't take anymore time. He grabbed Jess and ran.

A drop of rain touched his cheek. They had reached the road and the horses. He thrust Jessie strongly toward a tethered horse then shot one more time, turned and followed, determined not to admire his lady too much. He helped her on top of one of the extra horses, and they raced down the road, Charity and Trevor behind them. They had left the Chinese women behind, under Sheriff's Clayton's protection.

He didn't reign in until they were miles down the road and he had found a sheltered area approachable on only one side. A small cave wound its way into the cliff, offering shelter from the drizzle that had descended from the skies.

He leapt down from the horse then turned on Jessie. He glared at Drake, Trevor and Charity, silently announcing they stay clear of him for awhile.

When they were finally alone, "What the devil were you and Charity up too?" he demanded, stalking her, furious with the reciprocal glare in her gaze.

She pointed a finger at him and cursed under her breath. "I couldn't let them be sold."

"You wanted to see first hand what happened in a whore house? Well, be my guest. If those sailors had come a few minutes sooner, you wouldn't have any more questions."

She paled at that but wouldn't back down. "I would have defended myself. I am perfectly capable," she argued. "I've told you I have no qualms about using a gun, and I'm an expert shot. Charity has lined up several homes for the women to work in, and I think we can find some in Salem."

Roc laughed, a hollow bitter laugh. "How do you propose to get them there, sweetheart?"

"We have the wagons. The sheriff's men must have rounded up the sailors by now. We can go back and get them."

"Why?"

She straightened, indignant then furious with his assumption they would leave without the women.

"Why, Jessie?"

"Because they need me and Charity. Because the men won't know what to do with them, and if someone doesn't help them, they'll end up prostitutes despite all the trouble we went through to rescue them. I cannot let them be used. I saw my mother…"

He grabbed her shoulders, pulling her close. She shivered. "Jessie, you can not go back."

"I have to."

"No," he breathed. "You can not go back."

"I have no choice. They have done nothing to deserve the fate that could await them. I'll be careful, but I have to try to help. Do my part. I promised," she whispered, desperate to make him understand. "Roc, there was a baby." Tears shimmered like jewels in her amethyst eyes.

"I warned you, Jessica, and I meant every word. I'll go…baby?" he asked suddenly hearing her words. "Baby?"

"Yes."

"Jessie, don't push me. I'll go bring them back, the child, too, if that's what you want. Drake can come, but only if I have your promise to stay here with Trevor and Charity. Wait for me, please."

She thought a moment, turning her head to gaze at the stars. "Very well."

"Promise me, Jessie."

Frustration filled her voice but she vowed, gave him her solemn word. Trevor would take care of her. He was a good trustworthy man and her cousin.

"Come here," he said.

He pulled her into his arms for a fragile moment, feeling all her softness, inhaling the essence that was hers alone. Held her close, savoring the sweet memory of her then…

He let her go, walking to Trevor, interrupting the lecture he was in the middle of giving Charity. It almost made him laugh. He had heard himself say those same words time and again to Jessie. Trevor came when he motioned for him as did Drake. It took only a few minutes to explain the situation and to realize the foolishness of it, for the authorities would have already started back to Astoria.

Pierce and Rutgers were out there somewhere, revenge sweeter than ever, but he was leaving his wife with so little protection.

Despite his need for haste, he went back to Jessie. One last kiss, one more promise extracted from her and he could leave. Her eyes implored him, speaking of thoughts and possessions at the moment he would rather forget. Mysterious.

No, no mystery or magic. He loved her with all his heart. He had taken her innocence. Yet she had given back more than he could have ever dreamt possible. He had fallen into her web, spun happily around the length of her black tresses. The memory of her, the sweet tempest she evoked, would stay etched in his heart and soul.

"I won't be gone long," he said.

She touched his cheek then kissed him tenderly where he could still feel the print of her finger.

"Roc," she whispered softly.

"What, Jessica?"

She hesitated, gazing after him. "Nothing..."

He stared at her a moment, confused, then left her standing in the cave, watching. Trevor and Charity stood beside her, and she caught a last lingering glance of his back as he and Senator Drake rode back down the road.

Chapter Eleven

With no time to lose, Roc and Senator Drake set out to meet Sheriff Clayton and bring the Chinese women back to Jessica and Charity. It was a long ride, longer than either one of them had expected, but for once in his life, he gave free rein to his emotions and the well being of his horse, riding without thought.

When they reached the scene of the earlier ambush, there was no one about. Roc could see a few embers of the campfire still burning, but only a strange unearthly silence greeted them. He glanced at Drake, realizing a growing sense of foreboding had followed him since leaving Newport several days past. He inspected the clearing. It was empty, save for the coffee pot and cups littering the ground, dropped without a moment's thought when shots had unexpectedly rung hollowly at the campsite.

He dismounted, giving the reigns of his horse to Drake then searching the area for clues, evidence as to the direction the party assumed. Their tracks should have stood out, easy to find, but they didn't. By the time Roc picked up the trail, his emotions were ragged and on edge.

When he signaled to Drake to follow, he understood the gravity of the situation. He knew Trevor's feeling of betrayal somewhere in the ranks was not unfounded. Had the sailors who begun the ambush joined forces with the sheriff's men? Had they traveled together, following closely, waiting to spring the trap?

"How very clever," he told Drake, still wondering but losing no time in mounting his horse. He turned and started to walk the horses along the trail. Then he urged the horses faster, a horrible dread stealing into his soul.

He started to gallop then checked himself, cautiously thinking and remembering all that had gone on this night.

Drake rode abreast, appearing to study the man who had suddenly lost control then regained his equilibrium just as surprisingly. "You're a formidable foe indeed, Roc Newman. Perhaps I've underestimated you, hmm."

They had covered about a mile since their hasty start, and now Roc stopped and dismounted. He held a hand in the air, forewarning silence. He didn't need to do so. The wind whistled disconcertingly in the trees. On steady ground the two men moved silently through the forest, approaching the beach and the waves. Another ambush, Roc knew the signs. He was ready.

Drawing his gun, he started down the sand dunes, crouching low, motioning for Drake to follow. Slowly, and with the increased feeling of doom, he began moving. The ocean lulled and enticed, echoing a warning as the waves rolled across the sand. A shadow flitted across the moon, hovered a second before vanishing. Rain had given way to clear sky. He heard seagulls cry. Smelled the smoke of a campfire.

Moonlight illuminated a small circle of beach. His gun fell heavily to his side as all strength fled and he swallowed the fear threatening his soul. Fury seized his heart even as it pounded alarmingly and out of control. Rage stole his thoughts, and he stared unblinking at the small form sneaking across the beach.

No. She couldn't have. The thought and word compelled him silently forward, unthinking of the peril that waited, dangerous and close. No, how could she have beaten him here?

Jessie...

He cursed under his breath. Drake drew up alongside Roc. His hand rested lightly on his shoulder, holding him back. Drake's firm touch brought Roc's mind back to life. Roc dropped to the sand then rested, motionless watching the developing scene.

"How did she manage to get here ahead of us?"

Jessica darted between low rocks, sidestepping through the tide pools, impetuously endangering life and limb. She hesitated a moment, turned towards them, her chin defiantly proud, pointed haughtily in the air. She never looked more stubborn. Even from the distance separating them, he recognized the unholy glint in her eyes, the moonlight reflecting her determination. His heart leapt at the sudden realization she had just blundered inadvertently into the middle of the smugglers, pursuing them with determined menace. Bent on her crusade to right the world's wrong. With no doubt here, trickery was the game of the hour. And he had blundered heedlessly into the middle of it.

As had Jessica.

Impetuous Jessica, wild and untamed, reckless Jessica. He wanted to throttle her for racing into this, for not following his wishes. *How the devil did she get away from Trevor?* Hell, perhaps he didn't want to know. Then a force encompassed his soul, and he narrowed his eyes patiently waiting to see what would happen.

"My God, Drake," he whispered, "do you have any idea what this means? What betrayal is at hand?"

For the second time that night shots vibrated, creating tempest and chaos. Footsteps sliced the sand. Roc couldn't really hear but knew they came, vague shadows beneath the moonlight, vestige of an outline never clear but there; moving, rolling, rising up to shoot then surrounding. He watched Jessica. Roc prayed nothing would hit her. He should have made sure Trevor understood how determined she had become. He shouldn't have left her. Guilt curled within his soul in an anguished heap.

Suddenly, he realized he had left Trevor with two stubborn women. Trevor had managed well. Only one of them had escaped his attention. He wished there were not quite so many bullets flying and they were not so outnumbered. Wished also he knew friend from foe.

"Roc." It was Drake, speaking to him anxiously. "Riders over the next hill. Whose side do you think they are on?" The scattering of men and the subsequent lull in the battle gave clues, but neither Roc nor Drake was willing to chance anything in the darkness.

"Cover me. I'll get Jessie," Roc whispered.

Drake rolled to his knees beside him. "All right, but hurry. By thunder, she doesn't deserve this despite herself. Roc, you must save her," he groaned. "Roc, now, before it's too late. If you haven't noticed, the tides coming in; it's going to trap her. Someone wants to see her, or you, dead tonight."

"Quiet, Drake. Politicians..." Roc waved his hand in the air. "Has anyone told you, you talk too much?"

Roc didn't deny anything Drake had said, but he'd been intent on finding a way to get to Jessie without rushing heedlessly into a tempest of bullets. There wasn't. And the thought moved Roc to action. He crept forward slowly, belly sliding along the sand. Yes, he would keep her chained in safety when he got her home. Forever.

Yes, forever. He should have defied every principle he had and done that in the first place. He should have burned all her clothes; should have left her naked in his bedchamber so he could breathe. He should have sent Trevor in his place and stayed to guard Jessica and Charity then it would have been Trevor creeping along on his belly with the sand fleas biting him. But he wouldn't have realized how devilishly tricky his Jessie could behave.

Anguish doused his thoughts and harbored inside his gut. Jess, who had foolishly flung herself into an impossible play. Jessie, who had defied him at every turn. Jessica, who had wielded her way into his heart, into his soul. I will best you, she had warned him. I can beat you again. And she had done just that.

She had done that very thing, only she could not best Pierce and Rutgers on her own. She needed help. She needed him. She had dashed off after he had left somehow beguiling her cousin, and now she waited her fate. Or his. Because he doubted Pierce meant for her to die here. *Trevor needs you.* She'd said.

Then she'd gone the other way, to Astoria, heedless of the danger waiting.

Jessie. Ah, no, just when he'd believed in her promise. And now he could just make out the silhouette of a ship on the horizon.

"Roc, hurry," Drake cried again.

Roc surged forward, dodging driftwood and the sting of sand where misdirected bullets landed. Jessica's soft hair highlighted by the moon drew his attention. A bullet creased his arm. He had to make it, had to save her. She struggled frantically through the tide pools. Her feet slipped and she clung tenaciously to the slippery rocks, finally scrambling back to her feet, crouched low and running toward him. God, but she still didn't need him.

"Hurry. Run. Roc, Jessie!" Drake's cries pierced his subconscious.

Roc grabbed Jessie and pulled. She collapsed in a whimpering pile, unable to move. With a gallant gesture he hadn't felt until he heard her soft cry, he swept her into his arms and ran. They reached Drake, running hard.

Drake fell in behind, firing a round of bullets into the air.

"Stop shooting at shadows and run, Senator."

But they had scarce left the beach behind when they heard the fierce pounding of hooves, men coming at them from all directions save one. Roc mounted quickly then helped Jessica mount behind him. He headed south, disappearing into the darkness of the forest. He didn't know who was behind this, but he meant to discover the truth, as soon as he had Jessica and Charity safe, locked away, where they could create no more havoc.

But Drake was right. Now was the time to run, and he would have to send Drake and Jessica on ahead while he sent the men following on a wild chase through the Oregon wilderness.

He allowed the senator to come even with them. "If we can't lose them soon, I want you to take Jessie with you," he said over the thunder of the hooves. Jessica flinched within his arms and he realized he knew what she thought of the idea. Well, she didn't have a choice this time. "Go, the second I hand Jessie over to you, and tie her if you have to. Just make sure the knots are secure."

"There is no need for that." The muffled exchange rumbled across his back. "I'd never leave you."

"I know. I've learned the hard way. If it weren't for your machinations, I wouldn't have found myself in a hail of bullets tonight. Twice," he reminded her. "You will do this, or I swear..." he paused for breath. "Jessie, these girls are lost to us. You did your best but you can't change their fate, just go home to Salem, with Drake, and wait for me there."

Jessica started to protest, but Pierce's men were gaining on them, and he turned his attention to winding deftly through the forest trails.

"There they are!" someone cried. "After them. The captain promised a hefty reward for their hides, dead or alive."

"By thunder," Drake breathed.

"Go." Roc cried and the race continued. Through the forest, winding its way ever closer to Charity and Trevor. Roc must have known the pursuit had vanished for the moment. They had succeeded, gained a small measure of respite. At least he thought he would have time to send the rest of them on their way before he went after Raymond Pierce.

Then, once again, he gave his horse free reign. He pulled Jessica close, embracing her softness. Drake followed.

They rode on, the sun beginning to find its way above the eastern horizon. A soft veil of colors insinuated itself along the Coast Range. The cave where Trevor and Charity had stayed was in front of them, the ocean on their left and the mountains on their right.

~ * ~

"Good God, Pierce. That man can ride." One of the sailors whispered, searching the forest for a trace of the man. "The rumors must be true. He must have ridden with the Comanche."

"Hmph," Pierce declared, turning his mount toward the coastline and his waiting ship. He glared at the man beside him and began the journey back, empty handed and thoroughly frustrated.

Another loss at the hands of Roc Newman and he didn't like it, but at the moment there was little he could do about it. His timely escape now was at the forefront of his mind. Things could be worse, he thought grimly. At least he had retrieved his cargo and cut his losses. As he stared out at the ship, he laughed softly. Ah, he suspected he would meet the intrepid Roc Newman sooner than he planned. For it wasn't like the man to let anything go unfinished. He hoped Jessica would still be Newman's constant companion.

He dismounted and watched the loading of his cargo.

"What about Roc and Jessica Newman?" Rutgers asked, appearing suddenly at Pierce's side. "Should we go after them?"

"No," Pierce said smoothly, rubbing his chin. "I believe he will come to us and with him Jessica will fall handily into our schemes."

"Do you..." Rutgers began then stopped himself. "Yes, yes, I suppose you do have a point."

"Of course, I could be wrong, but it doesn't matter now. The tide will be going out in a few hours, and we're sailing with or without Roc and Jessica. Don't forget Lilly's still in business in Salem. For now, I've sent a few men ahead to keep up the search."

"But isn't that a bit risky?"

"Perhaps, but I like the odds. And Rutgers, I never gamble unless there is no risk."

"Indeed, Pierce."

~ * ~

Trevor had spent most of the night pacing and yelling at Charity. He wanted to ring her fragile little neck for the part she played in Jessie's escape. He could picture so many horrible things happening, and he didn't like to think of Roc's reaction when he found Jessie, and Roc would find her. He didn't doubt that for one moment.

Then, too, he could see Jessica rushing headlong and recklessly into the fray. Jessica would attempt to pull off the rescue by herself. And she would find trouble. Jessica always did and seemed to have become worse since she took on the persona of Jess Law.

Pierce could not best Roc. He was certain of it, at least not when there were no other factors to distract him. And, he admitted gingerly, Jessica was a disrupting factor. So, he would protect her at the expense of his life. But perhaps not, Roc was intelligent and capable; a man of wit and daring. Pierce was never alone and so, Roc would guard against an ambush, unless something preoccupied him.

He couldn't keep thinking about it. He should have followed Jessica.

He picked up a canteen of water and drank from it. All the while he glared at Charity. He wanted to blame her for this misadventure but didn't dare. In truth, he had no one to blame but himself and his inattention to his zealous cousin. He leaned against the cliff, trying to relax. But he could not.

He pounded his hand hard against the rocks and began to pace again.

Finally, impatience and frustration caused him to stop. He strode to Charity, brushing an errant lock of hair away from her face. He had tied and gagged her, and now he regretted his hotheaded decision, but he realized even then she had given him no other choice. Pierce had hurt Charity, subjecting her to fear and rape so cruelly, but she had hidden the pain well, conquering her insecurity and terror, vowing she would do everything in her power to keep others from the same fate. And Jessica had joined Charity in the crusade against her husband's wishes.

But now Roc was involved. And someone had betrayed them.

He hunched down next to Charity; he closed his eyes, allowing a moment of reflection. Charity had fallen asleep despite the night and the risks.

Unannounced, Roc, Drake and Jessica walked silently into this sanctuary he had created. Trevor stood, waiting for words, the incriminations to fly, but Roc said nothing for a long moment. He held Jessie in his arms, tenderly but the rigid set to his lips belied the mood. Roc stopped mid-stride, "Give me a moment."

Trevor and Drake watched with nothing to say. They both nodded.

~ * ~

"Jessica," he whispered, his voice deep. They were far into the cave, a private place; he knew no one would intrude except for an emergency.

He set her down. She backed away, hesitant, unsure of herself, yet anxious to make him understand. "Please," she murmured, wrapping her arms around herself, for security, not warmth then rubbing her arms as if she were really cold. She was so worried about what he might say or do she never realized he hadn't moved.

"You were expecting me to greet you with a smile on my face and open arms?" he queried at last.

"I...well, no, but..."

"Oh, yes, my love, you did. You see nothing untoward with what you just did," he told her.

She shivered. "No, I only did what I thought right, but I do understand the danger."

"Oh, yes, what you thought. Did you truly think, Jessica? Or did you run off wildly believing nothing could happen to you? Do you have any idea what kind of position you put the senator and myself in? Jessica, we were forced to defend you when you should have been safe in Trevor's protection. That should have never happened."

She closed her eyes against the anguish she felt, the terror she remembered, willing it all away but it wouldn't go. She couldn't forget. "All right. No, I don't believe any of us are immortal, including you. I didn't think I would run into an ambush. I thought the sheriff had rescued the Chinese women, and I didn't want to leave them with men. I didn't know. And I don't trust Clayton." she shivered, wondering at the fire in his gaze. She stepped back, distancing herself from the fury she saw and suddenly painfully aware he might never forgive her. And perhaps she didn't deserve his forgiveness. She had put them all in danger.

"Ah, Jess! Jessie...Jessica."

Swiftly, he pulled her to him, one hand encircling her wrist and his other resting on her hip. She looked away, unable to meet his eyes. His lip curled in a smile, but it terrified her. "Jessica," he whispered. The back of his hand moved to caress her cheek as if to memorize. He held her chin, tipping it back, feathering a kiss across her lips. Then his hand fell against the leather of her jacket, his fingers delving inside to the softness he had come to know so well and he caressed tenderly the fullness he found there. Surprised, Jessie cried out, a soft sob caught his attention, and he stopped his quest for a moment. But he seemed a man who would not be deterred.

He couldn't. He pushed her away. His breath ragged and barely controlled. His eyes narrowed, and oh, the silver glint froze. It seemed so cold.

"I promise," he murmured. "After all of this, you did not think I could do it alone. You could not trust me to bring the baby back and so you found a away to break another solemn vow. I swear, Jessie, you are your own worst enemy. Nine lives, though, you've about used them all."

"But, Roc, I..."

Escape was impossible. He pulled her to him again, catching her shoulders. "What does it take to penetrate your mind?"

"I don't know what you mean," she said, terrified that perhaps she understood all too well what he intended. Despite what Roc thought, she had never forgotten his warnings. His words were soft, very soft. So tender and gentle but they held a power all their own. "Don't..."

"Don't what, my dear?" he asked. "I want you to understand what will happen to you when we return. I want you to comprehend that I will have a terrible time trusting you. I want you to grasp the notion you will no

longer break promises to me. The chance to prove yourself has vanished."
His hand fell over her breast again, molding it, the fingers shaking but
caressing her erotically, seducing, claiming possession. "I want you to
understand you won't jeopardize your life. I need you in one piece, alive and
well."

He had backed her against the wall of solid rock. Moisture trickled
down the cave, soaking the back of her jacket and shirt. She gasped, still
stunned. She had been too mesmerized by the haunted look within his gaze
to fight him at first, but now she felt a tremendous indignation take hold of
her. How dare he assume such things? How dare he take control of her very
existence? Dash it all, but she wouldn't allow it. She had done nothing
wrong, a little foolish, but nothing wrong and he would understand.

"Roc, stop this, let me go. Please. You have to... When I was a child
my mother was raped. I watched…" Tears welled in her eyes.

"I don't know what to say, but it changes nothing," he said. She
tensed abruptly, trying to fight her emotions, wishing she could make him
understand. Impossible.

"Roc, you cannot, there is no time for games."

"This is not a game." He leaned into her, his gaze penetrating hers,
commanding. The long muscled bulk of his body pressed against her.

"Roc, stop..."

"Jessica." His power and great strength forced her to listen. "You
have to stop putting your life on the line. If not for me, for the possible child
you might carry right now," he whispered. Still, his fingers delved through
her hair. They fell to circle her neck. "What should I do with you, pray tell?
Ah, sweetheart, I want you. I want you alive and hot to warm my nights and
bedevil my days. I want the magic and the mystery that is so much a part of
you. But I will not spend hours on end worrying about you, rescuing you,
and I would expect you to keep the vows you have made. I would let you
continue with your investigations if you could keep the danger at bay. I'd
put your childhood nightmares to rest, if I could."

"I would like to believe you." She regained her courage, pressing
against his chest, imploring him to give her room to breathe. "I only said I
would love and honor."

"But sweetheart," he persisted, "those weren't the vows. I heard everything."

"No, dash it all, Roc, no...I didn't and I won't."

His mouth descended, soft at first and filled with the longing his fear had created. Her fingers splayed against his heart, pushed but suddenly began a rhythm of their own. She wanted to fight him again, but her body denied her, protested her reasons, yearned for his kiss. It was an unbroken seal of all that had gone on before and the promise of the future. He held her as if he would never let her go. Felt the gentle tremor of her body as she surrendered to him, inhaled the soft clean scent that always managed to entice him. His mouth molded over hers again. His tongue teased and delved, tasted the innocence only he knew. She prayed he'd understand, and perhaps he didn't want her to change but to stop risking herself. The kiss was achingly seductive, too short but sweeter than heaven. It lasted forever but not long enough. He drew away to study the woman he had called an accident.

Her fingers were still nestled against his chest, but her head had fallen back and her hair cascaded down her back. He ran his fingers through it, and she reveled in the feel of his hands sliding through her hair. She felt a strange menacing harbinger of the future and wondered desperately what he truly felt for her. And his words echoed in her mind. *Regrettable accident.* She tried again to resist the seducing touch that robbed her of logic.

His fingers left her hair; groped to capture her bottom in his hands and pulled her against his erection. He groaned, cursing her clothes, fumbling with the opening to her Levis. It wasn't enough. She wanted him to sheathe himself within her.

She whimpered softly against his throat. She tried to pull herself closer to him, savor the security and protection he offered. It was not her desire to provoke him or put herself in dangerous situations. They just seemed to happen before she could do anything to change them. He gave up the pretense, pulling her clothes from her body until he pinned her naked against the rocks, his own pants undone to allow him access. She moaned deep in her throat when he slipped swiftly inside. He clung to her, seeming desperate to possess and to control. Roc's kiss seemed surprisingly tender, yet growing more urgent and demanding with each passing moment. She felt the passion and the fire slowly consume her.

His lips continued their assault, exploring her mouth, her throat, the fullness of her breasts until they lavished the tips. She wanted him, burned for him, even though with each coupling, his command over her increased, and she found it hard to deny him that which he expected. A sob escaped her for she wanted him now, recklessly, wildly. Her mind and soul warred against his invasion, but her heart won each battle. Sweet wildfire, bold tempest, the magic churned, hurtling in upon her as the tides crashed upon the sand, holding her swirling, eddying, terrifying. She could drown in this, his seduction, before he would ever love her. He cried out her name then stiffened, pushing so very deep, so close to her heart, reaching it, and she shattered into a thousand tiny pieces. She began to shiver with the furious spasm of her climax, a point of no return, and she wanted to cry out that he didn't love her and this shouldn't happen. But she didn't.

The back of his hand brushed her cheek. Felt the tear. Then he rested his head against the cold rock behind her, a fierce contrast to his heated skin. He righted his clothing and began to sort through her own, handing them to her one at a time.

Then he turned his back on her. Abruptly vulnerable, cold, forsaken, Jessie cursed softly, watching him walk away from her. She wanted to reach out. Stop him. Tell him she loved him and she'd do everything he asked. But she watched and followed behind him.

He stopped, the opening of the cave framing him boldly. He turned to look at her, "Jessie, I'm beginning to understand your motives. I wish I could make you see, comprehend, perhaps even proceed with a little reason, but I know you, know you won't. You race blindly into everything. I don't know what to do." He hesitated, staring into the blackness and beyond. Waves lapped at the beach. The night seemed so calm, too calm. His senses, alerted he turned back to her.

Astonished, Jessie came to him, rested a hand against his back. Her sense of impending danger magnified. She hugged the buckskin jacket close, surprised at his realization. Her heart warmed.

"I have to follow my conscience. Before God, I couldn't live with myself if I didn't. Truly, I don't mean to defy you or anger you I..." Tears stung her throat and eyes. Her hand stifled a sob tearing from her throat. "I can only try. And I wouldn't have promised if you hadn't made me, Roc. My word is good when it's given freely." She choked back her fear and listened to the calling of the winds and the earth. The land seemed to have a language all its own. "Now what? What is happening out there? Are you leaving?"

He hadn't moved. "I have some business. Besides, I believe we'll have company soon. You, Trevor, Drake, Charity have to go before they arrive."

"Go where?"

He whirled, suddenly all his patience with her vanished. "Pierce has sent men to find you...me...he won't stop until he is dead or in prison."

"More men?" Jessie gasped, her face suddenly ashen.

"Yes, Jess, you have provoked him beyond patience and set something in motion that might be impossible to stop."

"And you..."

"What do you think? I'm going after them. You started this, now I'll finish it aboard that ship. I thought the most foolish thing you'd ever do was scale my house as if you were climbing Mt. Everest. But I was the fool."

She began to understand the ominous feelings clouding her thoughts. She had, in truth begun this, and he intended to finish it. But she couldn't allow that. She had to think of someway to help without landing in harm's way again.

And he meant to join Pierce and Rutgers on the ship. Oh, God, how could he. No, she was wrong. He didn't stand a chance if he invaded Pierce's territory.

Coldness transcended and wrenched her heart.

She had recklessly followed Charity into a dangerous intrigue. She had urged restraint but instead acted carelessly. She had endangered Roc.

Her stubborn mind was beginning to work. He believed she would placidly go with Trevor. What he didn't know wouldn't hurt him. He thought she would let him sail with those men, alone. That she would abandon him.

"What do you want me to do?" she asked. "I'll do anything you--"

~ * ~

But he stopped her, wouldn't let her commit another lie by omission or otherwise. He didn't want to hear a promise she wouldn't keep. He didn't want to hope she would be safe in Salem. Instead, he wanted to know he had kept her from danger.

Suddenly, he swept her from her feet and carried her to her horse. He'd tied the reigns to Trevor's horse, and he quietly but very efficiently tied Jess Law, P.I. to her horse. She wasn't going anywhere without Trevor. Charity and Drake were mounted and on their way. Trevor followed, leading a furious little bundle of wildfire through the woods.

Roc smiled.

The sound of hoof beats grew, coming steadily closer. Harder, racing, menacing and Roc hurtled himself onto his horse. It reared, pawing the air then landed hard on the earth.

Horse and rider burst through the trees.

Roc yelled, a fierce Comanche war cry shattering the early morning dawn. Seagulls rose into the wind, lending their lament to the sunrise. Roc turned his horse along the beach, running north against the wind.

He lunged savagely away from the beach. His horse's hooves pounded the shale and the mud, groping higher and into the forest once again. The whine of bullets and the screech of men became a terrible discord as Roc evaded missiles pummeling his way. He swerved into a small opening, slipped inside then through the rock to the other side before picking up his pace. They fell back, unaware of the path he had taken.

One of the men hollered an oath, cursing him for a devil as he managed to lose them one more time.

He prayed the knots he'd tied Jessie with had held. Prayed too, Trevor would not relent and untie her until they reached Salem.

He hesitated, looking back once more to see if he was followed. No one appeared. He saluted them, mumbled then dismounted.

Roc rummaged through his saddlebags, swiftly finding the clothes he sought, changed and with a quick swipe to his horse's hindquarters, sent him on his way.

~ * ~

Days later, traveling cautiously, the small party reached Salem.

Several of Roc's men had joined them on route, and so the ride home was safe and pleasant, if one could discount the worry. Roc had done the unthinkable, she realized, he had thrown himself into danger just as he rebuked her for doing the same.

Trevor babied her. Guilt, she knew, plagued him the entire trip back. He kept her tied just as Roc had insisted and had seen she arrived at their home without a scratch but securely bound. It was too late now to go back for him. The ship would have sailed hours ago, with Roc aboard.

They would recognize him.

He didn't stand a chance. And what would he do in the middle of the Pacific Ocean, swim for shore?

He would die and she would be alone.

He had to come back to her, if only so she could tell him she loved him. She did love him as surely as the sun rose each morning.

Now she might not have the chance, and it was all because he had so little faith she could handle her job. No, he never really looked at her and what she could do. He just always assumed she needed protection. So he took it upon himself to fight her battles.

But she had fallen into the trap at the end. If he hadn't come along and discovered her, she would have found herself on the ship instead.

There would be more smuggling, more slavery, and auctions.

"He will be fine," Trevor's soft voice floated through her reverie. He lifted her from the horse and carried her inside, knowing she could hardly stand, let alone walk.

He was in terrible trouble. She could feel it deep inside her, his pain and anguish. It was cold so very cold and not even the warm drink Trevor placed in her hands could warm her.

She would go back to Astoria.

She would interrupt the auctions; free the women held as slaves. She wouldn't allow this to continue. She would find a way to save them. It would become her crusade as Roc had labeled it.

But not tonight or tomorrow. She had plans to make, nothing reckless, or wild. Not again. She would fight and she would win, but she wouldn't let her own impetuous nature put anyone in danger.

It left her astonished, this sudden declaration to herself, but it did nothing to fill the empty void in her heart. Only Roc could do that, and he wasn't here.

"He did it for me. He was afraid," she told Trevor.

Charity came to her. Knelt down beside her and spoke softly. "Yes, Jessie, but you and I, we can make it all worthwhile. Perhaps we can make amends for what we caused. I want to go back."

"Yes," she whispered, determined and with right on her side.

"Good, then we are united in this," she said. Charity rose and walked to Trevor. She touched his arm tenderly then left the room, head lowered.

Jessie gazed out the window, west, to the ocean and Roc. She stiffened, her eyes narrowed and she made a vow.

A promise she would keep to herself.

Chapter Twelve

In some curious manner this all seemed preordained. Always controlled and well planned. He had indeed never entered into anything with such wild reckless abandon as he did this venture. A fitting climax to an otherwise restrained, albeit unpredictable life. Although exciting, this was not his modus operandi.

Ah, but he knew who worked this way. Jess Law. Jessie, somehow she had worked her wiles on him, insinuating herself into his soul, becoming a part of him, and she had embedded herself in his heart. Now to learn she had embellished her outlandish behavior into his mind. She was a menace and had in a few short weeks fragmented his life into a million tiny pieces.

This felt as if he had thrown himself into the Columbia River in January. His blood froze, his flesh broke out in goose bumps, his body shivered, and he knew a sense of exhilaration beyond imagination. But with the changing of the seasons, he'd forget the elation. The consistency of his life would return, and Jessica Lawrence would remain an unanswered mystery.

A shout from the workers below brought him from his nostalgic dalliance. Then all the fear and danger of the night came rushing back, presenting itself with a clarity he didn't want to examine. He knew the hazard. Saw the need to hide within shadows obscurely until the proper moment presented itself. Heard the commands he would have to obey in order to keep his real identity in tact.

He hailed the men as if he knew them, began to work with a lazy diligence, just enough to keep anyone from singling him out, but not enough to raise suspicion among the crew.

Someone was talking to him. Cursing the captain and the dandies who would sail with every luxury while they spent their time below. Quarters, dingy, suffocating and dirty were all they would know until they put into port again. No loyalty existed among these men, and Roc stored the knowledge furtively.

"Move along, now, the captain don't like no sluggards. If you know what I mean."

"Aye, I know," Roc replied, wondering what sort of man the captain was.

Roc followed the movement of the crew, studying each one and labeling them for future reference. Despite his earlier musing that he acted precipitously, he didn't. Every move he made now, he carefully calculated and manipulated to his advantage. He kept at his task. Felt the heavy cask boring into his shoulder. It was a smuggling boat, with a cargo that needed selling. But the destination, where would they head? Seattle? Victoria? The Yukon? All were promising sights for the sale of this delectable and profitable cargo.

If he were a gambling man, he'd wager on the Yukon.

Alaska was lawless and primitive still, despite the rapid influx of men and women. And there was gold.

"Aye, it's best you don't get on his wrong side. He's a mean one, he is. My name's Jake, what's yours? Don't believe I've seen you around." He stared at Roc. His frown deepened as if he pondered his statement. His brow furrowed deeply then he grinned, extending his work-worn hand.

"Billy," Roc said with no hesitation, but he ignored the welcoming hand. "My name's, Billy."

"So, Billy, what brings you here, or did the captain shanghai you too?" Jake was a young man, twenty or so. He was dark and almost too good-looking for his position. A deep scar slashed his cheek. A solid white line delineated it, glaring blatantly against his bronze flesh.

"No, I volunteered," Billy said.

"Maybe you're a fool," Jake studied Roc again, delving into his head as if he could read his mind. "Don't look like a Billy either," he said frankly. "You runnin' from the law?" His probing questions unnerved Roc, and he tensed suddenly.

Yes, Jess Law perhaps, any man would run from her, but she wasn't the law. He paused, adjusted the cask on his shoulder. "Maybe it's none of your business. If you want to live a long healthy life, I'd suggest you keep your questions and assumptions to yourself."

"Oh, that's how it is, is it? I think you should tread carefully, friend. You don't look like one of us, never will, I'd wager a guess on that," Jake said, still studying Roc, and his frown grew.

"I think you're probably right," Roc said slowly. His harsh tone set Jake back a step but undaunted, Jake continued to study Roc. "Maybe you should learn not to be so perceptive. You might regret what you uncover."

Jake roared with laughter. "Nah, I don't think so."

"You don't, do you?" Roc queried amused at the man's sense of humor and his audacity.

"No, that is the thought. You're more than meets the eye, and that's a fact."

"How about a little trust?"

"Around here, a little goes a long way, if you catch my drift," Jake said.

Roc nodded and prayed he wasn't about to make an unholy alliance with this man, an alliance that would cause more harm than good, but a friend aboard this vessel wouldn't hurt. Yet when the first set of hands fell upon his shoulders, it didn't surprise him. He wrenched away and turned just in time to see three men jump Jake before a fist smashed into Roc's belly. A friend, perhaps, but it wouldn't help.

"Son of a bitch!" Roc cried out, doubling over with the pain, desperate for air.

"Damnation!" Jake rejoined, incensed. He struggled next to Roc with several men holding his arms and another taking his turn upon him. "I'll see you rot for this, I will."

He hadn't gambled and lost with this man. Indeed Jake's friendship might well cost Jake his own life. Ironic it had come to this so soon. He had thought it would take at least a day before Pierce discovered him. When had he become so predictable?

Before he met Jess Law, it seemed, before she'd influenced him and she had come to prove to him her wild reckless behavior could reap enchanting benefits.

He tried to roll. The men holding him wouldn't allow it. The fist cracked his ribs then his nose. Another punch caught his back.

Oh, God. He hadn't planned for this. Jesus, but he needed time to think.

"Slow down, mates, Captain doesn't want him dead. At least not yet, Pierce told the captain, he wants this mate to suffer. Has a grudge to settle with him, he does."

Before blackness could overwhelm Roc, the beating stopped. He heard Jake's groan and knew he'd fared no better.

As Jake fell at his feet, silence suddenly prevailed. Roc raised his swollen lids and watched the captain of the ship and Pierce. They stood at the railing, overseeing the crew. Then Roc slipped to his knees.

He tried to stand. They had hammered his body unmercifully. This was a small price to pay, a brief dark hour in his quest.

"Bring him aboard," Roc heard the faint echo of sound, felt callused hands carry him, and heard the water lap against the boat. It was Pierce. He'd played into his hands, rushed swiftly into another ambush. Pierce had expected him, and he'd unthinkingly obliged.

"Well, this was easier than I thought it would be," Rutgers turned to Pierce, grinning madly, then looked to the captain. A blond, fair-haired man acknowledged Rutgers with a grimace of dislike. Roc saw the brief exchange. His head was pounding. He fell back into the bottom of the boat, sinking into sublime darkness.

Later, he opened his eyes cautiously. Someone had tossed him into a tiny cabin. Sunlight filtered gingerly through a small round window. He groaned and held his throbbing head in his hands.

"So, Roc, you've awakened from the dead? I've waited many years for this moment."

Roc stonewalled his adversary. The quiet encompassed the room and Roc took pleasure in Pierce's growing agitation. "Oh? So, you think you've won the war? Well, Pierce, don't become too complacent. You never know when the tides of fortune will reverse themselves."

"Hmm... I don't see a great deal to worry myself over now. Do you?

Besides, I will rather enjoy watching you humbled."

Roc's eyes glinted, silver cold, and deadly. Pierce stepped back, hesitant until he remembered the power he held over this man. "It doesn't matter."

Pierce hovered, smiling then shaking his head. The man continued to astonish him. Roc realized men stood behind him, waiting for Pierce's command. Pierce's men, not the crew of the ship, he noticed.

Pierce moved forward again, coming close, standing over him. He tapped his finger against his chin, the smile widening with each beat. "So, you don't believe I hold sway over what happens to you here, but you will learn soon enough."

Roc's features froze; he betrayed nothing. "No," he finally offered, calmly breaking the penetrating quiet of the room and the unearthly stillness.

"You are afraid of nothing?"

"No."

"Then you are a fool, no smarter than the rest of your kind."

"What did you do with Jake?" Roc's mind still bent on obtaining information, and now retribution for the beating.

Pierce smiled icily. "He is sleeping in the hold, shackled to the walls, where you will join him soon. So, what should I do with the two of you?"

Roc laughed. "It seems, whatever you wish. Although the captain of the ship may have other ideas."

"But the captain has no say over me. I own him and his crew. Besides, they have committed themselves too deeply to back out and take pity on a poor unfortunate soul such as yourself."

"Throw him into the sea for the sharks," one of the men suggested. "He is a risk to us and this venture even if you keep him in shackles for the journey."

"But I don't wish to deprive myself of the pleasure of watching him waste away. Life on a ship can be hard work. Don't you agree, Rutgers?" Pierce asked, resuming his previous position at least a body length from Roc. "He has annoyed me to no end with his constant attempt to interrupt my business. Then his wife, yes, Jessica Lawrence..."

"Newman. Her name's Newman now." Roc cut in hoarsely.

"Ah, yes...well, she has been trouble from the first moment she swept into town. And of course there's his father-in-law, I have a score to settle with him also." He smiled, leaning close to Roc. "Roc Newman can repay me with hard work on this ship. With shackles on his feet and wrists, and he will do it willingly." Pierce raised a questioning eyebrow. "If not then there are worse fates that could wait for him."

Pierce backed away from the feral gleam in Roc's gaze. The anger and the fury radiating from him seemed to give Pierce a moment's pause. But Pierce's men outnumbered Roc.

He had acted foolishly. Now he would pay the price.

"Put him in the hold next to the man he called Jake," Pierce commanded. "Take him and shackle him, secure him well. He is as wily as the devil himself. So don't take any chances."

Pierce's men set upon him, dragging him from the room until they could drop him unceremoniously into the hold. He fought though, with the little strength he could muster. He thought at least one rib had broken in the scuffle, and in the end they subdued him. It seemed the fall into the hold was endless. But when he regained his senses, he found he had joined Jake, his shirt now ripped open.

His mouth was dry from lack of water. The inquisition had lasted a long time. He had to find a way out of this. But at the moment no ideas came to mind. His body drained of energy, slumped against the wall. He reminded himself just before drifting off to the blackness again Pierce had only won a battle, not the war.

With each fantasy drifting through his mind, he remembered Jessica. Understood her determination to save a few wretched souls. For indeed, if there was ever a wretched soul in need of saving, he was one.

Jessie...

Dreams rushed through his black thoughts. He didn't remember them all. But many were vivid and menacing. He slept on; finally his thoughts drifted into sweet oblivion. A hazy fog surfaced, where he had no thought, no dreams, no fantasies of rescue.

The dreams turned inward and his fantasies seemed real enough to touch, to caress. He reached out his hand to test the length of black hair shimmering before him and mocked him with its proximity. He imagined mercurial amethyst eyes beckoning seductively.

Jessica? Jessie, is that you? For he could see black hair, so real, so close but always too far away to feel, she turned and he wondered that he could have ever doubted his imagination. Jessica, intriguing, fragile...mortal. Jessie with her impish look and her wild nature. Vulnerable.

Jessie, turning away from him, furious with him for protecting her. Furious that he could not understand her need for independence.

"I'll best you again and again and again..."

She had succeeded. Bested him. Pierce had been ready for him, expecting him no less. Had she planned this? Of course not.

Jessie...

He had no way to find her. He had never felt so frustrated and helpless, damned for not following his own advice.

Jessie walked out of his mind, fading into the lonely fog encompassing him. The cold that surrounded him then the heat and still he slept, unable to revive himself.

The fog and the mist cleared, and he looked into a penetrating light.

He had reached a turning point. The images he had seen brought him to a new sense of awareness, an understanding of life and the real promise of death for him and for Jessie. Perhaps she was right. Perhaps he had thought himself immortal. In the end it would make no difference. If anything, this new realization made him more determined to protect Jessie.

At all cost he would keep her from harm. Soon, he would find a means to get off the ship. But as rational thought returned and his visions cleared, he could feel cold steel surrounding his wrists and his ankles. Felt the raw edge of it where it bit into his flesh. Smelled the stench of sweat and days of hard work gone uncleansed. Bile rose to his throat but he fought it.

He opened his eyes, slowly at first, adjusting to the dim light filtering through the open door.

Someone had betrayed them all.

Words floated in and out through his exhausted mind. *I'll best you again...*

And she had. He'd fallen for the ambush. He'd ridden hard to secure himself this place in hell. He wondered again if she had betrayed him.

Once, she had worked for Pierce. Ah, the crime then the punishment, but she hadn't sent him to Pierce. Who else but Jessie, who had insisted so vehemently she could do the job herself?

~ * ~

"We've reached the end, I believe. No one wants them. At least not for respectable jobs." Charity said. She'd spent hours on the ledgers and the placement of the Chinese girls they had managed to grab from the cribs and a few shipments that had come into Astoria. Charity had managed to track some of the sales to a number of well-known brothels in Portland. Then there was Lilly's place. She knew Lilly bought women, but they had no proof.

Jessie, still furious with Roc for sending her off tied on the fool horse then racing into... What? Certain danger aboard Pierce's ship?

She cursed him even while she wasted away to nothing with worry. She felt sure Pierce had set a trap. Roc was so predictable Pierce must have known he would come. And she hadn't heard from him. Didn't know if he lived. All this time and she couldn't forget him and her love for him.

He had not trusted her.

She and Charity had slowly pieced together the puzzle of that night. The sheriff...the raid...and the blunders. Sheriff Clayton's deputy was on Sterling Rutgers' pay role. At first she had cursed Roc's stupidity, then the fear for his life penetrated deep and hard, as well as the anguish. He had left her believing she had only thought to best him. Perhaps he even thought she had betrayed him to Pierce.

Not once had he accepted her abilities, her strengths and weakness. He left thinking the worst of her. Oh...yes, she was furious with him. She wanted him to walk in that door right now so she could tell him what she thought. But no one knew where he was. Rumors abounded, some said the ship had sailed north. God, how she missed him.

Now she was determined to establish herself, her career, to show him she could manage without his protection. Eight girls would arrive tomorrow from Astoria. Charity was busily making the arrangements. They would take them on two wagons to Jacksonville. James Lawrence had arranged households for them. But that was it. If there were anymore, they wouldn't know where to give these girls homes. Charity had put her heart and soul into this, and when she looked up from her work, her frowning countenance sobered Jessie's thoughts immediately. "Jessica?"

"I don't have any ideas, Charity, short of bringing them all here," she said. "If we bought a house ourselves, perhaps teach each one a trade and the language. But I'm not sure."

She turned back to the ledgers again. Her pencil hovered curiously over the numbers. Charity could be unnerving, pacifying when she chose. Yet underneath was a strong will, stubborn and defiant. All the while agreeing with the opponent before turning to choose her own path. She was a true diplomat, a politician hidden within an alluring feminine form. "You have money for that?" she asked Jessie.

She did. After all of this, she had access to Roc's huge accounts, but she felt strangely reluctant to touch them. It didn't seem right she should take his money after proclaiming her independence so thoroughly. When he returned, it would give him one more thing to hold over her head.

"No, not enough for that. Very few people will hire a female private investigator. Not even another woman."

Charity appeared to have known the answer but it had seemed logical to ask. One never knew, and she had been wrong before. Roc had money, but the amount eluded most and she had known it was substantial by the expression on Jessie's face when she'd first seen the account. It came as no surprise that Jessica Lawrence Newman didn't see fit to use her husband's money.

"Ah, yes, prejudice still runs rampant here. An honest day's work should pay the same for man or woman. Now, that's a novel idea, and I doubt it will come about any time soon." Charity sat back, relaxing against the solid strength of the chair. "There is nothing else we can do, Jessica."

"But there has to be," she told Charity. "We can not give this up."

"I'm open to suggestions," she said flatly then she nodded. "Jessica, you know I won't quit. It's not in me to quit. Perhaps if I hadn't experienced their fate first hand." She shrugged. "Then there is Roc. If he's still alive, we have to assume somehow he has managed to stay in contact with Pierce and Rutgers without putting himself in danger. Rest assured they will return."

Fury welled within her. Jessie had cursed and paced, and she had lain awake nights dreaming of Roc, wondering what had happened to him. When all was said and done, she knew he would return, believed he still lived, for her heart would tell her of his death. Yet, at times, she doubted it. Rejected the thought because surely he would have found a way to send word. All these months she had heard nothing.

"Vanished...as if he had never existed," she whispered.

Charity watched her intently, gently holding Jessie with her gaze. "Jessie, Senator Drake warned us this would take time. This is not unusual. Roc would not risk his life or ours by sending messages that could find their way into unfriendly hands. Roc has disappeared for longer than this before..." her voice trailed away. "And so we must wait patiently. We must continue our work. If the rumors are true and the ship did sail to the Yukon, he could find himself stranded until the spring sun melts the ice."

"I'm not a patient person," she argued, "and I don't intend to sit around doing nothing. I want Pierce behind bars along with his lackeys. I want him found. He has no right to use women the way he does. Charity, he used you. Took you from your home and sold you for profit," she said. "I won't rest until all of this is settled. And Drake, he has done nothing, just sits back and tells everyone what they want to hear."

Charity smiled. "Jessica..."

"I mean it..."

"Jessica, he's a politician," Charity said curtly and she fell silent, suddenly contrite. She had acted as if she had an audience, albeit one that disagreed with her. Charity was not at odds with her. "Jessie, you are wasting your time and energy lecturing me and well you know it. Roc would want you to stay here, protected by his wealth and influence. Yet you continue to do whatever you want. He warned you to stay out of trouble but never told you his money was off limits. I don't want you to go against your principles, but do you truly think he would mind? I could set up a loan agreement. We could pay him back at current interest. Then--"

"Then he would still lock me in forever. I can't win but if I help one person, I've not lost, have I?" Jessie asked, raising a quizzical eyebrow.

"That's why we must do all we can, Jessica, now, while Roc is not here to tell you no. But truly I think he would applaud this scheme."

"Very well. I'll have the papers drawn this afternoon. We can both sign," Jessie said. "I haven't the vaguest notion how we'll ever pay him back though."

"Yes, that does elude me also," Charity murmured. "I have no job, at least not one that pays. And you have a job, but it wouldn't put food on your table let alone a roof over your head."

Jessie was surprised. Then she realized once again she had underestimated Charity and her determination. This had become Charity's reason for living, her crusade, more so with each passing day. She had uncovered the deputy who had betrayed them that night in Astoria. Had known the sheriff was innocent while everyone else suspected him, and perhaps even knew what had happened to Roc. She had surprising connections.

"What does Trevor have to say about all this?"

"Trevor doesn't speak to me," Charity said. "He has washed his hands of this affair. Since he can not control what I do, he'd rather not know."

"Ah, so much like Roc. Are all men so foolish? I'd have never thought Trevor would-"

"Believe it, he's worse than Roc, for he compares me with you and finds me decidedly lacking. I can't fight; I won't use a gun or a knife, wouldn't if I knew how and he has argued at great length with me about that. I won't allow him to teach me. In truth, just touching a weapon makes my skin crawl."

"You're joking?" Jessie asked incredulous. She couldn't help thinking about what she had taken for granted her entire life. Mastery. Belief in herself. When she had faltered, her father had offered encouragement. Even Pierce could not shatter that feeling.

Roc had nurtured it while he had threatened, warned, and made her promise so many things that went against her beliefs.

She prayed suddenly, furiously, Roc was alive, and when he returned would see things her way for a change. But that wouldn't happen. Not in her lifetime. So, instead she prayed Trevor would work with them and somehow she could persuade him to her side. She had wound him around her little finger before.

"Jessica, I'm not joking. Trevor has tried, but on the other hand I've come to realize a compromise has a place. We need his help and support and perhaps even his protection." She held up her hands warding off Jessica's comment. "I may need his protection. Don't refute this, Jessie. It is easier to accomplish a goal if a man backs you. Though, I imagine you will disagree with me until your dying day. If our ends are met, will it matter if a man helped?"

Jessie gasped, her breath, catching in her throat, barely controlling her temper. "Yes, it matters, Charity. It matters a whole hell of a lot. I'm going to have Roc's child and if it's a daughter, I want her brought up in a world where a woman can survive on her own. Where she doesn't have to prostitute herself if she doesn't have a man's protection or an inheritance to feed herself with. Charity, this is just the beginning. If we give in to them now, we will defeat our ultimate purpose. And a son? He must learn to respect a woman for her own worth not what she can bring to the marriage or her breeding abilities. More to life exists than simply bearing children and keeping house. An exciting world is out there, Charity."

Charity chuckled softly, and it seemed she admired the fire and passion in Jessie's speech. "Jessie, you can't right all the world's problems over night. Now I respect your energy, but without a man's support, a man's vote, we have nothing, just a great deal of talk and wishes. Back to business. We've wasted enough time with this stupid argument. The girls will arrive and we have to take them to Jacksonville. I will leave those details up to you since you are better suited for that endeavor. After this trip you'll return home, to Salem, then you must take care of yourself and let me do most of the legwork. Alexandra can come to your home when it's time for the birth. I won't have the babe harmed because of your persistence. We'll take each day one at a time and deal with this the best we can. I won't give up and even if we can't place a girl in another home, we can find some way to help her. Money won't become an issue."

She placed her hands on her swollen belly, feeling the babe kick. "All right, Charity, I'll do it your way, but only until the child is born then I intend to fight them with every breath."

Jessica Newman still wanted to see justice done, and she wanted to bring Pierce in herself, but at the moment they could only guess where he had gone. Pierce had sailed, with more than enough money to keep him for several years. When she thought of all the places he could disappear to, just vanish, it made her shudder. All in all she couldn't understand why he would come back. Didn't understand how potent a motive of revenge could become. It had only been Trevor's explanation, the history existing between Raymond Pierce and her family that had lent a small measure of light on the extent of Pierce's hate. He seemed filled with it, and Trevor feared for her safety just as Roc had.

Trevor was wise, she knew, and she clung to the hope someday he would understand her position. But he'd grown distant the last few months, pulling away from entanglement with Charity. Perkins, who had welcomed her into Roc's home when she'd returned had never accused her or reproached her for leading the man into such precarious circumstances. He seemed to take it for granted Roc would return safely.

The four of them, she, Charity, Trevor, and Perkins had made several runs to Astoria and back. They had raided auctions, brothels, and cribs in search of girls who wanted to find a new way. Not all of them would come, and those were the hardest of all. So damn hard to leave them, but they had no choice. To get Trevor's help in all this they'd had to promise that each individual would have to come willingly.

Then the raids had increased and she had lent herself to the work enthusiastically, thinking of nothing but the campaign. Every girl rescued seemed like a huge victory. She had not even noticed. Three months had passed before she had any inclination.

She had realized a difference, subtle, but there nonetheless.

She found none of her skirts fit. Her shirt stretched to the limit over an expanding bosom. But she hadn't been sick, so she dismissed the warning signs and went on with her cause.

After another month she accepted it. Life developed within her and without. The meaning changed. She wanted this child to grow up in a world where a person's sex did not determine its worth. The selling of women for the use of their bodies lay at the root of the problem and the evil.

She might never see her goals accomplished, but she vowed her children would continue the work. She was willing to fight for this cause. She was determined, no longer naive, floating aimlessly from one idea to the next.

Perkins had understood more than anyone. As she watched Roc's trusted servant move from one task to another, she knew he felt much the same as she did. She hoped for Perkins' sake she didn't let him down. He anticipated the birth of the child, perhaps because it was Roc's or maybe because his wife had died before giving him children. If this child was a girl, then Jessie was determined she would know from the first she could become or do anything she set her heart on. She would be a strong and independent being. The future would hold great promise.

The senator had asked her to back off now. They had thoroughly disrupted the smuggling rings, denting the profits considerably. Yet men still worked their trade. Women were sold.

Charity, of all people, preached patience. She meant it for her own good; she wasn't an invalid. Yet she had no idea how to convince those around her of the fact. Charity was a cautious diplomat; she valued other opinions as much as her own, and she was not beyond curtailing her activities for several months if that meant someone's health.

But Charity was also a force to reckon with. One who believed in humanity and the innate goodness of all individuals. She would work on other aspects of their cause until Jessie's child was born.

Always there was something else to accomplish.

Charity smiled suddenly, surprising her. "Jessie, you simply can not continue in such an undisciplined fashion for much longer. The world will not cease to revolve if you take a vacation. And if you don't, I believe, Trevor will try to put a complete stop to our activities. Now you and I both know he cannot succeed, but he can make life difficult."

She had to agree. Her cousin's mind was well known. Jessie raised an eyebrow then nodded.

"And now, if you will excuse me, I'll see to the rooms and the food. Perkins? Where is that man when I need him?" Charity laughed. "Trevor has sworn to have both wagons here. I've promised I'll find someone to ride shotgun, and of course he insists on at least five men. He and the senator have told me I can expect Pierce to turn up anytime now, and I ought to heed their advice, but I still don't know if he's even alive. Dash it all, one can't second guess that man and I suppose Trevor is right. But I did tell him

218

I could be hiring Pierce's men since they don't run around with a label on their collar proclaiming their allegiance. He scowled but relented. Told me he'd find the men. Ah, but I'm wasting time, aren't I? I'll meet you in the parlor before dinner. We can go over last minute instructions."

Jessie chuckled softly. Such a whirlwind of activity Charity could be when it seemed useful. For a moment, she wondered what had happened to her on board the smuggling ship. Charity rarely spoke of it. And when she did it was with a quiet conviction. But she had never revealed the entire story.

"Have you thought of anything we might have overlooked?"

Jessie stretched a moment, thinking, "No, you are meticulously precise. I am in awe, Charity. I'm anxious to return home to Jacksonville. I haven't seen my father since Roc and I were married. They don't know I'm expecting Roc's child. Of course they will object to my escapades, but they have long since given up restricting me."

"Yet, they encouraged your roguish ways, didn't they?" Charity asked. "But, Jessie, have you given much thought to Drake? It strikes me as curious the man brought the drugged wine to your house that night then locked the door to the bedroom so you couldn't leave. Tell me, could Pierce have bribed him? You know politicians, it seems every one of them has a dark shadow clouding their life somewhere."

Jessie cleared her throat, "I thought on it many times. But Drake is a friend. Honest to a fault. It amazes me he continually rises higher in the political arena because he always speaks his mind."

"So, he does puzzle you?"

She smiled slowly, catching the drift of Charity's question. "It isn't like that. He was just as surprised to find the wine drugged as we were. Yes, he took advantage, but he made no secret of the idea he wanted to see Roc and I married. Nor did Trevor for that matter."

Charity thought for a long time, seeming to sift information, question. "I have to rely on your faith in the man. Nothing strange or dubious has happened in the last months. Drake told us one of his constituents gave him the wine. He trusted the man, but he learned later a friend had given it to the man who gave it to him, and well...it's anyone's guess how many hands that bottle went through before it reached our table."

Charity's eyes narrowed.

"Drake is innocent in everything but locking that door. And at one time I didn't think I would ever forgive him for that, but now..."

Her voice trailed off. She inhaled slowly and looked around the room. The large empty room Roc filled with his presence. She missed him, his arguments, his loving. "Come back to me," she whispered. Felt the moisture gathering in her eyes. She bit her lip, wanting desperately to hold the tears back.

Charity touched her softly in understanding. "I'm sorry. I didn't mean to cause you anymore pain."

Jessie sniffed. She looked up from her lap where her eyes had focused on her tightly gripped hands. "Don't worry about it," she said then hurried outside the house. She walked swiftly through the gardens, past the gazebo. She stopped to watch the sky and the drifting clouds. Trevor appeared beside her. Perhaps she had wished him there. She didn't know but his presence gave her strength. They stood, frozen in time, somehow healing. Trevor helped fill the emptiness in her heart. Finally, she turned, "Charity needs your advice."

"That is a novel thought." Trevor began.

"Don't be snide, Trevor, I think she cares for you, it's just she's afraid," Jessie said, frowning slightly. "Only heaven knows what she went through on the trip here from Hawaii. She was an innocent, now...well, now she holds the weight of the world on her shoulders. I don't think she's strong enough to do that forever. Charity needs you but only if you're willing to listen and understand. It will take time. If you care for her, you will give her that time," she broke off.

"I do care, Jessica. It's just she makes it so difficult to get close to her. I reach out and she backs away."

Jessie nodded her understanding. "Just don't give up. But don't force her." She smiled, suddenly, quickly sweeping her lashes over her eyes, not wanting him to see her amusement. Trevor, with his cavalier attitude and charming ways, finally met a woman who could resist him. Ah, there was irony here, but she knew Trevor would win in the end. Who could resist her devilishly handsome cousin? Who indeed.

"I'll go see what she wants, Jessie, but beyond that I'll promise nothing."

She watched him go, his long loose-limbed strides moving purposefully down the garden path. Then Jessie turned and hurried quickly to the house. She strolled in the back way, hoping to avoid running into anyone. She had just entered the butler's pantry when she heard Perkins call out softly. "There you are. I've looked all over for you. I've packed everything you laid out; you're set to go tomorrow. The girls are in their rooms. The wagons are here."

"Fine, thank you, Perkins."

She ran quickly up the servant's staircase and down the hall to her dressing room. A fire blazed cozily in her chamber. She turned around the room then moved to the balcony. The sun had begun to set, and she realized if Roc was still alive, he must be seeing the same fiery show. Her thoughts turned inward and the tears began again. This time she didn't hold them back. They fell silently as she let her anguish have free rein.

Memories flooded her thoughts. Long lost memories, and she held onto the hope Roc would return. She prayed he would make it before the child was born. Did he care? The question hung on her soul and in her heart. *Regrettable accident.* He had never wanted the marriage. So, why would he want the child? But she knew he did want the child, just not a bastard. So, he had wed her. She couldn't dwell on it, but it seemed ever present in her mind, tearing her apart. Her emotions, frayed and vulnerable, left her trembling in the night and terrified in the days. Charity saw it but never spoke of it. For then she would have to reveal her own desperate anguish and Charity wasn't ready.

She had to think of her mission. It came first. It was the only way she survived each day. She had to deliver these eight women to her father then she would return and wait for the child to come.

But for this night...

She would let her mind wander. The moon rose. Rupert came to her, padding softly down the hall and pushing the door open with his nose.

She watched the night pass and the stars glow brightly.

~ * ~

Trevor had spent hours with Senator Drake since their return. He had long since discounted him of any treachery. They had discussed the betrayal and simply chalked it up to the scheming of Pierce and Rutgers. The offer of easy riches and an endless supply of women sometimes was too hard to resist for a man in search of easy money.

This evening Trevor came to Drake, frustrated and dispirited after his hour with Charity. Patience, Jessie had suggested it would do the trick, but he'd run out of that commodity weeks earlier when she stiffened her fragile form and told him she didn't want anything romantic to do with him.

Now he held out his hand in greeting to Senator Drake, ready to drink the night away. "Drake," he said.

Drake grinned slightly at the creases in Trevor's forehead, seeming to know exactly how he'd come by them.

"Had another run in with the little crusader?" Drake asked him then chuckled softly. "Are you going to let her drown herself in her misery and the past? Trevor, you have to make her talk about what happened or she'll never thaw."

"I've tried," he cut in, having had it with everyone's sage advice. "Jessie tells me one thing and you another. I'm no closer to her than I was weeks past when I found her hiding in the forest. I don't know how she got away from them." Trevor poured himself a cup of coffee.

"Giving up on the girls?" Drake queried.

Trevor wavered. "I don't know. Perhaps I'll see this with a little more clarity when I get back from Jacksonville. I've decided to go with Jessie. Not enough men out there I know I can trust. Besides I want to talk to James. Perhaps he can shed--"

"Trevor, I have a message for James. Roc sent it." The senator murmured, stopping Trevor. "I believe he's stumbled on to more of Pierce's syndicate; you will need to deliver this immediately. I know where he is and he is alive but that is all I can reveal at the moment. Read the letter with James and when you return, we can discuss this."

"You can tell me nothing else?"

"Any man who knows Roc Newman knows he has connections everywhere and is used to dealing among the underworld. Ah, yes, it places him in a unique position, doesn't it? It seems his mother was Italian, and that in itself explains many of his connections. She came from a wealthy family that was, at times, above the law. Roc's honest though. Above reproach."

Trevor stared at Drake, astonished. "But how--"

"I've known Roc a long time. He pulled me out of the slums of Chicago, or hadn't I told you that? Hmm...well, you see, I owe him my life several times over."

Trevor sipped his coffee, confused, finding it difficult to assimilate everything Drake had told him. He had more questions than he could think of, and he wanted answers to all of them. "Should I start the quiz or do you want to begin again and fill in the holes?"

"Neither. I don't doubt for a minute your trust in me has dropped measurably, but we haven't the time to worry. Faith, Trevor, you will simply have to deal in faith."

Trevor nodded. "So, you want me to take the message to James. Why not his wife? It seems he would want her to know he's alive and well, now doesn't it?"

"No. Two reasons. Roc isn't sure where her loyalty lies. He has reason to believe she could still work for Pierce, and this whole thing was simply a foil to disguise her ties with them. Money is a powerful aphrodisiac. And women have prostituted themselves for it more times than one would like to imagine."

"And the second reason?"

"If she isn't working with Pierce, if she were to read this missive, she'd intensify her crusade, endangering herself and the child."

"He knows?" Trevor demanded. His voice was rich with questions and the intrigue of this. If Roc knew, then this wasn't the first correspondence, and Jessie worried for nothing. Hell, he wondered how Jessie and Charity could do more?

"Yes," Drake said, interrupting Trevor's thoughts. "This is the third telegram he's sent. Don't say anything to Jessie. Don't give her more to think about. Let her take this trip, come back and have the child. She is not a foolish woman, only passionate. What she doesn't know won't harm her or the child."

"You're asking me to accept a great deal on loyalty alone, Drake."

Drake hesitated just a second, his gaze penetrating Trevor's own, purposefully as if he hoped Trevor could read his sincerity. "Roc is like a brother to me, I don't expect you to understand. I have only his best interest at heart, and Jessie's"

"All right," Trevor said pausing. "But I will not take my focus off you, and if you give me any reason to doubt you, you can feel assured you will regret it."

"Fair enough," Drake said. "I expected nothing less. I will hold you to your promise. Say nothing of this to Jessie," he reminded him.

Trevor turned to leave. "No, I won't tell her, but only because I agree with you. It is in her best interest not to know."

Chapter Thirteen

Jake was a Pinkerton; his name was Jonathan Conroy, Roc learned, and had grown up in the South, under the watchful thumb of carpetbaggers and crooks.

Jonathan's father had fought for the confederacy, and when the war ended had lost everything. Not even a premonition and a hasty investment in the banks of England could pull his life out from the under the ruble created when Yankees burned their way across Georgia. Jonathan's life had held the promise of wealth and prestige, a southern gentleman planter; Roc thought Jonathan would have died of boredom in that role. Jon had an uncanny knack for reading expressions and observing people to the point he recognized a phony immediately. And Roc, as Jake had predicted, stood glaringly different from the other sailors. Jon's other unique talent lay in his ability to adapt and blend as easily a chameleon. Fortunately for the pair, Jon had another man with him, another of Pinkerton's finest; he had somehow managed to be far enough away from the original confrontation that Pierce failed to spot him.

Roc spent the first part of the trip to the Yukon chained to a wall in the ship's hold. He frightened Pierce. But by the time they put into Vancouver Island, the captain had allowed him above deck. Ten of the women were selected and shipped overland somewhere for sale or prearranged buyers.

He could hear the whimpering of the Chinese women. Occasionally, one of them would be summoned above decks and light would filter through the opening. Shackled to the wall, he had no recourse except wait. It was his prison, shared with Jonathan, who in his indomitable way eased his mind and spirit. This had not been the way he'd imagined the journey when he first raced impetuously to Pierce's ship. His wisdom came in small doses, obtained by watching the crew members and Pierce's men as they went about their daily tasks. Jonathan had informed him he had another man on board and access to the law at each legitimate port they entered. But the smugglers rarely entered one of those safe ports, preferring instead to slip into unguarded coves beneath black skies. When they weren't forced above deck to scrub floors or man sails, they were kept chained below, the two of them, living on scraps of food.

Working the ship kept their minds and muscles sharpened to a keen edge; Roc's growing respect with this Pinkerton agent helped him through bouts of doubt and rage. Jonathan gave credence to their motto, "The eye that never sleeps." There were times Roc believed it true.

Somewhere along the route, Pierce and his steadfast companion, Rutgers, jumped ship. After cautious questions and careful surveillance whenever possible, Roc confirmed the rumors. Jonathan's fellow agent relayed the confirmation two days after leaving a small cove in Canada. Pierce had arranged for the sale of the remaining girls to a pimp in Fairbanks. From there the ship would sail farther north to mining camps and brothels in the Yukon.

Jonathan's agent had also wired an operative in Fairbanks and they were assured of safe passage off the ship. The Seafarer would find itself swarmed with law enforcement officers; Jonathan and Roc would leave. It seemed too easy, but now with Pierce and Rutgers gone, Roc would have to begin his search for them once again.

How curious. Roc had never imagined joining forces with the Pinkertons. He had always worked alone and succeeded admirably. Now he was in their debt and had decided to work with them. They were going to the Yukon.

But on a mysterious night when the air had taken on the decided markings of late autumn and potential for an early winter, Roc's musings had turned to Jessica.

A strange combination of events, some would call fate, allowed them to stumble into a wealth of information. He and Jake had wound their way to the bar at the Gold Nugget Saloon when they were approached by two of the saloon's waitresses. Moments later, they found themselves in the back room of the establishment, and he knew an auction was about to take place.

The room wasn't, large but it had arranged seating for about twenty guests, circular seating. A block stood in the middle of the room, draped with red velvet. Lights from a huge chandelier sparkled and cast the room in opulent splendor. Moments later, he heard a signal and he knew the entertainment was about to begin. Then a lady, exquisite, a Madame, he assumed, approached the center of the room.

Jonathan tightened. His hands gripped the arms of the chair. Black velvet molded to his fingertips. "It's been a hell of a long time. It's her, though, Midnight Annie. I'd never forget her face, the beautiful green eyes that give nothing away, nothing," he swallowed. "I'm astonished I can look at her now and feel so detached." He leaned against the back of the chair, crossing his arms over his chest. "Sweet Jesus, but she's still a beautiful sight to behold. I can remember when she ran in pigtails and swam buck-naked in the river behind our daddy's plantation. She never was one for convention. She had me fooled from the day mama gave birth to her."

Every muscle within Roc began to tense. This night had clearly slipped from their control. What had begun as a simple quest for information had landed them in a den of vice. And one of the ringleaders had turned out to be Jonathan's sister.

Midnight Annie...

"She's my little sis," Jon told Roc softly.

"Good, god." She wasn't just a Madame who had succumbed to greed. She was Jonathan's own damn sister.

After all the time they had spent together with nothing to do and all the stories they told, not once had Jonathan mentioned a sister. A complication, and perhaps he had wanted to forget this lady. She surely had traveled a path no brother would have picked for his sister. So, though Roc frowned for a moment, he quickly pieced the puzzle together.

"She's your sister, so exactly where does that put us? Assuming she will recognize you."

"Yes, and I don't know. Annie's never been predictable," he said bitterly. He crunched the black velvet beneath his fingers. "But, I'll learn the truth of her story tonight. She doesn't condone this sale of flesh. I'd bet on it."

"Any suggestions?" Roc demanded. He raised an eyebrow quizzically and studied his friend.

At risk to the operation, Roc thought. But in the bright light of the drab little room, Roc could see an unholy glint in Jon's eyes. Jonathan's expression had turned reckless, and the cautious sleuth assumed a new identity.

"This might compromise our goal," Jonathan warned.

"It might also give us the information we've searched months to uncover," Roc added.

It seemed Jonathon thought it over for a moment. It was one thing to risk his life but to botch a job and undermine the agency's reputation was not Jon's right to gamble. Roc knew Jonathan Conroy would make the right decision.

"We'll have to wait until the auction is over," Jonathan said.

"We'll both have to be ready." Roc paused and rubbed his chin. "When this is done, we'll follow her home."

Jonathan nodded confirmation and Roc assumed leadership for the time being. "God, I've forgotten how hard this was to accept. I'd thought I'd gotten over her rebellion. You know, she didn't deserve this fate, but her choice of husbands left her defenseless and miserable. She ran away. Wouldn't accept my help."

Roc studied his partner a moment, not sure how to respond. "Stealth is going to be critical. And you don't have to talk to her if you don't want to. I can handle it from this end. I have a wealth of unanswered questions, and I'd gamble my last dollar Annie can enlighten us to most of them."

"We'll still have to find Pierce and Rutgers. And the women sold tonight, what about them?"

"Perhaps she can help on both ends. Although I don't hold out much hope for the girls." He prayed Midnight Annie would help. They had bumbled along so far, reaching more dead ends than he wanted to admit to.

Right had to be on their side tonight. And if not, with the innocent victims of greed and avarice sitting around them so very sure of themselves they never bothered to check on the guests.

They saw the first girls led to the block. Heard the drone of the auctioneer as they cajoled for money. For a moment, Roc feared he would lose his dinner, but with loathsome practice he watched, and when the first girl stepped down and the second one led forward he swallowed the bile and concentrated, not on the preceding, but on Jessie, a breath of fresh air amidst the sordid squalor surrounding him at the moment.

The night droned on, and by the time the last sale was made, Roc had tensed and relaxed each muscle a thousand times in anticipation of the events to come. They left with the crowd, blending in, inconspicuous, hopeful. Jonathan leaned against the wall of the saloon, lazily watching the small mining camp move around him. Roc turned left then moved down the alley to the back door, blending with the shadows.

Time clicked by. Nothing stirred except a green-eyed cat surprised by Roc's presence. A slight drizzle began to fall. Roc swore softly, pulling his collar close around his neck.

"What?" He jumped. Jonathan had come up behind, undetected.

"She's leaving. Heard the commotion in the saloon a couple minutes ago. Annie owns a parlor house in the red light district. Best damn whorehouse in the Yukon. At least that's what some old timer told me a couple minutes ago. Guess you can't even get in unless you can manufacture gold nuggets."

"So, we need a gold nugget just to gain an audience with your sister. Hmm, unless, of course we abduct her," Roc said. "Or we confront her as she's leaving the saloon."

Jonathan was watching the saloon's back door swing open and his little sister lock it behind her. She had changed clothes. Now she wore a simple blue calico dress. Nothing like what he had imagined. Her innocent appearance astounded him.

"I'd rather kidnap her, but I think she'd make us change our minds within a minute or two. That leaves the second option." Awkwardly, he approached Annie. "Spitfire," he said softly, slowly moving from the shadows. "Do you remember?"

Annie turned. Her chin raised a notch and she stepped back, stumbling on a rock. She hesitated a moment. "I won't go home with you, Jon. Don't--"

Roc met Jon's eyes and smiled crookedly.

"I'm not asking that," Jon interrupted, swiftly cutting her off.

Jon stepped forward. Familial ties long forgotten bonded together. Roc's quickly exhaled breath shed a cautious light on the charged emotions hovering between brother and sister. Jon took her arm, escorting her down the alley toward her home. They walked slowly, and it seemed neither one wanted the confrontation that was now inevitable.

"What do you want, Jon?" she said, a harsh note of steel in her voice. "I didn't expect you to show up in my life again. I thought you learned the last time you tried to interfere." She turned on him suddenly. A feeble attack before she would let him into her home.

Within minutes, an older man appeared by her side. He was tall, and even in the deceptive shadows, he looked ready to defend her. His gaze lingered on Roc and Jonathan. Tension emanated from him, and his eyes turned hard and unforgiving. He looked to Annie for guidance.

"It's all right, Sean. This is my brother, Jonathan and..."

"Roc Newman," he said and stepped forward extending his hand. "Pleased to meet you."

"Roc, yes...well, these gentleman will be on their way soon. Jon just stopped by--"

"To talk, Annie. I have questions, and you're the only one who can answer them. I won't go."

She snorted. "Persistent as the devil himself. Don't things ever change? I told you that I won't come home, can't. There's nothing else to say."

"He's dead, Annie. Found himself in a high-stakes game and he cheated. They found his body in the river a few days later. You can come home. You don't have to be afraid of him. He's gone."

Annie sucked in her breath then paused a moment, "It's too late, Jon. Look what I've become, a soiled dove, and it doesn't matter. This is the only way I can make a living, and you know that. Even if I wanted to come home, Jon, which I don't."

"You could marry again," Jon said softly.

He watched the tear slide down her cheek. She turned away. He heard a bitter laugh and it seemed it echoed from a hollow used shell of a little girl he once knew. A girl filled with innocence, laughter, and joy, until she met a worthless excuse for a man who used her and threw her away. Her courage astonished Jon. And he wondered why he'd never realized it before. She had the strength to pick up the pieces of her shattered life. He didn't condone her method, but he couldn't fault her. Over the years he had come to realize she had made the only decision possible.

"No one would have me." Her voice sounded empty. Not even the pain and anguish of her loneliness penetrated the hollow sound.

Her mentor cleared his throat. "Best we get out of the cold, Annie. I don't think they mean you any harm, and I think you should talk with your brother."

Annie gave a quick shrug of her shoulder. They walked in silence. The parlor house reminded Jon of the elegant plantations that used to grace the South. It was a smaller version but just as beautiful.

She slipped in through the kitchen. It was warm and homey. The cook whistled a snappy little tune. The smell of newly baked bread hung in the air. It didn't seem like a home where men bought women for a night of pleasure.

Annie looked to the men then moved to the stairs. They all followed.

On the third floor, Annie slipped inside. Her private parlor was fashionable and modest. Nothing like Jon expected. Hell, he didn't know what to expect. He'd never had the fortune to find entertainment by the madam of a parlor house, although he'd paid for their services any number of times.

His opinion lay clobbered in the dust, and he suddenly had a new respect for all of these women. "When we're through here, Annie, you may not have a choice. All hell's going to break loose, and I don't want you hurt."

She motioned for them to sit. A knock at the door prompted Sean to rise from his chair and answer it. A lovely young girl strode in with tea and a few of the rolls that had smelled so delicious when they'd walked through the kitchen. Sean took it from her, set in on a table, and began to pour.

Annie ignored his remark at first. The discussion was light hearted, filled with reminiscing and tales of youthful exploits. Sean crossed his arms and leaned against the door, refusing for one second to take his hardened gaze from the two men. Laughter and music filtered up from the rooms below. Roc, patient and silent, waited for the right moment. The sky slowly turned from deepest black to a hazy purple. She had managed to steer the conversation in her own direction for hours.

She had manipulated this battle of wits and won easily. Her brother, putty in her hands, was no match for Annie.

Roc looked as if he was losing patience with this dalliance. Neither of them had ever thought they could have saved any of the girls bought tonight but he hated to admit the loss. Now, with so much time gone by, he accepted the facts.

Jon was lost in the past, despair written on his face. He blamed himself for Annie's plight and he would have moved heaven and earth to turn back time. But he couldn't. And now it seemed Annie refused to change.

"Son of a bitch, Jon, it's time we made a few discreet inquiries. I've run out of patience."

Sean stepped forward, blocking the path between Roc and Annie. Protecting. "You'll have to go through me, Mr. Newman. Me. A man. Not a woman," he threatened.

Roc lifted a brow. "I see," he drawled. "Your allegiance is misplaced. This woman is party to a series of crimes from California to the Yukon. You can't protect her forever."

Jon stood, feeling the tension between these two men. "Sit down, both of you." He turned to Annie and held out his identification. "I'm your only chance little spitfire. Talk to me."

Jonathan didn't waste any more time. He went straight to the jugular. Her gasp floated through the early morning dawn, and for a moment Roc registered impatience with Jon's sudden departure from the easily manipulated. Jon had attacked, surprisingly and swiftly. He parried Annie's defense until her shoulders slumped in defeat.

But Jonathan did not read the signs or if he did, chose to ignore them. He continued the assault, going for blood. Jonathan told her everything, sparing her no details, including the time she'd spend in prison if she didn't take this moment to reveal the needed evidence. Even then, Jon admitted, she might find herself under prosecution for crimes committed.

Sean moved to defend his employer again.

From intuitiveness honed to razor sharp edge in the ranks, Jonathan believed he had the winning hand. The cards were on the table, clear and concise, easy for anyone to read. And he knew Annie was bright, clear thinking. She'd give him what he wanted then move on with her life. He felt a moment of guilt for his sister, his beautiful little sister. Annie...ah, the sweet thing who followed him around, tormenting his every waking second and even a few nights.

"You win," Annie finally said. Her voice, quiet and so soft Jon thought he heard only the breeze as it fluttered through the partially opened window.

"Why don't I feel like it?" Sadness emanated from Jonathan's eyes and the weary lines around his mouth spoke of a youth long past and dreams left unfulfilled. "Annie, did you buy any of those girls tonight?"

Sean swore viciously. He moved to protect Annie.

It wasn't the beginning Jonathan had intended but he had to know.

Annie held up her hand, stopping Sean. He moved back against the wall.

"Yes," she said, meeting Jon's gaze. "And I'm not ashamed of it. I give each girl a choice. She may work wherever she chooses. I'm not a whoremaster or a pimp. If a girl wants to work in the kitchen, or as a seamstress, or..." she shrugged, "or leave, she may. All I demand is that she pay me back."

"So then she's here for life," Roc was on his feet. Sean had stiffened again. A battle threatened.

"No." Annie said. "Heavens no, all my girls are paid for their work. I run an honest business, and I've never taken advantage of anyone."

Roc sat back, folding his hands beneath his chin in tense concentration. Jonathan glared at him. Roc shrugged, not to be put off by Jon. After all, Jon must look at this from a far different perspective.

"What do you know about Raymond Pierce?"

Annie stiffened. "Nothing."

She lied. That much was obvious. But why?

"Annie, I can read your face like a book. You never could hide anything. Now tell me what you know of Pierce."

"Nothing. Nothing of interest. I know I don't want to deal with him. I know he supplies the girls and they hate him. If his name is mentioned, I get looks that would boil your blood. And it's not just the Chinese women. I have a couple of white girls who seem to know him. You should ask them."

Sean stepped forward at the mention of Pierce. His lips set firmly together. "If this is about Raymond Pierce, I'm on your side, Jonathan. I'd like to see the pimp behind bars. I've known him since before the war. White trash." His voice had turned to a low growl.

Roc crossed his arms over his chest. "I'm intrigued. The white women, what happens to them?"

"Over the years he's managed several parlor houses in different parts of the country. I believe he owns one in Portland that deals with him directly and Madame Lilly in Salem. He finds something to hold over them then slowly tightens the noose until they have no choices left. Blackmail, but he doesn't extort money, just services."

Roc's brow shot up. "So, the auction Pierce had planned for Jessie would have taken place in Salem, Madam Lilly's. The wine, the aphrodisiac and how it came into my home has become increasingly clear. Carefully planned and maneuvered, the wine was presented to Drake and it wasn't a secret the senator intended to dine with me that night, nor was Jessie held there against her will."

"He had his hand in several ports and several cities. We'll need testimony, Annie. I need you to come with me."

She hissed. Her eyes flashed a deadly fire then they closed. Her anger shuttered. She sealed herself against him. "My business--"

"Will be confiscated."

"You can't do that," Annie rose suddenly.

"I can, Annie, and I will. I want you out of this business, yesterday."

Her body shook. He could see the anguish, the pain, the fury; he wanted to take her into his arms and comfort her. But she wouldn't allow it. He had transcended the line drawn by her. He would force her to come with him, but after that he wasn't sure.

"How long do I have?" Annie rose, shook out her skirts and started toward a door at the far end of the parlor.

"One week," Jonathan replied without hesitation. "Once we have our witness back in the states, protected, we can concentrate on the capture of Raymond Pierce and Sterling Rutgers."

Roc stood and stared at Annie as she walked away. Annie turned before she left the room. "You may use any of the rooms on the second floor. Make sure they're empty first." Then she vanished and the parlor suddenly seemed stifling as if they had wrenched the life from the person they had thought to save.

The three men stared at each other. Roc assessed Sean slowly, a second time; he was none the wiser. *A body guard, yes. But a loyal man, perhaps loyal to a fault. Perhaps Annie had acquiesced too easily.*

Jonathan watched also, keeping an eye on Sean and the door Annie disappeared behind. Jon caught Roc's gaze and it seemed as if they were of one thought. Roc nodded. Jon rose and left the room. Sean followed.

Roc folded his hands behind his head, leaning back in the chair. He'd watch the sun rise then Jon would come to relieve him.

Neither one doubted Annie might run. They had given her enough provocation.

Roc closed his eyes a moment but it was long enough to catch a subtle movement from the back of the room, a soft fresh smell of green grass and pine trees conflicting with his idea of a whorehouse. Ah, but that was the difference. This was a parlor house. Then the movement was in front of him. Annie sat down, hands folded primly in her lap and she watched him.

When she spoke, he listened. Aware of her frustration and the lost years she'd spent in hiding. "I shall need help in selling this place. I won't run, if that's what all this is about. I suppose it's time to face my fears and return. But I doubt if I can ever fit into polite society again. Jon's a dreamer. Yet I have enough money set aside, and investments, legitimate," she added, "I won't have to ask for hand outs from Jon."

Roc didn't move, didn't say anything, but he heard more than she said.

"Sean has to come also, I won't go without him. It may take more than a week, but I'm telling you now so you won't think..."

"You're stalling," Roc interrupted. "Honey, your sob story's a good one, and if you didn't have Jonathan convinced of your innocence, you'd be on a horse back this instant, heading for the states."

She leaned over and took one of Roc's hands in hers. "You're hard, Mr. Newman. But I can't say it comes as any surprise. Even a determined man cannot stop the snow from falling and the earth from freezing. So the time of our departure may have nothing to do with me."

Annie, let go of his hand before smoothing her skirts then looked back to Roc. "You see. I tried to earn a living. Wasn't greedy. Just wanted to put a roof over my head and food on my table. But it wasn't possible. This was the only way. Mr. Newman, I was smarter than most. I managed to save my money until I could leave the parlor house I was in, until I could buy one of my own. I'm a good businesswoman. And despite your cold disdain, I have nothing to feel guilty about. Then suddenly my brother shows up on his white horse with his shinning armor and wants to take it all away. Tell me, sir. What would a man do in my place? No. I see. You don't have to. We both know he'd fight for everything he owned."

Roc did understand. At least he tried to. Jessie had told him enough times that a woman needed her own identity, an individuality beyond her husband's.

He cocked his head, studying the woman in front of him.

Indeed, he saw things he'd never dreamed of, and he suddenly realized his life with Jessie could use a little compromise. Yes, he would learn to compromise.

~ * ~

"I swear, Jessica Lawrence, you have never listened to a word I've told you." Alexandra Lawrence scolded her daughter. She was Jessica's stepmother, but she was the only mother Jessie could remember. Alexandra, or Alex as her friends called her, had raised Jessie since the tender age of six, and even though she'd borne children of her own, Jessie was always very dear to her. A few gray hairs twined themselves around the Scottish red, but Alex looked almost young enough to be Jessie's sister. She had followed Jessica back to Salem with no pretense at all. She wanted to be there when Jessie's child was born.

She was ranting on, but Jessie found herself curiously absorbed in her words. Never before had they held such meaning to her. It seemed as though Alex had experienced all the doubts and fears that now came to her mind. She seemed to hear the word compromise too many times to count. And partnership. Give and take. Everything she said held a measure of truth, but Jessie wondered how indeed one could compromise with an arrogant, self-assured man who thought his word was law. Still, she listened because memories resurfaced. Heard the arguments between James and Alex. Saw them make up. Felt the tension ebb and flow between them as they learned to trust one another and listen to the other's needs. Compromise. She didn't have room in her heart for compromise unless Roc could meet her half way.

She had so much love for Alex. She was lecturing passionately. All Alex needed was a podium and a room full of women to shout and holler and, of course, agree. But where were the men? Still sadly behind the times and set in their opinions.

"I wanted you to understand a woman could strive for independence and freedom, have it too, but not by sacrificing the pleasure of love. Jessie, I didn't want your nights filled with books and a lonely light to read. When we got Trevor's message, I was afraid for you, but James assured me he was good man and believed the two of you loved each other. Too suborn, he'd said, too pigheaded to admit it so soon but it would come."

She must have told her a thousand times, but Jessie didn't hesitate a moment. "It was just a regrettable accident, mother. I thought we would have the marriage annulled, but..."

Alexandra stopped waving her arms in the air and strode across the room to Jessica. She sat down beside her, turned her then rubbed her back. The back rub was soothing and relaxing; Jessie leaned into it and groaned. "You don't want that, do you, Jessie? An annulment?" Alex hesitated a moment before she continued kneading Jessie's muscles.

"I would have pursued it, except for the child," she told her mother softly. "He didn't want to marry me, and after all this time I haven't heard from him, not one word. He could be dead for all I know. Trevor pities me, Charity hovers with an 'I could have guessed as much look,' and Senator Drake keeps telling me to give him time as if he knew something. Time? How much time does a man need? I don't even know if he's alive." She questioned, and she forced herself to smile, even though she would give him forever if he asked for it, but he hadn't.

Alexandra watched her tired, forlorn features. She seemed to empathize with her for once she'd felt much the same. "He'll come back to you, Jessie. He's a fool if he doesn't know what a treasure he has in you. I swear it. Believe in the senator. He knows the man better than anyone on this earth, save perhaps you, but your grief is too fresh to see the situation through clear eyes."

"When?" she challenged Alex harshly.

Alex studied the stained glass in the middle of the fireplace. "When the time is right. When he either captures Pierce or gathers enough evidence to make him a fugitive in every state of the union. However, if I ever find him alone for even one moment, I will, truly, Jessica, tell him what I think of his high handed behavior."

Jessica smoothed her dress. "I love you, but you don't need to fight my battles. I'll tell him and enjoy every minute. I think the senator has heard from him. He let something slip the other day. I wanted to shake him until all his teeth fell out."

"You're right. James received a message, hid it when he saw me come into the room. Didn't think about it for a while then he said something, too, and well..." she paused. "Forgive me, Jessie. He's hurt you and I'm not helping, am I?"

"No, that's not true. You've put my life, with Mr. Roc Newman, in perspective. I have to make him understand or our marriage will never work. And I have to make him appreciate that if we have a girl, I will not allow him to brainwash her with his fanciful ideas of a woman's place. I want her strong and able to take care of herself under any conditions. I want her to know she can achieve anything her heart desires."

"Yes, well," Alexandra murmured. "I wish you luck and pray you don't find it an impossible task. Men sometimes are unbearably stubborn."

"Undeniably, mother. You just summed up the root of my frustrations with Roc," she said softly.

Her eyes brightened suddenly and Alexandra giggled. "And I'm about to become a grandmother. I hope it's a girl. I'm going to help you in every way I can think of. She'll be a holy terror just like her mama, and I hope Roc dotes on her."

"Like father did me? You and I both know he spoiled me."

"That's why he still calls you brat. With affection, of course."

Jessie smiled. "He does? But he's the one who taught me to shoot and urged me to get an education."

"At my insistence," she said with a little snort and a wink. "I'd do it all again too."

"Well, you can practice on your grandchild," Jessie informed her happily. "I..."

Jessie was about to tell her Roc called her brat occasionally, too, and it had absolutely everything with the way James and Alex had brought her up. She stopped herself, though, hesitant to disclose more of her faltering relationship with her husband. Where her father thought it charming, Roc thought she was truly a brat. Never would they find equal footing or common ground. They'd never find middle ground.

"And if he doesn't show up at least this little one will know love, Alex, I'll see to it."

"Ah, but he will come back, Do you think he could resist two such charming ladies? I think you will have a daughter just to vex him," Alex laughed merrily.

She would delight in encouraging her daughter to run him round in circle after circle. But at the moment it didn't really matter.

And having Alex here was good. It banished her fear of the birth and labor; instilled in her a reassuring feeling of peace.

Charity came to visit occasionally. In the privacy of Jessie's room, she told her of the increasing raids. Told her of the women she had brought into the home they had purchased with Roc's money. "Jessie, I have such a wonderful feeling of accomplishment. Oh, those beautiful women. But none of them want pity. Some of them were sold by their parents."

"Their parents?" she said softly. "Well, Pierce has vanished, or so it seems," Jessie told her wearily. "And Roc..."

"That man has no right to treat you so shabbily," Charity said fiercely.

"Everyone with the exception of his wife has received news from him," Jessie barely whispered.

"Put it behind you," Charity advised. "Don't expect something from him he can not give." Charity reached out her hand to Jessie then drew it back abruptly. Pain wrenched inside, and it seemed she wanted to offer compassion, empathy, perhaps love, but she couldn't. Jessie recognized Charity's response, understood and forgave. "Roc hasn't forgotten you, but he's not here, and you must remember the child. Take care, offer it the support and love for two."

Jessie gave it love. She cherished the babe within her body, loving it more with each passing day. She visited her favorite haunts, walked for long hours, and ate well, all the right foods. The babe grew within her and responded lovingly to her touch and absent crooning. Kept her awake nights with its tossing and turning. Left her helpless to rise from a chair, and when she'd finally make it to a standing position, she would swear for long minutes at the babe's absentee father.

Then she'd remember the message that had sent them rushing helter-skelter at cross-purposes. She recalled the ambush, the betrayal then the humiliation when he tied her to the horse and sent her home. He had turned from her then, scorned her and now he had been gone for such a long time.

She waddled furiously back and forth. A fighter since she could remember, the role he'd thrust her in left her terrified. She hated waiting, loathed forced patience, and detested him for leaving her alone. Wanted him back, today. This instant. Damn his sorry hide. Wanted him to enclose her in his strong embrace and reassure her the child would be born healthy and strong with two loving parents to spoil and raise her.

Yes, she knew this child was a girl. Dreams vivid and real possessed her at night. Saw the child racing down the stairway in reckless and wild abandon, long black hair flying, dirt smudged across her face and smoky gray eyes.

When the little girl vanished, it would leave her with other dreams, evocative and inescapable, felt his lips, his body, the warmth of his breath whispering across her. She couldn't bear the anguish, the memories, the hope he would come to her soon. She was going to have his child, and he'd abandoned her.

Just when she thought she could no longer endure, it happened. Midnight, the witching hour according to Alex, the contractions began, slowly at first. So slowly Jessie rose, donned her robe and walked to the kitchen for a warm glass of milk.

She curled into her favorite chair, sipped the liquid and watched the clock. It seemed easy, but as the sun began to rise and the pains came closer together and harder, she rethought her earlier conclusion.

Alexandra found her dozing in the parlor, a cup hanging from one finger, and a light sheen of sweat covering her face. It was time.

Jessie's eyes opened, startled awake by a hard contraction. "Oh!"

"Come on, sweetheart." Alex held out her hand. "Can you walk to your room or should I call for help?"

"Please, don't do that," she laughed then sucked in her breath suddenly.

"Come on then. I'll send Perkins for the doctor, and we'll get you settled into bed. First babies take their own sweet time."

Jessie calmly followed Alex, stopping every few steps, waiting patiently for the pain to cease before continuing. It seemed to Jessie eternity could have come and gone before she finally reached her room. But once resting comfortably, she was overjoyed. The end was near and soon she'd hold her daughter in her arms. She had never felt so relieved in her life.

But as the day wore on, her outlook changed measurably. The pains increased, consuming her body, unrelenting until she wanted to scream. Alexandra stayed by her side, holding her hand, encouraging her.

"Will this ever end?" she wailed desperately to Alex, her expression tense with pain, her hair damp and lying in wet strands around her face.

"Yes, dear, then you'll forget that it ever hurt. You'll forget because you'll hold a precious babe, born from your womb. And when it suckles at your breast, you'll know you would do it all again," Alex said longingly.

"Forget!" Jessie cried incredulously, staring at Alex. Alex brushed Jessie's hair away from her face and placed a cool cloth against her forehead. "Focus on something, dear," she reminded Jessie. "Don't forget to breathe."

She had never felt so miserable in her life. It hurt. And now the contractions had no separation. One continual pain surged through her. The world spun out of her control, and she was helpless amidst the chaos. Her skin prickled. Heat radiated around her. An inferno closed and constricted.

Figures moved knowingly in the room and, God, they all smiled.

Jessie hated them all. She couldn't begin to understand why they grinned when agony convulsed her. She cursed Roc, and it brought another round of smiles to the spectators. Her hands fell on the covers, and she clutched them desperately.

"Relax, Jessie, it's almost over," the soft voice floated magically and she swore at Alex. No one could relax and endure this she wanted to shout.

The day passed. The doctor fidgeted then joked she'd have to have the child before five. Everyone laughed, amused at his humor. Everyone except Jessie. She was nearing the end of her endurance. She'd had enough and made a promise to herself. That if Roc ever returned, she'd never allow him to do this to her again. He had no right to expect a second child. One would have to suffice.

"It's time, Jessie. Push." Alex smiled over her, holding her hand again. The doctor sat at the foot of the bed, encouraging her.

"Time?" she questioned, suddenly thrilled she could do something besides endure. She'd wanted to push hours ago, and the doctor had told her no.

"Yes, dear, just a few more minutes."

The doctor grinned. Jessie stopped fighting. She worked with the contractions, pushing. But it seemed to take so long, the agony forgotten in the exhilaration of the moment.

"Son of a bitch!" she swore. And it was for Roc, the memories, and the precious life he had given her that was about to make her first appearance into the arms of her family.

"Good for you, Jessica," the doctor encouraged her. "That's the way."

She felt the tension ebb, the pressure less than a moment before. She bore the pain unflinchingly and pushed again. The head had come; now the doctor turned the child and she felt the babe slip out.

She closed her eyes inhaled deep and long then sat up, gazing with awe and delight at the little girl. Alexandra had taken the babe from the doctor. She swiftly handed her to Jessie. They were flesh to flesh, and she'd never felt anything more beautiful.

The moment Jessie held her child next to her heart, she forgot the endless day of pain. Overlooked the months of waiting and the fatigue that consumed her and the toll it took on her body.

Jessie nuzzled the soft downy head then cautiously examined her little hands, counting the toes and fingers, gazing into her smoke streaked eyes that held just a hint of blue. "Isn't she exquisite?"

Alex laughed. "Yes she is, and now you'll have to give her back so we can clean her up. Then I promise you can hold her as long as you want."

Tears fell suddenly. She pushed them back, wishing so deeply Roc had made it back. But he didn't even know she had carried his child.

And she wondered if she could ever forgive him for this slight.

Chapter Fourteen

Bad luck had been their constant companion for months. Everything they had done had met resistance of some kind. Even the trip back from the Yukon, laced with danger and the unexpected, took longer than they had anticipated.

Now, driving rain beat down from the ominous black clouds overhead, leaving a soggy mass of mud and two soggy men in its furious pathway. Jonathan shivered and tugged at his poncho in a futile attempt to keep the wind and the water at bay. Roc stared out at the Columbia River, wishing he could find a warm berth in one of the ships lying at anchor.

But that would have to wait.

They had set up surveillance, Pinkerton style; nothing would deter Jonathan, and his ever-watchful eye, not even the undeniable fact they had managed to learn nothing from their espionage. No one moved about the docks. No one was foolhardy enough to go out in the Oregon downpour. Son of a bitch, it was the middle of June, summer.

The wonderful aroma of sizzling bacon and hot coffee wafted through the solid deluge, tingling their sense; many of Astoria's residents took refuge in the taverns lining the docks. Roc grunted, shifted position before glaring at Jonathan. He'd had his fill. Now it was time to sort through this mess and go have a good honest drink of ale, preferably somewhere cozy and warm.

Jonathan pointed to the white sails appearing at the mouth of the river. Roc grunted again but looked toward the Pacific. The sails meant two more hours of waiting, watching, and wishing for a more comfortable place to sit down.

"Does it ever stop?" Jonathan asked Roc. He moved and slipped in the mud, cursed, then looked at the sails filled with the storm winds. It wasn't the best time to cross the bar.

"The rain? Only when the sun comes out," was Roc's terse reply. "This hasn't amounted to much."

"Hrmph."

Roc whirled, searching with fumbling fingers beneath his poncho.

Jonathan caught the glint of silver and slowly raised his hands.

"Keep them high." The voice, soft yet hard as steel, threatened. Roc joined Jonathan, hands high.

"Pinkerton," Jonathan said when he saw the man's badge, "left pocket." He glanced down.

"Sheriff Clayton," the man said then pulled out Jon's identification. He motioned down the street and put his gun away. "Let's go some place dry where we can talk."

The three men strode down the docks and entered Clayton's office, just as a band of lightning streaked the sky. The office, neat and tidy, offered warmth and a hot cup of coffee. Clayton poured then settled himself behind his desk. He propped his feet up and leaned back in his chair.

"The smuggling?" Roc asked impatiently. "It's been almost a year since that raid failed at the warehouse. It seems you have a bit of explaining to do."

Clayton stiffened and dropped his feet to the floor. "No, I don't. My deputy was on Pierce's payroll. Left with the tide and Pierce." He leaned forward, hands on his desk. "Who are you?"

"Roc Newman. Jessica Newman's husband. Do you remember her?" Roc asked pointedly.

"Jessica and Charity..." His voice trailed off, but Roc didn't miss the slight edge to his voice.

"Ah, so you know the women then?"

A mask settled over Clayton's features. He hesitated. "I know them."

"Then you won't mind telling us if they've been around lately." Roc pressed on, intent for information, although they had thought to find out about Pierce. It seemed prudent now to ask about his wayward wife.

"Perhaps I would mind," Clayton murmured.

"The hell you say. Hey, we're talking about my wife. One who doesn't seem capable of staying out of trouble. If I find out she's continued with this," he paused for breath and control of his temper. Fear and anguish rolled deep inside, and he wanted to shake her. God, but he'd only been back a day, and she'd taken over his emotions again.

Jonathan broke in with a calm air of authority.

"We're on your side, Clayton," Jon said. "Pierce and Rutgers were our main concern until a moment ago. It seems Roc knew his wife rather well and would guess she's involved herself with the smuggling. Am I correct?"

Clayton frowned, his hesitation obvious. "Yes, but they've taken few risks. Most of the time Trevor Lawrence rides shotgun with a number of his men."

Roc felt the nausea begin. Few risks. Most of the time. The two phrases hit him hard. "The last time," he swore.

Clayton fiddled with a pencil on his desk then glanced up. "A..."

Roc thought he'd suffocate. Heat from the tiny fireplace overwhelmed him. His eyes closed and he said a quiet prayer, vowing to work with her when he caught up to her. And help her to realize she can't right the wrongs of her past. All thoughts of compromise slipped from his head, replaced by the gut wrenching fear for her life. "When?"

"Just after midnight three nights ago. She hadn't been here in months though. Heard she had a babe a few weeks back."

Roc sucked in his breath. "A child...they left on the road to Portland? I swear," he swallowed hard, "I swear, this time. Swear what? Swear I'll work with her, help her. And she had a baby--mine? Was it with her? No, don't answer. I don't want to know." His voice had turned to low growl, emotions in turmoil.

"They were well guarded. Trevor brought six men along. Lady says she can shoot as well as anyone. Never had a problem." Clayton shrugged. "At least not yet," he leaned back in his chair and folded his hands behind his back. "Woman trouble?"

"Not for long," Roc insisted, silver eyes gleaming hard as steel. He started to rise from his chair. Jonathan yanked on his arm, motioning him to sit down. "How many wagons?"

"Two."

"Trevor's along? Anyone else I might know?"

"Perhaps, but I wouldn't venture a guess," he told him cautiously. "You planning on following?"

"As soon as I can find a mount. She needs protection, all I can give her."

"Be faster by boat. A friend of mine's leavin' for Portland in about an hour."

Roc grumbled his acceptance then turned to Jonathan.

"I have to stay here," Jon told him. "Time to part company, eh?"

Roc rose, gathered his poncho from the coat hanger and slipped it on. "Take care, Jon, and keep me posted."

"You'll see Annie first. Looks like she'll find an empty house. Hope she stays..." He looked away. "Wouldn't surprise me if she chose to run though."

"You don't have to worry about that," Roc said. "Annie plans on staying."

Jon rubbed his temples. "I hope so. She convinced me, also, but I don't always trust my intuition where she is concerned. Never could. Last time I trusted her she vanished. Didn't see her for ten years." He rubbed the back of his neck. He hadn't slept in days, and it didn't look like a long rest was on his agenda any time soon. Roc was leaving and knew Jonathon had come to rely on his stability and good judgment. They would miss each other.

"She'll be there," Roc said, a confident smile, caressing his features. Then he sobered, remembering his mission and his purpose. "I heard she was planning on setting up a new business."

Jonathan flinched, realizing Roc teased. "She wouldn't dare, not after all I've gone through," Jonathan said.

"All you've gone through. I'm sure the lady can argue the point. I'd handle her with gentle delicacy," Roc urged.

Jonathan chuckled softly. "Listen to your own words, Roc."

"Thanks for the warning, Jon. When I find her, I'll remember your advice. Will try to take it and I'll certainly remember it."

Only a moment later Roc let himself out the door and was walking along the street toward the docks. He bought passage and strode aboard a ship bound for Portland.

He stood on the deck as if he was one with the ship, his poncho flying out behind, his face set and grim, intent on finding Jessica Newman and teaching her a lesson she wouldn't soon forget. If anything, Roc had hardened in the last months. The interminable wait in the Yukon had given him time to think and reconsider his relationship with Jessie. Forced patience while watching the snow fall and the passages close had given him an insight into his character and her crusades. Even now, distracted by the whereabouts of Pierce, and determined to find his wife, his volatile gray eyes sharpened as they studied the bank and watched for any sign of travelers.

Jonathan and Midnight Annie had helped him understand the cause Jessie fought for, women's rights. And he agreed in theory that most women could handle the power voting gave them. He also understood why Jessie was so adamant about helping the women who were enslaved by Pierce.

Annie questioned him, too, on how many men he considered wise enough to vote. He had thought long and hard. In the end, he had to agree that perhaps men didn't have a monopoly on intelligence. Annie's story sickened him. She should have never found herself thrust into such a life because she could find no other way. As she pointed out, it was men who created jobs and hired employees. He had given thought to that also. In any case, he decided he owed Jessica an apology. Until...

Until he discovered she still played a dangerous game. Until he learned she had involved a child. His child.

Damn, he didn't know what to do.

God knew he'd threatened enough. He'd already told her everything he might do, almost everything. The warnings evidently meant nothing to her. It was his fault, he thought, surprised at his admission. Simply put, he had been working against her, not with her. He expected her to comply to his wishes without asking what she wanted. Now it was time for them to come to an understanding.

She had befuddled and dumbfounded him, left him at a loss. His reputation had suffered considerably. Even Drake had found his confusion amusing. At this point he was capable of anything. And all he wanted was to love her forever.

Now Roc gripped the railing harder, watching as the last twinkling lights of Astoria vanished. He relaxed with the easy rhythm of the ship. He wouldn't catch his wife tonight, but in a couple of days. *Ah, just a few days was all she had left.* "Well, I wonder what she'll think when she sees me?"

The boat surged through the river, and Roc gave more thought to Jessica's instruction. No, that wouldn't do at all. "Hmm, but I grow impatient. I have, after all, waited ten long months." His soft words floated out to sea.

The driving rain had turned to mist as the foothills of the coast range came into view, and Roc held to pacing the deck with barely contained patience. After all this time, he would have her soon. He could touch her. Hold her. Protect her....

His eyes flashed, sparked then smoldered.

He'd never forgotten her. His nights, filled with seductive dreams, haunted him. His days, plagued with the sweet infuriating memory of her, tormented him.

She had become his undoing.

Ten months had become an eternity. Her words had thrummed in his head.

And now. Now she was on the other side of these mountains.

He chuckled softly; anticipated the battle then the sweet surrender. For there was no doubt in his mind who would win this contest. The little P.I. had done exactly as she'd pleased. She'd been traveling between Astoria and Salem, rescuing women who didn't have the sense God gave them to stay out of trouble. She'd not listened to his warning about Pierce. Even now Pierce could have returned. He could be stalking her at this moment.

"No, he wouldn't think of that," he told himself.

Nevertheless, the thought left a cold shiver in his heart.

~ * ~

"What's holding you up? Jessica..." Trevor Lawrence asked, distracted and concerned. Jessica's wagon had lumbered along. Now that the lights of Portland loomed just ahead, Trevor had anticipated a warm bath and a soft bed. It seemed, however, Jessica wouldn't make it over the next rise let alone to Portland.

Jessica grunted and tried to ignore him, choosing instead to focus all her energy on the horses and the steady but slow progress she made.

"Go away, Trevor. I'm doing the best I can under the circumstances. The wheel's lose. It may hold until we can get it fixed, but I'm not holding my breath," Jessica told Trevor, leaning forward and giving the reins an impatient shake as if it would solve all her problems. "I know you meant to find a little entertainment tonight, an adventuress or two, but unless you want to leave me here..." she shrugged.

Trevor growled.

"As I was saying, unless you want to go off on your own, I suggest you resign yourself to the inevitable. Another night on the ground." She clucked at the horses then turned her attention back to her cousin. "Trevor, it can't be that bad. It's not going to rain. See, the clouds have disappeared."

Trevor groaned. He'd never wanted Jessie to take this trip. Now it appeared it would take longer than he'd planned. He groaned again. The message from Roc had come two days before they left for Astoria, but nothing he could say short of betraying his friend would keep Jessie home in Salem. "I can't believe your optimism. The clouds haven't vanished, they've merely become a shade lighter than black. I don't ever remember it raining this hard or this long."

"Your memory is convenient, Trevor. I'm sorry, but we simply won't make Portland tonight. There isn't a thing I can do. The girls haven't complained. It seems you could try on some of their courage."

"Complain? Me? I'm the one who's going to have to wallow in the mud to fix the wheel." Trevor looked askance, studying Jessie. She had pegged him. And she was exceptionally stubborn when involved with this project. It seemed to him it was the only time she showed emotion except when she held her daughter.

Charity had devoted her life to this crusade. Jessie, also, at least for now. When Roc caught up with her, though, things would change, sparks would fly and he wondered who would end up the victor. It would happen sooner than he intended if he didn't get this caravan moving. Already they had spent more time getting to the city. Every time he heard hoof beats he cringed. His goal, when they began, was to get to and from as quickly as possible. Unfortunately, if something could go wrong, it did.

Trevor wanted to see them together but not at the expense of his hide. Once they passed Portland, the roads improved, but by his best estimate, it would not make a great deal of difference. Simply put, he calculated Roc would find them tonight or tomorrow. The wee thing in the back of the wagon wouldn't change the outcome of their first encounter. No, the presence of Skye Newman would simply add to the tempest. If the clouds boiling overhead gave any indication of the mood, he would rather not find himself nearby.

Perhaps Jessie would keep a mute tongue. But, no, he couldn't expect that. If he raised his voice once, she'd defend herself wholly, and unless Roc would find it in his heart to concede, the battle would rage. As it stood, little Skye might even find herself overlooked by her proud parents.

Trevor stroked his chin. Yes, life would have turned out far better if they could have reached home in record time as he had planned. And Skye, what of her? If Roc failed to see her before he took Jessie from the wagon, what then? Ah, perhaps he worried too much.

He was deeply concerned for himself if Skye was overlooked. He didn't want to find himself with diapers to change and a howling babe to feed. It was beyond his comprehension. Charity must know something about babies? His peered down the road to the woman driving the first wagon. Charity, ah, thank God. Charity loved the little tyke, crooned over her, took every opportunity to hold her, but had she ever taken care of a child? Trevor cringed and narrowed his eyes. She was a woman, she must know. He looked between the two females. Apprehensive was too mild a term to describe the thunderous thought suddenly choking him. Jessica hadn't known. Didn't have the faintest idea what to do after the child was born. Alex had patiently bathed the newborn and changed her diapers, finally teaching Jessie. The devil.

He wanted this problem to vanish. He suddenly discovered a man couldn't make assumptions about the opposite sex. They would surely encounter discrepancies and falter if they did. The old rules had vanished. He didn't want that to happen. He wanted rules and organization, and he wanted a woman to know her place.

He had thought to laugh at Roc and the confusion he had suffered at the hands of his cousin. But Jessie wasn't the only woman to have such curious thoughts and plans for herself.

Charity had them too. Charity and every other woman who attended the lectures held by Alexandra Lawrence, lectures touting women's rights. He groaned again and cursed himself for his leniency. He could have refused to take Jessie, but when the argument escalated, he had only thought to end it. He hated arguing with his cousin. It was so much easier to give in to her demands and pretend he hadn't.

"Perhaps we should make camp for the night," Trevor said. "I'll ride on ahead and have Charity stop too."

The drizzle they had anticipated had begun and the sky, as well as Trevor's thoughts, was turning darker by the minute.

Jessie looked over the area then turned to check on Skye. Skye, still sleeping soundly, was such a beautiful child, opening her eyes as if she'd somehow sensed her mother's presence. Perhaps she looked for dinner. Her little mouth pursed, and she blinked, taking in her mother's face, the only scenery she could see from her position. She gurgled happily and waved her little fists.

She was perfect. Her eyes had the same smoky glint of her father's, and she had dark raven hair.

Jessie stroked her daughter's cheek, and the little hands swung wildly, finally reaching her mother who let her hold on to her finger. Skye brought the warm object of her delight to her mouth and began sucking then she pursed her lips and howled unhappily. "Hush, sweetheart, this will only take a moment. Once we're settled, I'll give you what you want." Jessie laughed softly at the indignant look appearing on her daughter's face.

"I'll finish here," Trevor said. He'd ridden back and dismounted, tying his horse to the wagon. "Seems you've got another more important job."

"I can manage, Trevor, and Skye can wait. See..." Jessie turned. One of the little Chinese girls had picked Skye up and was cradling her, singing softly and Skye had quieted. She handled her as if Skye was a child she had lost.

Trevor frowned then conceded with great reluctance. "You forget

Roc would not look kindly on your escapades; then you had the nerve to bring the child with you."

Jessie snorted in disbelief. "I haven't forgotten anything. I simply choose to live my life as I see fit. And you forget I haven't heard a word from the scoundrel since he tied me to my horse before running off in the other direction. I don't know if he's alive, and he has no rights where I am concerned, or the child. Besides, look how happy Skye makes her." Jessie pointed to the Chinese girl holding Skye. "They sold her baby in the last port. I let her nurse Skye when her breasts are full and ache with need."

Her eyes were flashing and had turned dark with the rage filling her. He cringed. This was not going as he had planned. "Hah! You'll think otherwise when he comes home."

"When he comes home? Trevor, do you know something?" she asked incredulously.

"No, no." He grumbled then threw himself on the seat of the wagon, grabbed the reins from Jessie's hands and moved the wagon forward. In a matter of minutes, they had caught up to Charity's wagon.

~ * ~

Jessie mumbled under her breath. Of course he knew something. Everyone in Salem knew something, everyone except Roc's wife. She shivered, God, but he did know. And if she thought about it...

"Dash it all." She turned on Trevor. "He's here. Isn't he? He's alive! Tell me, or..."

"I don't know where he is," Trevor lied smoothly. "But he is alive, and if he isn't here yet, he's bound to be soon. I'd heed his warnings if I were you."

Skye wailed. The rocking of the wagon had stopped and she had come to anticipate the significance of that. The gentle singing of her caretaker didn't soothe her rumbling tummy.

"We'll talk about this later, Trevor." She jumped down from the wagon and stretched her arms up to take her wailing child. Her arms formed a protective cradle for the indignant little girl. A large oak tree stood out against the rolling hills, and the ground beneath was almost dry. Jessie headed for it then settled herself comfortably against the trunk. Skye gurgled happily.

~ * ~

Trevor found them both sleeping. The blanket Jessie draped across her for privacy had slipped. Skye's little head poked out from beneath it, her mouth latched endearingly to a nipple, and Jessie snored softly, her head against the tree. Trevor bent down and pulled the blanket back then cleared his throat. "Jessie," he said softly and shook her. She opened her eyes and smiled, adjusted her clothing then handed Skye to Trevor. He gingerly took the babe. Jessie rose, brushed off her pants and buttoned her blouse only to find her huge cantankerous cousin and her daughter grinning at each other.

"So, you've filled your little belly and you think all's right with the world, eh?" Trevor grinned and let Skye play with his nose as he nuzzled her rounded stomach. "Perhaps if you listen to your uncle, you won't grow up to be the brat your mother is," he chuckled softly, feeling the hair prick on the back of his neck. Trevor pulled his gaze away from the child only to find an irate mother glaring at him.

She watched him, and it tempted her to smile but that wouldn't do. No, not after what he'd just said to her daughter. Skye gurgled and crooned, attempting to draw his attention back and had now found his ear and was hanging on madly.

She was a stubborn child.

Too much like her mother. Ah, but Roc would not find this an easy job...parenthood.

"Well, Trevor," she said, "I'm making my own decisions, and I intend to raise my daughter as I see fit. Is there anything else you'd like to warn me about?"

Trevor cleared his throat then looked pointedly away. "No, cousin," he said, wondering just how much longer they had before Roc appeared over the horizon. He cleared his throat, "Far be it from me to try to tell you what to do."

Jessie grinned good-naturedly then ruffled his hair. She held out her arms for her daughter. Trevor handed the babe over before he looked between the two females and threw up his hands in defeat.

Why hadn't he the sense to stay home?

~ * ~

That night the wind howled and rain poured from the sky. They hauled the tents out again and Charity and Jessie shared quarters. Even though the heavens had seen fit to open, it seemed cozy. Jessie played with the baby until Skye became too tired. Then Jessie scooped Skye into her arms, fed her before lying down beside the sleeping child. They listened to the rain fall and soft moaning of wind as it danced between the branches of the trees.

Sometime before dawn the skies cleared and a light breeze chased the last remaining clouds over the valley. Jessie woke. The sky glowed. Where the sun peeked its head over Mt. Hood, an arc of peach colored mist clung to the slopes.

Jessie breathed deeply of the cool fresh air. It cleared her mind and brought a renewed vigor to the morning.

But Jessie had dreamt during the night. Dreamt of Roc and she had trembled in fear then rejoiced with pleasure. She had relived the enchantment he wove magically around her spirit, his touch, the heat of his caress. She wanted him yet he left her terrified. Stubbornly, she had held fast to her beliefs. Obstinately, she had continued the fight she and Charity had begun less than a year ago. Now she trembled, frightened by the man she loved because part of her knew she had thrown herself into dangerous situations and she had involved Skye. Perhaps he could have forgiven the first transgression but not the second.

The camp was breaking. The child needed feeding again.

Trevor paced, impatient to leave. "Hurry, Jessie! Trevor chastised. "I've got to get the wagons going. Let one of the girls drive and feed the babe on the way."

Jessie frowned, cradling her daughter close against the cool morning air. "I don't like that. It unsettles her for the rest of the day. Twenty minutes, Trevor. Twenty minutes. That's all I need...please, Trevor."

"Come on, Jessie. Don't give me that soulful puppy dog look. The devil." Trevor ran his fingers through his hair, swearing. "You win. Twenty minutes, Jessie. Not once second more. You're holding us all up. It's a fine way to start out the day. Behind schedule."

"Who got you up on the wrong side of the bed?"

"Jessie...nineteen minutes," he warned. "Don't waste them. Skye's the only one who will suffer." He gave her a pointed look then turned, denying her the chance to retort.

Jessie snorted and settled herself, with Skye nursing hungrily. She watched Trevor pace and check the harness then pace some more. Every few minutes he would chance a glance in her direction.

Fifteen minutes later, with Trevor fuming and Skye tucked sleepily in her makeshift bed, the wagons began to roll.

"Thanks," Trevor grumbled. It was almost an apology and Jessie smiled.

"For what, Trevor?" Jessie goaded him. "Let's get home. I'm just as impatient. I've had my fill of sleeping on the ground and bouncing on this hard seat," Jessie said firmly, chanced a look back at her daughter, and clucked the horse forward, determined to keep pace with the other wagon. Three more days, she thought. Three long tiring days and they would be home. Yes, she did understand Trevor's impatience.

Trevor watched her sympathetically. "Do you remember, cousin," he said cautiously, "that long ago night you spent grappling with and fighting with Roc Newman over a safe full of papers?"

Jessie smiled knowingly as she focused on the road ahead. She stiffened and her gaze flew to Trevor.

"How could I forget?"

"Did you know you sought more than documents?"

"No."

"Jessie, that was incriminating evidence. Proof meant to put Pierce away for life. Roc thought you worked for them," Trevor said slowly.

"Does he still?"

Trevor avoided her question. Everyone had a tendency to avoid her questions. She wanted Roc to give her a chance.

But she couldn't forget, and she didn't think she could forgive. And somehow, she knew Roc wouldn't understand her need for autonomy.

She had to find a way to make Roc comprehend her motives and her desires, to enlighten him to the new modern way. Somehow, during Roc's time away, she'd come to terms with the nightmares that had haunted her since she was a child. The memories of her mother's rape and death were no longer the driving force behind her actions.

"Perhaps, Jessie, you should stop your childish ways. Isn't all this just a big tantrum? A wild bid for attention?"

"Trevor, you don't believe that?" Her face had lost all color. "If you think...and you know me...then..." Her expression shuddered against realization. She didn't know what to believe. She urged the horses faster, fighting off the anguish and pain suddenly surfacing with Trevor's innocuous question.

She closed her mind and her heart to the thoughts that hurt, wishing she could escape somewhere. Instead, it seemed, she had inadvertently tied herself to the wagon and this horrid road.

Jessie was terrified of seeing him again. Because she had behaved outrageously, because she had endangered Skye by taking her along, yet she had to follow her heart. No, she chastised herself. Selfish, childish, and just plain foolhardy, you deserve whatever comes your way. But please God, don't let that be Roc.

Evening came slowly, plodding along at its uninterrupted pace. With setting of the sun they found themselves camping just south of Portland, on a good road. She felt a moment of relief and safety, the first time since leaving Astoria. She cuddled Skye and played with her in the flickering firelight. The campfire, warm and cozy, offered a feeling of peace, and Jessie began to think nothing could go wrong.

Trevor sat down next to her with a cup of coffee and sipped it slowly. The lines around his eyes had begun to relax. His lips curled in a mischievous smile. He bent to tickle Skye's tummy, and she gurgled outrageously.

"You will have a great deal of explaining to do when Roc comes home," Trevor said. "And I worry about you. It's why I've acted such a bear on this trip. I had this horrid premonition Roc would descend upon us, riding his black stallion and swinging his black whip."

Jessie giggled. "You're scandalous. A black whip?" she laughed hard, eyes watering.

He laughed too "I dreamed he tied you to his horse again and rode off into the forest." He raised an eyebrow, teasing her.

Jessie hit his arm and laughed again. But a cold shadow whispered over her, and she turned back to the fire, suddenly frowning. "Enough, Trevor. I doubt if I'll see him for months. After all, he seems to care more for everyone else than he does for his daughter or me.

The mood turned from merry to sad in a blink and Trevor grimaced. "Jessie, you must learn to take more care in your dealings. I should have never allowed you to come let alone bring Skye. If anything had happened--"

"Nothing happened," she snapped.

"And we aren't home either," Trevor said.

"But I have you for a bodyguard and six of your men. Nothing will happen," Jessie assured him.

"You don't know that."

"No, but, it would take an army to get past you and your men," Jessie paused for a moment.

"Or a friend," Trevor whispered.

The chills came again. Yes, a friend could indeed get past him. Roc could do that and if he came, what then? "Roc?"

Trevor nodded. Jessie stood, trying to hide the trembling of her body. She picked up Skye and walked unsteadily to the tent.

Jessie stopped for a moment. As if in answer to all her fears, the wind as well as all the night sounds seemed to stop and she trembled once more. Jessie wrapped her arms protectively around her child and tried to stop the chills traveling down her spine.

She should have stayed home with Skye.

The trepidation continued long after she tucked Skye into her covers and settled down, protectively shielding the tiny babe. She stared at the wall of the tent for a long time before finally dozing.

~ * ~

The sun rose on another fine day. Steam rose from the ground. The heat of the sun rapidly dried the roads, and it seemed a day perfect for many things. Roc mounted his horse and rode, feeling the fresh southern breeze, the perfume of the rhododendrons and wildflowers that grew haphazardly and the heat of the sun upon his face. Roc's confidence grew with each passing minute. Signs loud and clear indicated his rapid approach to the little caravan. He had ridden from Portland, slow and continuous, changing horses often, continuing well into the night.

He stared down the valley, rolling hills bordered the road and on either side the hills gave way to mountains. Cumulus clouds road the Cascade Range, threatening thunder storms later in the day.

He heard them before he could see the dust from the wagons.

His patient ingenuity had paid off. She was there, less than a mile from him.

It had been such a long time.

He had missed her. Yet before he could love her, or even welcome her into his embrace, they would have to come to terms.

Chapter Fifteen

"Son of a bitch!"

The words exploded then vanished. A roll of distant thunder spooked the horses, and lightning flashed in the distant foothills. The horses panicked and shot forward.

"Jessie..." his words trailed off and his heart lurched to his throat. He was a wild man, watching as Jessie groped for the reins the horses had pulled from her hands. The wagons bounced and it seemed they hit each hole and rock that lay in the road.

She was there, scrambling against the furious motion, leaning over the edge, stretched as far as she could. But still her fingers remained inches from the dragging reins.

No, Jessie.

Terror gripped him. He cursed, swallowing his fear then sending his mount charging down the road after the wagons. *Damn you, Jessie. Stop before you kill yourself.* God, but she still managed to infuriate him, plague him, and she stubbornly refused to give up.

Beautiful and passionate, her raven hair shimmered beneath the few golden rays of the sun splitting the clouds. Dust swirling, horses hooves pounding, frantic, she finally reached the reins and struggled back to the seat ready to battle the horses and their fear. She should have shown fear. Instead she pulled back, crying out the horses' names before crooning softly to them.

Trevor had reached the lead wagon and brought it to a stop then turned his attention to Jessica. Her wagon raced by and Roc could hear Trevor curse. It took only a few more minutes before Jessie's wagon had slowed, the horses puffing.

Then he grinned with satisfaction and slowed his horse. He could have never ridden that far in time to save them from that perilous flight. It didn't appear anyone was hurt. Trevor was apparently determined to keep the wagons moving. Intrepid fellow, Roc thought, but how he had allowed Jessica to talk him into this?

His horse nickered softly and he pushed his black poncho off his shoulder. "Ah, my little kitten, we'll see...we'll see. Tonight," he said softly. "You will understand and we'll make new promises to each other. I vow, Jessie, that we will."

"Hmm," he moved his horse to the cover of trees then continued his curious scrutiny of the people below. Charity had joined in the discussion. She jumped off the wagon and stood her ground, glaring blatantly at Trevor. It seemed she refused to continue. Trevor gave in and led the two of them off the road to a small clearing. He motioned for his men to bring the wagons.

Jessie followed behind the horses and her wagon. The sway of her hips enticed him, and he moved casually, readjusting his position in the saddle.

Roc's lips curled derisively. He had never really decided what he would say to her. Ah, tonight they would begin anew.

Trevor glanced his way again and saw him doff his hat to him in salute then nodded in understanding. "We'll be home tomorrow whether we camp here tonight or push on. The horses need a rest and so do I."

Jessica stared questioningly at her cousin. Even as he turned his back on her and blithely sauntered away to tend to the horses, she glared at him. It appeared to her something was afoot. He had stared at the hillside foolishly with a horrid look of chagrin painted on his features. Then he'd turned back, issuing orders; no one could sway him.

A silence pervaded the easy chatter and gossip that usually marked the end of the day.

~ * ~

Silhouetted against the dying sun, Roc Newman rode, arrogant and handsome. Jessie turned and choked back a startled gasp and a shocked, *No*. A moment of fear and a simple reminder of her impulsive nature plagued her heart and her mind as her gaze focused unerringly on him. The world began to turn and spin. She fought for control and thrust her chin high. She had nothing to be ashamed of. Let him make the apologies and the explanations.

Trevor's men stepped aside and let him pass. He rode through the group, ignoring Jessie and headed straight for Trevor. The strange visions and the terror she'd felt at night in her dreams when she slept stared back at her. For indeed, Roc was dressed for the night, and in his hand he brandished a black whip.

He turned slowly. His gaze, now aimed at Jessica, gave warning she would soon regret this trip.

"Trevor, I came for my wife." His voice was harsh and rang through the little clearing. "Don't try to stop me." The horse sidestepped, tension collected around him and Jessie trembled. She shook her head, an unconscious plea, to no avail. She backed up, still staring at the black rider and his whip. Her courage faltered.

Trevor nodded then spoke before Roc could capture the object of his intent, Jessie "I can't let you do that," he began.

"You have no choice in this."

"I want your promise you won't hurt her," Trevor's eyes suddenly as hard as Roc's and as determined.

"I swear to you on my honor," Roc commanded his regard and his trust, "that I will not touch her in anger. I will not harm her, she'll suffer no pain." But his masked expression offered no further explanation and Trevor asked for none.

A long pause followed while the two men studied each other and the meaning in their words. Jessie watched, speechless. How could he hold it against Trevor? He was her cousin, had grown up with her, had held responsibility for her over the years only conceding that to him a year ago. Then he'd vanished and the task had fallen on Trevor's shoulders once again.

~ * ~

"Trevor, believe me. I mean her no harm." He turned to look at his trembling wife. She had moved further into the trees, slowly inching her way into the brush and the forest behind. Her face a white mask of fear. Damn, he didn't want her to fear him.

Before he could speak again, Trevor had searched for Jessie, comprehended Roc's intentions then held out his hand. "I understand and I won't interfere. She is, after all, your wife. But I'd like a moment with you first to explain."

Roc sat, resting his arm against the saddle, nonchalantly. He waited mindful of his wife who stood, her back stiff.

"In private," Trevor muttered.

"And give my wife a chance to run? No, I don't think so," he said and continued his watchful demeanor. She had suddenly returned to her wagon and was rummaging through the back. "Ah, but what do you suppose she is up to?" he asked Trevor. "I could have sworn I would have to charge through the bushes."

Trevor swallowed hard and ventured a glance at Jessie. Charity had come up beside her and they were whispering together. "Easy," Trevor warned him. "Remember your promise."

"Yes," he said. Then he held her with his gaze. His heart trembled and the anguish he felt for her riddled within. God, but he dreaded this night. He had thought of it so many different ways and when he'd ridden after her from Astoria, he hadn't known how to deal with her. He meant to describe the auction at Midnight Annie's place even while he needed to hold her close and chase her fears away with his love.

Her innocence had endeared her to him, but now he had to rid her of it. It got in the way, made her naïve, and she wouldn't live the year out if he couldn't make her understand.

All he had wanted to do was love her. He had missed her, longed for her in the lonely nights. But he had returned and found her risking life and limb, without a thought to the consequences. Yet he understood why but that didn't rid him of his terror or his nightmares.

He tightened his hold on the reins, feeling the same pain and fear for her life that caused him so many long, tortured, sleepless nights. He turned his attention back to Jessie and she had vanished.

But her friends had given her path away.

For a moment, he hesitated, wondering just how he should proceed. The wait had seemed interminable, but she had just made him realize how much he terrified her. Horror was not an emotion he wanted his wife to feel for him.

~ * ~

Jessie gulped in air, panicked, and pushed another long branch from her face. Her foot caught on a gnarled old root and she stumbled, groping for support. She wrapped her hand around the vines of a blackberry bush and grimaced at the pain. Blood pooled in her hand and streaks of red painted her wrists. Her heart flew furiously against her chest. She rested a moment, looked around to get her bearings and moved on.

All around her the forest had come to life. Sounds, some familiar and some frightening, closed in around her. Sweat popped out on her skin and she ran on, ignoring the reason for her flight, disregarding the lazy sound of a horse pursuing her.

The sky seemed blacker and the stars seemed brighter, for the moon had become a tiny sliver in the sky. Tension tightened in her and spiraled. Her breasts heaved from exertion, fury, and the fear of his retribution. When she first saw him, she knew. Had indeed recognized the unholy flash of vengeance in his gaze.

She forced herself to continue. Her legs would carry her no farther, but she couldn't let him win. A second bolt of energy surged within; adrenaline pumped through her system, hooves pounded furiously behind. She thought if she could scramble through the bushes just ahead, his horse would never follow. It would balk. A last desperate surge of energy and she was almost there.

"Jessie stop," he called. But she didn't stop. Her terror pushed her past her endurance.

This time she felt his arm wrap around her middle. She was pulled against his chest, jolting her back to reality. She could never escape him.

He turned her, holding her at arms length. She felt ready to stand her ground this time. Saw the amusement in his eyes as she tried desperately to stand straight and tall. They were alone, irreversibly alone. She could feel the strength of him, smell the scent that was uniquely his, longed for him to hold her and soothe the fears, for truly, she hadn't meant to break her promise.

"What do you want?" she cried out.

"Jess, Jessie, Jessica...."

"Let me go. You have no reason to do this."

He smiled as he pulled her to him. His mouth slanted and came down across hers.

She pushed against him, her fists beating against his chest. She managed to jerk her head away. "Don't," she cried, trying to wrest free from his hold, tried to throw him, her body heaving against his, her eyes ever more amethyst and defiant. "You left me...didn't write...I thought you were d-dead...and now...now you come back and think you can step into my life without even asking. Let me go."

"Do I think I can come back into your life without asking? Oh, yes, Jessica, I know I can. And as for letting you go," he hesitated a moment, "never."

Roc, ever confident, always so self-assured, so convinced and determined to have his way, studied her with bold assessment, his gaze raking over her body, seeming to familiarize himself with her, growing ever bolder. She felt the heat of his gaze and her rising passion then gasped, desperate to breathe.

And his fingers wound through her hair, slowly pulling her head back so he could memorize every detail.

A harsh oath escaped him. Her struggles continued and they forced him to pull her closer. He cursed again, sweeping her into his arms and striding to his horse, setting her upon his back. She was determined to fight, the task would not be an easy one. He caught her wiggling derriere with a resounding but firm hand and held her still.

"Jessie, please stop fighting me. I don't understand..."

Oh, but he did. She would not call it quits. Before he could mount, she had inched her way again over the horse until she balanced precariously. He clung to her then pulled her swiftly back.

He held her still, and with deft moves he covered her mouth with his, silencing her. His kiss singed and burned, yet she responded. For a moment, he held her away from him and lifted his finger to her chin. She watched and the silver flame of his eyes snagged her attention. She cowered, moving as far from him as he'd let her, having no idea what he intended.

He shifted back, settling her in front of him on the horse. Snug and secure and hating every minute, she cringed against him as he pinned her against his chest. He held her firmly and she wiggled, trying to dislodge his hand, but he allowed her movement to carry his hand higher so he caressed her intimately, and it seemed even through the layers of clothing he could feel the heat and her desire awakened.

"Jessie, please, I mean you no harm. We need to talk."

"You don't listen."

"This time I will. I promise," he told her, riding toward the wagons.

A few minutes passed and he held Skye in his arms.

To Trevor, "We will be back in the morning."

The ground below turned and the movement made her dizzy. She closed her eyes against the roll and sway and the blur. He moved the horse quickly through the rugged terrain, gently urging the horse on when it shied and refused to go farther.

Finally, Roc halted. A stream flowed near by. He dismounted and helped her down, leaving her sitting beneath a huge old oak as he moved about, handing over the baby before tending to his horse first then the campsite. She stared at him as he gathered wood for a fire. Smelled the smoke and heard the crisp blaze and the snap of the dry wood as it caught the flames. Still, she remained alone, clinging to a ragged hope he would forgive her soon.

Eternity moved slowly and she listened for his other movements, rustling now with his provisions, the clank of utensils, and the sizzle of water evaporating on the hot rocks. Now she smelled coffee and baking beans. Her stomach rolled and cried out for food. She could hear the clank of the tin as he dished up the food and she nearly drooled. Then he handed her one before giving her a cup of coffee. Her breasts, now engorged with milk, longed for release. Her body ached and she had never felt more miserable.

She needed to feed Skye but she suddenly felt shy. "Roc, I need... Skye needs."

"Of course, go ahead."

"Privacy?"

He paused with his fork halfway to his mouth then set it on his plate. "Jessie, I'm your husband. Please feed our child."

Tears of frustration began to well in her eyes, but she forced them back. Stubborn pride climbed from the depths of her despair. But she proceeded, and a few seconds later Skye suckled at her breast.

"That is the most beautiful sight I've ever seen."

When Skye finished, he took her, holding her and cooing nonsense.

A little while later Trevor appeared from the darkness. "I'll take her back now. She'll be fine." He disappeared into the night.

"Jessie," he said. "I'm going tell you about Midnight Annie and the auction in Alaska."

He had moved so he towered over her. A hard mask covered his expressions and she flinched.

"You don't have to do that. I'm sure... I'm sure I can imagine what goes on."

He sat beside her, taking one of her hands to hold in his. "It was horrible, Jessica," he said, his tone harsh. "I don't believe your mind could envision what happens to those women, what could happen to you."

"I could live the rest of my life without hearing about it."

"Jessica..."

She smiled, a bitter smile then shook her head, knowing he was different. Events had changed him. "Who is Midnight Annie?" A strange curiosity took hold.

"A madam. I met her in Alaska." He stared into the night, his thumb rubbing gentle circles on her hand.

"You've strayed a long ways from home." Her heart went out to him even as she wondered what hardships he might have endured during his quest to find Pierce and bring him to justice.

"That's another story." When he looked at her, his eyes appeared sad and weary.

"What about this lady? A friend? Or foe?"

"If I tell you about her and what I saw, will you cease your adventures?"

"Roc, this was the last trip Charity and I were going to take. I promise. But no one can foresee the future."

He held up his other hand. "Stop, I don't want to hear promises. I'm trying not to ask you to obey, and I'm not going to threaten you." He reached out to touch her cheek. "God, has it been a year?"

Tears slid down her cheeks. He wiped them away with a gentle touch she had longed for but had not expected. "The longest year of my life."

He told her so much, details she didn't want to know about; white gossamer dresses, drugs, like the one that had been put in her wine. The madam had been understanding and loving to the women, offering them honest work if they wanted and expecting nothing in return.

"I just want you to understand, and I want to keep you safe. I want to feel the sweet wildfire of love I know you can give me. But after all I've put you through..."

He stood and vanished into the woods as if he couldn't stand the sight of her, as if he needed to put distance between them.

"What you've put me through? Roc, I've defied your wishes at every turn. Can you forgive me?" she whispered into the empty space of the dark night. She felt as if so much had been said and nothing had been resolved.

Chapter Sixteen

Jessie sat on the rock near the fire. A wild fear and a horrid confusion invaded her mind. No matter what else, she'd find a way to compromise. She loved him, and she had never meant to lose his trust. She had only pursued the calling of her heart.

He had never understood her. And now, sweet Jesus, where was he? She had no idea what this was all about. She'd thought he would never return.

She just wanted to explain. Make him realize...

He appeared out of the woods, suddenly stepping into the firelight. She stiffened, wondering which man would was standing in front of her.

He stepped closer, letting his shadow fall across her.

Apparently, he had gone for a swim; with water dripping from his hair, his black shirt clinging to his chest, he looked liked the man she thought she had once known. He walked around the campfire with a natural grace; regal, powerful, foreboding.

So very different from the man she remembered. He had changed so much. She cringed at what he must have gone through on the ship as a prisoner. Perhaps now would be a good time for him to tell her more.

She had so many questions. Had no idea what had happened to him when he raced a way from her that long ago night. No one had told her or even thought to prepare her for this moment.

Trevor had known though. He had known Roc lived and he would return.

Roc strode toward her, his gaze solidly riveted on her, but he kept a slight distance. He smoothed a seat on his bedroll, patting the space next to him in invitation.

"My ploy was exposed soon after I boarded Pierce's ship. Spent most of my time on board in the hold with a Pinkerton agent." His voice was harsh.

"You blame me."

"No, I was careless, but I suppose my identity would have been discovered soon enough."

"I don't know where we go from here."

He arched a brow, staring at her. Her eyes closed as if she could deny his experiences by the simple gesture.

"It is for your life," he said slowly. "You must take every possible care not to fall into his hands. Yet, despite what I said earlier, I need to hear your promise and know you will obey. I just can't get past that."

"I have, Roc. I have taken care and no harm has come to me. I won't mindlessly promise to obey. We can have discussions though, a bit of give and take as if we're both adults."

He swore and turned away from her and began to pace. She wondered what he thought. He stopped suddenly then turned to watch her.

"Pierce was not in town. I forgot just how stubborn you are. I had to remind myself that even if you agreed now, I cannot trust your word. I've walked that path too many times."

"So we are back to the beginning."

"We are," he said.

She had told him from the start only vows she gave willingly she would keep. He could not force her to a promise then expect her to keep it. Indeed, she had nothing to feel guilt or shame over.

"You can you know, trust me. I've changed since you vanished without a word."

"Perhaps, but I'm going to walk you through the auction. I want you to understand first hand what might befall you."

She felt a brief moment where everything seemed clear, and she knew with restraint she could endure anything. She simply had to remind herself he was her husband and she loved him. Yet, a deep sense of foreboding swept through her.

Clarity swiftly vanished, for she saw the deep lines of anger knit across his brow.

"I don't want to talk about it. I don't want to know, and I don't understand your anger."

He ignored her. "First, you'll be dressed in a wispy fabric which will swirl around your legs, fluttering with the hot evening breeze, teasing and uncovering various parts of you to everyone's view. Since the day I first met you, I have wondered how best to handle your impulsive and reckless nature. I have toyed with many ideas, but never, Jessie, never could I bring myself to hurt you. I won't lay a hand on you in anger no matter what you do. If I could just find a way to get you to listen..."

"I always listen," she whispered vehemently, but the tone of her voice stopped him. It was hard and unforgiving.

He had made his decision.

He swore softly. "The material Pierce will drape across you will leave you exposed and vulnerable." The determination in him was terrifying.

"Roc, I beg you," she said. "I don't want to know. It hurts so much. Your first explanation should suffice."

Her words seemed to strengthen his will. "You must understand. Damnation, Jessie, you've given me no choice. You will try so hard to be brave. You will stand above them, trembling. You will try to jut your chin out, showing Pierce your scorn. Their gazes will roam the length of you, over your breasts, soaking in the ivory flesh the material does not cover." His voice was hard. "They will touch you anywhere they please. I'm sorry," he whispered.

"You need say nothing more." She blinked back tears, understanding a great deal more then inhaled quickly. "I see."

"Next, the men are allowed to examine the merchandise."

"The women are not merchandise, but living breathing human beings with rights and privileges. I would not let them do this. I swear it."

"You will have lost those considerations," he said quietly, his voice hard. "And they will give you no choice."

"I won't play your game, Roc. You can stop anytime. I don't need every detail."

"Jessie--"

"I would scream if anyone touched me."

Still his face showed no emotion, no anger, nothing. "You could do that. But no one who might care would hear."

"No, you don't know how loud I can scream."

"Ah well, but now it's time. Jessie, do you know what still awaits?"

"Nothing awaits. You're going to cease this and take me back to the caravan."

A brow arched again. "You will flinch away from exploring hands, trying hard to maintain a distance between them, the men who are there to buy you. Each man who has the cash is given the opportunity to see and examine what they are there to purchase."

Impulsively, she caught her lip between her teeth, shivering, despite the heat of the night and the horrid flush that had covered her body. She remembered the drugged wine and the way it made her feel.

"They will make you open your legs, Jessie."

She shook her head. "No," she whispered vehemently, tears streaming down her cheeks. A soft sob escaped her.

"I think," he began, "that you should know what will happen if you refuse their request. He nodded to the four stakes he had planted in the ground. Then looked to her for a sign of recognition. Nothing.

"I've no idea..."

"How curious. Can't you even imagine? Think Jessica."

And it seemed as if a beacon of light entered her mind. She shook her head wildly, denying her thoughts.

"Yes, Jessie." He nodded. "That's where you'll be placed, your ankles and wrists bound to a stake."

"No," she shook her head again. "They wouldn't."

The wind whipped from her lungs at the very thought. Her face lost all color and she begged him with her gaze then her voice. "No, Roc, I asked you to stop. I don't want to hear this." She covered her face with her hands, a sob ripping through her.

"I don't want this to happen to you" he hesitated, his will faltered. "For now, I'll leave it to your imagination."

This was a nightmare. Jessie could not believe. Absolute hardness and lack of compassion in his eyes touched some cord deep inside her. He meant to continue, she could tell.

She would make him pay for this, and she suddenly understood the need for revenge.

He continued his dialogue, seeming to leave nothing out.

But neither could she fight him, or the stinging words of truth he spoke.

He stepped back from her, suddenly watching her for a moment, waiting.

"Next..." he said.

Her eyes grew wider and she searched the woods, confused. But no one came and she breathed slowly calming her frayed nerves and quavering senses.

"Now, Cat, since the first man is done, another man will get his chance to observe your charms close up. It will all begin again."

"No, you can't mean--"

"Yes," he said. "Anyone who has enough money."

God, she thought she would die just thinking about what could happen.

Belittled. Degraded...

Forced into prostitution and enslavement.

No, but she would not give into this ridiculousness. Never and she braced herself against the servility he spoke of. In some strange way it made her more determined to save the helpless women. Yet, she understood the consequences and knew she would need an army behind her.

"It's your lucky day, Cat. You've been sold to the highest bidder. Now someone owns you, body and soul."

Her face went pale, understanding at last the implications of his words and her impulsive behavior. He was a concerned husband, trying to convince her not to put her life at risk.

"Now, I would like to make love to my wife. I need to put all this in the past. I've never wanted to hurt you, but I had to make myself clear. I watched an auction. It was worse than I described."

His heated palms drifted evocatively over the swell of her breasts, moved down her ribs and narrow waist, memorized the smooth slight flare of her hips, trailing slowly to the beckoning juncture of her thighs. Teasing the soft, hot flesh and her dark silky hair, heard the sound of her surrender as she rose to the pressure of his hand. Anger warred with obsession in Jessie's mind and in her heart; her hot flushed skin prickled with desire, but stubborn pride surged to the breaking point and frozen, she stared at him with surging passion. He tore her jeans off then slid his long fingers into her dampness, into the beckoning haven that lured; he pointedly stroked the velvet softness and watched her writhe beneath his assault. Jessie moved lightly into each gentle thrust of his hand, unable to deny the pleasure he gave her.

"Roc, please...I...want you, now," she whispered.

~ * ~

Jessie offered so much, and he hungered for her like a starving man. He could feel a pulsing ache creep into his body. She had surrendered completely, and he wondered then if that was his intent. He had found her and seduced her but what of his purpose? What of her real and threatening danger? She had promised nothing.

He withdrew his fingers and moved away from Jessie to lean on his elbow. The time for her promise was here, he intended to get it from her now before...

Had he been able to convince her?

No, he wouldn't. He had to get control of himself. This beautiful woman who had annoyed him from the first moment he laid eyes on her could send his soul to the devil. This woman who had the attention of two white slavers who sought revenge and would not rest until they had Jessica Newman sold to the highest bidder. Who had refused to heed his warnings and in that had forced him to this conclusion he would have avoided. He spoke again, his voice faltering but his tone brusque and harsh. "You won't like me." But he could not leave her like this.

"Roc...please..." she gasped. Her body shuddered.

He ignored the plea. "Promise me." And he scrutinized with deep regard the glorious woman he had loved for so long, proud and willful, her outward nature and enigma, paradoxically confusing.

She pursed her lips together, closing her eyes as thinking.

"Your promise?" he asked softly.

"I comprehend everything." Her eyes were wild and frantic. "But all I can say is that I'll make each decision with care and I'll consult you whenever possible."

"Jessica," Roc murmured, "that's just not good enough. If Pierce gets hold of you, you'll give up more than your freedom."

She struggled against Roc's words, "It has to be. It's all I can give you.

She lowered her lashes, letting them rest against her pale skin.

Then he slowly relaxed, anticipating her acceptance of his wishes.

The following silence filled him with frustration, and he watched the tensing of her body and slight tilt to her chin and recognized the signs. He was no closer to his goal. He swore then and instead of carrying out his promise, eased away. He waited, hovering over her until her arms rose on their own accord to circle his back. His hands closed on her hips, and he tenderly kissed her, and when she'd finally surrendered to him, his eyes shut briefly and he groaned deep in his throat, holding back his desire to sheathe himself within her.

He brushed kisses across her face, again and again, heedless of time or space, hating himself for his failure, his lack of restraint. Her perfect breasts feathering the texture of his shirt as he loved her.

Jessie cried out her despair and her fear for herself, responding passionately to his erotic seduction despite her efforts against it. She was wild. Her traitorous body defied her thoughts and dissolved within minutes to a throbbing need.

Mercuric and selfish, he had thought only of himself, as though Jessie was no more than a pawn set on earth for his own purposes. It had been so long and he had missed her intensely. He could not help himself and swore once more at his loss of command. He swiftly rose to tower above her. His chest heaved and labored as he denied himself. Desire ravishing his thoughts, he gazed at the smooth white flesh, her flat stomach and the glorious black hair. God, she deserved better than him.

She was twisting, arching upward, and he had left her pulsing with pent up desire. Roc stepped back, cursing himself, and this ungodly promise he had determined to extract from her.

He groaned and swore again. He lay beside her once more, barely touching, one hand finding her, teasing and building the sensation until he brought her to climax. She cried out and he swiftly kissed her. It was nearly his undoing. She was shivering and trembling with his caress. Her eyes closed as she reached the pinnacle of her pleasure, and he thought he died a thousand deaths.

It seemed as if he'd journeyed to hell and back. She was glaring at him now, eyes blazing. Her stubborn pride had returned full force, and he saw the bitter hate born from this night. She understood his manipulation of her.

He smiled then, a determined smile, knowing the charade would have to play to the end. He needed a promise. He stood, turned quickly, and walked from the clearing, leaving her desolate and forlorn. He blamed Jessie for the chaos in his mind, blamed her for the horrid mess they'd made out of their marriage, for this hot, fierce need to protect her at any and all cost to their relationship.

A sob tore through her and it pierced his heart, sending the anguished stab of the knife deep into his soul. It seemed he could hear Jessie's heart beat in a frenzied staccato pounding madly against her chest. He knew she hated him and everything he stood for. At this moment he hated himself. Even with his warnings and threats of such treatment and all the women she had helped live again after enduring similar situations, she had never expected this. He had succeeded. And despite it all, she had willingly given herself to him, wrapped her arms around him, inviting his touch.

From a distance he watched her close her eyes, saw the anguish in her expression. Hoped she could find a way to deal with this, his unrelenting thirst to wrench her unbendable pride, her independence and her freedom from her. But he hadn't truly intended that, had meant only to keep her and his daughter safe.

Then he walked back to the clearing. Knew the soft tread of his boots sounded loud and threatening. While he'd been gone she'd dressed.

Jessie.

Why the hell was she so damn stubborn, he wondered furiously? She had more strength than he had ever imagined.

He bent over her, brushing her tangled hair away from her eyes, outlining the fragile bones of her face. He saw the flush cover her body again. He reached for her hand and pulled her gently to her feet then into his embrace, holding her for but a moment.

He had never felt so cold. Unshed tears stung his eyes.

"Perhaps we can come to an understanding tomorrow."

He wouldn't because he hated himself and his inadequacy, and his guilt...and he wouldn't allow himself to back down now. But he kept his voice steady when he told her good night.

~ * ~

Neither slept well that night. Jessie fell victim to self-pity and loathing, softly sobbing until exhaustion claimed her. Roc listened and cursed himself again for his callous behavior, searching his brain for another way, finding nothing, then swearing at her pride. All he wanted was to pull her close and soothe her battered spirit.

Morning brought fresh air and sunshine, but it didn't lift her heart and encourage a new beginning. Roc rose swiftly and stood before her, waiting for the words that would set her free, but she withheld them, her pride once more getting in her way. Oh, she had learned her lesson, his tale had not sifted through an empty head, but her pride disavowed any admittance of wrongdoing.

I cared for you, she cried out silently to him. Tears began again. "I missed you. I had already planned to stop this crusade and relentless pursuit of danger. You didn't have to do this," she whispered and he never heard.

"Jessie," he said softly, handing her a plate of food. "Eat."

She accepted the food but only pushed it around. The fork fell to the ground, and she stared at it.

Lifelessly, she gazed at the forest and beyond, as if searching for some way to vanish. It seemed she lacked the courage now. "Roc?" she whispered softly. Her eyes lowered, the gentle sweep of her lashes falling delicately across her cheekbones.

He looked up. His expression masked. For he didn't trust her, didn't trust the soft beguiling tone of her words. After all, he had hoped for compliance, a swift end to this nightmare, even prayed for it, but he had never expected it.

"What now?" He studied her and she looked so vulnerable and hurting, he berated himself then cursed. Still he could see no other way...

"I promise," she looked at him then. And he felt a new wave of guilt surge within and damned himself for the weakness.

"No, Jessie...that's not enough. What do you promise?"

She stiffened at the harsh reality his words elicited. Tempted once more to deny him the victory and her willing surrender then silver flamed in the steel gray hardness of his eyes and she felt the horrible reality of being someone's whore. She broke out in a cold sweat, trembling and shuddering so she could only gasp for air. His gaze held no compassion only a stubborn determination to convince her.

"I..." she began but he cut her off.

"What Jessie, say it, don't prolong this any longer than necessary."

"Promise to obey."

"Ah, my little love, who will you obey?" He gazed at her, wishing he could have accomplished this some other way.

"You," she whispered. Her eyes shut. Like hell, she cried silently.

"Look at me." Her eyes opened.

"That's good. You won't try to rescue any maidens in distress."

"No."

"Good," Roc said very harsh.

She fought the battle raging within her, fought the tempest that fired her thoughts and her pride, but she allowed him to have his way in this.

And she vowed...that she would have her revenge.

Chapter Seventeen

Jessie rode in his lap, exhausted and listless, eyes staring blankly ahead.

It was going to be challenging and formidable, difficult to undo the damage he had done. He cursed himself for a fool, berated himself, but in the end he'd simply had no choice, could think of no other way. Ah, the dread of it was that it had worked too well. In the end he had not only tamed the little hellion, he had stripped her of her spirit, tore everything away down to her soul then kept going. But he wondered...no, he shook away that thought. It couldn't be.

This woman in his arms was not his Jessie. She had died last night, and he had caused it, afraid if he had shown her a gentle and caring side she would not have understood. Afraid compassion would ruin the advantage he had gained. Afraid for her life, but what kind of life would she have now if he could not undo this great wrong he had heaped upon her?

He had within him a great power and he had wielded it, to his regret.

So Jessie was going to have a taste of his devotion. He was going to make absolutely sure she knew he had not meant to change her, had only meant for her to understand what could happen to her.

He began by carrying her into their bedchamber and ordering a hot bath and a magnificent feast for both of them then called Charity and Annie. He stayed out of Jessie's sight, allowing Charity to work her magic, waited patiently, hoping time would begin to heal the wounds and there would be no lasting scars.

He paced, sat, stared at the fireplace then paced again. A walk in the gardens didn't ease his mind nor did the rapid gallop he commanded down

State Street.

Charity would have sent him to hell when she finally confronted him, but Perkins swayed her anger and consoled her, explaining Roc's good intentions.

But it was only Trevor's restraining hand that kept Charity from murdering Roc. And they all prayed Jessie would recover soon.

Annie arrived in town on the train. She accompanied Charity, and she was notably compassionate to any abused woman. Her line of work had given her an adept insight to this type of withdrawal and a proficient knowledge in healing the mind and the spirit. She would shower them with love and empathy, encouraging them to talk of the ordeal and she would listen.

Maybe he had told them too much; on the other hand, perhaps he hadn't told them enough. Guilt slid down his spine, and he wanted to handle this himself, but he'd already done more than necessary.

So he stayed away. And when the afternoon wore on, his patience thinned, he discovered he had to reason with her, go to her, see for himself that she would regain her fire and life and tempestuous magic he'd come to adore. The indomitable spirit that was Jessica Lawrence, Jessie his wife, and Jess Law the independent woman who had defied the role society had thrust upon her with determination and resilience.

Jessie, still sequestered in their bedchamber, whispered low and secretive with Annie. "Can't hide from him forever, Jessie. He's your husband, you know. From the sounds of it, he didn't hurt you. If that had been Pierce, Jessie..."

"Don't say it," Jessie told her softly, leaning back against the headboard of the huge bed that they had once shared. "I know it would have been a thousand times worse, but..." she whispered. "He took it upon himself to be God, the judge and the executioner. I had already decided I wouldn't go again. But did he stop to ask?" Her fury at the indignation and the ordeal he had put her through had surfaced hours ago. And if Roc had heard half of what they said in that room, he would have bounded up the stairs and hauled her back for another lesson instead of wallowing in guilt.

"Well, now, did you tell him that? From what you've said to me, you didn't. Now, Jessie, if I heard you right, you let your stubborn pride get the better of your good judgment, and you refused to tell him what he needed to hear. I don't condone the method, but it seems better than beating you half to death like some men do or even allowing you your own way that would have eventually landed you in a heap of trouble. The danger is not over yet either. From what I've heard, Pierce is back in the country. So, perhaps he had good reason to fear for you. Now I think both of you owe each other an apology. Roc, for putting you through that hell, and you, Jessie, for pretending to make him miserable."

"He deserves to feel the same anguish I did."

"Ah, but that's the crux of the matter, Jessie. You don't feel near as bad as you led him to believe."

And it was most obvious that Midnight Annie had seen through her charade quite handily, and berating her every minute of enjoyment she had in seeing him suffer. She hadn't exactly been able to watch him, but she could hear his cursing and the pacing. Had watched him gallop his horse without heed, mindlessly away from the house, before seeking solitude in the gardens. Yes, she'd enjoyed that, but Annie didn't think it very well of her for continuing with the pretense. In the beginning she'd helped her, but now...

Now, as Annie succinctly put it, it was time to ease his torment.

But she didn't want to. He hadn't suffered nearly enough. Another twenty-four hours would do him good.

It wouldn't happen though because Annie had told her specifically that if she didn't get dressed, go down for dinner, and tell him she was alright, then she'd send him up here to discover for himself.

She shuddered at that idea. Quite frankly, she didn't know what to tell him. Didn't want to see him, and the very thought of another bout of punishment sent all her courage flying.

It was a simple matter at first. She had truly felt bashed and bruised, in spirit and soul, her heart bleeding and her mind unforgiving. But she bounced back swiftly. After a hot bath, a good meal, and holding her beautiful daughter once more in her arms, she realized the ordeal had taught her things she would never forget.

But she still wanted him to suffer at least a small portion of her agony.

"What's it to be, Jessie?"

"I don't know," she said. "I'm afraid." She rose from the bed and wandered aimlessly around the room. Pictures of her daughter and one of Roc stared back at her. Sunlight filtered through the lace curtains and left a myriad of dancing patterns on the lush Persian rug at her feet. She looked down below and saw Roc leaning against a huge oak tree, gazing intently up to her room then the attic window. Air hissed from her; she swiftly stepped back, praying he hadn't seen her.

"You shouldn't fear him," Annie said softly. "Roc Newman is a good man. Gentle and understanding. He was worried about you."

"He threatened...never did anything about it though...except make love to me. Every time he got angry..."

"He what?" Annie laughed.

Jessie turned and stared at her confused. "Made love," she said.

"Give me a man like that any day and I would never let him go."

That was interesting. Jessie kept her thoughts to herself while Annie rambled about men and their propensities.

"Perhaps you're right, Annie," Jessie said with a sigh. This time she stepped up to the window and remained in full sight, allowing Roc to memorize every detail of her.

Pleased by the concerned expression on his face and the anguish in his gaze when it touched hers, "Annie, don't you think there's more to a commitment than making love. I mean...we never talk. I'm afraid he'll never take the time to listen, and I can't live that way."

Annie walked to her then and offered her a warm embrace. Roc had moved into the house. "Jessie, I know it's hard, but you have to put a stop to this," she warned her. "If you expect him to listen, you have to speak the truth."

She frowned petulantly, remembering the night before and what he'd done to her in the name of education. Bah, he deserved to suffer. "Perhaps in the morning."

Annie flashed her another quelling look. "You'll regret waiting so long. Tonight, Jessie. This charade has to end."

Was she pressing her luck? If so, she knew Annie's words would come true, but she couldn't seem to control that boiling fury that simmered deep inside hunting for revenge.

"I'll deny anything you tell him..."

"Jessie." Annie cut her off. "Don't you dare, besides what makes you think he'd fall for the ruse? He's not a fool and once I explain to him that you're fine, he'll know. One look at you and he'll know. Indeed, I find it hard to believe that he's not knocking down the door right now, the way you two stared at each other just a moment ago."

"Arrogant and overbearing, Annie, two traits I can't live with and he possess them both."

"Tonight, Jessie," Annie said.

Jessie gazed innocently at her fingernails, absorbed in nothing but avoiding Annie and the threats she'd made. "Oh, I suppose so," she sighed, "if you insist, but I don't guarantee he'll like what he encounters."

"That poor man will be beside himself, and you intend to make him dance like a puppet on the end of a string. Two wrongs won't make this turn out any better."

"No, it won't. But I don't care in this case," she murmured. And smiling coyly, still she tapped her finger against her chin.

"Go ahead, Annie, do your worst. Tell him I've recovered and I'm ready to see him, or whatever you feel is necessary."

That should make him come running.

Senator Drake had come to visit while she was talking with Annie. The Senator brought Roc up to date on all the latest news. Rumor had it Pierce was back in the country.

Jessie could hear the slight rumblings of their conversation. It floated up from the open window below her room. At the mention of Pierce, she choked back a cry.

~ * ~

Roc, standing below the balcony by the front door, heard the soft sound and walked down the porch.

He saw his wife, framed once again by the lace curtains, turning from his attention. Struck by the look on her face, he needed to reassure hr.

He stared at Senator Drake for confirmation then looked back to the window. "Your time is running out, sweetheart, I only have so much patience. And although I am much at fault here, I don't believe...ah, what do I believe?" He groaned out loud, hands on his hips, as he watched her move far enough back he could see only her shadow. He strode forward.

She wanted her retribution too. Ah, well. Maybe he would allow it. He had wallowed in his guilt long enough, but if it made her happy to watch him suffer, he would play along. He had never really stopped to think she had faked her condition, or in truth never suffered the loss of spirit he had attributed the vacant look in her gaze to. But then perhaps she had. Ah, but she had recovered easily, his Jessie. Yes, it seemed almost impossible she wouldn't bounce back swiftly from the ordeal. Indomitable and proud, yes.

Yet, he had never stopped to think she might understand and perhaps comprehended the point he had tried desperately to make.

A shattering realization seized him. Dear God, he thought, if Pierce ever managed to kidnap her and put her on the auction block. Damnation, no! He'd die a thousand deaths.

He stared at the window. His breath seemed to catch in his throat. His wife and his daughter were there. His life. His love.

He would resolve this tonight.

Tonight he would tell her all that filled his heart and soul. An apology and a humbling of himself belonged to this woman.

Even the knowledge Jess had recovered did nothing to ease the waiting. He had seen his daughter, held her for the first time and felt a father's protective nature burst through his callused hide. But confronting Jessie terrified him, though demeaning himself in front of her would surely give her cause to laugh again.

He was also afraid he had made a terrible mistake, because if Jessie were to refuse seeing him tonight, she might never find it in her heart to forgive.

And although Roc had succeeded in his mission with Jessie, Charity and Annie might just want to see him brought down. No, that wasn't a problem; he could reason with the two of them if need be. But his guilty conscious was another matter.

He could well imagine what his Jessie, Jess Law, had in store for him. Thumb screws, or the rack if she could find one, perhaps she had found steel shackles she could use on him. And, he supposed, he deserved it.

So, while he thought Jessie was surly thinking of ways to torture him, he sat with Senator Drake, trying to sift through all the information that had come to bear on the Pierce and Rutgers case. "Well, Drake, we know about the cave under the lighthouse at Newport. Trevor discovered that," he reminded him. "And I hope you have men covering the area. Do you think one of us should be there?"

"Don't worry, Roc. I have my best men stationed there. Sheriff Clayton is supervising and Jonathan Conroy, the Pinkerton agent has come also." He hesitated a moment.

"It doesn't feel right," Roc said harshly. He had done everything he could. He wanted to secure his families future, but the threat still hung over his head, a heavy weight of doom forcing his hand at every corner. He would not feel safe until he saw Pierce and Rutgers caught and prosecuted.

That feeling swamped him, sent chills to the pit of his stomach. Despite all he had done to secure Jessie's safety, some hint, premonition, or perhaps plain honest to God fear, rose constantly inside, telling him he had not done enough; he could think of nothing else.

He had placed a guard on surveillance the moment he came home. He thought she would have noticed, protested. But she hadn't.

"What doesn't feel right?" Annie asked, appearing suddenly behind the men.

"Nothing, Annie...nothing. I don't know how to fight this enemy."

"With all your intelligence and strengths," Annie confided. "She's all right, you know. She's waiting for you but she's mad. And I think she has some plan to make you pay for last night's devilry."

An auction. How swiftly he had come to that conclusion. And how brazenly he had set about to instruct her.

He glanced up the stairs toward the room they had shared once. He'd been hoping for sometime now that she'd descend. He'd heard her moving about, speaking with Annie and Charity then he'd seen her through the curtains looking oh so smug.

And he realized now with a fierce certainty that he had fallen very deeply in love with his wife, and therefore, the fear for her life had been all the greater. Bittersweet remorse had resulted in the culmination and surrender of his wife as he wrenched the promise from her.

He had given nothing in return, nothing. Ah, Jessie, I owe you so much, but to admit it might truly reverse what I accomplished.

And the process had taken most of the night. Jessie was so stubborn in her resiliency, in her refusals to give in. And she had held herself with such dignity, regal, in fact.

"Devilry? Hmm, I could find that interesting," he said.

"You deserve it."

"Of course I do, but I'll never admit it to Jessie."

"You may have to," Annie told him, grinning wildly.

"What does--?"

"I could only guess," she interrupted. "But I have a feeling she'll enjoy it immensely. The look on her face was one of pure delight."

"Delight?"

"Yes, Roc, she gave up on your suffering alone. I think she intends to witness it first hand, perhaps give you a dose of the same education you gave her last night. You had to have a great deal of arrogance to carry that through to the end. Jessie had already decided to quit the raids and there in lies the rub. All you did was unnecessary. Did you realize that?"

"No," Roc told her. "I had no idea."

"It was her pride alone that made her hold out that promise. She didn't want to surrender."

"I didn't hurt her, Annie. I had to see that she would never get near Pierce again. For all I knew, she would go after them alone. They are back and I feared for her."

Annie Conroy was smiling, grinning from ear to ear. "An auction. I would have never thought of that. Now, I don't mean to say that I didn't think you carried it too far. But...well," she narrowed her eyes. "I don't know what I mean. Roc, it was wrong, but--"

He waved his hand in the air. "Son of a bitch, Annie, make up your mind."

"I trust in your judgment, since she seems to have recovered swiftly."

If he could only trust in that same knowledge. "You'll not interfere tonight then, Annie?"

"Why, you have something else planned?"

"No, but if you hear my screams, promise me that you won't interfere."

"Oh, I think not. But truly, Roc, are you crazy? You will give Jessie a freehand at administering restitution? It's a dangerous proposition, Roc, one that could prove life threatening, if the look on her face when I left was any indication."

Roc smiled slowly. "Well, I thank you, Annie, for the warning. But I have a rendezvous with a little wildcat tonight, and whatever she wants I'll give her. Tonight, or I'll never find the courage again, and someday when I'm least aware, she'll attack me and seek to set a noose about my neck. I've got to do this now. And prove my repentance."

Annie stared at him, incredulous, a slow smile curving her lips. "Well, now, I can understand that and give you a great deal of advice, but I don't think you'd listen."

"I intend to go to her, vulnerable and as helpless as she was."

"Impossible," Annie shook her head. "You can try but it's not possible. You, a powerful man, could never understand or become vulnerable simply because you have a different way of looking at life and living. Now, Roc, I am glad that I had this little chat with you. I've respected you since that first night we met, but I don't think I ever knew what lay so deep in your heart. You're a good man and a fine husband. Jessie could have done worse, much worse."

"Thank you, Annie. I take that as a compliment."

Annie frowned, looking up the steps. "What was all this about? Has Pierce surfaced, Roc?"

Roc tapped his fingers slowly against the table. "Not yet. But he's back. No one knows where yet."

Annie choked back a muffled cry of fear. "You've yet to find him. That means..."

Roc felt his heart thunder against his chest. The fear in Annie's eyes did not go unnoticed.

"You're afraid for yourself," Roc said. "He's after Jessie."

"And anyone who has betrayed him. I'm at the top of the list, thanks to my big brother," Annie concluded bitterly. "I wanted rescuing. I've never denied that, but I had intended to do it without putting myself at risk. Jon's hasty and sudden intrusion into my life left me in a tenuous situation. "Hey...don't worry about me," she waved off his concern nonchalantly.

"I will," he said softly. "Your brother helped me." His glance veered to the steps.

"I left her in the dressing room at the front of the house," Annie said, a lost look coming over her features. "Be careful."

Roc smiled slowly. "Oh, I intend to, Annie, I intend to."

Annie giggled softly. "Good night then, Roc." She kissed him lightly on the cheek. "It was good to talk to you. I hope you live through this meeting."

"I mean to see the next day," Roc chuckled.

Then Annie returned to the sitting room. Roc grinned again, started through his house for the stairs that would lead him to his wife and whatever she had planned.

The room was dark and empty when Roc opened the door. A shaft of moonlight filtered through the partially opened curtains. Whisper soft breezes stirred the air and left a hint of rose to entice the senses. Curious shadows lingered on the wall and floated across the braided rug, pulling him further into the sitting room, beckoning him deeper into illusions of fulfillment. Where was she?

He stepped gingerly at first, but charmed by the velvet cloak of night and devilish intrigue that so often surrounded his wife, he moved swiftly through the first room, into the bedchamber. Still absorbed in the novelty that seemed to enshroud the hour, alerting his natural instincts, honed to a razor sharp edge and prepared for this trial of his wits, he waited.

Pillows piled high on the huge bed issued a capricious invitation, nodding compliance, beckoning and propositioning him, every intuition, screaming beware, take care, watch.

He stopped at the doorframe, ever cautious, scouring the silent dark tomb for warning, a hint of the future. Muscles tensed and ready to spring, Roc felt the cold steel of a gun press against his back.

Nothing more. And he silently applauded Jessie for the deception and the skill with which she carried this out, but he didn't move. Waited instead for the weapon-toting brigand to offer asylum or issue the ultimatum, promising the sweet revenge Roc had anticipated with untold apprehension.

The gun barrel nestled his spine. He stiffened slowly, voluntarily giving the impression he intended a fight. His grin contradicted the act, but he suffered the paradox because she could not see.

Time lengthened to an eternity, and they battled in their own way, each saying a wealth of explicates that only the two of them could understand.

He nearly broke the silence.

He'd wanted to discover the depth of her scheme, of the vengeance she planned but as yet he had no clues. She should have said something.

But she hadn't.

She was standing behind him, a gun at his back, a complete surprise to him. She was silent, unconcerned. Completely in tune with the night.

Patient.

He began to turn. Intimidating. Threatening. The prod of the gun gave him pause. Hesitating, he stepped away from her. His silver gaze touched her.

She gnawed at her lower lip, dropped her lashes subtly for one moment. The act seemed to renew her courage, for when she looked up, again a hardness shadowed her gaze.

"Over there." She waved the gun toward a wooden block.

His lip curled, a grin creased his expression but swiftly he masked it. "What if I refuse?"

Her gaze flew to his; confusion flashed a second in her eyes. "You won't," she told him, her voice calm and controlled.

He raised an eyebrow, "Oh?" then shrugged and moved to the block.

"Take off your clothes," she said. The gun wavered a moment in her hand then the resolve surfaced and she held it steady, pointed at his heart.

Son of a bitch, he thought absently. I hope it's not loaded. Then he complied, his volatile eyes ablaze. "I might need some help with my boots."

"You'll have to manage on your own."

He bent down to tug on them, gave up and sat on the block, still working diligently at the task. He looked up and shrugged, undermining the stoic reception she gave his plight. "Don't know if I can..." he grunted and one boot dropped to the floor. His lazy smiled stifled the flurry of oaths she had almost unleashed upon him.

"Keep going." She moved to a chair by the window, sat, and watched as he struggled with the other one. "Now your shirt."

He complied, almost eagerly, and it seemed an impossible task to keep the smile from curling his lip and throwing his head back to roar with laughter. Ah, this was indeed his Jessie, his fearless, prideful Jess Law. An eye for an eye but oh, he so willingly gave it just to know the little dickens had indeed returned to torment his days and haunt his nights.

He stood naked now, on the makeshift auction block, fully aroused, and it was all Jessie could do to keep from ogling him. Oh, dash it all, she couldn't let it happen this way. Determined to maintain control, Jessie pulled her gaze from his blatant manhood, gasping for air at the same time.

She remembered the hot torrid night he'd just put her through, and simulated his actions, walking around him then, raking him with her eyes. And she began to quiver inside, felt the first melting sensations, knew then that this would never work. Heat slid the length of her spine as she anticipated the consummation of this and his tender loving.

She gazed at him in silent wonder. Her desire increasing, crystallizing and blossoming, afraid of her weakness, the urge to touch him, explore.

"I think the examination comes next," she told him swiftly, ignoring her response, this man, her lover, her husband, a man who sorely needed a lesson in humiliation. But, she realized, this was not the method to use.

"Oh," he said smoothly. She heard the murmur, the slight chuckle he held back.

"This isn't working."

"My thoughts exactly," he murmured huskily. His eyes raked over her, and she felt as if he'd torn her clothing away as if he caressed her skin, stimulating every inch of her.

"Roc," her pulse ticking alarmingly, she closed her eyes against the vision. She truly did not want him to gain control of this. If anything, she had to make him understand, had to make his feel vulnerable and helpless and she had to cleanse her soul. But unfortunately, this wasn't humbling him, only arousing him to a state she simply could not find the strength to ignore.

"What?"

"It's time for the bed. The stakes...remember."

She flushed, thinking of what that entailed and that she'd have him spread out, helpless, at her mercy.

"If I refuse?" he asked.

"I was hoping you'd say that."

"Oh...but how will you mange the gun?" he questioned. "Or have you ignored the possibility that I might wholeheartedly want to comply, to allow you access to me."

Dash it all, his smile was wicked. "You won't," she said sternly, motioning to the bed where she had tied black silk scarves to each post.

He didn't reply. His voice was husky when he finally said, "All right, Jessie."

He stepped down, slowly walked to the bed and sat down in the middle. It creaked slightly under his weight. The scarves lay nearby, supposedly threatening. His volatile gaze lingered a moment then flashed to Jessie.

"Tie yourself."

He laughed then. She pointed the gun at him again. His hesitated only a moment then he tied each leg to a separate post.

Lazily, he leaned back on an elbow.

"Now?"

"Tie one hand. I'll do the other."

"Ah, sweetheart this will never work."

A flash of anger sizzled through her. "You humiliated me and I want you to feel the shame, the horror of it all. It's not fair."

He shook his head slowly. "Life's not fair, Jessie. I wanted to do this for you, but it won't work. All I feel at the moment is an overpowering need to possess you. To love you. I want to do it right tonight."

She pointed the gun at him. It wavered slightly then dropped from her hand. She watched helpless as he untied the bonds at his ankles.

She inhaled swiftly. "What now?"

"Come here."

The effrontery of that man.

"This isn't the way it's supposed to happen."

He arched a brow. "Please."

Jessie rubbed the back of her neck. Nervous energy poured into her. How did this man always turn everything around in his favor?

"You want me to come to you?"

"Oh, yes, with all my heart." He smiled pleasantly.

Then he patted the bed beside him. As if under a spell, Jessie moved toward the bed and his invitation, no longer capable of protest or in need of coercion. She began to fumble with the buttons on her shirt, making no headway. Her eyes narrowed. A soft moan whispered near to him, but he didn't touch.

"Please..." she said.

"Please what?"

"Damn you, Roc Newman..." her whisper, husky and surprisingly desperate caught him off guard, "Help me."

He had waited for that plea and he swiftly complied. Naked and soft, he swept her against the length of his body, gazing tenderly into her eyes.

"Oh, my love, this will work," he promised.

A last drop of reality surfaced, and she began to protest.

Too late to deny him or herself, suddenly he covered her. And he whispered. "If I promise to listen, my love?"

"Impossible," she told him.

"Even if I swore to good intentions, begged your forgiveness." The heat of his body consumed her need for vengeance; the need to see him humbled before her.

She had no answer.

"I will learn to compromise, to listen, perhaps even to understand," he told her with a tender smile.

His lips brushed across hers lightly, enticing a response that some part of her still reached out to deny but didn't.

A new beginning.

Oh, yes.

Perhaps Roc Newman could learn a lesson from her as well.

Chapter Eighteen

She allowed him the intimacy, allowed him the sweet surrender he had sought so often simply because he gave her no choice.

Stubborn pride abandoned her, left when she needed it most, and if she had stopped to think, she would have never attempted the humbling of Roc Newman. She would have realized the absurdity of that task. Instead, she capitulated to the enchanting seduction and endless magic he wove within his caress.

His audacity and arrogance amidst the threat of submission seemed bold beyond compare, but he knew she would never have used the gun. Stupid, foolish idea to think she would conquer, hold him prisoner to her whims, when he could have disarmed her in one swift move. Crazy woman, misguided, ill-advised, yet she lay beneath him now, trembling and anticipating the sweep of wild currents within, the inevitable conclusion of the tempest fueling the mysterious attraction between them.

Haunting...

Except that he no longer haunted her nights with vivid memories of his caress, no longer. No, this man of her dreams was real. Oh, yes, he was so very genuine. And perceptions had never before felt so intense, or so natural. He was a sensitive lover, had always anticipated her needs, and he swiftly found the most sensual, delicious spots to stroke and tease. Embraced and caressed with magical and intimate knowledge of the woman beneath him. Pursued carnally with the moist wet heat of his mouth.

"Roc, please," she cried, her body openly responding to his erotic attack. And he smiled with the comprehension that once again he would possess and cherish this woman. His woman. He intended to appease her, to pay honorarium, and plead forgiveness.

He'd spoken from his heart, meant every word. Intentions and forgiveness aside, he meant to compromise with her. Somehow, some way they would find a means to settle their diametrically opposed philosophies. For surely now that she had a child, a daughter to occupy her time, she would settle domestically into home life. The enchantment flourished within her. The whirlpool of mystery surrounded her, pulling her longingly into the wild uncharted depths. Ascending like sultry rose on rain kissed air, pulsing through her, assuming an expeditious and precipitous control. She clawed at his shoulders, sheathing her nails into his powerful muscles, slid upward into his hair. He hoped she would surely drown in his magic, enfolded into the soft welcoming depth of the sea, but then she shuddered and soared into the nether world on wings of the falcon and she thought then that perhaps she would die a moment in time.

He slowed the magic, his length tenderly moving, parting her, anticipating the wonder of it.

She was ready, expecting the union, moist and hot, and so very tight. He thrust into her, his lover, his wife, his possession. He filled her completely, rejoicing in the moment and the truth, knowing that she accepted him.

"Oh, my love, I need you. Always..." he whispered huskily. He managed to slow the tide that had built within them, cradling her close to his heart, prolonging the conclusion of this. He began the seduction anew, building the magic again, bringing her to the pinnacle she had climbed only a moment ago. His thrusts, slow and deep, his control overwhelming. A small sob escaped her. His mouth explored her, her ears, her breasts, even as he intensified the sensual assault. His voice, soft and melodic, heated her flesh before his lips devoted themselves to other desires.

"Jessie, how I have missed you. I'm sorry for last night. Truly I did not want it to turn out that way. The only thing I could think of to convince you..."

She pulled him down so their mouths came together. Her lips and tongue delved within tasting him, exploring, and he realized she no longer cared and was eager to meet him half way. He rose above her, watching the union of their bodies, the sheer wonder of it. Then he closed his eyes, and the mystery consumed him, sweeping all else from his thoughts. He moved with no hesitation, stroking deeper, hungry and insatiable. Everything forgotten for the moment. Forgiveness, compromise, understanding, all assuming an inferior place in his mind. He possessed her body and soul.

Then the summit, turbulent, frenzied, shattered around him. He battled the culmination, fighting the fierce surge of release that caught him unaware, anxious that he had fulfilled the sweet promise for her. But inflamed and so long denied he could not slow the tremors of desire and passion shooting through him, and he was powerless, left without choice but to drive into the softness that was uniquely hers. And when it ended, he fell upon her, weak and helpless, unable to move still in awe of the moment. He pulled her into his embrace; felt the hesitancy, perhaps fear, and wanted to deny its very real existence. His voice, husky and deep, "God, Jessie, I don't have words. I swear that we'll find a way."

Her eyes were wide and she didn't answer. Tears pooled within the mercurial depths, shimmering. He rose above her, satiated but curious at her silence. His gaze stroked and caressed the length of her, her breasts, the long slim legs that had clung to him only a moment ago, the slightly rounded abdomen. He owed her so much. He had taken her innocence in a manner unforgivable although through no fault of his own, denied her the very essence of herself then abused her ego, her soul, her very spirit. Still she gave of herself, tenderly and with such wild loving abandon.

He stroked a finger across her cheek, catching a tear just as it slid from her eye, softly, from the full upper lip down her neck to the valley between her breasts. "God, but I have dreamt of this," he murmured. He caught another tear. She stared at him, holding her bottom lip with her teeth. Her brows knit together, in pain or thought, he wasn't sure.

"Did I hurt you? Sweetheart, tell me..."

She shook her head, still gazing at him. "Will you ever learn?" she asked tenderly. "That seduction, the enchantment you weave so easily, none of it, Roc, none of it will change..."

"Hush," he said gently, his smoky gray eyes flashing a silver warning. "I don't want to change anything. Haven't you listened, understood my pleas for forgiveness."

"I've heard no begging or groveling." She pushed on his chest, rejecting him and she spoke again. "You were supposed to feel the same things I did. I wanted to humiliate you, strip you of your pride, instead... instead I fall to your seductive charms. You, you never gave me a chance. You assumed the worst and did your worst."

"Jessie," he spoke suddenly, "I am trying to understand. I would like to reach some type of compromise with you. But if our roles were reversed, what would you have done?"

"Well, I would have asked first. I had no intention of ever going on another raid. You have done nothing but command and demand and wrench promises from me since I woke in your bed that morning. I am not a regrettable accident. I never wanted to marry you either, and look what it has gotten me. I never wanted to marry anyone simply because I didn't want them telling me what I can and cannot do. You are despicable and if you think that I'll forgive you so easily, you're wrong."

"Oh."

"Oh? Oh! Is that all you can say? I want you down on your knees, Roc."

His biceps bulged and she noticed a tiny blue vein outlining the muscle. His jaw tensed and he appeared wired and ready to pounce. "I do not go down on my knees for anyone," he snapped suddenly.

"I'm not anyone."

"Indeed?"

"In...deed." She jumped from the bed and snatched his long shirt from the floor, quickly wrapping it around her shoulders then buttoning it down the front.

"Modesty doesn't become you, Jess, especially in front of me," he told her sweeping her into his arms and tossing her back on to the bed.

A wild light glinted from her eyes, disheveled and sensual she clung to the shirt and her modesty with innocence and a beguiling fear that sent Roc's pulse flying through the ceiling. "Don't you dare," she cried out suddenly, surprising and ripping him back to his broken intentions.

"Jessie, I dare what I want. You know that," he told her, puzzled. "This isn't what I want...more arguments. You're precious to me. You've given me a life and a family who I would protect." She had never looked more vulnerable and at the same time courageous. Such an exquisitely small little thing to have such undaunted bravery.

She stared at him. Confused, he held her head between his hands and made sure she they had eye contact. Her eyes, violet fire, met his. "Roc Newman." she said in barely discernible whisper, cold to his skin, "I never asked for your protection. I never asked for anything from you."

"What the hell? Jessie, you're my wife. That's my job," he yelled at her, still puzzled by the sudden turn of events.

"Get out of my bedroom. You're not welcome here tonight," she told him.

It was a lie, she had orchestrated this to her own ends, and now that it did not go as she thought it should, she wanted to get rid of him. But he wouldn't concede to her demands. She was his wife, and even though he had meant to plead his case before her, she was still his wife and he would not allow her to gainsay him.

"Have you forgotten so soon, Jessie? You seduced me. Ordered me at gun point to disrobe."

"But not for the reason you thought," she shot back. "I didn't accomplish what I set out to do. You had no right to enjoy it, and you still managed the entire tableau. And..."

"Possess that which I hold dear to my heart?" he suggested.

"You are a supercilious fool," she told him then jerked back to stare at him and wonder if he meant it.

"I don't know what you mean," he persisted.

"Of course you don't," she lashed out. "Ah, let's see. You tied me to a horse then embarked on an expedition that took you God knows where. I certainly don't. You extracted promises from me, which you knew that I could not keep. Then you insisted on a reenacting an auction for the sole purpose of educating me. An education I didn't need."

Jessie hesitated a moment. She didn't want to think about the hurt and the pain that he'd inflicted, and a catch seemed to form in her throat even as she berated him. He had sent her wildly and yes, she had to admit to a wondrous sensual pinnacle and now...

Now he claimed she was dear to his heart.

"I confess. I did all that and more. Would do it again if I thought it necessary," he told her patiently. He pulled her across his lap, holding her close.

"But then you came back and assumed control over my life," she said softly. "Would protect me from my enemies, shelter me, enslave me in my home if I let you have your way. Don't you see that you won't always be there for me? That I have to stand alone sometimes."

"No," he said cautiously.

She grimaced. "I give up." Her hands fell to her lap before she looked at him. "Annie said you lived in her parlor house."

"Yes, several months," he said, a slow smile curling his lip.

Heat eddied to her face and at that moment she wanted to dive beneath the covers. "Well, your confession...?"

"Does not go that far," he interrupted, ginning deeply and he looked so very amused at her insinuation.

"I like that," he told her. "Yes, I think I could come to enjoy that not so subtle rush of color to your exquisite cheeks. Jealousy becomes you, sweetheart."

"I am not," she cried vehemently.

"Ah, but you are," he leaned back on one elbow, surveying his conquest. "And I could tell you stories. Stories that would make this slight blush turn deepest red." He caressed the side of her face oh so gently, and the chills that followed made her gasp.

"I don't want to hear them," she said disgustedly.

"Good, because I intend to keep my past exactly where it should remain, in the past. I have done nothing to break our vows, unlike yourself," he paused, watching her for the violent reaction he felt assured would follow that last proclamation.

"You arrogant bastard," she said. "I haven't broken one vow."

"Obey? The time in Newport and your promise to stay there and wait for me. Even under this roof, when you told me you wouldn't go after your cousin. Trust me. I recall those words."

"You didn't touch one of Annie's girls, in all that time?" she asked innocently.

"No," he said without hesitation. "It never even occurred to me," he went on honestly.

He sat on the bed, looking over his beautiful wife and grinned like a

Cheshire cat. "No, not since that first stormy encounter," he said. "I haven't had even one thought of another woman. Haven't wanted any one else in my bed."

"No one?" Jessie asked again.

He didn't hesitate. "Jessie, you may find this hard to believe, but it never occurred to me. With you I have found more than satisfaction, or gratification, you've become a way of life, a part of my soul that I can not do with out."

"I am not a regrettable accident then?" she murmured.

"A fortunate one."

"Fortunate," she repeated.

"Yes, my love. I admit that night was indeed an accident, but I am wholeheartedly grateful for the events that led to it," he said softly. His voice sounded cautious and she wondered about that, wishing he would give in to her. Instead, it seemed as if he tread lightly, guarding his heart and his soul.

But she didn't believe him. She had told him he needed to beg.

"That's not enough," she told him calmly. "You want to direct my life, and the first time we disagree you will do your worst. You can't help yourself."

He lifted his shoulders lightly, "Jessie, if we are trying to reach an understanding, then you must know I am willing to make a few concessions for the sake of our marriage. But..." He paused then continued, huskily. "From the moment I first saw you, I wanted you. Even that black night when I watched you scale my house so easily."

"I was shocked at my own prowess."

He grinned. "Me, too, but I was also enthralled. In all my travels I have never met anyone who could compare. I have always thought of women as a bit of fluff for my pleasure, but you Jessie. No, I could never compare you to a piece of fluff. Nor would I want to."

Jessie had the look of the devil about her, feeling an unbelievable surge of power race through her. "But you did believe I had a great deal of audacity assuming a man's role. And you still managed to weed through all that oddity to make love to me."

He nodded, conceding once again. "Oddity, be damned, Jess. I lusted for you like an untrained schoolboy." He growled deep in his throat. "But that isn't how I lust for you now. I never wanted a woman to control. I never wanted a wife, period. But then you danced into my life, and I was left in dazed confusion and dripping of ice water. I seek a compromise, a way for you to maintain your spirit the part of you that is unique, the part of you that tumbles my life into shattering little pieces, keeping me forever primed for any surprise. I have fallen in love with you and nothing, not even a nefarious plan hatched by Mr. Pierce will keep me from protecting the woman I hold dear and close to my heart."

She searched his expression, seeking a lie, a telltale glint of an untruth but found only honesty and a compassion she'd never witnessed before. She was shivering so hard the bed shook along with her. She could think of nothing to say in return except her confession of love and she wasn't ready for that.

"Is that true?" she whispered softly.

"Jessie, with all my heart."

She trembled again, debating her words of love, ready to forgive him. But she still wanted restitution for his crimes against her, still determined he would kneel before her.

"You'll let me keep my office on State Street?"

"A compromise, Jessie, but I won't let you run impulsively off after dangerous men."

"You'll peruse all my clients then...a yes, and a no...at your whim?" she murmured softly, a hint of sarcasm in her voice. She leaned back, still thinking of this curious compromise, a strange one indeed. And she knew she could live with it because she didn't intend to act impulsively again. But she didn't want him to think this an easy game.

"What!" she choked out suddenly. It became a yowl of outrage. He had startled her, attacking so swiftly, tying her hands and anchoring them solidly to the bedposts behind her. He sat back on his haunches, his knees straddling her hips and smiled, a lazy powerful smile. One that told her she had carried this too far. He had laid bare his soul and she had taunted him.

"I will study every damn one of your clients, my love and yes, I will tell you if you can take their case. Don't ask me to compromise more than that," he growled.

"It doesn't sound like much of a concession," she said perversely.

"It's as much as you're going to get."

She smiled slowly and cursed herself for this uncontrollable fit. "Wanna bet?"

"Ah, lady, now you have gone too far," he warned her. "I do intend to watch over my wife, and I do intend to discipline her if she endangers even one hair on her beautiful head."

"Untie me," she sounded close to panic.

"No, not until you agree."

She closed her eyes, cursing silently. It seemed that only a few hours ago they had done this same thing. Stubborn, foolish pride, she berated herself. He'd done it to her again, at her insistence this time. His form of retaliation lacked creativity, but it didn't matter. It worked.

He was crazy. He hadn't meant to let his temper rule his actions. If he kept this up, he would have to go down on his knees for her. All those months, fearing for her, knowing that she could stumble into anything. Sometime he had been a fool for the right reasons, but it had accomplished little to sneak away on that ship. He had been a fool last night for the right reasons, but now he had no excuse.

Except that she had the canniest way of making a confusing puzzle out of all his thought. She seemed to turn the meaning of his words around to suit her and the strangest of all was that she made sense.

And now...

Pierce lived free. He was still a threat to Jessie, albeit removed at the moment. Now there was only waiting.

And he didn't do that well. Still an almost impossible task for a man used to action and one who would give his life to protect a woman who dashed off on causes without a thought to the consequences. He had to find Pierce, see him prosecuted and escorted to prison. He had to do it soon.

Life had smiled favorably on him. He had found Jessie, a quirk of fate perhaps. If Pierce had not hired her to steal the evidence from him, he would have never encountered the fiery little hellcat.

And perhaps she had come to love him also.

If he didn't guard her well, he might lose her. Danger still threatened.

His body shuddered. He gripped the sheets tightly to stop the fear within him before Jessie noticed.

He had Jessie. And if they could survive the months ahead without incident, they might well see the promise of a lasting future.

He untied the scarves then rubbed her delicate wrists. A fit of anger had caused another lapse in judgment.

He gazed at her, coming down on his knees beside the bed. She reached out to stop him, but he shook his head. A smile curved his lips, and he picked her hands up in his, kissed the top then the palms. Jessie watched him.

"I am sorry," he said reverently. His volatile gaze caught her with a shimmering fire. "I shall try very hard to understand you, and find a way to compromise."

"I wish I could believe..." she said with a slight tremble to her voice.

"Believe," he repeated, frowning ruefully.

"I can only promise to take one day at a time." she said gently.

He smiled then, unbuttoning her shirt, slipping it over her shoulders so she lay naked beside him once more, drawing her close and into his arms.

Dazed, she permitted the intimacy. It seemed she felt the knowledge of his commitment pour from him into her.

"Jessica, Jessie...my sweet woman, for months all I did was dream of you, fear for you, and try to understand the strange ideas zooming through your mind. I should have realized I can't mold you into a sensible woman. I don't want to. But Jessie, it is difficult," he told her. "I've seen too much hatred, too many women used by self-seeking men. You are too naive, too trusting, and, sweetheart, it wouldn't take much for you to fall into their hands. Do you think for a moment I could forgive myself if that happened? Jessie, I might never find you...God..."

"But--"

He silenced her with a finger to her lips. "Not to mention the motive Pierce has. Revenge is powerful and hard to fight."

"But he's left. It's been almost a year, Roc. Do you think he'll come back? For me?"

"Yes. I know he will. Pierce has a vendetta to see through. Even if he is safe in another country, he won't accept that he failed to reap his revenge on your father. Pierce is meticulous, a perfectionist; he's has always seen his endeavors through to his preconceived conclusion. He will come."

He hesitated. Traced her lips with his finger then rolled onto his back and stared at the ceiling. He had never felt so afraid for anyone.

"I almost lost you to him that night the senator brought the wine to the house. But thanks to Perkins' quick thinking... I shudder to think what might have happened. Madame Lilly had a spot for you that night."

She gasped, surprised by his revelation. He knew no one had spoken of this to her. Perhaps if she'd known. He wanted to tell her everything now, reveal his heart and the feelings he'd held within for so very long and the knowledge that might have curved her audacious behavior. If she had known.

"You should have told me. I think I might have listened to your warnings. I'm not a stupid woman, Roc. But you kept so much of the truth from me I saw only that I could help someone less fortunate than myself. And I was furious with you for presuming to run my life."

"I thought it was for the best. I didn't want you to worry," he told her softly. "Though I did feel a small measure of guilt. When I had you with me, I knew no harm would come to you. And I always felt you would see things my way."

"But I didn't."

"No, you didn't.

But different presumptions about life, a woman's role in society, a man's rights and privileges concerning his wife still separated them. And he could not bring himself to beg forgiveness for something he had thought necessary.

"Where do we go from here?" Jessie murmured uneasily. "I won't let you run my life."

"Ah, well, perhaps I won't try. But you have to promise me something."

"What is that?"

"Caution, Jessie. I want you to promise caution and wariness. No more risks, at least not until we catch Pierce. Promise?"

She nodded, had, in truth already vowed that to herself only she added prudence. Did not intend to do much for the next few months except play with her child and love her husband.

"Roc," she spoke softly, rising on her elbow so she could see his face, watch the silver smoke of his eyes. "I know your fear. I realize that I have done so many stupid things and perhaps there's luck here. I am safe and you weren't here to protect me, guide me. I can take care of myself, but I don't want to any more. I need you and I will promise to take care with my life. I don't think I could survive another auction. God, Roc, no wonder the poor women I found that day so long ago looked hollow and empty."

"Forget that," Roc said, his gaze still upon the ceiling. "It won't happen to you."

The tone of his voice, his words, she trembled. And he hoped she would never forget and that the memory would linger.

"But you won't rest until Pierce makes the first move," she told him swiftly. "He has to come back to the states. He has to show himself. Until then you can do nothing."

His gaze precipitous and all consuming, "Pierce will come." Once again he felt the heavy threat of doom weigh upon his shoulders. A horrible foreboding of the future, chills sweeping down his spine.

She caught his head in her hands and turned his face to hers, gently holding his gaze. "Roc, you can not guard me all of the time. Justice will be done. If he comes back, you and I both know he will face prosecution. All the law informant agencies in the country wait for him to make a mistake." She touched his lips with hers, softly, with the greatest regard. "The ever watchful eye will eventually see him."

He laughed, gazed at her, enchanted with her unending spirit. "I do intend to keep watch over you every minute of every day and night. If not me, then Trevor, or Drake."

"Perkins too?"

"Even Perkins, Perkins adores you. Has thought of you as his daughter for a very long time."

"I won't do anything rash," she said suddenly, realizing the full extent of the danger she placed on other people. "I would do nothing to put that man in jeopardy."

"Ah, then you care more for him than yourself, Jessie. I'm glad I've finally found the tool to keep you in line."

She hit his shoulder and he grunted. He saw the words for what they elicited. He had indeed touched a nerve of guilt with her. Touched also on the helplessness she so often felt, a vulnerability she strove so hard to overcome.

He rose on an elbow, hovering over her, reversing their positions. "I will not let anything happen to you," he promised her.

"I know you'll try, but..."

"We've time to plan," he told her.

He ran his fingers through the length of her hair, enjoying the moment and the endless time it seemed they had. The newfound understanding they had both come to. Bent then, and brushed his lips across hers, a whisper of passion and longing. A breath of love endearing before deepening the kiss suddenly as if he had to taste her, possess her, if only to insure her safety. He dipped his hands lower, gently arousing the softness that was hers, over her breasts, her belly. His gaze met hers.

She touched his cheek, ran a fingertip across his jaw.

"What is it, sweetheart?"

"Well," she murmured, "you haven't begged my forgiveness yet.

He cursed soundly.

"And," she added prudishly, "you think I will fall into your arms each and every time you wish it. Think of that long endless night I sobbed out my grief, the emptiness I experienced and I thought you had deserted me, become a callous unfeeling brute. I want you to beg, Roc. You owe me."

"I thought I already had."

"Not enough, Roc. You have at least ten more hours to go," she promised. "I want the same amount of time."

"You want me humbled, submissive, docile perhaps."

"No. I want you on your knees."

"As you command."

He had flipped her over and yes, he was on his knees. "No..." Jessie wailed, but it was too late. It was not his intention to beg forgiveness.

"Is this what you desire?" he whispered, but she heard the amusement lace his tone and despite it all she almost said yes. Before she could respond, he had reached for her hips, lifting her to him, her legs parted. He began to beg for her surrender, not his forgiveness, his gentleness, the tender intimate caress, making love with her as if it were the last time, tracing, feathering his lips his tongue his fingertips over her hot sensitive flesh. He left nothing to the imagination.

She howled at first and he laughed softly next to her ear then nibbled tenderly the lobe. "It won't work," he finally breathed. "I tried, sincerely, I did, but it won't work."

Beneath him, once more, she forgot.

She tried to turn back, to become a part of this, but he wouldn't allow her. He held her breast, kissed his way down her spine, lingering on the softness of her bottom. She murmured softly.

And sighed when he gently sheathed himself within her once more.

As he began to move with a slow enticing rhythm, he crooned his apology with words of love intermingled.

All the while knowing it wasn't enough. Comprehending she wanted him to listen and to understand, to find it in his heart to give her freedom even while he claimed her love. He wondered if he could do that.

Moments later he had collapsed on top of her, replete, content to hold her and enjoy the peace he found with her. She felt the heat of his gaze and she laughed softly, hitting his chest with her small hands. "Beast, you know we haven't solved any of our problems. Yet, this seems to be your answer to everything," she told him prudishly.

He kissed her tenderly on the nose, running his hands suggestively along her legs. "And you have objections?"

"I didn't say that," she whispered. "We still haven't reached a compromise."

"You don't want a compromise. You want me to give you your way, brat. I won't do that," he warned.

She snuggled closer to his warmth. He watched the shadows play across her features and smiled grimly. He wouldn't compromise, no matter how beguiling she appeared. He'd do what he thought best and damn the consequences.

She felt his hands within her hair and he turned her. "Jessica, I have vowed I will try to understand. Compromise, that's another issue all together, but when I believe it won't endanger your life or that of our child's I will allow you to seek whatever crazy course you desire."

"Even if you disagree?"

"Even then. As for last night, I do admit I should have asked first, and I do beg you to forgive me. I didn't want to do it," he said fervently.

"All right then. I will try to meet you somewhere in the middle," she said softly. "But I can not promise I will always keep my temper or that I might try to defy you if I disagree."

He laughed out loud, "Jessie, you are impossible. I wouldn't expect anything else from you." He pulled her into his arms.

She rested then against him, watching the gentle rhythm of the morning slowly lighten the room. He listened to the soft cadence of her breathing and felt the slowing of her pulse as she drifted close to his heart. "Oh, Jessie, I missed you. Not a day passed that I didn't dream of holding you like this," he murmured. "Sweet Jesus, but I have no wish to change you. I love you just the way you are."

He hesitated, glancing toward her, praying she would reciprocate and speak of her own love. But all was silent.

She slept even while he had poured his heart out to her. How like a woman he thought, wanting clarification of everything then falling asleep when it came, forcing him to say it another time.

But he didn't know what tomorrow would bring.

Pierce would return, and until then he would have to learn patience.

He prayed she would never discover the real horror that could come her way once he did return. For Pierce was a very determined man.

Chapter Nineteen

Life developed from that point in time, blissfully serene, agonizingly boring, and for a while it seemed a tenuous compromise had formed. A delicate balance existed between two indomitable and stubborn personalities.

The weeks following would become the eye of the storm. Devastating calm before the last violent fury overtook the little patch of land and did its best to destroy everything in its path. Autumn swept God's country with a scintillating display of artistry. Indian summer, so warm during the days then dropping off to cool nights, camouflaged the danger. They picnicked along Mill Creek and rode their horses along Battle Creek Road.

Perhaps life had always held such sweet promise, perhaps she had nothing to fear, and maybe even the past was a fleeting memory and elusive image that would not rise from the dead to haunt her future.

Or perchance Pierce and Rutgers would find contentment in their new life and not come back for the sworn revenge.

When she watched Roc astride his horse, Jessie thought he was invincible. Piratical, even with his raven black hair flying in the wind, bronzed muscle rippling in easy cadence with the horse. He had left nothing to chance, twenty-four hours a day he was by her side, but he could not do this forever. Eventually, he would have to find her a bodyguard. Ultimately, he would have to stop shadowing every move she made.

But his compromise had only gone so far. He insisted on having his way. He perused her clientele thoroughly. Selected and discarded assignments ruthlessly, and she could do nothing except protest, for he had taken control of her business. She had never imagined a year ago her life would come to this. Nor had she thought Skye would create such a wealth of enjoyment for them. Skye already had Roc at her precocious mercy. Jessie could only wish she had the same power over this man she loved. Skye loved the gardens, and when Roc placed her on her back staring upward into the towering trees, she gurgled and cooed delightedly.

Guilt surpassed all emotions when she watched the two of them. The time seemed to have come and gone, and she could not bring herself to tell him how much she loved him. She would lie in bed at night, determined to talk to him and speak about how she felt but the words never came. The contentment of the season would not last, soon winter storms would arrive and she didn't know how to detain them.

Distractions, she had told herself not insecurity with their relationship, had kept her from that last final commitment. When he would come to her in all his masculine glory and sweep her into his arms, she would tell herself, later, later she would talk to him.

And she would feel his strength pour into her, but in the aftermath when he held her possessively next to him, the time never seemed right. It would break the spell he had woven, and she didn't want that.

Slowly, she came to realize he did try to give in to her. All the ideas she had, the wild passionate crusade he seemed to support along with her. But he had never thought about women's rights before, never thought there was a need. And as for equal, he had always held a woman's value above his own.

Finally, he came to acknowledge he was one of a few. He had seen first hand the plight Annie Conroy had survived by sheer determination and stubbornness. He knew the danger Jessie would have to survive if Pierce ever managed to capture her.

In each other's company, in that glorious cloak of autumn, and the shadowed darkness of the night they revealed many things, but Jessie could not find a way to expose her love.

"Annie knows how to tell it like it is," Jessie told him one day. "Annie wanted me to tell you all along, you know. She didn't think you should suffer."

"Indeed, I know. It was you who vowed revenge," he told her, clearly amused.

She punched his arm affectionately and gazed out at the little stream. You knew then? Knew that I had not lost all spirit."

"No, but I prayed. And then when I saw you behind the curtains, staring at me...well..."

"Well?"

"I saw that unholy glint in your eye." Roc leaned back, resting his head on his hands, the sun kissing his face. "And I knew you'd be in the room waiting for me. And the gun...wasn't loaded."

"No."

"Of course," he said smugly.

"Beast. And you let me think...monster. How did you know?" she asked him incredulously.

"Didn't, at least not until this minute," he said huskily.

"Oh." she hit him again and moved away. She tossed the grass that she had picked and smiled when he sputtered and swiftly moved to capture her hands. But she had anticipated the retaliation and had pushed to her knees. Jessie struggled to her feet and scampered away from him. He growled playfully and lunged for her.

She shrieked, "Don't touch me."

But he chuckled softly and grabbed her around the waist just before she dodged behind a huge old oak tree. His voice was deep and husky, enticing, and the very sound swept a deluge of spicy tremors sizzling throughout her. "Ah, sweetheart, but I can not help myself. I have to touch you."

Before she could protest further, he had ensnared her in his magical web of enchantment. And she forgot Annie, and Charity, and all the crusades that she had vowed to fight for. She wanted only to love this man.

And surprisingly the days following were filled her with a peace and contentment she had never thought possible. Roc followed her everywhere, and when he couldn't, he set Perkins at her feet like a faithful hound dog. Rupert proved as worthless as ever, chasing after teasing squirrels and chattering birds.

Annie and Charity pretended to look the other way, but they too made sure Jessie never found herself alone.

"What do you think you're doing?" Jessie demanded one day when she stumbled over Charity for the third time.

"Nothing...not much," she amended after receiving the chilling end to the glare Jessie flung at her. "I mean...Roc suggested that I help in the kitchen."

Jessie snorted. "Foolish man. Does he think to poison us all?" Jessie wagged a stern finger then turned her back on Charity and finished kneading the bread. "You can't protect me, no one can. If he brings enough men with him, you and I sitting in the kitchen will prove a slim barrier."

"He doesn't want you alone."

"Dash it all, I need some privacy," Jessie sighed, exasperated with her now doting husband.

Charity smoothed back her hair. "You're both right."

"Who's right?" Roc queried, stepping boldly into the woman's domain. He circled Jessie's waist before stealing a kiss.

"Both of you," Charity said.

They discovered Pierce had entered the country, but their informants had lost track of him.

Roc worried more than ever, tried to hide it with a lackadaisical attitude. "I think I like this new role, housewife and mother," he told her, trying not to laugh. But his voice grew husky. "I could order you to stay in the house all day, but you would immediately disobey me, so I've simply conned your friends into keeping an eye on you."

He kissed her lips again. "Be prudent, Jessie," he warned. "Honestly, I can't think straight when you're alone. And now that Pierce is back, I may have to leave. I don't want to worry about you."

But she knew he was terrified for her, yet she did comprehend the threat, the danger, and the lengths Pierce would go for revenge.

To Jessie's relief, Roc had quit urging her to heed his warnings. Had quit following her to the office and perusing the cases she accepted.

To Roc's comfort, Jessie declined anything but the most placid action.

Trevor moved in with them and acted the doting cousin with the adorable little Skye. Trevor, she knew, was just another bodyguard.

Yet he adored her, worried over her, and she acknowledged he gave her a feeling of security when he hovered. She didn't look over her shoulder quite as often or jump at every strange sound.

She overheard Senator Drake and Trevor arguing one day. About her, she presumed, what they could or could not tell her.

"I've heard that Sterling Rutgers was seen down by the docks in San Francisco," Drake informed Trevor. "I don't want Jessie to worry."

"She already is. If you tell her, perhaps she'll stay in the house. The devil, but I'd find it easier to keep track of the little scamp," Trevor said.

"Scamp? You mean Miss Jessica. By thunder now that we know Pierce is back, I want security doubled," Drake went on to say.

"She won't stand for that."

Jessie decided she best step in before this got out of hand. "He's right, Drake. I don't want any more men tagging along behind me and lurking outside the house," she said gently. "Trevor's here, Annie and Charity too. There's a guard outside the house and Roc."

Drake cleared his throat, clearly disapproving, but unable to rescind the orders he had already issued.

She told Roc about the conversation that evening. He frowned and for a long time said nothing. Then he turned her toward him, "Pierce has taken up residence just outside San Francisco. He has boasted that he would exact his revenge soon. Nothing specific, but I'm sure he refers to you and possibly Charity."

Tremors of fear tapped a painful staccato down her spine. She had experienced more than she wanted at the hands of Pierce.

The long languid autumn days had established a new understanding. They had within their grasp a beginning that held a wealth of promise.

But now that Pierce had returned, foreboding nightmares, dark and powerful, consumed her nights and a restless unease taunted her days.

She knew Roc wanted to lock her away in that familiar attic room but didn't dare. Knew she would find a way to escape and blame him for the damage done.

The torrid memory of the night Roc brutally dramatized an auction returned, testing her fortitude and blind faith in her husband. He had promised to protect her. With vivid premonitions of the future, she realized he would fail.

"I'll stay in the house," she told him.

"Willingly?"

"The truth, Roc? Yes, I--"

"Good, then I can concentrate on finding him. He will come, and I'm sure he intends to weave Lilly into his plot. Rutgers won't be far behind either. And he might not know I escaped his ship and have returned. I imagine once he realizes you are alone, he will come without hesitation."

"Alone?"

Roc nodded slowly. "Yes, Jessie, I'm going to him."

"But...I thought you said you'd stay here?"

He stroked her hair. "Stay safe, Jessie," he told her softly. "Don't take any foolish chances. Promise me?"

Willingly, she did so.

Just as he had told her, Roc left the next day. He woke with the sun, pulled her into his arms, and kissed her a swift good bye. She awoke, sleepy-eyed and reluctant to see him leave. It seemed the end. Curious thoughts chilled her inside and out.

"Do you have to leave?" Jessie murmured.

He nodded, "Yes."

Nothing she could say would change his mind. He headed south, Trevor beside him. And she wished she could ride with them.

Jessie stared at Charity who had come at Roc's bidding. Her protection, that and the army of men Roc had arranged to guard her and his home. Safe, a perfect haven of protection, a bastion against Pierce. But if Pierce wanted her enough, he would find a way inside. She didn't doubt it. Not even Perkins and his famous yell would stop them.

And he would come. Now that her husband had left, Pierce, and Rutgers, perhaps even Lilly would come for her. She watched terrified as Roc's back disappeared around the bend in the road.

When she turned to move inside the house, Jessie could scarce breathe. Her words caught in her throat, and she fell silent, gazing at the stained glass window, forging their pattern in her memory so she would never forget. Perkins moved in behind her, waiting silently. Charity rested her hand on her shoulder, a hopeful, curious reassurance. Annie walked up the long walk to the house. All came to protect, to safeguard what Roc held dear.

"Jessie, this will all work out. You'll see. Roc will return before you even know he's gone," Charity said warmly.

Jessie slanted her a baleful glare, curious that she could lie so handily. "Can you feel? The air, it turned so cold."

"Jessie, don't even think it." Annie said.

Jessie didn't want to, but fear enveloped her, sending tremors deep within. With no amusement, she turned to confront the entourage assembled around her. But Annie had read her thoughts. She arched a brow to Jessie.

"Annie," she said softly, trying very hard not to show her fear. Terror, so at odds with her usual courageous show. An act that was exactly it. She had never delved farther than the surface for answers. Now, sweet heaven, she knew what awaited her and she froze. "Perhaps Roc has made me a bit paranoid. But I can't help myself. I don't like this. It's too contrived. Suddenly, Pierce shows up in California and Trevor and Roc take off after him. Don't you think...?"

"Stop," Annie said. "It's not in his nature to wait for the inevitable. Trevor went in case of trouble."

"They left her defenseless," Charity snorted.

"He's close," Perkins added. "I know Roc thinks he's in Eugene, but I've seen his henchmen. The ones who cracked my ribs the other day. Hope Roc's hunch is right."

"I don't understand. For the love of God, he left because of a hunch?" Jessie wailed, feeling surprisingly like the spoiled brat he'd equated her with so many times.

And so they stared at each other, pondering the question.

Charity gnawed at her lower lip, speechless. Perkins left to make tea, his answer to every problem, mumbling his way from the parlor. Annie fiddled with the lace curtains, wishing desperately Jonathan had come to Salem. "A good Pinkerton agent would come in handy at the moment." Annie laughed softly then as if she realized how far her life had turned around.

The day lingered, hovered; silence encapsulated them all. With the amenities finished, and the sun obligingly set, Jessie retired. She paced the length of the upstairs, reworking, envisioning everything Roc had said and done. Hours dragged on endlessly. Finally, unable to erase the cobwebs from her mind, she gave up to the exhaustion plaguing her.

She woke restless and disillusioned. Cool breezes swirled in from the open window. When she rose to close it, the gardens seemed to beckon, called to her. Jessie slipped into a coat then cautiously made her way down the stairs and outside. A silver moon hung in the sky. Fresh fallen leaves aromatically captured her senses. When she closed her eyes, vivid and evocative images of Roc framed her imagination.

Left with no choice but to endure, she returned to the house. She slept again, waking later to discover an unseasonal frost upon the ground and in her heart.

The new day dawned with another glorious show of autumn color. Jessie didn't see anyone when she left the security of her upstairs retreat and entered the dining room. The house was strangely quiet. The back door banged shut. Swift strides brought her to the kitchen.

It was at that moment she saw him. Or at least she thought she had.

He dipped back into the gardens, vanishing completely. She knew he still lingered though. Felt his cruel gaze. Wished her imagination would not terrify her so.

And his gaze touched her, shivers swept throughout. He was out there, and she couldn't see him. A coward that had waited until defenseless she would become easy prey.

Dinner that evening was painful and silent. They all felt his presence although not one of them could confirm he was in town. Drake had come reassuring them. If Pierce were in Salem, Drake's informants surely would have told him.

"Then you've heard nothing?" Jessie queried, searching his face for answers. Sure that he wouldn't tell her even if he knew.

He shook his head. "Jessie, I've made a few discoveries and some discreet inquiries. I sent Perkins to see a curious Lady named Sabrina. A lady who dabbles in drugs and potions of all sorts. It has taken nearly a year to get even that much knowledge. I haven't seen Perkins since this afternoon when he set out on the mission."

"If he's in trouble, we'll never find out."

"Oh, all right, but when he comes in I want to speak with him."

"We all do," Drake finished.

Jessie stared at him for a moment surprised by the tenor of his voice and the fierce determination he couldn't hide. The worry etched deep in the lines of his face. He knows something, she thought. He knows and the secret kills him.

She wanted to wrench the truth from him.

For a moment she remembered that night so long ago. She remembered looking up from the dirt, Roc straddling her thighs, and she saw the senator beaming down at her, a twinkle emanating from his sky blue eyes. She remembered the horrible embarrassment she felt when she heard Trevor laughing somewhere behind.

And now nothing around her held any humor, only fear and terror, the incessant waiting that plagued her, seized her, squeezing her heart. Ah, but she wished for the magical days of fall that had just passed so easily. The happiness that had warmed her heart, the love he had cherished and nurtured until she could deny him nothing, not even her obedience. Yes, that was the clincher, she obeyed now and he had learned to expect it. Jessie grinned, her heart suddenly lighter, but when this was over, when Pierce no longer threatened, Roc would not find her quite so easy to manipulate.

"Jessie?" Drake called, "what on earth..."

"Oh, I was just thinking." she told him.

"I don't suppose you care to talk about it?" Charity asked,

"Nope," Jessie lowered her lashes swiftly to hide the slight curve of her lips and the angelic yet devilish thoughts she couldn't seem to hold back. "No, I don't think so."

Drake laughed, watching the transformation. "No, why Miss Jessica but I would like to hear what has you looking like a cat that just licked all the cream from the bowl."

"Drake," Jessie murmured, giggling, "you have no shame."

He chuckled "Perhaps not, I was thinking that a bright light had entered and lifted all our spirits. I suppose I was only hoping."

Jessie sighed, disappointed his words held so much truth.

The back entrance creaked open then the door closed quietly. Footsteps shuffled through the kitchen into the butler's pantry then hesitated a moment. Perkins stood at the entrance to the dining room. He seemed resigned, though, motioning to Drake that he wished to speak with him alone. Jessie's temper seized her. She had every intention of knowing what Perkins had discovered. They would not keep it from her.

When Drake rose, so did Jessie. She followed the two men into Roc's den and sat down. The look on her face clearly issued a challenge.

Her eyes narrowed. As Perkins looked to Drake for assistance, he tapped his fingers nervously on Roc's desk before turning his attention to Jessie and clearing his throat, waiting for her to leave.

She remained firmly ensconced in the chair.

And she was not very surprised when they began an innocuous conversation about absolutely nothing. Drake asked Perkins if he'd had a nice day and Perkins replied nonchalantly.

Then Drake's blue eyes suddenly darkened, "And now, Miss Jessica, you can leave. You may not want to hear any of this."

"Of course I want to hear," she said swiftly.

He scowled. "Pierce is here. Ah, but you mustn't take any chances. Rumor has it that something unusual will be up for sale. Messages have been sent over the Northwest. Rich men, Jessie, only rich men are coming. Do you have any inkling what this means?"

She waited for the room to quiet, the silence issuing a stern warning. "Yes, I believe that I do."

"I doubt that, but it's not in me to argue with you. Roc is gone. He won't be here to help so you must take care. Now if you'll excuse me, I have my own plan to set in motion."

He left then. Perkins stared at her, not saying a word.

Jessie trembled inside. She knew. Oh yes, she knew, indeed, and it developed now just as Roc had feared.

She moved through the house a wraith, silent, questioning and wondered what on earth she could do to prevent this from happening.

Midnight came. The witching hour, and she imagined she could cast a spell on those horrid creatures that tormented her. The papers Perkins had held so fiercely in his hands left an indelible impression in her head. In the darkness she moved cautiously through the house to the den. Jessie lit a candle then sat down at Roc's desk, hands folded softly in her lap. She inhaled sharply then closed her eyes. When she opened them, she began her search. Only a few minutes went by and she found the prize. Perkins had left them on the desk, and she paused a moment wondering if perhaps he had thought...no...

Jessie paused a moment. Not Perkins. Ever-loyal Perkins.

She whipped through them once, glancing over everything then went back to the beginning. Later, she sat back, eyes closed, thoughtful.

Lilly and someone named Sabrina had contrived the love potion that changed her life forever. She blinked, a small smile forming on her lips. Perhaps she should make a point to thank them.

No. On second thought she had best stay wary of those two.

Perkins had written it all down. It seems Pierce had conspired with Lilly. That came as no surprise. He had done the same with Annie, selling her women before moving on. Only Lilly was different. She had helped Pierce with her abduction.

"Sweet Jesus, no," she murmured.

She rubbed her temples. "I want this to end," she said softly, still staring at the words that haunted her. She read on, "Sabrina wanted to see her."

A shiver of dark foreboding chilled Jessie's body.

"I can't leave the house," she moaned. But then Sabrina could meet her here.

Perkins would object. The senator would object. But of course they didn't have to know. She'd send a message tomorrow.

The assault came faster than anyone had suspected. Perkins had gone out for a moment and the two guards, easily disposed of, lay unconscious on the ground. Jessie, alone in the house, unsuspecting, composed a message to Sabrina. It was never sent.

She looked up into the calculating gaze of Raymond Pierce, gasped and immediately rose from the chair to run. The gasp caught in her throat, and the message to Sabrina slowly drifted to the floor. Surrounded by men with each exit blocked, she slowly slipped back to the chair. She had known it would come to this. Tears of fear and anguish flowed within; her stomach clenched and rolled. Two deep breaths gave her courage to meet this head on.

"How did you get in?" she asked Pierce, resigned now.

He laughed. "You didn't think to keep me out indefinitely? You're alone, little cat, completely abandoned. With just a bit of patience I have succeeded."

Jessie's chin tilted forward, even while her hands trembled. She gripped her skirts tightly, hoping to still the quavering. No one to come to her rescue. No one here. Impossible.

She stood once more. "What do you want?"

He didn't answer for the longest time.

Jessie looked at the men around the room. Sweet Jesus, even if Roc were here, he couldn't have stopped this. "I want you to leave," she said softly.

He laughed. And it was low hollow laugh. "Not without you."

Once again she tilted her chin high and drug in deep cleansing breaths of air, preparing for the horrible truth. Her gaze lingered on the desk in front of her. Surely, she could find a weapon but nothing, not even a letter opener. She stepped forward, boldly intending to call his bluff and leave the room. His men closed around her. This shouldn't happen, she thought wildly. She had obeyed. Stayed in the house. Respected Roc's wishes and acted only with careful thought.

As the seconds wore on, the fear escalated. Pierce's horrid smiling face leered at her, and she knew he imagined her on the auction block. "I don't understand," she lied, stalling for time and the appearance of her friends. She prayed then for Roc, prayed he would understand and forgive her. Lord, but when he discovered her missing, she prayed he would realize she had done nothing wrong.

"Of course you understand. Reciprocity," he told her. "Sweet and simple, you're the object of it."

"And if I refuse?" Jessie asked.

"You have no choice," he looked to his men, they stepped closer, closer still and she shuddered.

Pierce nodded his directions. One man grabbed her wrist, but her struggles were useless against their strength. Her hands were tied behind her back and her mouth gagged. A sickly sweet odor emanated from an old rag held to her nose and she lost consciousness.

By the time Perkins returned, only minutes had passed since Pierce had come for Jessie, but it might have well-been days. No trace of her existed. Perkins searched the house, woke the guards then hurried to the telegraph office to send a message to Roc. He couldn't have gone far. And he had promised to stop in every town along the way. For the first time in years, Perkins cried.

Roc had to get the message in time...

It wasn't too late.

His heart raced. He closed his eyes. He was so very glad they had made this arrangement.

He swallowed his fear then, determined to find Senator Drake and apprise him of everything.

~ * ~

Jessie groaned and sat up. Her head throbbed sickeningly and she barely held onto the contents of her stomach. The carriage she rode in lurched suddenly, and she cried out from pain and fear. She looked up to see the backs of Pierce and Lilly. The carriage, surrounded by horsemen, bounced along the dirt road.

The woman turned to stare down at her, then back to Pierce. "She's awake."

Jessie's arms and legs were still tied but thank heavens she could talk, scream...

"Don't even think it, Jessica," Pierce growled.

Lilly squinted her eyes at Jessie. "Your husband won't find out soon enough. You know that." Lilly laughed. "And by then...who knows?" she shrugged. "You might like your new owner."

The carriage rolled to a stop. Two men rushed to help Lilly down before scooping Jessie out of the carriage, quickly making their way to the back door of an elegant three-story home. Moving quickly through the kitchen on to a narrow flight of steps they continued, up and up they climbed, finally stopping in front of a door. The man who carried her kicked it open then nearly doubled over, he entered the tiny attic cubicle.

A narrow cot sat in a corner and above it a window boarded over enticed thoughts of escape. It smelled of mildew and sweat, the heat almost unbearable. They left her on the bed, closed and locked the door behind her.

She lay back and shut her eyes, thinking frantically, searching for some way out of this unholy predicament. Sweet Jesus, but she'd seen enough in rapid flight to the house to know that they were in Astoria. Pierce had kept her drugged for days and Roc...

Oh, God, she wanted to cry out for him, but it would do no good. He was lost to her now. The blame would fall on her shoulders, and she couldn't deny it. The worst part of all this...she knew what would happen to her. She trembled, agony wrenched within.

All his safeguards were for naught...

She struggled with her emotions; the tears that burned seeped from beneath her eyes. It couldn't happen. She wouldn't allow this.

And she knew she had to save herself, must free herself from the ropes that held her vulnerable, defenseless.

The door opened. She grimaced against the beam of light falling on her.

Pierce stood before her. He carried food and drink and a length of white filmy material. "Oh, God..." she moaned softly.

Pierce grinned, set the tray on the floor and whipped a gleaming knife from his belt. One swift flick of his wrists and the ropes slithered to the floor. "Put this on," he commanded.

"When? How much time to I have?" she asked softly, afraid to hear the answer but desperate to know.

Pierce reached down for her, gripped her arms, and jerked her to her feet. His smile knifed through her. "It pleases me," he said. "The terror in your eyes. Sweet, sweet revenge. I've waited a very long time for this night." He paused then, watching her, waiting for her to say something, but she only lowered her lashes. "Midnight," he said then threw her to the cot.

She didn't look up. Just waited for him to leave.

She heard the lock click shut. Watched the flame of the tiny candle flicker weakly in the darkness, small comfort for her fears. She remembered again the awful shame Roc had put her through that night so long ago. Even then she had known he loved her, and it truly had not been so bad. Even then she had sensed the remorse he had felt, the disgust she had driven him to such a thing. She remembered, too, the night they had made up, all that she had forgiven him and all that he had said.

Yes, Roc was right. After this night he might never find her.

~ * ~

Roc received the message in Eugene, information that sent him into a wild rage and Trevor into a bout of swearing. He'd been so sure he'd find Pierce here, so very sure. As an intelligence man he had trained diligently to foresee everything, to anticipate. Never, ever had he expected this. He sent an urgent telegram to Astoria, to Conroy, urging him to take heed, that Jessie had indeed fallen into Pierce's plans, despite all precautions.

While Roc contacted Conroy, Trevor bought train tickets home.

When they entered his house, they found it in an uproar.

Perkins, beside himself with guilt. Drake pacing the length of the downstairs hallway. The women calm, resourcefully planning the rescue. Annie had contacted Jonathan as soon as they discovered Jessie missing. The guards sat in the study, bleary eyed, heads throbbing, but otherwise unscathed.

Pierce had kidnapped Jessie.

Jessie...son of a bitch, but he wouldn't get away with this.

Kidnapped from his home.

Fury seized him. He swore, impatient with the wait, with his frustration and lack of foresight, and could find no answers. Finally, they set out; Roc, Trevor, Senator Drake, all of them, raced toward Astoria.

Terror walked in Roc's heart; pounded against it, treaded heavily throughout.

Because he had so little time. So damn little time. Pierce had threatened and had wanted vengeance. He had waited patiently for the right opportunity and seized it.

Perhaps he would arrive in time. Perhaps nothing would happen to her. And Pierce would find somewhere to hide. He could surely disappear forever.

And he would have sold Jessie to the highest bidder. Damn, but he had failed. Roc swore furiously. He would never find her, never hold her again. Jessie, Jess...

Dear God, the highest bidder.

He couldn't stand the thoughts, couldn't think about the future. The auction, the men, no...

Not his Jessica, she would never endure the horror, but Jess Law might. He prayed.

"Don't think about it, Roc." Trevor saw the anguish, the pain that washed through Roc. The guilt.

"I can't help myself."

"You have to," Trevor said tensely.

"We have to pray for her, pray Conroy can infiltrate the auction. Oh, God, Jessie."

And so they rode. Faster, urgently, listening to the train wheels speed along the tracks.

On and on toward the coast and into the hot sultry heat of the day.

They reached Portland and rode to the Columbia River, booked passage on a ship just leaving the port.

Closer, past logging camps and homesteads they sailed toward the ocean.

Night closed in upon them. The parlor house stood bleak against the hill overlooking the mouth of the river.

One light burned on the third floor.

Midnight...the auction was nearly over.

Chapter Twenty

The mystery, the terrible intrigue, graphically prosaic, but woven amongst the lives of so many people. She had envisioned his coming, had prayed for it.

Roc had come.

But he had not come for her, indeed, he had come for Raymond Pierce and Sterling Rutgers. A driving need that had possessed him for such a long time. Even before their first encounter.

Yet now, even as she watched him, standing amidst the chaos of her life as the tempest raged within and around, Roc in his majesty, lightening sizzling throughout him, so invincible and commanding.

Even as she saw him, she felt rough hands yank her from the floor and the coarse feel of cloth covering her mouth.

Her nostrils flared, seeking fresh sweet air instead of the cloying sweetness that filled them.

She struggled within his grasp. Pierce. Pierce had found her huddled, terrified, and still praying Roc would see her shadowed form in the dim light.

Yet even as the cloth closed over her face and the drug penetrated her lungs and her senses, lightning flashed overhead and filled the room with brilliance. Jessie saw Roc once more, alone upon the stage, shadows still hovering around him.

Confusion and drowsiness warred with her desperation to stay alert. Even against the sultry heat of the night, she felt the lethargy, reaching out, embracing her. She closed her eyes and began to slip away. Ice, white, blue...

Her mind battled. Fog and rolling mists simmered quietly inside her mind, deathly and overpowering, it left her with a vague understanding. She rested, slipped inside herself, now surrounded by dim memories of a happier time, but she knew it wouldn't last forever. Knew she would wake, later, when Pierce ordained it.

"Newman." she heard the distant thunder of his name and smiled.

Yes, it was remote and foggy, but she could hear his shouts. Could hear the purposeful strides thundering toward her. Bullets whined overhead. Thunder crashed around them. The building seemed to move and sway. Closer and closer the pounding of his steps came, crashing alarmingly inside her. He moved through the multitude of men that battled now, following them. She heard his breath deep and strong, on fire with rage, defying the tempest, the deadly missiles, and the men surrounding them.

Pierce stopped suddenly; before her eyes a large panel moved and they traveled down a long winding staircase. His men followed. She heard the grating of the hinges as the door closed.

Roc wouldn't find her. He wouldn't be in time. They were vanishing again, and one more time she was going with them.

"Pierce." The voice echoed and rumbled through the narrow confines of the passage.

So far away, so very far away, yet the promise and the hope that one word gave her knifed through the fog holding her prisoner and she groped upward. Trying to surface to breathe in the intoxicating scent, the will to battle.

"Stop him." Pierce bellowed and one of the men in the back of the pack left. Moved up the passage to meet his fate.

She could hear them fighting in the passage. Too dark for guns now, the battle was hand-to-hand. Sounds of vicious blows pummeled the halls and shook the stairs.

Pounding boots fell on the steps. Shouts, yells, cries of alarm as the battle moved closer.

She could imagine him now. Visualize the silver smoke of his eyes. She could hear the beat of his heart and his raged breaths, and the fury smoldering beneath the pent up violence.

His breadth and height filled the narrow passage, barreling through the bodyguards' straight to Pierce. She felt the fury even before he unleashed it on his enemy. Felt the surge of fire and heat and anger. Pierce dropped her just before the shattering blow came. She had no strength or feeling in her limbs. Frozen and numb, she watched within a hazy tunnel. Roc, and behind him Trevor, more men followed.

Roc scooped her into his arms, covered her with his coat, and ran until he broke through another door into the stormy night. Rain poured around them, men ran across the lawns, whistles and horns, shouts, bullets and still the heavens unleashed their worst, joining in the fray.

Fortunately, nothing hit them. Pierce flew from the door seconds ahead of them and more men joined him. They ran through the night toward the docks.

He had come. Somehow he had arrived in time; now, he had another opportunity to catch Pierce and Rutgers. She wanted to tell him how much she loved him, but she could not find her way out of the fog. So close but so impossible to surface from this treachery surrounding her. She wanted to tell him she had done nothing wrong, had not caused this, that she had learned the lesson.

But she had no opportunity. Even as he placed her upon the ground, Sheriff Clayton appeared, and his soft voice pierced her conscious thought. "We're after them now. They're getting away, Roc."

Jessie cried out for him, a silent plea, wanted to push the coat off, but fell back into the sweet bliss of warmth. Then she was shocked back to semi-reality when she heard wild shouts. Roc surged after Pierce, unwilling to let him escape one more time. He left her in the care of Perkins who tenderly cradled her in his lap.

She sighed into the warmth.

~ * ~

The smugglers moved swiftly to their ship, cut off before they could reach it. Pierce slipped through an alley in the hope of moving beyond Roc's threat.

And so Roc and Trevor and Jonathan began a rapid search through the streets of Astoria, hoping against all odds they would find Raymond

Pierce before he had a chance to do more harm.

He would not get out of this port. Clayton had stopped all ships, barricaded all roads out of town. Pierce was trapped. Only a matter of time stood between him and Pierce.

Roc stood on the boardwalk, listening to the water lap beneath the pier, desperate beyond measure. The storm had moved on and the stillness left a curious feeling in the air. Strange and innocuous, he shivered with dread despite the knowledge Jessie was safe now.

Jessie...

His heart catapulted and constricted in his chest until he could barely breathe. Perkins lumbered down from the hill. His baldhead catching the faint light from the moon and reflecting it back. "Where is she?"

He had left her in Perkins care.

Jessie? Fear pounded alarmingly in his soul. Jessie? What happened?

And he fought the fear surging into his brain. No. Pray to God this means nothing.

"Pierce has her."

~ * ~

She woke from the images painfully. The dreams, the illusions that she had thought would keep her safe. Remembered the flight down the narrow passage, Roc's warm embrace, the tender caring Perkins administered then she had slept.

Jessie smelled tar and sweat. A gentle rocking motion lulled and comforted for a moment, but she realized she was on board a ship. Silence greeted her. Alone and held against her will in a dark cold cell.

She had thought...

No, her imagination had precluded her rational thought. The drugs had made her believe the dream. She tried to focus, but the bleariness wouldn't go away. And what was the dream? Ah, she had thought Roc had come for her, Perkins too.

Her stomach rolled and the heat against her sensitive skin frightened her. The potion, the drugs...

She had thought Roc had come. Lies, disillusioned dreams. He had not. And what of Skye?

A soft sob filled the bleakness. She had tried, had tried so very hard to do the right thing. Nothing had turned out for her, for them, always pitted against each other. A regrettable accident and he hadn't even come. Had someone bought her? Even now she didn't know where she was or what would become of her. The auction, the horrid nightmare had only begun, not ended.

"Ah, Jessie. You have come back to me. I had wished to see this ended, but it seems I'll have to try another time. You'll come with me for now."

Impossible. Perhaps a smattering of truth existed in that elusive mist she couldn't quite grab hold of. Perhaps Roc had come and rescued her, but...

"Confused? But then I wouldn't have expected you to remember." He shrugged.

She wriggled against the wall to a sitting position. Her hair hung limply in her eyes, and she wanted to shout at Pierce, ask him what happened, but she could only murmur through the foul gag he'd tied around her mouth.

He laughed softly, seemingly amused with her condition and her attempts to speak. He settled back against the hull of the ship and closed his eyes, pretending to sleep.

She listened to the soft sound of lapping water, wishing for some way to climb out of this horrid place. He was nothing like Roc, nothing, and yet he always landed on his feet two steps ahead of him. And nothing they did made a difference. He had, through his wit alone, captured her twice, right out from under Roc's fingertips. Roc had failed to protect her. Had promised but it hadn't worked. She was bound here in some ship. Now Pierce needed only to give the orders and no one would ever see her again.

"He won't ever find us, my dear. Once I have found a new home for you, he won't want you anyway." He opened his eyes and leaned so very close to her. "He won't come for you, Jessie. No man wants someone else's leavings and even if he finds you, that is what you'll be. If he finds you, he will find a well-trained whore."

He slipped the gag from her mouth, expecting an icy retort, but she said didn't speak.

"Ah, sweetheart, nothing to say? No answer that will cut right through me?" He laughed again.

Bitter and cold, her heart sank. Everything he said sounded so true. Roc wouldn't want her, wouldn't forgive her for taking chances. But she hadn't. Pierce had found her in her home, where Roc had promised she would find safety. Now no one would ever find her or want her. She couldn't let it happen. Never.

He was touching her breasts. The diaphanous gown clinging to her shoulders a slight barrier to his assault. Her flesh crawled. "I would, if we had time, sample the merchandise. A first hand recommendation rarely hurt a sale unless of course a virgin."

"No," she interrupted struggling away from his hands.

"Ah, but we both know that you're not a virgin, don't we Jessica? And that night, well, I had different plans for you then.

"I'm sure you did," Jessie spat out.

He shrugged. "Well, I had different plans for tonight also, but, you see, Roc did come. He changed them once more, but I still hold you, my pet."

"Not for long," she told him, suddenly realizing the boat wasn't moving and why. "You'll not get away with this. He's out there, isn't he? He will search every ship in port before he lets them sail. I know he will. He will find me tonight. I know it."

"This part of the ship is sealed. He'll search, yes, but he won't find us."

Jessie glowered at him, shivering under his icy gaze. She didn't want to talk to him, didn't want him here, wherever here was. But she had to find a way out. "I can't breathe, Raymond, please. I...untie me."

He laughed again. "Very well." He undid the ties around her ankles and loosened the ones around her wrists. Jessie swallowed hard, looking at him while he leered then threatened her. "This is my ship, Jessie, my men. They are loyal to me. Once we sail, you will have only one person who can protect you from them."

He stared at her, waiting for the knowledge to sink into her mind.

330

"If you cause even one problem, I'll give you to them. Do you understand, Jessica. I won't feel a twinge of guilt."

She nodded her head, sick. Then leaned back against the hull and shut her eyes once more, searching for the opening. It was, she thought, well concealed. Almost as well hidden as the escape panel in the parlor house last night. "Why me?" she asked suddenly. Her eyes now wide and demanding. "I know you hated my father, but this, I just never believed."

"You don't have to understand. It's nothing," he told her. "Only a pay back. James Lawrence stole my land. I steal his daughter. Simple restitution."

"Father never stole a thing in his life."

"Ah, my pet, but it's a matter of interpretation, isn't it." He fastened his gaze on her. "You'll bring a handsome price you know that."

"And you simply don't have enough money without me?"

"We both know that is not the incentive. It is the mere fact that James will suffer; will forever hold himself responsible. And then of course your husband, I hadn't counted on the fringe benefit when he came into your life."

"Sweet Jesus, but you must hate them."

He moved closer. She could feel the heat of his body, the smell, the sweat, and the fear. Her eyes opened wide with the realization he was a very good actor. He was afraid and in that instant she felt a surge of power, knew she could endure anything because they both knew Roc would never let her down.

She cringed against the wave of nausea that swept through her when Pierce reached out to touch her. But she understood the situation now. Comprehended nothing would sway his course, that he thought only of himself, and that he could kill her just as easily, if he thought it necessary. Only caution would do, not her usual wild impulsive way.

"I despise your father," he told her calmly. "He bested me at every turn, took land I had coveted for years. Created a dynasty that should have been mine. Hate? A word hardly strong enough to describe my feelings for James Lawrence."

"So, you use me as a pawn?" Jessie asked. "I hardly fit into the scope. I'm not even a real daughter to him."

"Liar." But Pierce looked suddenly startled. Perhaps he hadn't known. Perhaps now she had leverage against him.

She didn't know how, but she was going to use it, this new development. Would use it to her advantage to escape this man. The knowledge failed her no matter how desperately she tried, no matter how terrified she became with each passing second. Something had to happen, a diversion, something before they set sail, something before he had her on the open sea.

She thought until her head hurt. A silent tomb, he had found, for she doubted even a scream would reach the deck. No one would know he had hidden her deep in the bowels of this ship. No one, not even Roc could find her here. But if she pounded on the walls and screamed?"

Footsteps thundered above.

If she gave away this sanctuary, he would kill her. But then she had thought that death would serve a better purpose than enduring the horror Pierce had planned for her. Now without rescue, she faced that horrid degradation again. Revenge was a powerful motive to this man, a means to an end.

Very well.

She had made up her mind. Her body quavered but her mind did not. She rose swiftly, pounding with all her strength against the wall that she had leaned against. Screamed his name, over and over again. "Roc! If you are there, help! Below, Roc...below you!"

His hands were on her hair, yanking her back. She screamed again just before he hit her. His fist slammed into her jaw and the force of it sent her flying across the tiny room. She landed hard against the opposite wall, the wind knocked out of her, gasping for air. Jessie slumped to the cold floor. He strode toward her, the hate and evil in his heart twisting his features. He wrenched her from the floor prepared to hit her again but paused.

"Jessie! Jessie!"

Her reply caught in her throat. He had come for her. The footsteps, the pounding, Roc.

She pushed against Pierce with an incredible force, determined Roc stayed, if only to search more thoroughly. She managed to scream one more time. To hear noise from above, yells and shouts that she thought she would never again hear. She had not believed any sound would penetrate those walls.

Sweet Jesus, but she loved him.

"Roc. Take care!" she cried and prayed that he had heard.

She stopped suddenly, for Pierce had clamped his hand around her mouth and nose, tightened his grip until she felt all air cut off.

"Leave now, Mr. Newman, and your wife might live. I swear if you don't," he hollered, "I'll kill her."

Jessie maneuvered carefully and swung her elbow hard into his chest, pushing away from him, gasping for air. He came at her and she prepared to battle. She rested softly on the balls of her feet, wary, studying his every move. Watched the smile on his face, the horrid grin stretch on forever. And she knew she didn't have a prayer. Understood now that night so long ago Roc had let her have the win. If only she could run farther than a few feet.

Pierce came at her, and she had no room in this small place. He had her again, struggles useless against his strength. She bit, kicked, frantically she beat at him. He turned her in his arms again, and this time the blow to her head was vicious. She slumped silently to the ground, her breath slowly rushing from her.

Silence, freedom, a curious blackness came over her, and it seemed she drifted through space. Still she could hear the shattering of the wall, feel a hot breath sting her cheeks, but she could not respond. She would die and she had never told Roc, never told him how much she loved him.

~ * ~

Pierce checked her pulse, nothing. Ah, but he had not intended this to happen. Revenge too short, he had wanted it to last a lifetime. He had wanted James Lawrence to search and ache for his daughter, never find her. But now this would have to do.

He slipped from the hidden door, gun in hand, intent on sneaking from the ship. His men would never conquer the troops Roc had behind him. The sheriff's forces, the Pinkertons and only God knew who else.

Roc shattered the last remaining barrier to the room only to see Pierce's back disappearing through the opposite wall and Jessie lying on the floor.

Trevor stumbled into Roc's back.

For a moment, as Roc burst through the wall, fear seized him. Rancid odors assailed him. Disgust and terror filled his soul. Jessie, son of a bitch, Jessie lay on the floor, so very still and Pierce would get away with this if he didn't go after him. Torn once more, he leapt after Pierce.

He shouldn't have to choose between these two.

But a bullet seared his arm. He could feel the heat of it and he crouched low, following. He had no choice but to go after Pierce. Even now he could feel Trevor behind him, supporting him.

Roc heard the activity on the ship above. Pierce bellowed orders to his men, but they were engaged in a battle of their own unable to lift anchor. Roc moved up the ladder, shielding his eyes from the bright light of a new morning. Another bullet whined past him, and he backed up against the wall before answering the shot.

Then he rushed onto the deck, hiding behind barrels and anything else he could find. Suddenly, someone jumped him from behind; he whirled casting the fellow over his head and onto the deck. He dispatched him with a swift kick to his jaw. Two more flew at him. He fought with renewed determination, battled with only one aim in mind, sent a man flying over the railing into the cold depths of the Columbia.

Then he saw Pierce.

He had slipped off the ship and was attempting to escape down the docks to an alley.

He shouted to Conroy, who stood at the bow overseeing the battle. One remaining man stood between him and his quarry. He was young, a dark haired smuggler with pale blue eyes. His pulse ticked fearfully at his throat. He was afraid, but he had no time for mercy. Pierce was rounding the corner and soon it would be impossible to find him. He looked back to the young man, yelled, and pulled out his gun.

The man raised his hands in surrender.

Pierce would never get away.

He sprinted after Raymond Pierce with such fury he reached him as he thought to hide in an old building. He spun Pierce around ready to fight. Even as he did, Trevor came up behind him, stopping him. Conroy appeared on the other side with handcuffs.

Pierce sneered at them. Then he spoke. "You can't save her, she's gone."

Roc's mind reeled, unwilling to believe the taunts Pierce issued, but remembered how very still she had been.

"You'll hang," he said calmly. Then panicked, he turned, ran back to the ship, back to Jessie. The town had woken and people lined the streets. Trevor and Conroy would see Pierce did not get away.

Roc picked up speed, heading for the ship and his wife, praying Pierce was wrong. He raced forward.

Jessie was sitting on the deck, slumped against the mast. She was still wearing his coat and the long white gown that hid nothing. Her hair fell across her shoulders in a silken mass.

"Jessie," he swallowed her name, terrified. She looked as if death had touched her soul, her face swollen and black. He rushed to her, trembling as he explored her cheek, her jaw, and saw her wince with the pain. His caress so gentle, he couldn't believe the agony she endured. He had promised to protect her, and he'd failed. He knew better, should have never left her with Perkins. Never. The old man meant well but he couldn't fight, couldn't have defended her even though he tried. "Relax, sweetheart, you're safe now."

He lifted her into his arms, her face ashen behind the darkening shadows.. Her trembling hand rose to touch his lips. "I'm all right, you know," she said before slumping into his arms.

"Jessie," he whispered again and again, and the horror swept over him. The terror that she had endured. He touched her lips then kissed her lightly, so afraid he would hurt her more. God, how could this have happened?

Fury seized him, overwhelmed him.

"Jessica, Jessie, Jess..."

Curiously, he knew she felt his pain, wanted to deny it. Knew also she wanted to tell him it wasn't his fault. It was over.

He lifted her in his arms. He was carrying her. Walking with her to a safe place, a haven of peace. Her breath caught. Tried to speak to him but exhaustion fell upon her.

"Jessie," he whispered, "I'm so sorry." He kissed her forehead and her nose, avoiding the bruises.

She licked her lips, watching him. "Roc, it's all right. I understand. You could not have changed anything, you know, even if you'd been there. Pierce would have found..."

But he was suddenly swearing. Cursing himself and his stupidity. Promising his own reciprocity now that Jessie was back under his protection. Beat Pierce as he had done Jessie.

An eye for an eye.

Roc looked up, startled by the approach of his men and Trevor. Drake stood in the background. A faint smile touched his features. Conroy strode behind with Pierce at gunpoint. Roc rose and pushed through the gawking crowds straight to Pierce. "Bastard!" he bellowed, his voice rough and threatening.

Conroy moved to the side. Roc hauled back his fist and shattered Pierce's nose. He didn't give a damn if Pierce's hands were secured behind his back. Defenseless and vulnerable, let him have a clear understanding of how it felt, defenseless at the hands of a powerful foe. He drew back his arm to hit him again. This time he blackened Pierce's eye and the man staggered back against Conroy. He leered at Pierce, grinning even in his defeat. "Don't want a soiled dove, ah, mores the pity. Let me see how many men?"

Roc felt the fury rip throughout, reached for him sure he could beat him to death.

"Roc?"

He hesitated and that gave Conroy the time to push Pierce away from the crowds toward the jail. Roc turned to meet the soft voice. Jessie. She stood before him, ethereal, her raven hair tumbling all around her. Her diaphanous gown blowing gently in the breeze, huddling beneath the buckskin jacket he had given her. Her eyes filled with pain yet pleading also, and she was seriously gnawing on her lip.

Son of a bitch, he didn't want her to see this. No more violence. He wanted only to shelter her forever from this horror, but somehow he knew it as an impossible dream.

"Leave him be, please," she whispered gently. Her hand fluttered softly, toying with her skirts. It must have hurt her to hear Pierce's accusations, but she made no move to deny them.

He turned back to look for Pierce but saw his back moving inside the jail, Conroy behind him. Roc looked back to Jessie, his body rigid with tension.

"Roc, please?"

Her eyes so bright, her voice almost commanding.

Jessie didn't realize. Didn't understand the need to seek payment for what Pierce had done to her. What he had intended for her fate, a degrading dehumanizing fate that would have killed her.

"No one touched me," she whispered softly, sensing he stood on the edge of decision. "Leave him."

Slowly, he let out a deep breath and relaxed, purged of the fury and the desperate fear. Roc turned and gathered Jessie in his arms then held her away from him, studying her features, memorizing every detail. His thumb traced her lips. He kissed her. Gently. Once, twice, he touched her cheek and her eye. "Ah, but I won't let you out of my sight ever again," he said, his voice trembling.

She touched his jaw and laughed softly despite the pain. "No, you will let me out of your sight. I will not allow you to smother me."

She was wrong. No more compromise. He would lock her in the house. He would see no harm came to her ever again. Should have done that in the first place.

She would not protest.

And he had better not hold his breath.

"We'll talk about it," he said.

He swept her into his arms and toward the waiting carriage. Perkins seated on top, prepared to drive. The sun beat down, drying the vestiges of the tempest.

"The sky is so blue," she murmured.

"And the clouds have disappeared," he agreed.

"We have nothing to fear now." Trevor came up behind them and closed the door. Roc glanced up and smiled.

"He'll stand trial in Salem, Roc. He's looking forward to a long stay in prison."

"Good," Roc said. He turned his attention to Jessie again. Trevor moved to the front of the carriage and joined Perkins.

Roc shifted her in his lap. The carriage moved slowly, gradually picking up speed. And he wished beyond a doubt they could make it home by nightfall.

So they rode, and stopped at all the stations, changing horses, taking a quick meal before moving on. Trevor and Perkins and even Drake took turns driving. Jessie rested within his arms.

Roc had nothing except his wife to concern himself with. He would never let her go. Would disavow all his earlier promises.

"Roc, I was in the house," she began so softly he could barely make out her words. "I did nothing wrong."

"The house was guarded."

"They didn't tell you?" she asked incredulous. "Didn't tell you that Pierce had five men with him? That you couldn't have stopped him, no one could."

"Perkins said as much. But Jessie..."

"I know it's easier to believe I had defied your wishes and run off by myself."

"No, yes."

Jessie emitted an unladylike snort and fell back against his chest, closing her eyes. "Nothing will ever change, will it," she sighed. "Roc?"

"Hmm?"

"Did I ever tell you that I love you?"

He sat up straighter, nearly dumping her on the floor. Roc turned her head and lifted her chin. Their gazes met, clashed; set an inferno blazing within. "No."

"I do, you know, but I was so angry with you that night." She gulped for air. "I wouldn't admit it. Didn't want to give you the satisfaction." And after that, well, it seemed so very hard to say.

"Even when I went down on my knees and begged your forgiveness?"

"You never did that," she laughed softly. "And you never will." She touched his lips and shivered. "Oh, Roc, I would do anything for you. Even stay in the house, but..."

"But you would give me no peace arguing with me. No, my love, I've changed my mind. I love you too much to keep your wild beautiful spirit locked away."

Her words caught in her throat, eyes widening with shock. "Hush, don't say anything you might regret later."

"Regret, never," one eyebrow rose. "Fortunate to have you, Jessie, just the way you are. Beautifully enchanting, wonderfully impetuous, you leave me gasping for breath, frustrated beyond endurance. Should I go on?"

He didn't give her a chance to respond. There, within the wonderful light of day, a dawn, was a new beginning, he kissed her. She tasted of life and loving and the promise of a rich happy future.

"I love you, Roc Newman," she whispered, returning the kiss.

"Ah, but if we continue with this, I'm afraid that I'll not find the strength to stop," he murmured. "Can we wait until we make it home?"

"It's so very far away." Her words slowly died as he tempted her lips and her heart with another kiss.

"Not so far, you've slept, and I've held a silent vigil over you." He smiled and kissed her nose, then her eyes, traced her throat, her lips. "Sweet Jessie, in truth we should be home in a few hours."

Dusk shed its beautiful curtain of colors, shadows lengthened then the carriage rolled to a stop near the front door. Annie flew from the door with Charity close behind. James and Alexandra had come. Dark circles hovered beneath his eyes, for he had shouldered the blame and the guilt of it all. "I found her and everything is fine," Roc told him.

James gathered her in his arms, tears flowing from his eyes. He had cursed and swore, but he'd never given up on Roc. Faith had reached out to him, blind faith, nothing more, but he had known somehow his indomitable Jessica would come through this unscathed. Well, he grimaced studying her, not quite, but she was alive and he was holding her.

It seemed Roc took charge once more, issuing everyone inside, shielding her from the onslaught of questions.

Then a hesitant voice suddenly echoed within the parlor.

Jessica froze, for she had never thought to see Madam Lilly again.

She had returned with Senator Drake.

"Roc, Jessie," she said clearly distraught. "I am sorry and I wish an apology would suffice for all that happened here but...I doubt that it will." She looked to Drake for encouragement, strength, but he had little to offer. "I, well..." She stammered, trembling beneath the blatant glare.

"What she's trying to say is that Pierce met her sister a few years back. A twin. It seems the sister married a Senator from Massachusetts. Quite nasty for a politician to find out one has a Madam for an in-law, so..."

"Blackmail," Roc said slowly, beginning to understand.

The drugged wine, the betrayals, the intimate knowledge of everything transpiring within their house. Drake?

"I set her up," Drake went on. "This last year she worked for me. I gave her information and she helped me in return. The wine, Jessie, I'm sorry. I didn't know then, but I'm not sure I would have stopped it. It was only through Lilly that we knew of the auction, the time and the place; she supplied all the details, otherwise..."

Drake nodded, wishing he could have told Roc sooner. Then he met his gaze and Jessie's, his sky blue eyes sparkling. "It has all worked out. Now let's have a toast to celebrate our good fortune. Put this all behind us." He clapped Perkins on the shoulder, pointing the way to the wine.

Somehow they all made their way into the house. Puzzled, laughing, and outraged all at the same time.

Annie appeared with Skye in her arms, handing the child to Jessica who hugged her tiny daughter. Roc wrapped his arms around both of them for a moment, seeming to delight in his family.

A paradox of thoughts, so much that might have been avoided if they had only known, but Pierce had persisted and come after her even when he had escaped safely from the country.

Stars began to appear in the evening sky.

The moon a silver slipper...

Finally, everyone left, finding their way for the night.

"It was a night just like this that I called you a pest," Roc said gently then swept Jessie up in his arms. He gazed down into her eyes and smiled.

"You called me a brat too." She wrapped her arms around his neck, pulling his head down for a kiss. "A regrettable accident, another time."

He groaned, "And you will never let me forget will you?"

"Nope. You'll have to go down on your knees and beg, perhaps then I'll forget."

The night darkened and the stars burst upon the night in a brilliant display of dazzling lights. He stopped midway up the stairs to wonder at the beauty of the gardens, of his home, of the night and his lady. "I love you. You have brought joy and happiness into my life as well as Skye. And it would never have come about except for a fortunate accident."

"Oh!" she whispered. "It was no accident and you know it. Drake planned and executed it very well. And it matters not because I love you. I think I have always loved you."

"And I am delighted we have now reached an understanding," he chuckled softly.

"Oh, no," she cried. "What..."

His lips touched hers."

"Yes, Jessie? What do you ask?"

She thread her fingers into his hair, grinning. "Fine, believe what you want. Think that you have tamed me then. Make love to her, listen to her purr through the long night, and watch that love grow so that it will conquer all...

"Yes, sweetheart, never conquer, share...we will share everything. And I would never seek to tame you because you are my door to heaven."

The soft breezes of the evenings enclosed them, and flamed the passion within them, and the night wove the web of enchantment.

About the Author
achristay@aol.com

Born in Medford, Oregon, novelist Christine Young has lived in Oregon all of her life. After graduating from Oregon State University with a BS in science, she spent another year at Southern Oregon State University working on her teaching certificate, and a few years later received her Master's degree in secondary education and counseling. Now the long, hot days of summer provide the perfect setting for creating romance. She sold her first book, Dakota's Bride, the summer of 1998 and her second book, My Angel to Kensington. Her teaching and writing careers have intertwined with raising three children. Christine's newest venture is the creation of Rogue Phoenix Press. Christine is the founder, editor and co-owner with her husband. They live in Salem, Oregon.

Other books by Christine Young
Available at Rogue Phoenix Press

Catching Meara
Book One in the McKenna Clan Series

Meara Thorton was a feisty, world-class computer hacker—cornered by the FBI and shockingly given the chance to be their newly acquired technical analyst. Brilliant and intuitive, yet aching with the loss of everyone she has cared about, her restless heart led her to discover a love she fought and a world she didn't know could possibly exist.

Sweet Sexy Sadie
Book Two in the McKenna Clan Series

From the first time Sadie's eyes met those of Brody McKenna in the hot Sierra Madre Mountains, theirs was a potent attraction—not gentle, slow, and easy, but hot, hard, and all-consuming. The daughter of a dysfunctional family, Sadie had dreams no man could wrench from her with hot sex and an all-consuming passion. She'd challenge this alpha male with all the strength she possessed. But her red hair, fiery temperament, and indomitable spirit obsessed Brody...and he knew he had to find a way to show her he was more than he appeared and convince her to make a life with him.

Sweet Misbehavin'
Book Three in the McKenna Clan Series

Cast adrift after fleeing the home of Jokul, the ice demon, Atantsi, a firestarter, grew to womanhood as she moved through time to keep the demon from finding her. Though stubborn and courageous, she was ill prepared to use powers she had not been taught. Her first sight of the intoxicating Carr McKenna left her breathless, and her second encounter gave her hope for a future she never thought she had.

A playboy, a second son and a shifter, a man who thought his life would be carefree, Carr McKenna was shocked to discover the woman he'd paid as an escort is a firestarter who is running for her life. He is the leader of all the McKennas around the world and that he has multiple powers. His passion for Margo and the need to defend her might cost him his life as well as hers.

Sweet Talkin' Sugar
Book Four in the McKenna Clan Series

Lyonesse McKenna, was dreaming or was she? From the instant Lyn saw Deacon McClain across a black jack table in a crowed Las Vegas casino the unmistakable attraction sent Lyn's senses flying into overdrive. Her family of shapeshifters believed in soul mates. She'd always been skeptical yet she couldn't help but question the way her heart sped when he looked at her.

When Deacon appeared in Las Vegas he knew his first job was to save Lyn from a Sea Demon, but the next order of business was to convince her he would someday mean more to her than she'd ever expected. But her stubborn nature and unbendable spirit consumed Deacon...and he had to chase away all the demons real and imagined in order to win her heart.

Dakota's Bride
The first book in the Lakota/Pinkerton Series

When Emma St. John received her brother's letter imploring her to escape her stepfather's vengeful scheme and to trust Dakota Barringer with her life, she was willing to chance it. But the handsome, brooding riverboat owner Emma found in Natchez a danger of another kind. For Emma soon found herself surrendering to an unrelenting desire.

Raised by the Sioux when his parents were killed, Dakota had been betrayed once before by a white woman. He wasn't about to trust another, especially one claiming that her stepfather, a powerful U.S. senator, had framed her as a murderess. But he couldn't let Emma's intoxicating effect on him. Now Dakota would risk his very life to protect the innocent beauty who had seduced him with her tender love.

My Angel
The second book in the Lakota/Pinkerton Series

A BEAUTY IN BUCKSKINS
When her father decided to send her to a finishing school back East, Angela Chamberlain refused to be confined to stuffy drawing rooms. Instead, the daring spitfire who could shoot like a man and ride like the wind longed for a life of adventure and romance—and she knew exactly who could give it to her. Devil Blackmoor was a hired gun with a dangerous reputation. But Angela was willing to go to the ends of the earth to capture the handsome devil's heart.

A DEVIL IN DISGUISE
He'd come to America looking for excitement, but Devil Blackmoor got more than he bargained for when he encountered a beautiful rebel who answered his kisses with a wild innocence that touched his very soul. Yet standing between them were more obstacles than either ever dreamed. For Devil had strapped on a gun for the wrong man. And that made Angela his enemy. Now he'll have to choose between his duty and the woman he loves more than life.

The Locket
The third book in the Lakota/Pinkerton Series

The year is 1894. Seeking revenge for crimes against his family, Misha Petrovich follows a path that leads straight to Ariel Cameron's boarding house in Mist Harbor, Oregon. A family heirloom in Ariel's possession leads Misha to believe she is guilty. The locket has been handed down to the oldest girl in the Petrovich family for generations. Ariel is innocent of wrong doing, but her father is not. Misha is torn by his feelings for Ariel and his need for restitution against her father. Knowing that the relationship between them is fragile, Misha does everything in his power to protect Ariel's father. His efforts are to no avail when her father is shot. Ariel comes to realize Misha's steadfast courage and determination to protect her and her father despite what has happened to his family. Ariel's love and devotion heals Misha's heart.

The Talisman
The fourth book in the Lakota/Pinkerton Series

Running from a marriage that lasted one night, Dr. Moriah McKeown discovers the land she has settled on is coveted by determined and lawless men. Yet the proud young woman who once vowed never to abandon her home has second thoughts when her adopted children are threatened. Her only recourse is to enlist the aid of a dark, dangerous gun for hire.

Haunted by the past and a betrayal he will never forgive, Ian Civanovich uses his fast gun and his reckless courage to forget the faithlessness of a woman in his past. He will trust no female—nor will he rest until the threat hovering over Moriah McKeown is put to rest.

Forever His
The fifth book in the Lakota/Pinkerton Series

Struggling to come to terms with the part she played in Jacob St. John's death, Etta Barringer resigns from Pinkerton Agency and seeks peace and solace in a Rocky Mountain Cabin.

Jacob has vowed to discover the reason Etta has betrayed him, sold him out to his enemy and left him for dead.

Isolated in their cabin, they discover their love for each other and learn to trust. But the trust is shattered when Jacob learns she is married to his sworn enemy; the man who left him in the desert to die.

Allura
The first book in the Twelve Dancing Princesses Series

Allura McClellan is horrified by her father's decision to take out an ad in the Times awarding her to the man strong enough and smart enough to win her hand and uncover her secrets. She's an intelligent young woman who takes great delight in the freedom allotted to her by her father. She's well aware that marriage would effectively curtail the adventures she's shared with her sisters and cousins.

Hunter Gray is nothing like the other men who've arrived to vie for Allura's hand in marriage and everything that goes along with it. However, he is the first to refuse to concede defeat and pursue her despite her attempts to disguise her true appearance. It's her temperament that is of more concern to him than her looks. Hunter has worked all his life with the hope of someday owning his own land. Now that it looks like there's a very real possibility that everything he's ever wanted is within reach nothing is going to deter him – including Miss Allura's disagreeable disposition.

The Wager
The second book in the Twelve Dancing Princesses Series

Amorica Hepburn was sent to London to find a husband. Finding a man was the last item on her agenda. With her two cousins, Amorica wagers she can dissuade her suitor before the others. Despite her efforts she discovers a chemistry that cannot be denied. Suddenly she is the arrogant man's wife, pledged to a marriage neither desire. But swept off to his ancestral home above the Dover cliffs and into his strong embrace, Amorica is soon possessed by a raging passion for the husband she had vowed to despise...

Damian Andrews couldn't afford to trust the emerald-eyed spitfire who happened upon his secret. Amorica's hatred of all men of his kind only inflames the war that rages between them. Still, he can not control the intense desire his stubborn bride inspires, or make her surrender to his will until he has conquered the headstrong beauty on the battlefield of love...

A Marriage of Inconvenience
The third book in the Twelve Dancing Princesses Series

A REGAL BEAUTY
When the duchess decides to wed her to a wastrel and a fop, Ravyn Grahm takes matters into her own hands and declares her engagement to another man. Instead of fessing up and telling her great aunt what she has done, she goes through with the pretense. Aric Lakeland is the bastard son of an earl and has a dangerous reputation. But Ravyn is willing to do most anything to keep the duchess from discovering the lie.

A DEVIL-MAY-CARE SMUGGLER
He'd bought land in America, looking to put down roots and end his life of adventure, but Aric Lakeland got more than he bargained for when he encountered a beautiful heiress who made a promise she didn't want to keep. But the promise could not be undone and standing between them were more obstacles than either ever dreamed. Aric had made plans to spend the rest of his life in America and that was at odds with Ravyn's plan of living in England and running her father's estate. Now, he'll have to choose between his dreams and the woman he loves more than life.

Highland Sunrise
The fourth book in the Twelve Dancing Princesses Series

He Made Her An Offer...

Life has thrown Christel McClellan some experiences that could have devastated a less determined woman. Beautiful, self-assured and fiercely independent, she is trying to forget the loss of her stillborn child. But is the child alive?

She Couldn't Deny...

Life is carefree for Ryder MacLaren who loves to see what is on the other side of the sunrise. Laird of Clan MacLaren, he is wealthy, handsome and happily unencumbered...until stunning Christel McClellan enters his life. When he hears her story, he believes the child she thought dead has been sold to a wealthy buyer.

Storm's Passion
The fifth book in the Twelve Dancing Princesses Series

SHE MADE A PROPOSAL...

Life strikes Storm Graham a shattering blow when she learns her father has bartered her to a man she detests. Storm is beautiful, self–assured and fiercely independent, and refuses to be a pawn in her father's schemes, yet she can find no way out of this bargain made in hell. Going on the offensive she asks the wealthiest man on the eastern coast of England to marry her, never believing she might fall in love.

HE TRIED TO REFUSE...

For Hadden Johnston life has provided everything he ever wanted, including a sanctuary for homeless children. He is wealthy, handsome and happily unencumbered...until stunning Storm Graham marches into his life and proposes a marriage of convenience. Yet this type of marriage to a woman who inflames his senses is far from acceptable. If he's going to be tied down, he will move heaven and earth to have this woman warming his bed.

Rebel Heart

HER REBEL SPIRIT DEFIED HIS OUTSIDERS SOUL... She was velvet and silk, eyes the color of a summer storm and amber hair. Victoria DeMontville, because of a promise and a codicil to her father's will, was forced to marry one man to protect her from another. She hated Cameron Savage with a fierce passion. But to hold on to her genetic research and find a cure for the deadly Signe virus, she must pretend to love the enemy at her door, come with weapons of fire to melt her icy heart...

HIS OUTSIDERS TOUCH IGNITED RAGING PASSIONS... He wore a mask, disguised as the Phantom, a true legend come to life. Even as war and debate over new genetic research engulfed them all, he would find his greatest adversary in the beauty who'd branded him an outsider and barbarian, the woman he was born to possess, his soul mate.

Straight to Heaven

Running from demons, Alexandra McMurdie stumbles into Forbidden Ground where up is down and elements of nature are contested. Though a strong independent woman in the twenty-first century' she is unprepared for life in the 1800s. Her first site of the formidable James Lawrence makes her heart skip a beat, giving her cause to reconsider her desperate need to find a way home.

Born with a silver spoon, James' life was torn apart during the War Between the States. Moving west he vows to put the life he once knew in the past. When he discovers a half-frozen woman near Gold Hill, his heart begins to thaw. His love for Alexandra and his need to keep her from a man who has pursued her through time might cost him his life as well as hers.

A St. Patrick's Day Tale
Christine Young, C. L. Kraemer, Genene Valleau

Tumble through time…

…to Ireland in 1817, when tensions are high between Protestants and Catholics and faey people guide the fate of villagers. A lovely Catholic lass stumbles upon the weakly ritual fisticuffing between Irish lads. She falls into the lap of a handsome young Protestant. Family ties, grudges, and two conniving faeries threaten their budding love. But the faeries outsmart themselves when they hijack a time machine that has mysteriously appeared in their forest and are whisked to…

…Eugene, Oregon in the 20th century, amid a property feud between the local faeries and night elves. The conniving faeries from Olde Ireland try to stir up more mischief. However, a warrior gnome convinces the magic folk to control their own destiny, and forces the intruding faeries to take refuge in the time machine again, spinning their way toward…

…A modern day castle in western Oregon. An eccentric inventor is determined to reclaim his wayward time machine and save his beloved wife from her latest misadventure. If only they can travel safely past the black hole…

A Valentine's Anthology

The Lending Library-a fantasy by Christie L. Kraemer
Faeries try to fit into the human world when the forest where they make their home is destroyed by a mysterious enemy.

Chasing Rainbows-a contemporary romance by Genene Valleau

An eccentric aunt, an inventive uncle, a mother who wears poodle skirts, and a brother who wears pearls provide a hilarious backdrop for the courtship of a young woman who yearns for a "normal" family.

The Gift-an historical romance by Christine Young

A man and a woman on opposite sides of the Civil War get a second chance at love after one final battle returns soldiers to their war-torn homes to rebuild their lives.

Writing as AnnChristine

Safari Moon

Solo St. John, a wildlife photographer, is preparing for a trip to Alaska. Suddenly, Solo finds women of all sorts invading his privacy, his home and his office, all cooing nonsense words and blatantly throwing themselves at him. Solo doesn't know why, and he has no idea how to rid himself of the persistent women. He finally decides to beg a favor of his best buddy Nyssa Harrington.

In love with Solo for the past ten years and knowing he doesn't return her feelings Nyssa doesn't want to talk to Solo. She knows if she accepts his phone call, she will not be able to resist the temptation to hope again.

A Valentine's Anthology

Sharks by AnnChristine

Will Lily and Jacob, best friends forever, find love or will they discover friendship is not enough for a relationship to take the final step into marriage.

The House on Berkley Street by K. J. Dahlen

When Serenity is asked to find the truth in a forty-year old tragedy, someone in the town of White Oak, Texas doesn't want the truth told. Can they stop her before she finds out what they have kept hidden for so long?

The Placebo Effect by Solstice Stevens

First, there was the poison. Then, there was a four story jump and the basketball hoop. Jessamyn Hamhill's life has been one validation attempt after another . . . until now.

www.ingramcontent.com/pod-product-compliance
Lightning Source LLC
Chambersburg PA
CBHW061925170626
46813CB00006B/2302